the Walker

Jane Goodall

the Walker

HODDER

A Mark Macleod Book

Published in Australia and New Zealand in 2004
by Hodder Headline Australia Pty Limited
(A member of the Hodder Headline Group)
Level 17, 207 Kent Street, Sydney NSW 2000
Website: www.hha.com.au

National Library of Australia
Cataloguing-in-Publication data

Goodall, Jane, 1951- .
  The walker.

  ISBN 0 7336 1851 0.

  1. Serial murders - England - London - Fiction.
  I. Title.

A823.4

Text design and typesetting by Bookhouse, Sydney
Printed in Australia by Griffin Press, Adelaide

Plymouth, September 1967

It was fifteen minutes walk from school to the station, or a bit more if you were carrying a heavy bag. Nell was carrying two bags: one with the week's clothing and her growing collection of cosmetics, and the other with the weekend's homework. The homework bag was heaviest. She changed the bags from hand to hand, to share out the drag on her arms, and every twenty paces (she counted them) she stopped to rest briefly and blow on the whitening palms of her hands.

This was going to be a heavy year. Some of her teachers said ten O levels was too much, but Nell thought ten sounded like a nice number. Mum told her to take eight and Dad said you only needed five to get into the navy, but they weren't here—so there. Aunty Pat said ten sounded impressive. The twins had five each and she was very proud of them.

Nell had to be a weekly boarder this year and spend the weekends at Aunty Pat's, which was all right really because she liked being with the twins and anyway she was used to it because Dad was always being posted somewhere overseas and sometimes Mum went with him. The twins were Rita and Julie, and when she got home they were all going out to the cinema together in Exeter to see *Doctor Zhivago*.

'Julie's seen it twice already,' Rita said on the phone. 'She's got a crush on Omar Sharif. You'll fall for Tom Courtenay, I know. He's the intellectual type.' Nell quite liked her cousins thinking she'd go for the intellectual type. She put the bags down again and flexed her hands. The new maths book was the worst thing to carry, even between classes. It was big and old and a bit smelly with a thick hard cover and an ink stain on the edge of the pages in one corner. Nell thought at least six people must have used it before. She didn't like used books, with dirty pages and other people's underlinings all over them. The biology book was almost new. It had glossy pages with photos of frogs pinned out for anatomy. She had a new French dictionary and an old French grammar. The English texts were old, too, but she was going to buy her own copies of those: *The Mayor of Casterbridge* and Book 6 of *The Prelude* were the ones Miss Crabbe announced they would be doing this term and she said that all the girls should try to have them.

Miss Crabbe was called Crabby, but she wasn't. She even smiled when they said it. 'Hey, Crabby, are there any good sex scenes in this book?' She was a lot younger than the other teachers and looked a lot happier. She had a Sandie Shaw haircut and wore purple tights and in summer term she wore a Mary Quant dress. This term she came to school in a trouser suit. The girls crowded round her after assembly. 'You could be a model,' they said.

It took Nell twenty minutes to get to the station and that left only ten minutes to wait for the Exeter train. She hated waiting for trains. Or buses. But she specially hated waiting for the Friday train at the end of the day, when it was getting all gloomy. She positioned her bags near the edge of the platform and brushed the front of her school mac with her hands. It had been dry-cleaned for the new term but still looked faded and limp, and it flapped around in the wind. Nell wished she had a trouser suit like Crabby, with a big foldback collar and two rows of buttons. In her school bag was a copy of *Honey* magazine with all the autumn clothes in it. She'd bought it after school on Wednesday—the day it came out—but had saved it for reading on the train.

There weren't many people waiting on the platform—fewer than usual for the 5.10. Some of the trains had corridors but the 5.10 from Penzance often didn't. It just had separate compartments with a door at each side of the carriage, so once you were in, you were in. Nell knew better than to get into a compartment where she'd be on her own, so she usually tried to pick out someone on the platform who'd be safe to travel with. Some other girls if possible, or, failing that, any woman would do, really. That's what her mother advised her. But the only other people waiting today were a man with an umbrella, who would probably go first class, and a couple of boys from the high school. A lot of Nell's friends would have got in with the boys. They didn't look exactly dangerous, but Nell didn't want anyone thinking she was 'boy mad', least of all the boys themselves. It was always better to play hard to get, Rita and Julie told her.

When the train drew in, a student in a green duffle coat got out and held the door for Nell, his long hair blowing across his face. She checked quickly inside. There was a dumpy, middle-aged woman in the corner opposite who seemed to be asleep, and that was good because Nell didn't want to get drawn into aimless chat. She shut the door, put her bags on the seat and pulled the window up a bit. The man in the duffle coat had pushed it right down, so it must have been freezing with all that cold air rushing through. She arranged her bags on the seat beside her and got out her magazine.

The autumn fashion colours were amazing. Twiggy was wearing a dress in rich chocolate corduroy with mustard tights and a rust coloured blouse from Biba in some shiny material that draped into big gathered sleeves. Over the page was the perfect trouser suit: deep burnt orange with a blue pin-stripe. The jacket was long—'military length', said the description—and had a lovely curved shape, fitted close around the ribs, then flared out to the hem. The trousers were flared too, and the model wore high heeled boots under them. *Jean Muir trouser suit, £14.50.* Nell could not afford more than £12.00 even if she saved up most of her dress allowance for the term. Perhaps when she went to university in a few years time she'd be able to buy a trouser suit from her student grant and throw away her old school mac, which was smelling horribly of dry-cleaning fluid.

She kept turning pages, then stopped to read an article about Lynn Redgrave. It said that Lynn had always been the ugly duckling in her glamorous family, because she was plump and self-conscious while her sister Vanessa was being called 'the most beautiful actress in England', but now everybody was raving about Lynn in *Georgy Girl* and saying that she could be the most talented of all the Redgraves. Nell lost interest in the article. She hadn't seen *Georgy Girl* and, besides, her eyes were stinging. Maybe from too much reading.

Her gaze slid across to the window. The dark was closing in outside and the lights in the carriage were reflecting on the glass, so she had to put her face right up to it to see. The bushes were black shadows along the railway line, with an eerie glow around them because the sky was still letting through shafts of light that showed the high points of the moors further away. If this was Dartmoor, they must already have passed Ivybridge, but the train wouldn't stop till Torquay. The glass was cold against Nell's forehead and the rattling of the train made her teeth vibrate. She drew back and saw the compartment reflected, with the hills and the trees rushing through it like ghosts.

•

The woman in the opposite corner was still asleep. What if she missed her station? Nell began to wonder if she should ask her where she wanted to get off, but she didn't like to disturb her. Anyway, she was enjoying the time to herself and the woman looked like the chatty type. Perhaps it would be best to wait till they were near Torquay, then tap her on the arm. Just in case. Nell wouldn't like an old lady to miss her station and have to go all the way back from Exeter in the dark. She stared at the reflected image of the hunched figure, with its head slumped into its chest. How could you let yourself go like that? Why did women just give up when they were about thirty-five, and start wearing those boxy sheepskin coats and thick woollen skirts right down to their knees?

The train went over some points and jolted from side to side so Nell's magazine nearly slipped from under her hand. She caught it as it was about to fall, and that was when she noticed something running along the floor of the carriage. At first she thought it was a trickle of water, but it was thick and dark, and then another streaked across after it, and another, and another. Nell lifted her feet off the floor in a sudden reflex, as she recognised that the liquid was dark red and spreading everywhere.

Although she hardly realised it, she was already screaming as she looked at the woman opposite and saw the bib of red stuff soaking into the sheepskin collar, gathering in the woollen lap and seeping steadily through onto the floor. Nell threw down the window and screamed for help out into the night, fighting for breath against the great thumping beats of her own heart. It was a full two minutes before it occurred to her to pull the emergency cord.

London, August 1971

1

London was awash with pale sunlight and Joni Mitchell was singing 'Chelsea Morning' in Nell's head as she watched a real Chelsea morning through the cab window. After she'd sat through what amounted to three continuous nights on the plane, relieved only by short episodes of shallow sleep, she felt as if she were dreaming and wide awake at the same time. Here she was, back in England.

Ten weeks of living in Adelaide, even in what were the winter months over there, had accustomed her to a light that was fiercer, thrown from the brilliant blue disc of an unbroken sky. It was hard to believe that the same sun shone here. This was an altogether different light, reflected from stone walls, broken into mottled patterns by the leaves of the trees, gleaming across the bare back of a passing cyclist.

It was Friday morning and Nell's watch said 8.30, so in Adelaide it would be dinner time on Friday evening and Mum would be frying the chops. Mum didn't like her going back on her own, not after what had happened, but everyone agreed she had to take up the university place she'd been offered, and her parents couldn't move from Adelaide because Dad was the head of the new training program there. She'd be all right anyway, she told them, so now she was going to have to prove it.

She leant forward in her seat, relishing the space around her, watching the people walk at different paces along The Embankment, or leant over to stare at the river. A hippie sat on the wall and strummed a guitar. They passed a pub that seemed to explode with flowers from hanging baskets and window boxes. Some of the houses had window boxes, too, filled with pink and red geraniums. Living in London was going to be fantastic.

'Pretty, init?' said the driver. 'That's the *Draper's Arms*. Gets fancier every year. Bit of a competition now, see, to be the fanciest pub in Chelsea. Trying to be part of the Flower Show. I've heard Adelaide's the Garden City—is that right?'

'Yes. There's parks all around it, in a ring.'

'That's nice, then. It's going to be a scorcher today, they reckon. Eighty's the forecast. But I expect that's nothing to you.'

'Well, it's winter in Australia now, so it can get quite cold.'

'So I've heard. I got an uncle over in Australia. He lives in Perth. Loves it out there, apparently. But I love London. Lived here all my life. Maybe it's because I'm a Londoner... You know that silly old song? Collingham Gardens is nice. You'll like it there. Lovely old houses. Got a flat, have you?'

'Yes. Well, my cousins have. I'm moving in with them.'

'That's nice, then. I hope they take care of you—little Australian girl like you could get swallowed up in London.'

Nell saw in the driving mirror his eyes, raised to see her reflection. A warning signal flickered somewhere on the edge of her consciousness. 'I'm not really Australian. Just my parents moved there a few years ago, so I went out there to stay with them after I finished my A levels.'

'Ah, that explains it. I didn't think you sounded much like one of them. They're all supposed to live in Earl's Court, you know. Kangaroo Valley, they call it. But anyway, you want to take care in swinging London. Few sharpers about, if you know what I mean. They older than you, these cousins?'

The warning light was on now.

'Yes. They're judo champions, as a matter of fact.'

'That right?' The cab drew up at a junction. 'I'm a bit of a judo champion myself.' The driver turned and winked at Nell before he drove off again and took a right turn.

She felt the panic wave start to rise and remembered the counsellor's instructions. Breathe through it. Just concentrate on your breathing. Let the breath out through your lips, smooth and steady. The cabbie went on talking.

'I'm only kidding, of course. My brother was the fighter. He used to tell me I couldn't knock the skin off a rice pudding—but I always knew my way around. That's the thing in London, see. Got to know your way around. Get yourself an A to Z. There's a tube map on the back. Then—doesn't matter where you are, or what time of the day or night it is—you can find your way home. This is Sloane Street, where the trendies live. What do you think of those platform shoes, then? Ridiculous, init? Wonder they don't fall over and cripple theirselves.'

Nell was counting her out breaths: one, two, three. She could feel sweat on her forehead and her mouth was dry. This was how it happened. Just as she was feeling happy, when she thought she was safe, some slight thing would open the crack through which it came back at her. The killer was still around, she knew—delivering milk, or selling ice creams or driving a cab—and he knew Nell. Schoolgirl Nell Adams, all the newspapers reported, finds murder victim on train. And there was her picture, on the front page. So he knew her name and he knew her face. His own, sought obsessively now in dreams and waking nightmares, was always obscured by the straggly brown hair blowing across it. It was worse in dreams. The focus zoomed in, like a close-up in a film, and just as the hair was about to blow clear and reveal the killer's eyes, she woke, sweating, with a strangled cry in her throat.

The cab turned another corner, then another. Sometimes she dreamt that a middle-aged woman in a sheepskin coat was looking for her; the woman wanted to explain politely that her throat had been cut, and to show where the wound was, pointing with a plump finger at the great smiling gash. Once, she dreamt she was back in Aunty Pat's house in Exeter watching television and turned to see the woman asleep in the armchair next to her, but this time with her head thrown back...'

'Here we are, then: Collingham Gardens. That's one pound and sixty-two new pence, my duck, or thirty-two and six, as I was brought up to call it. And here come the judo champions, by the looks.'

Julie and Rita were bopping around on the pavement, waving with rapid hand flaps and calling out.

'We thought it was you. We saw the taxi turn in on the other side of the square. We've been looking out for you for an hour.'

They pulled her out of the cab and hugged her, then began hauling her suitcases up the steps to the front door as Nell found a five pound note to pay the driver. She took three pounds in change and returned the coins to his skinny hand. He was okay. Just a friendly old bloke.

'Thank you, my duck. You take care now, won't you? Have a lovely time.'

•

The flat was up two flights of stairs, and had a small front balcony overlooking the gardens in the square. French windows led out from the sitting room, which must once have been vast, with its high ceilings and ornate plaster work. Now it was divided with a partition, to make an area for the bedrooms. These were so small they were almost like cubicles, side by side, each with its single bed, miniature chest of drawers and bedside table. The one at the front was the best, because it had a big window that overlooked the trees. The back one, the worst of the three, was rather dark, with a small window from which you could see onto an alley lined with rubbish bins. The middle one had a skylight and was slightly larger than the other two, so that there was room for a narrow table along the wall opposite the bed.

'This is yours,' said Rita, 'because there's room for the little desk, see? Julie and me are going to swap every six months, so each of us gets a turn in the front bedroom. You'll have one of us on either side of you, so you'll feel very safe. The only problem is those little windows above the doors let in quite a lot of light, so it's hard to go to sleep if someone has the light on in the sitting room. Means it's best if we all go to bed at the same time. Oh—bathroom! Through here.'

Rita led the way out into the hall and opened a door at the far end.

'We share it with the other flat, unfortunately. They sometimes complain if we take long baths or if they think we haven't cleaned it properly. So we bought a Mickey Mouse bath brush. Look! Isn't it wonderful? It's from Habitat. So's the aubergine bathmat—there are towels to match—Mum gave them to us last birthday. What about a cup of coffee?'

Julie already had the kettle boiling on the top of an old gas stove. The kitchen was long and narrow, with cracked lino on the floor. Nothing looked very clean. The sink was a stone laundry tub, containing a red plastic washing-up bowl packed tightly with mugs and cutlery.

'Sorry.' Julie picked out some mugs and rinsed them under the cold tap.

'We're terrible about the washing up. We were going to have everything all tidy for you, but somehow it didn't quite happen that way.' She spooned instant coffee into the mugs. 'Get the milk out, would you?'

The fridge was huge and its heavy door opened with a handle that operated like a giant stapler. Besides the solitary milk bottle, Nell could see nothing in there except a small wedge of cheese and some very old looking butter.

'We took a couple of days off work so we can show you around. Isn't it fabulous weather? Rita wants to go to Biba's. Don't you, Rita? Their new store is just fantastic. You'll love it. All the clothes are hung on these curved hatstands, with boas draped around them. After that we have to show you Mr Freedom—there's this giant satin shoe right in the middle of the shop and all the clothes are satin—blue and red and green satin all mixed together. It's brilliant. Then we could go to the ice cream parlour in Kensington Church Street. They have these flavours you wouldn't believe—like blueberry cheesecake and rocky road. Or you can even have a vanilla fudge sundae, which is to die for—but so fattening.'

Julie patted her flat stomach and handed Nell a mug of hot brown liquid. Nell's hand shook slightly as she accepted it.

'You okay?' asked Rita. 'You look a bit—'

'Yes. I'm fine. Just jet-lagged, that's all. I lost a couple of nights' sleep on the way over here.'

'Really? But that's terrible.'

Rita led the way back to the sitting room, where there was an ancient and bulbous three-piece suite. The armchairs were covered with a swirling pattern of mustard and orange that made Nell's head swim as she stared at it. She sat down carefully, so as not to spill the coffee. The twins sat on the sofa, which had been covered with a turquoise Indian bedspread. A wave of giddiness caught her and she put the mug on the floor just in time to prevent an accident.

'So tell us about Australia,' said Julie. 'What's it like out there? Is it really boiling hot all the time?'

'Well, not at the moment. It's winter, actually.'

'Really? I can't imagine that! Can you, Rita? Winter in August.

How funny. So why couldn't you get to sleep on the plane? Is it very noisy?'

'Not exactly; just cramped. I find it hard to sleep sitting up.'

'What? You mean they don't even give you a bed on those long flights? You poor *thing*!'

Nell suddenly found the image of a dormitory plane unbearably funny and started giggling.

'What? What's so hilarious?' Rita's face had lit up, ready to share the joke. But Nell was too far gone to answer. She giggled till the tears streamed down her face and then she got the hiccups, which she tried to control with gulps of coffee.

2

Dressed and ready to go, Briony Williams was looking out over Camden High Street from her first floor flat, waiting eagerly for the sound of the police siren. It was now 7.20 am. If the car got here this side of half past, they'd just about make it to Gower Street in ten minutes, with the siren on. Shafts of sun were appearing on the pavement, glinting across the tops of the cars. It was going to be hot.

She heard the car before she saw it and was downstairs locking the front door as it drew up. Two uniforms were in the front seat and Detective Superintendent Macready was in the back, wearing a heavy grey overcoat. Briony wondered if it was because he hadn't checked the weather, or because he always went out dressed like that.

'Morning, sir. What a beautiful day!'

'Morning,' he huffed, before turning back to look out of his window.

Briony watched the road ahead, with the lines of Monday morning traffic parting in response to the siren. Had to be some job, and it was timed right for the start of the week, which was a bit too tidy, somehow. She thought of remarking on it, but glancing sideways at Macready got the distinct impression that he was not in the mood for remarks. Donna, one of her new colleagues at Vine Street, had warned her, 'He's tight with everything, including words. Typical Scottish.'

He'd been on the panel for Briony's promotion and—well, talk about give nothing away! She'd prepared like a mad thing for that interview, researching late into the night. She'd compiled dossiers on six unsolved murders, going through every detail to identify possible neglected leads, and the rest of the committee were visibly impressed. Macready had said nothing, until right at the end of the interview, when he'd leant forward, clasped his hands together on the table and fixed her with a steady gaze.

'Do you not think, DC Williams, that you might need to have flesh and blood knowledge of these cases in order to be able to contribute anything useful to the inquiry?'

She was convinced he'd voted against her, but she got the promotion. Then the next thing she knew, Macready had actually asked for her to be transferred to his new divisional team at Vine Street. Now here she was, barely a week after having started the new job, the youngest female DI the Met had yet assigned to a major investigation.

Gower Street was closed off at the Euston Road end and there were four police cars and an ambulance behind the cordon. Briony was poised to be out of the car as soon as it had drawn up, but Macready was of the slow and steady school and it was protocol to stay behind him. He brushed down his coat as he stood up, closed his door carefully, then spoke to the driver before proceeding up the steps into the building. The officers guarding the entrance to the laboratory saluted Macready and held the doors open. He strode forward into the room, ignoring the offer of a white mask from a female officer by the door. Briony accepted one and tied the tapes securely around the back of her head before going any further.

The lab was like a large hall, with its floor set about three feet below ground level, and long windows that stretched high above ground, flooding the whole place with light. The lamps around the gurneys set against the walls under the windows seemed superfluous. Bodies and parts of bodies, all variously opened up for examination, were lying on the gurneys. A detached leg was arranged with the thigh skin pinned back, cleanly revealing all the muscles. Waiting for attention on the neighbouring table was a plump male cadaver from which the head had been removed. Severed hands lay in a stainless steel tray of preservative, each attached to its identification label by a red thread tied around the index finger.

Between two of the tables was a small doorway that evidently led directly onto the street by some stone steps. Fingerprinting officers were at work on the door itself, painting the areas around the lock. That must have been where the murderer got in. Briony went to take a closer look. It was a fairly solid door, with metal bands around the top and bottom. The dry weather would have favoured the intruder, because forensics were going to have a lot of trouble getting any footprints off the flagged stone floor.

The victim was at the far end of the room, on a massive oval-shaped table that was obviously used for demonstrations. It was drawn away from the wall so that there was room for several people to stand behind it, and surrounded now by a silent audience of professionals. The photographer's flash was going off with a steady rhythm, but Briony couldn't see what the camera saw. Although a space cleared instantly for Macready when he strode forward, nobody moved aside for her.

'Excuse me,' she said through her mask, but produced only a muffled noise. When she tried to edge forward into what looked like a clearer space, a uniformed arm shot out to bar her way. Then the officer pointed to the floor, where there was a large tin vessel, like an old wash-tub, from which a trail of intestines led upwards to the table. That tub didn't belong in the lab. It was a battered, domestic thing. Briony could now see the mid-section of the corpse, where the disembowelling had been done with an oversized knife, left protruding from the abdominal cavity. The knife was not a professional instrument—she could see rust on the blade and the crudely shaped wooden handle was marked with what looked like a bloody handprint.

Macready moved around behind the table, making a sign for the photographer to stop. Briony noticed that no one else was wearing a mask and wondered if she should take hers off. But it was too late.

'Perhaps some of the officers would be courteous enough to move back a little,' he said, 'so that Detective Inspector Williams can get a clear view. And perhaps, Detective Inspector Williams, you would care to remove your mask, since this patient's condition is unlikely to be adversely affected by your breathing on him.'

Briony could feel herself blushing as she fumbled at the tapes. As she pulled the mask away, she registered an unfamiliar chemical smell that hit the back of her throat and made her cough. 'Formaldehyde,' Macready remarked. She tried to suppress the cough, but it erupted again as she looked at the body on the table. For a second, it seemed as if the thing were rearing its head to look at her.

This effect was due to a clamp under the base of the skull, which lifted the head several inches from the table with a very convincing turn. The jaw was dropped wide open. One eye was also open, but the other had been scooped out with a fine bladed knife that was still wedged deep in the socket. A thick bolt was screwed through the centre of the forehead. The abdomen was a gaping cavern, with the large knife skewered in the liver.

'This is Richard Godwin, FRCS,' said Macready quietly, 'Professor of Anatomy and Physiology. Aged fifty-eight.'

'What's FRCS mean?' asked the photographer, in a distinct cockney accent.

'Fellow of the Royal College of Surgeons,' answered Briony promptly, keen to take any opportunity to establish her credibility. 'Who found the body?'

'We'll go into that later. I'd like this room cleared now while the pathologists do their work. And please keep the press behind the cordon. I don't want any of them sneaking up to the building. All details of this are to remain strictly confidential.'

The photographer moved around the table to take shots of the tub, then began to pack up his camera.

'Got a right one here,' he said.

'Are you referring to the victim or the perpetrator, Jimmy?' Macready was wearing a half smile, the first Briony had ever seen on him. 'There is no doubt that this was carried out by someone with a sense of theatre and a great deal of confidence. This cannot be our man's first job and it will not be his last.'

'What if it was done by a woman?' The question had leapt out of Briony's mouth before she knew it was there.

Macready studied her for a moment before replying. 'Female murderers—murderesses,' and his Scots accent enabled him to capture all four syllables of the word, '—do not exist outside the imaginations of fiction writers. Women do not commit murder. They are occasionally guilty of manslaughter, but that is invariably the result of carelessness or bad driving.'

Okay, thought Briony, rule number one: don't get fazed. Rule number two: keep coming back. She looked him in the eye. 'It's Hogarth, isn't it?'

The photographer, a slightly built young man with an impish expression on his face, turned and stared at her. 'It's what?'

'Williams is keen for us to know she studied art history in her A levels,' said Macready. 'There's an etching, Jimmy, by an artist named William Hogarth, upon which this work of mischief we're looking at is undoubtedly based. Did they not teach you art history in your photography course?'

Jimmy shrugged. 'Well—s'posed to. I thought it was a bit boring.'

'Ah!' Macready's eyes lit up as if someone had just given him a vital piece of information. 'We detectives,' he said, 'cannot afford to find anything boring. Can we, Williams?'

The team assembled in the incident room at Vine Street that afternoon was small, considering the nature of the crime: three assistant detectives including Briony, two detective constables for surveillance work (one of whom was Briony's new friend Donna), Jimmy the photographer, and two other scene-of-crime officers who were in charge of the forensics. Macready had a reputation for running a tight ship with a handpicked crew. The same forensics team had been with him for fifteen years and he insisted on Jimmy as his photographer for every case. Steve Latham had been a controversial DI appointment six years earlier with a degree from Oxford, brought in because Macready had said he needed someone whose brains were bigger than his boots. Donna told her this and warned her that if you only worked once with Macready, it was a heavy mark against you. He picked carefully and expected you to be good. If you were, he didn't let you go—so, if he did let you go…

'I get it,' said Briony. 'My first job as a DI and I land up on a tightrope. Don't fall off and if you can turn a couple of somersaults on the way, that'll be fine.'

'Something like that.' Donna grinned. 'That's what you get for being promoted before you've done your time on the beat.'

Donna was one of two detective constables specialising in undercover work and on her fourth investigation with Macready. There'd be no fear of her failing to come up to the mark, thought Briony. She was as sharp as a tack—about people, anyway. And she could size up instantly what was going on in a room and change her tactics to suit: sometimes just blending in with whoever was there; sometimes attracting everyone's attention with the way she looked and moved. She wore her long hair loose and came to work in an assortment of coordinated outfits from the best boutiques. Briony wondered how she looked on her days off.

Everyone fell silent as Macready came in. He had taken off the overcoat now and, sitting with his hands clasped together on the desk in front of him, he revealed a complex arrangement of cuffs and leather buttoned sleeve edges. The silence grew uncomfortably long as his gaze travelled the faces in the room, one by one, his expression unchanging. Then he took a gold fob watch from his jacket pocket and checked the time before starting his address.

'This could prove to be a very difficult case or very easy. The murderer, in what may seem an excess of confidence, has left us no less than three weapons, on one of which he has apparently been considerate enough to leave a handprint. He is clearly someone familiar with the college, who had access to an external door of the laboratory with a key, and he is also clearly someone who has qualified himself in anatomy. However, this only means he could be one of several hundred students who have passed through the college in the last five years or so. He may have changed his identity since then.

'There is a strong element of fantasy in this crime. It might have been inspired by hallucinatory experiences, but it was not executed under any such influence. Whoever did it knew exactly what he was about in every detail. It is almost certainly not the killer's first murder, so we need to start the search through archives for any unsolved case that may have features in common. If we can find his earlier work, that will greatly increase our chances of finding him, at the risk of wasting time on extensive searches that are likely to produce red herrings.

'For the time being, the priorities in this investigation will be tracing the murder weapons and interviewing all those students of the college who are at present in residence and may have valuable information as observers, witnesses or possible suspects. As I'm sure you are aware, this is not term time, so those who are around are mainly here to do research or to study for exams. We need a statement from every one of them, with an alibi and details of anything they have seen or heard about that could possibly be relevant.

'There will be another briefing as soon as we have the autopsy reports. Now I would like to confer with the assistant detectives on this case—Latham, Palgrave, Williams—in my office, please.'

It was clear that the three men knew each other well, and it was hard for Briony not to both feel and look awkward. Inner circles were not easy to enter, especially when they kept reminding you that you were the wrong sex.

She wasn't sure what to expect of Palgrave, who had cast a couple of stern glances in her direction during the briefing. Was her Marks and Spencer's cotton jacket too racy for him? He had to be somewhere in his fifties, maybe even a few years older than Macready, and had obviously done his time in uniform, so might well resent the fact that she hadn't. He showed a lot of wrist as he shook hands— the sleeves of his limp suit were too short, and the cuffs of his shirt too starched. He was tallish, say five foot eleven, but fine boned and somehow brittle looking. His thin hair was parted sharply and cut high over his ears, which stuck out slightly. It was the hair in his nose that needed trimming, Briony couldn't help thinking.

Steve Latham, whom Donna had pointed out to her as Macready's protégé, made a very different impression. He offered her a cigarette with a slightly shaky hand, which went to sweep his hair out of the way as soon as the pack was back in his pocket. 'Nervy' was the word Briony's mother would have used about him, but at least he gave the impression of being a bit with it, which was more than you could say for the other two. His suit had a touch of Carnaby Street, and the fitted shirt he wore under it might have looked good if only he'd ironed it. Briony noticed that he hadn't shaved, either. She guessed the call this morning had caught him still in bed, and that was no doubt why he wasn't there when she and Macready inspected the scene. Well, good. If he was human and a bit rough around the edges, maybe she wouldn't be the only one to fall short of the clinical precision the boss seemed to require.

Macready gestured for them to take seats opposite him.

'Palgrave, you will be supervising the collection of statements and coordinating the searches as usual, including the weapons trace. Latham will be coordinating the work of suspect elimination and will be developing strategies with me. Williams... This is Detective Inspector Williams's first case with us. I have decided to put a woman on this team because I believe that the female of the species has higher abilities in certain areas.' He paused for a moment, like someone saving up a punch line, looking at the three of them in turn with one eyebrow slightly raised. 'Namely, in interview work and in records.'

Briony came back a bit too quickly. 'What sort of thing in records, sir?'

'Searches, archive work. That sort of thing.'

'Surely much of that can be done by the clerical staff. But I'd like to conduct the interview with the person who found the body. I think—'

Macready cut across her. 'Latham and I will conduct all interviews on the primary list and that is the first on the list, but you may sit in if you wish. It will, I expect, be an educative experience. We'll be preparing a secondary list of subjects for interview, but for now you can start with the filing. Since it is more than likely that our man has killed before, we need to go through records of unsolved homicides in the Greater London area over the past eighteen months. We may need to go back further and range more widely, but successive killings by one person most commonly occur within a discrete geographic area and less than eighteen months apart. The use of formaldehyde is worth attention. It is rarely employed as an anatomical preservative these days, but it certainly makes an impression, does it not? It will give us an initial lead in identifying cases with possible connections to this one.'

There was a pause. Steve Latham leant forward, smoke leaking slowly from his nostrils.

'Maybe he used it to suffocate the victim. Formaldehyde on a handkerchief, pressed over the nose and mouth, is a really easy way to put someone out. He wouldn't have been able to do all that fancy work on a struggling victim. Is it easy to get hold of?'

'Formaldehyde?' said Palgrave. 'Dry cleaners use it on permanent press fabrics. You'd get it in diluted form easily enough. It's used in a lot of household cleaning products. There was a case of domestic poisoning a few years ago—woman washed her mother-in-law's sheets in it. Nasty stuff. Causes rashes, asthma attacks, nausea. It took the old woman seven weeks to die. GP failed to identify the cause of the symptoms.'

Steve interrupted. 'But if we're dealing with a mass murderer—'
Macready interrupted.

'This is not mass murder, Latham. Mass murder is what occurs when a bomb goes off. What I am suggesting is that this may be a case of repeat killing. Or *serial killing* is a term I have heard in use recently at Scotland Yard.'

'Whatever we call it, sir,' said Palgrave, 'when this gets out it's going to generate a lot of work at the station. There's going to be scared people wanting information and all sorts of cranks ringing up offering to give it. And the press will be all over us.'

'Those are matters I will leave in your very capable hands, Palgrave. If you need to transfer more officers into the area, you have my authority to do so.'

Latham took a deep drag on his cigarette and lit another from the glowing stub.

3

Vine Street Station had reopened in a hurry to help cope with the spill-over of cases coming through West End Central, where things had become pretty well unmanageable if the Met gossip was anything to go by. But Vine Street looked like a place that should have stayed closed, hidden in its ugly little back street, keeping its naked light-bulbs and yellowing walls and brown lino floors to itself. It was just round the corner from the electric carnival of Piccadilly Circus, but seemed like another world, a world passed over by the whole energy surge that had transformed London's streets in the past five years.

When Briony got back to the incident room after lunch, there was no one there. The mismatched, ill-arranged furniture looked strange on it own, like a jumble sale waiting to be priced. She had definitely been given the worst desk—newcomer's privilege—a hefty one with drawers that jammed and a sheet of particularly lurid green Fablon covering the top. The chair, a squat thing with heavy wheels, was too low for it. She steered it out into the middle of the room, and gave it a kick that sent it off to the far end, amid a collection of empty cardboard boxes and the scrolls of butchers paper used for sketching out enquiry lines. With one of the scrolls tucked under her arm, she moved around trying the chairs behind all the other desks until she found one that felt right. This she wheeled back to her own place. A couple of yards of the butchers paper served to cover the offending green Fablon, and provided her with a convenient surface for notes.

She sat down and phoned the records department at West End Central.

'Now let me get this straight,' said the voice on the other end of the line. 'You want unsolved homicides going back to January 1969. What area?'

'I told you, all of them.'

'What, the whole of Central London? You gotta be joking.'

'I'm not joking. I'm carrying out the instructions of Superintendent Macready on a murder inquiry. Those are the records requested.'

'Well, where are you going to put them? It'll be a bloody truck-load. We got some cases run to three boxes each on their own.'

'I don't need them all at once—'

'Then why don't you ask for what you do need? We're busy here, you know. The whole collection's being rearranged. I spent the morning stacking boxes that don't even have any labels on them. I'm not in the mood for fancy requests.'

'Look, I'm trying to explain to you—'

'I don't need no explanations, darling. Why don't you sort yourself out and give us a ring when you know what you're doing?'

Latham came in just as she slammed the phone down.

'Problems?'

'Bloody records section.'

'Say no more. They've been reorganised and they're in more of a mess than we are. I came to tell you we're interviewing Colin Oldroyd—that's the guy who found the body—in ten minutes, Room 7 down the corridor. They've just finished taking his statement—poor sod looks completely shell-shocked. Don't blame him.

What a freak out. What's your name, by the way? I can't call you Williams all the time.'

'Briony.'

'Nice. Celtic. You look kind of Celtic. I'm Steve. Cigarette?'

'I don't smoke.'

'Why's that, then?'

Briony shrugged. 'Just...never took it up.'

Steve shook out his match and took a deep addict's drag.

'You will, believe me.'

•

The interview room was small, hot and stuffy. Briony noticed that beads of sweat had collected in the stubble on the side of Steve's face.

'Open the window, Latham,' said Macready, who by now was reduced to his shirt sleeves. 'If we are not going to suffocate we'll need some fresh air.'

'There isn't any. It's what the papers call a scorcher out there. Shall I see if I can find a fan?'

'No. They're too distracting. Just open the window.'

Steve was right. There wasn't enough breeze to stir the dust from the window ledge. Briony hung her own jacket on the back of a chair, which she then positioned at the end of the table furthest from where the subject was going to be. When Colin Oldroyd was shown in, the two men introduced themselves and shook hands, so she did too, making sure he met her eye and took in her confident smile. Her colleagues might be able to force her into a back seat temporarily, but she knew her interview skills weren't matched by anyone she'd worked with so far. And it remained to be seen whether Macready and Latham had as much to teach her as they seemed to think.

Oldroyd was one of those sandy-coloured men she could never find very interesting: pale hair, beige cord jacket (held hooked over his shoulder on one finger), light trousers, desert boots. Aged somewhere between thirty and thirty-five, Briony guessed. He spoke with a trace of Yorkshire accent.

Macready pushed a typed document across the table towards him.

'Dr Oldroyd, this is a copy of the statement you made to Inspector Palgrave when you came in. We would like to ask you about some aspects of your account. Inspector Latham will begin.'

Latham coughed and fumbled with a couple of bits of paper containing scrappy notes, before he got his first question out.

'You say you were not the first to enter the laboratory this morning when you arrived at...7.15. That there were already two students at work in there.'

'That's right. Postgraduate students. We would not allow undergraduates in there unsupervised. Research students are issued with keys to the external door because they may need to work late at night or early in the morning. We're trying out a new preservative that enables us to maintain a cadaver out of deep storage for thirty-six hours, so the research students who are undertaking complex dissections will work almost round the clock. It's perfectly normal to find people in there by seven.'

'Could they have failed to notice anything amiss in the laboratory?'

'Easily. Researchers are not encouraged to examine each other's work in there unless they're invited to do so. There've been complaints in the past about work being copied and even stolen.'

'Stolen? How is that?'

'It's usually the undergrads, of course. Typically the ones who don't do any work, then panic before their exams. Happened to me when I first came. I did some difficult work on the thoracic area—isolating the major blood vessels, which is very tricky to do without damaging them—and when I came back next day a young smart alec was digging away in there with a scalpel, trying to claim he'd done all the work himself. He was due to be assessed for his finals and he was worried about failing. It all came out in the inquiry.'

'An internal inquiry?'

'That's right, yes. By the college board.'

'Why do you think you noticed that something was wrong when the other people in there didn't?'

'Simple. I have some supervisory responsibilities in the lab. It's my job to go round and check that the equipment's in place, instruments have been properly cleaned, bodies are being handled with respect and so on. I noticed immediately that there'd been some funny business.'

'Funny business? Why would you refer to it as funny business, Dr Oldroyd?'

'Because that's what I thought it was. At first glance, any road. A student prank. They happen from time to time, though I've never seen one of that order before, I can tell you.'

'Did you recognise that it was Godwin?'

Clearly in distress, he shook his head several times. 'No. It was just—well, you saw it. It hardly looked human at all. The face was all pulled out of shape.'

'So what was your first reaction?'

'I was angry. I thought it was a disgrace.' Oldroyd stopped and took an audible deep breath. 'From time to time—as I say—some bunch of undergraduates get themselves in a bit of a party mood and decide to play games with one of the bodies. They dress it up, or arrange it with an extra arm and leg, that sort of thing. Some of the younger ones—that's their idea of a joke. But, of course, we take it very seriously. Every effort is made to identify the culprits and they're always disciplined. It's reported to the head of department initially. Then he reports to the ethics committee, which considers the case and usually issues an official reprimand. That's kept on record. Any further misconduct of any kind and they're out. They're all supposed to have passed tests in medical ethics before they're allowed into the human anatomy lab. If they lack respect for the people whose bodies they're privileged to examine, then they shouldn't be allowed to call themselves doctors.' Oldroyd had gone red in the face. 'Well, that's my opinion, any road. Sometimes I think there's a bit too much tolerance these days, what with the sit-ins and all that kind of nonsense...'

Macready poured him a glass of water and Steve gave him time to drink it and start on a refill before asking the next question.

'Presumably, then, the college has records of all such cases.'

Oldroyd made an emphatic sideways movement with his head. 'My word.'

'Who should we approach about access to those?'

Oldroyd stared at his water glass, sliding his fingers around on the condensation.

'Normally it would be the head of department.'

'And who is that?'

Oldroyd's voice choked as he tried to reply.

Macready evidently decided this was the moment to take over. 'It is Professor Godwin, is it not?' Oldroyd nodded, and his mouth twitched. Keep him focused, thought Briony. Don't let him get emotional. There's more he can tell us.

Macready framed his words gently and quite slowly, almost as if he were speaking to a child.

'So you thought at first, understandably, that this was someone's idea of a joke?'

'Yes. Thing is—although I didn't instantly see it was Godwin, I recognised the Hogarth picture instantly. Godwin used to show a slide of it in his lectures on the history of anatomy. There's a print in his study. So I suppose it stands to reason that some of the young larks might have drawn on it for inspiration.'

'And what made you realise this was no lark?'

'Well... two things, actually. When I went in close, of course, I noticed the formaldehyde, which is not something our students are supplied with. I don't know where they'd have got it in concentrated form. Then the—well, what they'd done to the body. It was too complicated and technically too difficult. The work on the torso is fairly standard stuff, but driving an inch-thick bolt through the front of the cranium, without cracking the whole thing apart, that's a pretty advanced exercise. I doubt I could do it myself, and I've had some experience in cranial surgery.'

There was a pause.

'Then all of a sudden, I did recognise the victim. I couldn't believe it at first. I'd seen him only the day before, eating a ham sandwich in the pub at lunch time, and looking pleased with himself because he'd just been given funding for a new laboratory. He bought me a beer to celebrate. He has a wife, you know, and grown up children—a son and a daughter—although I've never met them. He used to talk about them. His son's reading philosophy at Cambridge—he'd be in his second year, I think...'

Keep him focused, Briony urged again, mentally. Get him back on track.

Macready came in briskly with his next question. 'Can you think of anyone who might have a grudge against Professor Godwin?'

'No.'

Rubbish, thought Briony. He was the one who shopped them to the ethics committee when they had a muck-up day.

'One last question,' said Macready. You obviously have quite a knowledge of the students and staff in the college, Dr Oldroyd. Do you have any suspicions of your own, perhaps, about who might have done this?'

'Not right now. I suppose I'm a bit...stunned. I'm not thinking straight. But d'you mind if I ask you something?'

He seemed to hesitate as he said this, looking sideways at Latham without moving his head, then at Macready, who prompted.

'Please feel free to say anything more that may be on your mind.'

Oldroyd took a deep breath. 'Are you the murder squad? It's just—I thought something like this—it would be a job for Scotland Yard.'

Macready could not prevent a smile from growing across his face.

'Ah, the famed murder squad. Dr Oldroyd, I have been appointed to form a major investigation pool here at Vine Street. I will make sure that the very best personnel available are brought in to this inquiry.'

'Of course. Thank you. I hope you don't… I didn't mean…like I say, I'm not thinking straight.'

Macready escorted him from the room and Steve and Briony followed at a discreet distance.

'I guess you must find this all a bit overwhelming,' said Steve.

'Well, you shouldn't.'

He made an exaggerated frown. 'Eh? Shouldn't what?'

'Shouldn't guess.'

He dragged on this cigarette.

'All right, then. Tell me what you make of Oldroyd.'

'Is he a suspect?'

'Of course.'

'I'd say he's not a risk taker in any way. He was comfortable in his world. Doing well. Why should he want to turn it upside down? He's not imaginative enough to be involved in anything like this. He sees himself as the one who prevents trouble. He's not going to make it. But he didn't give us the full quid on Godwin. Somebody should have pushed him harder on that question about grudges. We're going to have to look into that.'

As they gravitated towards their places in the incident room, she realised it was Steve's chair she'd just swapped for the dud. She put her hand over her mouth to suppress a giggle as he sat down, and inspected the new close relationship with his desk top.

'Just a minute.' He looked at her with piercing blue eyes. 'Who's been playing Goldilocks around here?'

4

Nell woke in the dark again. Yesterday, like the day before, she'd fallen heavily asleep at four in the afternoon and now again she'd woken up before three in the morning.

'Damn,' she whispered, as she shone the torch on her watch. It would be three hours before there was even a glimmer of daylight, four hours before she could safely go for a walk outside, five before any of the shops or cafés were open and probably a good deal more than that before either of the twins woke up.

With the torch pointed at the floor in front of her, she made her way as silently as possible out through the sitting room to the balcony, where there was an old wicker chair. It creaked loudly as she sat in it, then again when she leant forward to pick up the magazine Rita had left under it. The pictures in *Vogue* looked funny by torchlight, especially as this was the summer edition. Verushka was posed against sand dunes, arms across her naked chest, wearing nothing but a white sarong and heavy gold bracelets. Even framed in the circle of orange torchlight, the sand dunes made Nell think of Adelaide with a sharp pang of longing. You could see the dunes from the window of her parents' flat in Glenelg. How could she have left there, so suddenly and totally?

Flying was the weirdest thing. Your body just couldn't understand that it had come all this way and it was still back there somewhere in another time zone, another climate. She switched off the torch. Even the stars were different. The sky looked lower, denser. The moon was a pale sick thing, nothing like the great gold disc that hung over the sea at Glenelg.

Was she really going to like it in London? After that first intoxicating dose of English summer, the city was beginning to lose its magic. Nell remembered her first trip to London—on a shopping spree with Aunty Pat and the twins after she had finished her O levels—so it must have been three years ago. Everyone was still trying to help her forget what had happened the year before. And it worked, for a while. They were all caught up in a great wave of excitement that seemed to surge through the crowds in the streets. It was in the music, the clothes, the shops, the cars, the way people moved and talked. Groups of students sat on the grass in the parks, playing guitars. Some people just leant against the sunlit walls of the buildings and watched the world through wire-framed glasses with blue lenses. Julie had to have a pair of those.

Bob Dylan's voice cruised in the background at Just Looking in the King's Road as Rita helped Nell pick out an Ossie Clark shirt. She still had it, but it was a size too small now. At that time, she was driving Aunty Pat mad by refusing to eat, and that inspired the twins to do the same. The girls had turned heads in their new clothes. Julie counted the wolf whistles. She wanted a boyfriend with a red MG. Rita wanted the tall guy in the velvet suit who cut her hair at John Michael's. Nell wanted John Lennon.

But somehow, that new world seemed to have got old very quickly. Yesterday London came across to her as a tired, irritated, disappointed place, run by hustlers and pushers, though Julie and Rita behaved as if they hadn't noticed the change. Julie worked for Brook Street Bureau, an employment agency that found temporary office jobs for the hundreds of girls who flooded into London every week to start a new life. Rita was hoping to be made a junior buyer at Harrods Way In boutique, if she did well on the sales team this year. The twins hadn't asked her much about university. When she left a small pile of Penguin novels on the coffee table in the sitting room, Julie moved them out of the way, onto a shelf crowded with junk.

Nell picked up the torch and went back into the sitting room to fetch them. *Anna Karenina* was the one she'd been reading on the plane and had now got quite deeply into. She was about two-thirds of the way through the story where Anna had the nightmare about the railway accident. Nell recognised things about Anna, like the sudden changes of mood, the broken trains of thought, the need to take drugs at bedtime to make her sleep, then more drugs to dull the aftereffects of the nightmares. Panic symptoms.

Now you had counsellors to help with those. Nell could still hear the friendly advice in her head:

You were unlucky to be the one who was there at the time, but this terrible thing was nothing to do with you. It didn't choose you. You were there by chance—it could have been anyone. But it's over now. It's in the past. Nothing like that is ever going to happen again.

But Anna knew something different. She knew that the horror was for her and no one else, and that it was going to come back. Nell felt the old wave of terror rising in her own body, in sympathy.

5

Briony was the first person in the incident room next morning when she arrived at 7.30 to start work on the files. Twenty-four of the vital seventy-two hours were gone and she had to make up for lost time already, but she was still trying to figure out how to place the order with the prickly guy in records.

The forensic report confirmed that formaldehyde had been used in a gag across the victim's nose and mouth, partially suffocating him before his throat was cut. Twice. With two elegantly parallel gashes. Formaldehyde might, as Macready said, be one of the killer's trademarks, but you'd have to go through case notes of each murder in detail to find out whether it had been used. That would take time. Lots of it.

If the files were cross-referenced for a murder weapon—as they were at the Holloway Station where she last worked—she could order the records for all the homicides that had involved a surgical scalpel, or an iron bolt, or a rusty butcher's knife. But since whoever did this was so versatile in his choice of instruments, maybe he'd used a whole different set the time before. She needed to identify anything that might be a common factor. Perhaps the photographs would help. There were a few polaroids already on the display board, but she needed the whole collection, which might be ready by now, with any luck.

She went down the corridor to see whether Jimmy was in yet and met Donna Caldwell arriving for duty in a little navy blue two piece with a deep pink shirt, her eyes made up with metallic blue gloss under a pair of wire-framed glasses.

'Hey, what's with the secretarial look?' asked Briony, whose cheesecloth shirt was looking limp and very off-white, in keeping with the Vine Steet decor.

Donna blinked her eyes, dolly-bird style. 'This isn't me?'

'No, not really.'

'Med students are supposed to be a bit conservative. The handbook for new students says, "Medicine is a professional discipline that attracts responsible and serious minded students. Undergraduates in the medical faculty tend to dress less casually than students in other faculties." My brief is to hang around the canteen and the common room and go to a few lectures. Will I pass?'

'Pass what? They have pretty high standards in anatomy, you know. I have to find Jimmy. Do you think he'd be in yet?'

Donna looked at her watch. 'Jimmy's usually at Lyons corner house at this time, eating sausage and egg.'

'Come with me. Students are never around before ten. You've got time for breakfast, haven't you?'

•

Vine Street was narrow with three-storey buildings on either side and it hadn't caught the sun yet, but when Briony and Donna turned into Piccadilly, summer was in full swing. Office girls poured out of the tube station in bright cotton dresses, and two men drove past in an open topped sports car, wolf whistling loudly at them. Baskets of pink and purple flowers hung from the curled tops of the lamp posts and Eros looked as if he was about to get lift-off into the blue, along with all the pigeons milling around his pedestal.

Donna stopped to exchange the spectacles for a pair of pink framed sunglasses with matching lenses, then looked up, smiling brilliantly.

'I love summer in London, don't you?'

'Yeah. Wouldn't it be great to just go and lie around in Hyde Park near the water? What are we doing chasing killers, Donna?'

'I know. I think it's mad sometimes, working for the police. Then I think… All these people, looking forward to an ordinary normal day, worrying about whether they're going to be late for work, or thinking about who they're going out with tonight. And somewhere among them is the guy with the knife, thinking about when he's going to use it next.'

•

There was a queue in Lyons and most of the tables were already taken. Donna pointed to where Jimmy was sitting in one of the booths along the side wall.

'You go and chat him up and I'll get the breakfasts. What do you want?'

'The lot, whatever that is.' Briony pointed to the menu and gave Donna a pound note. 'And a big mug of coffee.'

Jimmy was steering a piece of sausage through a lake of egg yolk and HP sauce. He didn't look up or give any sign that he saw Briony hovering by the table.

'Hello. Mind if I join you?'

He snapped up the sausage and gestured with his fork to the seat opposite. 'Be my guest.'

'I came to ask you about the photos.'

'Oh yeah?'

'How long have you been doing this job?'

'What job's that, then?'

'Police photographer.'

'You mean how long have I been working as a scene of crime officer for SO3?'

'That's what I mean.'

'Four years.'

'And how many murder cases have you dealt with?'

'As a soco? Ooh...' Jimmy counted on his fingers rapidly, going through both hands several times. 'Na. Couldn't say. Not on a quick count.' He swung his fork from side to side, as if weighing up the probabilities.

'Look—you don't have to take the piss out of me. What I really want to know is—You must get an impression from the photos—you know, when you're processing them and pinning them up—you must get a particular point of view.'

'Sometimes.' He cut off another piece of sausage, speared it and put it in his mouth.

'So what's your impression this time?'

'Like I said.' Jimmy spoke through the sausage. 'Nutter. This one's a nutcase.'

'But you can do better than that. What's his particular thing, this nutcase? What's he trying to achieve?'

'Different from all the others, you mean?'

'Yeah.'

'Question for a psychologist. Not my department.'

Briony suppressed an impulse to snatch the fork from his hand. 'Of course it's your department. Everyone on an investigation has ideas and observations. You know what I mean. When you look at the photos, what's running through your mind?'

Donna came into view, carrying a loaded tray.

'Here's your breakfast,' said Jimmy. 'I was wondering if we could get a break in this interview. Hello, Donna. Did *you* bring her here?' He pointed at Briony with his knife. 'She's giving me the third degree.'

'Yeah, she's like that.'

'I just want his impressions. So you were about to tell me, Jimmy—your impressions, based on the photos.'

Jimmy pushed his plate away and fished a pack of cigarettes out of his coat pocket.

'He worked it all out in advance, how it would look. Most killers, they got no idea how it's going to look. I seen a couple of cases where they tried to make some kind of picture—like for a film shot or something—but they never got it right. Killing is messy and I often think—well, most of them never quite expect how much mess they're going to make. But this bloke, he knew exactly what to expect. He planned every detail and got everything right. Now, that gives me the creeps. It's not human, you know? Most people are animals when they kill. This one's more like a machine.'

'Thanks,' said Briony. 'That's exactly the kind of thing I was after. Really helpful. Look, I've been asked to go through the records to see if I can identify anything else that might be his work and—'

'What records exactly?'

'That's the problem. I need to find a way of cutting down the search and I thought—if we could start with just the photographs, that might be a way to do it.'

'You've got a point there,' said Donna. 'Now eat your breakfast.'

Jimmy indicated her overloaded plate. 'And if it's all a bit too much for you, you'll find me very helpful.'

•

It was almost nine when Briony got back to the incident room, and Jimmy set about arranging shots from the crime scene and the autopsy room on the display board. He obviously had no more time for questions.

Briony looked at each of the photographs closely, then stepped back for a general impression. It was true. There was a completely controlled picture here, a tableau. She had never seen anything like it, but something was nagging at her memory, all the same. An arranged scene of murder. Witty. Ostentatious. Bodies used to make art. Was it some case that had been described to her? One of those she'd studied at Hendon? The ringing bell faded. She was about to go and scribble down the train of thought so that at least she could try and track it to its source later on, but she was interrupted by Macready's entrance.

He swept to the front of the room and launched into his report at such a pace she couldn't write fast enough to keep up with the details.

'Cause of death was a lateral knife wound, left to right, which severed the trachea and the carotid artery. A second gash, parallel, was more superficial and may have been done for effect. The rest of the wounds were done post mortem, after the victim had bled so much that the body was almost drained. Time of death was between 11.30 pm and 1.00 am. The last persons we know to have been in the laboratory other than Godwin were Dr Gregory Francis and two of his doctoral students, who say they left shortly after 10.00 pm and that it had been Godwin's intention to leave shortly afterwards. If we assume that the killer took his opportunity as swiftly as possible after the departure of Godwin's colleagues, the time of death leaves us with something of a puzzle. Why the ninety-minute wait? Did Godwin know the killer? Was there some kind of conversation?

'Weapons. Four implements were used for the infliction of the injuries. Forensic reports on these are not yet complete, but we know from the autopsy that the bolt piercing the frontal bone was one inch in diameter, which is beyond the size range available from any ordinary hardware merchant. The instrument used for the disembowelling was a common butcher's knife with an unvarnished wooden handle which, curiously, made the perfect surface for a handprint. The other items were a pair of standard issue dissecting scissors and a scalpel, the latter being left in the eye socket.

The right kidney and eye are missing from the body. Scissors were used, as they would be in any professional dissection, to sever the optic nerve and the renal arteries. The eye was removed with a clean circular cut, as were the bowels, stomach, peritoneum and pancreas, leaving the way clear for the extraction of the kidney, which is not the most accessible of organs, since it lies against the posterior abdominal wall. Our man is a skilled surgeon. Highly skilled. It is likely that he has had clinical experience with cranial and abdominal procedures. The bowels and intestines were removed from the body—possibly by hand—and cast over the edge of the table into an iron tub. The tub itself does not belong in the laboratory, but has been recognised by one of the cleaning staff. The word TURN was daubed in blood on the side of it. It was taken from an unlocked storage cupboard in the maintenance room off the hallway. Here.'

Macready pointed to a diagram of the building interior, which showed the wide hallway with the laboratory on the right, next to a storage room where the cadavers were kept, then the maintenance room, opposite which was Godwin's study.

'The post mortem injuries would have taken forty minutes to complete, even for someone with extensive surgical experience. Are there any questions?'

Jimmy's hand went up. 'Were there any prints on the scalpel, sir?'

'Apparently not.'

'They would be easy to wipe off a stainless steel instrument,' said the forensics officer.

Steve was frowning. 'So why would he bother to wipe them off the scalpel if he just left a bloody great handprint on the knife handle? The handprint's a bit—well—showy. In fact, I'm thinking maybe it's not his print at all. There's a whole tray of hands in there, detached hands, in some kind of preservative.'

The forensics officer had gone pink in the face. 'We'll have the tray checked, sir. It's just that we had no reason to think that—'

'Of course you didn't.' Macready cut in briskly. 'It is not your job to do the thinking, Mr Wye. Please also arrange for a detailed examination of Professor Godwin's office. We have ordered a cordon there, I take it, Palgrave?'

'That was done yesterday, sir, as a precaution. We thought there might be clues.'

'Good. Now, on the matter of public information, in case any of you should face questions from the press, details to be released at this stage are the victim's name and the time and location of the murder. We are describing the corpse as "mutilated", but for the time being there will be no information whatsoever as to the nature of the injuries. And we will be offering no descriptions of the scene of the crime. I hope you are all absolutely clear about that.'

The room emptied rapidly after Macready's exit and Briony felt a bit odd to be the only one left, as if she had been excluded from the action. She stared at her own scrawly handwriting in the notebook, then went across to the display board and stared again at the photographs.

6

A personal visit to the records at West End Central had got Briony no further. The murder files for the past six months generally divided into two kinds of cases—domestic violence and street fights—and they made depressing reading. They gave entry into a world in which teenage youths smacked each other over the head with beer bottles and women were killed in their own kitchens with whatever happened to come to hand: the carving knife, teapot, the electrical cord on the hair dryer. No, she thought. The crime she was investigating did not belong in this world.

After two hours she was down to four unsolved cases that carried even the remotest possibility of any connection with it. One was a gangland killing, in which the victim's throat had been cut. He'd bled to death across the bonnet of his car. A wealthy stockbroker had been carved up with a scalpel, but whoever had done that certainly had none of the pictorial sense Jimmy was talking about. It was an ugly and indistinguishable mess. The strangest weapon was a school handbell, used to whack the caretaker during a robbery in a well known boys' college. Only one case involved multiple post mortem injuries. A teenage girl from Hammersmith had been abducted, taken to Epping Forest, tied up and sexually assaulted, then killed with a well aimed blow to the left temple. After that, the killer had evidently gone ballistic. There were knife slashes across the breasts, abdomen, thighs and buttocks. Thirty-two of them in all. Whoever did that was still walking free, but after eighteen months the case had been put in cold storage. None of these showed any significant points of comparison with the Gresham College murder, but Briony kept them aside for further checking.

Once she'd returned the trolley with the first batch, she felt she didn't have the stamina to order up another, so she headed back to Vine Street, feeling badly in need of tea and a chat with someone. She looked at her watch—not four o'clock yet, so Donna wouldn't be back.

As it happened, Steve was at his desk in the incident room, with a small collection of old books.

'What's all that?' she asked.

'Stuff about Freemasons.'

'What?'

'Freemasons. I think there could be a ritual element to this killing and they're into ritual. Couple of hundred years ago, they used to virtually run everything in some areas of London. If Godwin was a Freemason, that would be our most promising lead yet.'

'What's the boss's opinion of that?'

'Sceptical. Macready's own father was a Mason. He says in ninety-nine per cent of cases it's just a kind of gentlemen's club. When I pushed him about the other one per cent, he said I had an overactive imagination stimulated by a taste for sensational literature. But it's true some of their literature's pretty sensational.' He opened one of the books and turned the pages with his yellowing fingers. 'They have these myths, including some ancient murder story that's pretty far out.' He held out the open book to show a small crude drawing on one page. 'These three guys were disembowelled—they had their intestines chucked over their left shoulder.'

'But our killer got his idea from the Hogarth drawing. And the intestines weren't over the shoulder: they were thrown in the tub.'

Steve fixed her with ironic blue eyes. 'Hogarth was a Freemason. So anyway, Briony, what have *you* been doing to help the cause of justice?'

'I've been looking through unsolved homicides. They can get to you, those cases. Some poor woman getting coshed with her own teapot. Sometimes the really ordinary killings are the worst to think about. They just seem so—'

'Sure. Can't afford to let it get to you. But this thing with the disembowelling, it must have been pretty important to the Masons, because in the initiation ceremony, they have to make this gesture as if they're throwing something. There's a picture of that, too, see?'

The eyes fixed on Briony again. 'You know what? I don't think all that teapot stuff is going to get you anywhere. Sounds like a blind alley to me. Better try another tack. Anyway, I'm taking these notes to Macready. See you later.'

Briony was left there, staring at the pile of books on his desk. Steve gave the impression of being the kind of person you could talk to, but it was all on his terms and, anyway, he was starting to make her feel uncomfortable. He either ignored her or put her under a searchlight. She went over to look at the photographs again.

'There's another lot here. Going to help me pin them up?' Jimmy had come in behind her, soundlessly, and Briony nearly jumped out her skin.

'Jeez! Don't *do* that,' she squawked.

'Do what?'

'Creep up behind people. I've just been looking through all these cases about people being bashed on the back of the head with the school bell or throttled from behind with the hair dryer cord.'

'Well, these won't help to calm you down, I tell you. Maybe you should go and get a breath of fresh air.'

'I just did. I had to go over to West End Central. Here, what do you want me to do?'

Jimmy had a whole sheaf of autopsy photographs, five times the number he'd taken on any other case, he said. Macready wanted every wound, from every angle. So now, of course, there wasn't enough room on the corkboard.

'Shit,' said Jimmy. 'We'll have to get some more boards brought in. I might have anticipated this. It's all chaos here. They were in too much of a hurry to get the place operational.'

'So wouldn't it have been better to have the incident room over at the other station, since we have to keep going back there for everything?'

'It's chaos there, too. West End couldn't cope with the volume of work—that's why they reopened Vine Street—so now we got chaos in two places, stead of one. There's the Met for you. Tell you what, let's just use the wall.'

Jimmy pulled a table over to the wall opposite the windows and stood on it.

'We'll have to use masking tape. There's some in the cupboard over there. And scissors. Lucky they put gloss paint on the wall, eh? My grandad used to paint the walls with gloss paint. Lovely sort of mustard colour not unlike this. Okay, pass me the first one.'

He arranged the shots in rows of five and by the time they'd got to the end of the third row, Briony was getting used to the ragged edges of flesh, the black hollows, the tumbled mess of intestine.

'Do you keep copies of these?' she asked.

'Well, of course we keep copies. Don't you know the drill? Always an extra copy for records.'

'That's not what I mean. I mean do you keep your *own* copies?'

'Not my type of souvenir.' Jimmy wrenched noisily at the roll of tape, and bit a piece off with his teeth.

'Look, don't get me wrong—'

'It's okay, I'm only kidding. You mean do we keep copies in

photographic? Well, sort of. We don't have prints, because there's no space to store them, but we keep the negatives in a cabinet in the dark room—they're all at West End, of course. But going back, say, three years there'd be a couple of dozen photographers used that dark room. West End was the headquarters for every homicide investigation from Tottenham Court Road out as far as Ealing and Wembley. Until they decided to throw open this dump again. Okay, next row. The screw in the skull, I think. What a weirdo, eh? Fancy taking all the trouble to do that. He must have really had it in for this poor bloke.'

'Can I get access to those negatives?'

'Not officially, but I guess I could get them for you. If you pay for my breakfast.'

7

The offices of the *Evening Standard* were unusually busy on Tuesday and Caroline Staines had to ask three times for the copy on an article she had submitted that morning, well before her deadline. She did not receive it until 3.30, after the inside pages for Wednesday's early edition had gone to press. So it was already too late to deal with the sub-editor's act of violation: a diagonal line scored in blue pencil through the middle paragraph of the piece. She read it through again.

> This was no ordinary act of vandalism. It was committed in the grounds of one of London's finest, most historically important churches. Christchurch in Spitalfields was designed by Nicholas Hawksmoor, a student of Sir Christopher Wren, as part of a major programme of rebuilding following the great fire of London. The building was completed in the 1720s, along with that of several other Hawksmoor churches in the City, most of which are in walking distance of each other. Situated in some of the most depressing and derelict areas of London, Hawksmoor's churches lift the spirits with their

soaring spires and the exquisite harmony and symmetry of their proportions.

As an arts graduate with two years experience doing research for the *Sunday Times* Insight team, Caroline never responded well to having her work vetted by an uneducated hack. On this occasion, she was furious. When for once there was an opportunity for her to write about something she really understood, out came the blue pencil. Repeatedly she had pleaded to be moved to the arts pages, or at least to the general news pages. Crime reporting was a sordid, futile occupation. As far as she could see, very few of the people who did the horrible things she had to report on ever got caught and most of the horrible things happened in the worst parts of the city. So she had got to know Clapham Junction, Kings Cross, Spitalfields and the Mile End Road a good deal better than she had ever wanted to.

Besides, she was never given the really important stories. Anything for the front page went automatically to one of the senior reporters. That's what had happened with the Gresham College murder, which no one had even had the courtesy to tell her about before Tony, the staff photographer, rang to say that he couldn't be there for the interview with the rector at Spitalfields yesterday afternoon.

'Bigger fish to fry,' was his excuse, and she'd had to interrogate him to find out what he meant.

Anyway, it had turned out to be a disappointing assignment for Tony. A shot of the arched entrance to Gresham, surrounded by uniformed police, was the closest he got to the action. He'd had to admit that the visit to Spitalfields this morning provided him with more interesting work.

She took the prints out of their envelope and went through them again. A massive rectangular tombstone, taken from a low angle so that it reared against the open sky, had the word DEADSHIT scrawled over its inscription. The paint had run thickly from the lower edges of the letters. Three smaller, rounded headstones stood side by side under a tree, each bearing the message TURN. This was the shot she had recommended to go with her article, but of course they had ignored her advice and chosen instead the image of a beheaded angel standing over a table-top tomb that had been drenched in red paint, looking as if an animal had been sacrificed on it. The angel's head sat in the middle, its eyes blotted out with the paint. The effect was muted in the black and white print, but it was still shocking. Far too shocking to print, in Caroline's view. How typical that they had gone for the most sensational picture.

Caroline could see movement behind the mottled glass of the door to the sub-editor's office. She had half a mind to go in there and confront him, but the phone rang.

'Miss Staines? Thomas Burroughs here, from Christchurch.'

'Ah, Reverend Burroughs. I've just been checking the proofs of our article. It'll be in the early edition tomorrow, on page 5.'

'Good. There was... As a matter of fact, something else has come up since you were here.'

'Further damage?'

'Not exactly. The police made a brief visit, about half an hour ago, and one of them noticed that the top of the tomb was slightly out of alignment.'

'You mean the one where they vandalised the angel?'

Burroughs cleared his throat. 'Yes. The top is removable, though with difficulty, since, as you may imagine, it is of some considerable weight. It seems that someone has at least attempted to remove it.'

'What do the police think?'

'I'm afraid to say that they do not seem very interested. They were here for barely ten minutes and evidently have no plans to return, although I did try to press upon them that—As a matter of fact, there is a bit of a story attached to this particular tomb.'

'Oh yes?'

'I would prefer not to discuss it over the telephone, Miss Staines, but since you have shown a genuine concern about this situation and the police have not, I thought—'

'Yes, of course. I'd be delighted to come and talk to you again. This afternoon?'

'Tomorrow would be better. At half past ten?'

'I'll be there. Thank you so much for contacting me. I do appreciate—'

'I appreciate your interest in our church, Miss Staines.'

As she put the phone down, the sub-editor's door opened and a florid, bespectacled face appeared around the edge of it with a beckoning hand.

'Caroline? A minute, please.' The face disappeared again.

She got up and smoothed her skirt down over her hips. Lennie Meyer always made her wish she was wearing a maxi, but who would want to wear a draggy long skirt on such a beautiful day? The sun this morning had inspired her to pick out a white trimmed purple mini-dress from her wardrobe.

Taking a large writing pad to hold over her knees while he talked to her, she walked across to his den and knocked lightly on the half open door.

'Caroline. Yes. We got one or two things to sort out here. Sit down.'

He looked up from his open copy of today's midday edition to watch her as she sat, crossed her legs and arranged the notepad strategically.

'You won't need that. You're not here to take dictation. Now. Got a new story for you. Pickpockets over in Battersea. Having a bumper season, apparently. Local cops will give you a briefing at ten tomorrow. Don't be late.'

'But I've got an appointment somewhere else.'

'Where might that be, then?'

'It's in Spitalfields. There's some further developments in the story about the churchyard vandalism.'

'Are there, now? Well, that's the other thing I wanted to talk to you about. We've decided to drop that one.'

The pitch of Caroline's voice escaped any attempt at control.

'But you can't! I mean—I've got the proofs—it's already gone to press.'

'It nearly went to press, but I pulled it. We needed the space for something else.'

'Mr Meyer, I've already told the rector of Christchurch the story's going in tomorrow.'

'We'll be very sorry to disappoint him, I'm sure. Tell him to put it in the parish news. The only good thing about that story is the photograph.'

Caroline took a deep breath and thought quickly as she stared into the popping eyes behind the thick spectacles. Confrontation wouldn't work. She'd have to try another approach. She really wanted this story. She had an instinct about it.

'But a new angle's come up. I got a phone call this morning from Reverend Burroughs—that's the rector—who says they now think one of the tombs may have been robbed. Please—I know—you're going to say *so what*, but just let me finish.' She adjusted the position of the notepad, turning it sideways so that a smooth, slim knee was in view. 'There's some kind of story attached to that tomb, apparently. A mystery. At least let me find out a bit more about it. I'll reschedule the appointment with the Battersea police for midday and get the copy to you on that one by three. Together with the new version of the vandalism story.' Caroline swallowed her pride and watched the bulging eyes as she crossed her legs again.

'You think you can twist me round your little finger, don't you?'

'I just think there may be a really good story there.'

'I'll be the judge of that. I'll expect both stories on my desk before you go home tomorrow.'

'Thank you, sir.'

An involuntary shudder went through her as she closed the door of his office. But at least she'd got what she wanted out of him. She picked up the phone and rang Tony. 'Can you be at Spitalfields at ten thirty tomorrow?'

'Spitalfields? You're still trying to flog that one, are you? I thought Lennie had spiked it.'

'He has. But I just persuaded him to give me another chance.'

8

It was strange starting work at eight in the morning in the dark room. The light box threw up the images on the negatives in sharp relief and cast a suffused glow that made the room even more unreal. They had got into a routine of unrolling four strips at a time, then sorting them quickly into those that were of no interest, and those that might be worth a closer look.

Jimmy held a magnifying glass over a particularly dark image in the middle of the top strip.

'What about this one? Look, they packed the poor sod in a suitcase.'

'Put it in the review pile. And this one.'

'That's just a drowning, isn't it?'

'It's got the homicide code.' Briony noted down the serial number. 'We need to check the injuries before we can discount it.'

'Isn't there an autopsy reel in there with it? Should be.'

'Oh yeah. Sorry, I missed it.'

'That's a strangling,' said Jimmy. 'I seen a few of those.'

'Case of the needle in the haystack, isn't it?' she sighed.

'That's a fair description of just about every murder investigation I've had to do with.'

They worked on in silence and by nine thirty had checked through over a hundred rolls of film.

'Here, wait on.' Jimmy bent closer to the light box, so his face was suddenly glowing. 'Look at this one.'

'I can't make it out.'

'It's a hanging. Look, someone's been hung out to dry outside the pub. See?'

'I still can't really make it out. What's all that?'

'Not sure. I wasn't on this case. Must have been one of Pete's. He retired at the end of last year. You know what I think it is? Flowers. Flower baskets.'

There was a knock.

'Shit,' said Jimmy, 'pardon my French. Just when I found something interesting at last.' He opened the door to the desk sergeant.

'Jimmy? Superintendent Macready wants you in his office. Now. Bring your camera, he said. And I have to find Detective Inspector Williams. Do you know where she is?'

'She's here.'

'I see. Cosy.'

Jimmy closed the door again. 'Tell you what, you go on ahead and let Macready know I'm on my way. That'll give me a chance to at least start the processing on this roll.'

The air in Macready's office was full of smoke, even though the window had been thrown wide open. He raised one eyebrow at her as she came in. On the desk was a transparent envelope of the kind used in records to preserve single page documents, together with some crumpled wrapping paper and a small Tupperware container—about three inches deep and four inches wide—with a baby blue lid.

Before Briony could stop herself, the words were out of her mouth. 'You might have told me I was missing the Tupperware party.'

Steve Latham coughed in a way that sent the cigarette flying out of his mouth. Palgrave tucked his chin in towards his throat and stared down at his thumbs, which were posed against each other to make a church steeple.

As she moved closer, Macready peeled back the lid of the little container to reveal a grey gelatinous mass.

'Frogspawn?'

'You surprise me, DI Williams. Did you not study biology for your A levels?' Macready turned the plastic envelope around and pushed it towards her.

The uneven letters of the message were scrawled in thick black crayon:

Keep an eye out for me. Walker

'He sent us the eye?' Briony looked more closely at the thing in the container. 'Godwin's eye?'

'That is yet to be confirmed. Forensics will have their work cut out for them today, if you will excuse that unfortunate turn of phrase. Latham, it's time to pull yourself together. I need your thoughts on this, please.'

Steve peered closely at the wrapping paper.

'Sellotape. Not string. Everyone uses string differently. It's like a signature. He's smart enough to avoid giving us the obvious clues. Address written with a cheap blue biro that misses the start of the letters, like the ones they issue here. Everything he's used—biro, packaging, notepaper, crayon—is the cheapest standard stuff. Nothing to trace.'

'Except the Tupperware,' Briony cut in. 'You don't buy that over the counter. What I mean is, they don't sell it in shops. You buy it at parties. Tupperware parties.'

'That's right.' Palgrave had been nodding slowly. 'My wife gave one once, a few years ago.'

'The company sends a rep to the party with a range of samples and the guests can order them. So, theoretically, there should be a record somewhere of every Tupperware purchase.'

'A job for your team, I think,' Macready said to Palgrave.

Steve was still frowning at the sheet of brown paper. '"Detective Superintendent Iain Macready". That's what gets me. How did he know who to send it to? That's inside knowledge. It wasn't in the press, was it?'

'No,' said Macready, 'but the newspaper report mentions Vine Street. It would not be difficult for an interested person to find out the name of the investigating officer. How, for instance, would you go about finding out such a thing yourself, Latham, if you needed to know?'

'I'd probably make a phone call. Pretend to be someone delivering a new reading lamp. You need it, by the way. That one's a monstrosity.'

Macready looked at his watch. 'Let's keep to the point, shall we?'

'I'll find out what calls have come through,' said Palgrave, 'and get the desk sergeant to document any incoming calls related to the case.'

'Thank you, Palgrave. Latham, you're still frowning. You had better speak your thoughts.'

'He wants you to know that he knows your name. That he's keeping an eye out, too. That he's a couple of steps ahead. We need to be very careful about what gets into the press, because he'll react.'

Briony leant forward. 'Surely we're withholding too much information. If we don't release any of the details that might help someone who knew something to make the connections, we might miss out on a vital contact. What I mean is... And also, if he's looking out to see what kind of publicity he's getting, we can anticipate him. Feed information through the press, to manipulate his reactions.'

'Risky...' Steve turned away from her to blow smoke over his shoulder. 'Much too risky, I'd say. I'm willing to bet he's already planning his next horror show. Anything might serve as provocation. By giving him nothing to go on, though, we might lure him into a bit more correspondence. He's a show off and we're his audience.'

There was a knock on the door and Jimmy poked his head in. 'I was called, sir.'

'Yes, Jimmy. A task for you here. Do you want us out of the way?'

Jimmy had brought a small camera, but no other equipment. He looked over the items on the table, checking them from different angles.

'Best thing to do, sir, is just take a basic set here and do some more when you get this down to forensics.'

The flash went half a dozen times.

'Okay. Done.' And in two steps, he was out of the room again.

Macready turned to Palgrave. 'So Latham thinks our man is looking for an audience,' he said. 'Do you agree?'

'Fancies himself,' said Palgrave, who had been nodding steadily again. 'Murderers who send messages are a breed apart, in my opinion. They're the ambitious ones who want to make it onto the front pages.'

'Like Charles Manson, you mean?' asked Briony.

'He didn't send messages,' said Steve, 'did he?'

'Well, no, what I meant was—' Briony was blushing. 'Like him in wanting to be famous.'

'Did he?' Steve clearly wasn't inviting an answer. He was frowning again. 'There's a Sherlock Holmes story where someone sends an ear through the post in a cardboard box. And, as everybody knows, Jack the Ripper sent the police a kidney.'

The old desk lamp went out with an audible *ping*.

There was silence for a moment, while everyone seemed to be adjusting themselves to the changed atmosphere. Macready spoke first.

'He calls himself Walker. Of course, there may be no connection to his real name.'

'But if there isn't,' said Steve, 'then he's chosen the name for another reason. It means something to him.'

'Not necessarily,' said Palgrave flatly. 'It's a common enough name. Could have picked it with a pin from the telephone directory. Is there anything more from the autopsy, sir?'

Macready shrugged. 'Not a great deal. The pathologist has confirmed that Godwin's blood was used for the writing on the wall. And he favours the view that the iron bolt is a specialist item. He's requested expert opinion from an engineer.'

Briony found herself about to say something else stupid at this point, but managed to contain the impulse. She'd made enough blunders for one conversation, apart from the Tupperware. Macready would be so glad he had a woman on the team. *Well, Inspector Williams knows her Tupperware.* She stopped listening as the others continued to throw comments back and forth. She wanted to be out of there, out in the sun, hopping on a bus that was going just anywhere. Anywhere else.

•

Rule number one: don't get fazed. Rule number two: keep coming back. Briony went to her desk and began doodling on the butcher's paper. Steve was right, the Met issue biros were el cheapo. This one missed every second stroke, but still left ink all over the tips of her fingers. She drew a line of little pigs, with tails curling on and on around the edge of the paper and wrote the word PIGGY in the middle of the page. That was what Charles Manson's family daubed on the walls of the room in which they'd left two murder victims trussed up with pieces of cutlery sticking out of their plump bodies. A perfect picture.

Jimmy stuck his head round the doorway.

'Had a stroke of luck. I got some prints drying up there, but I need to make a load more. I reckon it's the same weirdo done this one. Plus I checked the autopsy roll. I got no prints from that yet, but just from the negs, there's a double throat wound. The right hand has been severed.'

'I'd better look up the case file straightaway. Have you got the serial number?'

'Yeah. Got a bit of paper? I'll write it down.'

Briony gestured to her desk and held out the biro.

'What's this, then?' He grinned broadly at the drawing she'd just made.

'Nothing. Some doodles to help me think. Just write the number, will you?'

'Little piggies. Very sweet. Not a bad drawing. That what they teach you in A level art?'

'You heard of Charles Manson?'

'Course I have. What planet do you think I'm on?'

'After one of the Manson murders they scrawled "PIGGY" in blood on the wall. There was something nagging at me about those photos of Godwin. Some connection. I dunno.'

'You going out this evening?'

'No.'

'Just as well. Reckon you need an early night.'

She got one, thanks to a power cut at ten that switched off the TV, the kettle and the reading lamp in one hit, leaving her in darkness except for the ghastly orange veneer cast over everything by the street lamp outside. She stood in the middle of the room, staring at the weird silhouettes of all her things, then wandered into the kitchen and opened the fridge out of habit. No light inside it. No food anyway, so what did it matter?

She rang the electricity board and got a recorded message.

'Power supplies to some Central London areas have been affected by maintenance work. Normal service will be resumed as soon as possible.'

In time for the winter season of strikes, thought Briony. She checked the hot water tank, which was lagged to save on the heating bills. Last winter, during the worst of the strike, when the power was three hours on, three hours off through the dark evenings, at least she'd been able to have a candlelit bath—which was just what she needed now.

As she lay in the steaming water, the images surged through her mind, all in the full technicolour missing from the photographs. A woman's body, lying face down on a blue and white lino floor, her blood mixed with shattered teapot fragments. Another woman's body hanging in a crude harness of wires from the side of a building. There were extravagant garlands of flowers draped over her head and shoulders. Little piggies with curly tails. Naked bodies with knives and forks stuck in them. Briony's head throbbed.

She'd studied the Manson murders at Hendon and couldn't stop them coming into her mind, relevant or not. Okay, so it was just the brain on overdrive, throwing in whatever came first in the rush of associations.

A visiting lecturer from the FBI had taken them through the Manson case, dishing out bits of advice as he went. 'Don't try to figure out what's going on inside the killer's head. Your job is to find out who did it and get the evidence to nail him. Full stop.'

All very well, she thought, but when you knew the killer was probably planning his next murder, you had to try and second guess him, didn't you?

9

Caroline didn't want to rush the interview with Reverend Burroughs, so she arrived ten minutes early, clipping smartly up the path to the rectory with her photographer trudging three steps behind.

The rectory sitting room was sparsely furnished and surprisingly modern. There were no photographs or ornaments and no pictures on the wall, just a plain black crucifix above the fireplace. Since there was only one armchair, they were invited to sit at the small table in the window recess. Tony looked too large for the space. He obviously felt uncomfortable on his shallow wooden chair, sitting opposite the fine boned and very straight backed Reverend Burroughs and staring at the vase of daises that stood between them.

'I think if you don't mind I'll go and take a few more shots outside,' he said, scraping the chair as he got up. 'Then I should be getting off, unless there's anything new for me to take.'

'Well, I don't suppose there is, really,' said the rector. 'I'm afraid this may have been a bit of a waste of your time.'

'Quite possibly,' said Tony. Caroline didn't seem to register the tone of voice or the look that went with it. She was already totally absorbed in the new details of the story.

'So you mean this is not the first attempt to break into Bartholomew Tremlay's grave?' she asked, as the door clicked shut after Tony.

'Certainly not. There was an attempt about five years ago by a couple of hippies. I actually caught them at it and scared them off, but the police never tracked them down. The desecration of graves doesn't seem to rank very highly in the constabulary's ledger of crimes. And on that occasion there were no obvious signs of vandalism, as there have been this time—and as there were on a previous occasion, I may say. That was in the summer of 1888. The parish records give an account of the damage. The tomb was found with the cover stone askew and badly chipped. Pigs' blood had been poured inside it and thrown over the angel. So you see that what we have out there now looks like a repeat performance.'

'How did they know it was pigs' blood?'

'Valuable commodity at that time. They didn't just let it run down the drain, you know. It was stolen from a local butcher who planned to make puddings with it.'

Caroline didn't feel like pursuing this line of enquiry any further, so she took a new one. 'The hippies who broke into the tomb—did they actually take anything?'

'There was nothing to take.'

'How do you know?'

There was chilly pause as the rector straightened himself further, and turned his head to look out of the window.

'I do hope your friend won't disturb anything out there. I haven't entirely despaired of interesting the police in this matter, so we must be careful not to interfere with anything that might provide clues. The parish is in possession of a number of rare documents, one of which is Bartholomew Tremlay's diary, kept between 1720 and 1724, when he died. Since the building of Christchurch was not completed until 1729, Tremlay may have been buried in the churchyard before it was actually consecrated. Besides being a friend of Nicholas

Hawksmoor, who, as you know, was the architect of this church, Tremlay was a scientist and a member of the Royal Society. In his will, of which the Society has a copy, there is an express request that his diary be buried with him, together with certain notes and instruments for his experiments. Those who opened the tomb in 1888 may well have been looking for them, but they did not find them.'

Caroline was scribbling as rapidly as she could, but several times had to ask him to stop so she could catch up with the essential details.

'Reverend Whitcombe, who was rector in 1888 at the time when Tremlay's grave was first attacked, was a keen botanist and himself a member of the Royal Society. He was a supporter of the ideas of Charles Darwin, which, curiously, he regarded as perfectly compatible with his Christian beliefs. As a matter of fact, he was one of those who campaigned for Darwin's burial in Westminster Abbey, though I daresay this is not something you wish to discuss in the columns of your newspaper, Miss Staines. Whitcombe had taken something of a scholarly interest in Tremlay's anatomical researches and was aware of the importance of his papers, which he retrieved from the tomb himself in 1885. They were subsequently installed in the parish archives, from which I myself have temporarily removed them, for safekeeping.'

'So why would anyone be so especially keen to get their hands on them?'

The rector's pale eyelids fluttered slightly at the interruption. 'Do you want my theory or Whitcombe's?'

'His first, then yours.'

'Whitcombe thought Tremlay's ideas eccentric. More than that. He calls them "lunatic and dangerous". He seems to have been very anxious that other lunatic and dangerous persons should not have the opportunity to be inspired by them. Tremlay went in for an odd mixture of science and magic, which was still common enough in his time. His experimental notes show that he was obsessed with trying to create a homunculus.'

'Sorry, could you spell that?'

Burroughs did so. 'A homunculus is a miniature man. Some kind of alchemical idea.'

'So is it really lunatic and dangerous?'

'Merely absurd. An old fairy tale. What *was* lunatic was Tremlay's obsession with it. In his diary, he writes incessantly about some being he is convinced he has let loose on the world. The Walker, he calls it. First he imagines it is following him, then that it is about to take possession of him. In his last year, he starts to write as if he is this creature, which he claims has gone on a killing spree.'

'So did he? I mean, did Tremlay murder people?'

'I'm inclined to doubt it, but I suppose it's not out of the question. Given the number of murders, homicides and supposedly accidental deaths in this area at that time, it would be very hard to find convincing evidence one way or the other.'

'What would anyone want with these papers now?'

'Many people are fascinated by what they imagine to be dangerous secrets. Including yourself, perhaps, Miss Staines, and most certainly many of your readers.'

Caroline made a mental note to use this argument in defence of her story when she got back to the office. 'But surely the police need to know all this. If someone who's a bit unbalanced is getting fixated about Tremlay and his hom—?'

'Homunculus.'

'Anyway, who knows? They might get some nasty ideas.'

'As I explained, Miss Staines, the police appear to be too busy to investigate the matter. Perhaps you may encourage them to do so by publishing an appropriate account of it in your newspaper.'

'Let's hope so.' Caroline looked at her watch. 'Oh, goodness! I'll be in touch. Thank you so much for your time, Reverend Burroughs.'

There was no sign of Tony in the churchyard, so Caroline

assumed he had gone. As she was walking down Commercial Road towards the station, she thought she heard him walking behind her and turned round, but couldn't see him among the miscellaneous shoppers on the pavement. She quickened her pace. She really was a bit late and was going to have trouble meeting her deadlines.

10

When Briony woke up in the dingy light she thought she must have forgotten to set the alarm, since she was used to the sun streaming into the room by the time it rang. But then she heard the rain, full and steady.

She made her way over to the window and took in the whole gloomy scene: dripping awnings, umbrellas and macintoshes, windscreen wipers. On a bright day, Camden High Street looked a good place to be, but on a day like this, it reverted to its true character as a miserable outreach of the city, practising all forms of slightly murky business in half derelict buildings that no one ever bothered to clean. It's the new trendy suburb, believe me, her friend Sheila had said when they originally took on the lease together three years earlier. Sheila had moved on within six months, to live with a boyfriend in an apartment in St John's Wood, but by that time Briony had developed a conviction that she belonged here. She liked being able to look out over the street and was comfortable with the fact that it was never quiet.

She picked up her watch from the dressing table. 7.30: that was the latest she'd woken in the past week, so it meant she'd had 'a good night's sleep'—something she'd never really seen the value of all those years when her mother kept fussing about it.

Suddenly she felt better about the job ahead of her. She and Jimmy had surely made a breakthrough yesterday and she was looking forward to examining the file in detail to find the clues that might have been missed in the original investigation and make the connections. With luck, she should have something really significant to report to Macready before the end of the day and that would restore his faith in her. Steve Latham would see that she was not there just to be patronised and Palgrave would have to admit that if she'd been given rapid promotion, there was good reason for it. There was good reason, wasn't there? Briony looked at herself in the mirror and raked fingers through her disappointing hair. Limp, as always, just like the weather.

Twenty minutes later, she was walking fast to the bus stop with her mac held tightly across her chest and her wet-weather hair trapped under a scarf. Rain caught against the lenses of her spectacles and occasionally ran under them.

When she arrived at Vine Street, Macready was poised in the doorway shaking out a vast black umbrella and stamping his feet.

'Galoshes are the thing for this weather,' he said, 'I can't think why swinging London has not discovered galoshes, can you?'

She looked at his hand-stitched brogues. 'I've heard yellow wellies are all the rage, sir,' she said.

'Ah, indeed. I can't quite see myself in those. Come to my office, will you? In about ten minutes. I have an interview list for you.'

'Yes, um... sir, could we possibly make it a bit later in the morning? The thing is, I think I—we—may have found a relevant case in the records. It looks as if it could be the same killer, but that's just going by the photographs. When I've been through the file I should be able to report to you with all the relevant details. I'm getting it sent up this morning.'

Macready rolled his umbrella expertly, deposited it in the stand, then turned to her, the eyebrow raised. 'Good. Have it sent direct to my office. I'll get Latham to start work on it.' He set off up the narrow stairs and took them two at a time, his unbuttoned coat slapping against the walls on either side of him.

For a burning second, she understood the impulse to hit someone over the back of the head with something hard and heavy and imagined Macready collapsing theatrically on the stone steps. That would scotch his theory about the female of the species never committing premeditated murder. As she turned off towards the incident room, she'd already made up her mind about one thing. Steve Latham was not getting his hands on that file till she'd had a really thorough look at it herself. She went straight to her desk, still in her dripping wet mac, and picked up the phone.

'This is Detective Inspector Briony Williams. You've got a file on order for me: C 228. To be sent to Vine Street.'

'Yes? What about it? There's no deliveries till 11.45.'

'I'll come over and get it.'

'Suit yourself. Hope you got an umbrella.'

Briony headed for the cloakroom to try and repair some of the damage the weather had done to her appearance and met Donna coming out. Donna's hair was sleek and shiny, her make-up smudge free.

She smiled broadly. 'Hi! I was hoping I'd see you this morning. Got time for a coffee?'

'Wish I did,' said Briony. 'I've got a bit of an awkward morning. Tell you why later. Could we have lunch together?'

'I'll be gone by then. I've just come in to file my report, then I have to be back at the college by ten.'

'Donna, tell me something. How come this weather doesn't turn you into a drowned rat like everyone else? You got a chauffeur to take you to work?'

'Bill dropped me off on his motorbike. If you want to keep your hair dry, get a helmet. Perfect for the job.'

'I'll remember that,' said Briony. 'When can we get together, then? I'm starting to feel like the only woman on the planet. What about having coffee tomorrow about this time?'

'Could do. Or—tell you what—we could go to a film tonight. *Ryan's Daughter's* on at eight.'

'Won't your boyfriend want you to go with him?'

'Bill? Nuh. He's away. I probably won't see him for a week now.'

'So what's the attraction? I don't suppose you're short of choices.'

'Oh, we're not going steady. Meet you at Lyons at seven?'

Having done what she could to tidy herself up, Briony went down and knocked on Macready's door.

'Ah, Inspector Williams. Come in. Sit down. These are your interviews: two are with students who have remained in residence during the vacation and who have no alibi; three are with members of the public who claim to have seen someone loitering in the area. And this one is the most sensitive: Godwin's wife. We need to get her to talk about his friends, acquaintances and so on. See if she can identify anyone with a grudge.'

'Yes, sir.' She got up to leave.

'Oh, and Williams?'

'Yes, sir?'

'You mentioned a file that is of interest.'

'Yes, sir. Records say the next delivery is around 11.45.'

'Very well. I'll look forward to reading it.'

Briony went back to the cloakroom, collected her mac and head-scarf, ran down the stairs with them under her arm and stopped by the front door to put them on. It was tipping down now. She snatched Macready's umbrella and headed out.

The umbrella did its work well, because she arrived no wetter than she had been when she set off. In the doorway of West End Central, Briony imitated the routine she'd watched Macready perform outside Vine Street, opening and shutting the umbrella several times so it flapped like a crow, then rolling it briskly with both hands, before pitching it into the stand with a sharp *clunk*. The best way to understand someone was by copying their gestures, her sister always said. It was a game they played together as children and both had become very good at it. So what did she understand about Macready from that little performance? Apart from the obvious things—the decisiveness, efficiency, sense of command—there was a touch of the showman and perhaps an edge of brutality. An umbrella was a weapon, after all.

•

The murder was committed on 14th August 1970. That was just over a year ago, and the investigation evidently reached stalemate by December, when the pre-Christmas bombing campaign in Central London diverted every available member of the CID into anti-terrorist work.

Not that there was evidence of any promising lines of enquiry having been abandoned. There was only one serious suspect, a twenty-eight-year-old called Greg Kendrick, who worked at the pub. After several cross-questioning sessions they hadn't made much progress and since there was no forensic evidence pointing to him, no arrest had been made. There was a picture of him. A round, friendly kind of face, but the expression lines showed tension and the eyes stared mistrustfully at the camera. She'd seen that look before on people who just couldn't believe how their lives had suddenly been turned upside down. It was not the look of someone in control. Kendrick was a bulky five foot seven and evidently very strong, since his work involved hauling massive flower baskets on their chains, up over the iron girder that ran around the roofline of the pub.

It was in one of these that the victim had been tied, with chains across the torso, running between the legs and then up across the back, round the neck and over the face. The throat was cut so deeply it was really the chains that held the head in place. The first shot was taken from the left side, showing the arm and hand hanging limp and free, so she couldn't have struggled much. Something must have been used to take the fight out of her. Formaldehyde? But the front-on view revealed that the right hand had been severed. Another trophy, perhaps. Entwined with the chains were flowers, crushed and wilted by the violence they'd been drawn into, but they were all over her, trailing in garlands from her shoulders and over her hair and trapped in the wires around her ankles. The rain had poured over the whole arrangement for two hours before there was enough daylight for a passer-by to see that something was amiss in the glorious display he was used to admiring on his way to work.

Briony went through the documents in the file, laying them out in a fan above her notebook, and checked her watch. She was going to have to work fast, if she wanted to cover up her little act of disobedience by getting the file back to Vine Street in time to be inserted into the 11.45 pile of deliveries.

The victim was Sabina Melies, aged twenty-seven, born in Puerto Rico and working in London as a translator for the Spanish embassy. That was about it, really. If anyone had done the research on her, they hadn't put it on record. The whole investigative process looked decidedly shoddy. Briony copied passages from the autopsy report, the forensics report and the witness statements. The right hand had been severed in one clean cut and so had the left ear. Two trophies: another parallel. One for us and one for him. So if he had sent one to the police, what happened to it? She flicked through the pages of the station report and, sure enough, there was a reference to a parcel, four by four by two inches, received at the station on 17th August. Too small for the hand, so it had to be the ear. So what was in it and where was it? No further info.

The crime scene description lacked detail and specificity and was barely two pages long; it could have been made from the photographs, since there was nothing in it that you couldn't see in them.

Luckily, the photographs gave a pretty comprehensive record, but the fact that it had rained between the time when the victim was first hung out there and the time the body had been discovered meant that two vital elements might be missing. There was no mention of formaldehyde in the reports, nor was there any reference to a word painted at the crime scene. Traces of either or both could have been washed away by the rain.

The interview notes for Kendrick were irritating. Heavy handed and incompetent. Too much repetition. It was the kind of interview that would make anyone's mind go blank: good for intimidation; hopeless for information. He should be interviewed again, certainly, but with what line of questioning? As soon as Macready and Latham got the file, they'd set the plan of action without consulting her, so she needed to have her thoughts clear before they did. One point was certain. Whether Greg Kendrick was a suspect or a witness, he was going to be crucial to the case they were dealing with now. The transcript indicated that Kendrick had been trying to communicate some suspicions of his own. The investigating officers seemed to have taken these with more than a pinch of salt, assuming they were an attempt to throw the focus away from himself. Briony's own hunch was that Kendrick might well be worth listening to and she wanted to be the one to do the listening.

Bide your time, she counselled herself in her mother's voice. It was something she'd never been good at. Rushing in was her style, but she was starting to realise that it worked heavily against her in this situation. She checked her watch again.

When Briony emerged from the building with the bulky file, duly signed off and sealed in a despatch envelope addressed to Detective Superintendent Macready, her thoughts were racing all over the place so she hardly noticed that the rain had cleared. She set off at a brisk pace, working out her next manoeuvre: it wouldn't be foolproof, but since most of the staff at the station were far too busy to be interested in checking on each other's activities, she didn't expect any difficulties.

When she arrived back at Vine Street she went straight to the front desk, with the file concealed under the mac she now carried over her arm.

'Is the morning delivery in from West End Central?' she asked. 'I'm waiting for a file.'

The sergeant moved a large pile of documents from a table behind him onto the counter.

'Do you mind looking for it yourself? I'm trying to do three things at once already.'

It was easy enough to slip the file in among the other documents then 'find' it as she sorted through.

'This is it,' she said. 'Detective Superintendent Macready's waiting for it. Can you make sure it gets to him?'

'If it's got his name on,' said the desk sergeant wearily, 'it'll get to him.'

The afternoon went better than she expected, partly because all the people on her interview list except Godwin's wife were in the same part of London. Both the students were in a residence hall near Russell Square and the three witnesses lived in the area around Gresham. After asking the college secretary to arrange an interview with Anne Godwin at her home in Highgate the following morning, Briony walked to the residence hall and found the warden, who seemed to have been left off the interview lists, but turned out to be the most informative person she spoke to all day.

11

Nell had been lying there for a while, listening to the rain drumming against the skylight and hearing snatches of the conversation going on between the twins next door.

'But how's she going to manage? She's going to have to get around on her own. She'll have to catch the tube and stuff. What if she has an attack in the tube?'

'She could get the bus.'

'Nobody can manage in London without using the tube.'

'She needs a boyfriend. Someone who'll look after her.'

Nell didn't care what they were saying. She tried to figure out what day of the week it was. Wednesday, perhaps.

The stuff she'd taken made her sleep as if she was part of the mattress. It was a heavy, muffling sleep with no images. No dreams. No feelings except a kind of dull security. No more waking up in the small hours. Yesterday she got up at eleven and bumped into everything on her way to the bathroom. Right now she would have liked to just lie here doing nothing and thinking about nothing, but the voices in the next room were cutting in and forcing her to follow them through all the things she didn't want to think about.

'So what did the doctor say about it?'

'Panic attack.'

'But I thought she'd got over those. She hasn't had one for over a year, she said. Maybe she got overtired, d'you think?'

'That's what the doctor said. But he wasn't much use by the sound of it. Just gave her a load of Moggies. And she's eating them like sweets. They'll turn her into a zombie.'

'Could we get in touch with that nice counsellor she had before, do you think?'

'The one in Plymouth? How? How would we find her?'

'Mum might know her phone number or something.'

Nell rolled the pillow round her ears and tried not to listen, but the conversation went on inside her head anyway and as she thought about all those things that were expected of her—that she would go out there and get boyfriends and catch tubes and fix up a bank account and meet all those new people at university—she felt so hopeless that she started to cry. Pull yourself together, she told herself, pressing the corners of the pillow against her eyes.

'We could take her to the cinema... What's on, d'you know?'

'*The Devils*. I'm sure that would do her a lot of good. That's the trouble. Everything's got something in it that's likely to upset her. Should we wake her up, do you think?'

'Probably. I'll make a cup of tea.'

Sitting up now with the pillow between her knees and her chest, Nell told herself to get going, but she was still there when the tea came. Julie sat on the bed beside her.

'Sorry I'm such a drag,' Nell said. 'Why don't you two go out for a while? I'll be fine here. I'll just get on with some reading.'

'No,' said Julie. 'Look—I know you think we don't understand you, but I don't think you know what's good for you. You should come out with us and get some fresh air.'

'It's pissing down.'

Julie picked up the bottle of pills from the bedside table and peered through the brown glass, frowning.

'Why did he give you Mogadon? I don't like the sound of this stuff. A woman at work takes it and she's just—not there, you know. You say something to her and there's this blank look on her face. You're so brilliant, Nell, passing all those exams and everything, don't just let it—'

'Let it what?' Nell turned like a hawk.

Julie hunched her shoulders into her neck and made a little ducking movement with her chin.

'Well, you know… Why don't you come out with us? Rita says she thinks the rain's going to clear. She went to get some milk just now and said there's a bit of blue sky. Come on. We have to go back to work next week. Don't let's waste these days. We had all these things we wanted to do with you when you came.'

Nell watched Julie's hands make small flapping movements as she talked. The nails were bitten. What did she have to bite her nails about? Did Rita bite hers as well? Maybe Julie had a boss who nagged her, or maybe she'd fallen for a guy who wasn't interested, or she might have been worried about her mum, who was living on her own now. Thoughts started to reorganise themselves slowly in Nell's mind. It was as if, since she'd been back, she hadn't really seen the twins at all, just let them wash over her with their plans and their chatter. But now she'd drawn them into something that was peeling it all away, so they didn't know what to do. One part of her wanted to take Julie's hand and tell her it was okay, so they could both cry and she could say she was sorry, just really sorry to bring all this trouble with her, when they were being so kind and sticking by her. But she couldn't say those things. They were all locked away somewhere and she couldn't get at them, so instead she threw off the bedclothes and put her feet on the floor, letting her hair fall over her face so she could avoid Julie's eyes.

'I'll get dressed,' she said. 'I won't be long.'

The rain really had stopped by the time they got outside and the patch of blue had grown bigger.

'So—' said Julie, unbuttoning her PVC raincoat and whirling around on the pavement, 'where do we go, girls?'

'Hey, watch it! You're splashing me,' squawked Rita who, since the rain was over, had put on a pair of light blue bell-bottoms and turquoise sandals. 'Nell, you have to decide where we're going.'

'Trafalgar Square.'

'I've got a better idea,' said Rita. 'Covent Garden. We can look at the markets there. Or we could do both—take the Piccadilly Line to Covent Garden, then walk back to Trafalgar Square.'

'Can't we walk all the way?' asked Nell.

Rita rolled her eyes to heaven. 'This isn't little old Exeter, you know. You can't just start walking one side of the city and expect to come out on the other half an hour later. It could take two hours to walk to Covent Garden.'

'So?'

'So we're catching the tube.'

It was all right in the tube, really. Nell felt a bit tense, especially when a great crowd of people got in at Knightsbridge, but she concentrated hard on the advertisements opposite her. One was for the Brooke Street Bureau. It showed just the feet of two girls talking to each other, but wearing beautiful knee-length boots and maxi coats.

'What would you pay for a pair of boots like that?' she asked Rita.

'Oh—twelve quid at least. I know this place where you might get a pair for ten. I'll take you.'

'Okay. Maybe when my grant comes in.'

'You're going to have to buy clothes for university, you know. Anyway, you used to love shopping.'

Nell pulled at her old navy T-shirt. 'I suppose I can't go through the autumn term in this. Perhaps I should get one of those coats, do you think?'

'In a few weeks. But it's still summer. I'll find something for you in the markets that won't cost much. I know what you need.'

Rita was true to her word. When they got to the markets, she went to work in earnest, flipping through racks of droopy shirts on wire hangers and turning over piles of jumble. Julie stopped to watch a busker who was eating fire, bending his head back at an alarming angle as he pushed the flaming stick into his mouth. Nell wandered over to the flower stall. When her mother bought flowers in Adelaide, they were tied into neat little bunches of carefully mixed colours, so that you could take them home and just stick them in a vase on the table. Here, they were piled up in dense heaps, tumbling onto the floor, where they got tramped on and shredded. She picked one up to rescue it, then collected several more, choosing them one by one from the chaotic mass on the table. They were white carnations, with tinges of pink on the petals. Soon she had a great armful of them and had just paid for them when Rita came bounding up.

'Perfect, absolutely perfect!'

Nell saw a flash of brilliant red, before something was pushed over her hair. Rita turned her by the shoulders so she faced a reflecting window, in which she saw a girl in a red beret with clouds of dark hair around her shoulders and an armful of white flowers.

'See?' said Rita. 'Oh, I wish I had a camera!'

'You wanna picture, eh?' A tubby American in a safari suit and white hat, grinning from ear to ear, made his way up to them.

'Here. I'll take your picture. Just wait while I put a new film in here, because I can't let you take this one away with you—my wife wouldn't be very happy about that, not when it's got the one of her on London Bridge that she's busting to show to all the neighbours when she gets back home. Okay now, get happy!'

The flash went off several times.

'The two of you together? Oh, three of you, eh? Say, are you sisters?'

Julie giggled. 'Well, as a matter of fact—'

'Yes,' interrupted Rita. 'Now—you must let me pay you for the film.'

'Oh no, I couldn't let you do that. How about you just let me have my picture taken with you, eh, girls? Come on now, huddle.' He handed the camera to the boy serving on the flower stall. 'Here. Would you mind? Before my wife comes back and finds me with the ladies. Shame to waste the rest of the film. It'll be a souvenir for you, right? Very good! And now a couple more of the one in the red beret. You know what, you look a picture holding those flowers. You should be in Paris!'

He wound the film on, opened the camera and handed over the little yellow cylinder.

'Here y'are. Worth a thousand dollars. You made my day, ladies.' He raised his hat in farewell as a woman with bright gold hair and spectacles to match bustled up and grabbed his arm.

Nell was transformed by the flowers and the beret, which kept the ragged corkscrews of hair back from her face. Everyone looked at her and she found she liked it. She felt like a completely different person.

12

The residence hall was an ugly red brick building with patterns of paler brick set into it, but this was the only attempt Briony could see at any kind of decoration. Inside, the place was bleak and brutally functional: no carpets, rugs, curtains or pictures; just bare concrete floors and badly plastered walls showing several generations of paint. It looked as though you could do the cleaning with a firehose.

A flight of narrow concrete stairs with a rusting metal rail led up to the next floor. High spirited undergraduates were not going to be sliding down that. At the top of the stairs was a crossroads of narrow corridors, with the way ahead of her leading to a dark wooden door that had WARDEN painted on it in bronze letters and, underneath, the name *S J Perrin* written in large italics on an ancient square of cardboard. She knocked and watched the shuffling movements of the inmate's approach through its milky glass panel.

The warden was an elderly man—over sixty, Briony guessed—and his heavily lined face seemed to be working in several directions as she introduced herself and her business.

'Detective Inspector, eh? My word. So you're the police, are you?

I thought there was supposed to be some bigwig from Scotland Yard in charge of the investigation. Cup of tea?'

'Do you have any coffee?'

'Oh yes. I should say so.' Breathing heavily, he reached down to forage on a low shelf. 'I should have guessed. The younger generation don't drink tea any more, do they? Here it is. Gone a bit sticky, I'm afraid, but if you give it a good scrape with the spoon it should come out all right. Do you mind putting your own in the cup? I never know how strong to make it. Sugar?'

'Just one. What can you tell me about a student called Alan Logan?'

'I can tell you he's not here very much for a start. Supposed to be studying for exams, but if he is he doesn't do it in his room. Shall I put some hot water in that for you? He failed his second year but they let some of them re-sit at the end of the summer vacation, which means they can go on into third year when term starts. I'm pretty sure the milk's all right, but give it a sniff before you pour, just in case. My guess is exams are the last thing on his mind at the moment.'

'Why would you say that?'

Slurping his tea noisily, the warden sat back heavily in his chair, then fixed on her with his faded blue eyes.

'You're young to be a detective. Do they have many women detectives?'

'A few. Women are a very important part of the Met—the Metropolitan Police Force.'

'I know what the Met is. Women's Lib, eh? Seems to be everywhere, but I didn't think the coppers would be so quick to take it up.'

'Women were being recruited into the Met long before Germaine Greer hit the headlines. Haven't you heard of Superintendent Becke?'

'Who's he, then?'

'She. Shirley Becke. The most senior woman in the British police.

Retired a couple of years ago. She spent her whole career recruiting women. But I'm getting you off the subject, Mr Perrin. You were going to tell me about Alan Logan. You said exams would be the last thing on his mind. What did you mean by that?'

'Not much, tell you the truth. If you want my honest opinion, he's not the person you're looking for. I get to know them pretty well, the young fellers around here. He's a mixed up kid, Alan. Lazy. Gone a bit off the rails. He's the type who needs a job with strict hours and simple responsibilities. He can't cope with the degree, so he smokes that funny stuff all day long. Pot. And he can't cope with the fact he's going to disappoint his father by failing. His father was here before him, in 1948—I been here since just after the war, you see, twenty-five years—which is why I know the story a bit. But I tell you, it's a common enough story.'

'What about Eddie Cantrel?'

'How many names you got on that list Miss, er—sorry—Inspector Williams? You see, I think you may be wasting your time. Like I say, I get to know the lads here pretty well and I can tell you there's no one on the residence list now who would be capable of doing what was done to Professor Godwin. I heard about it from Colin Oldroyd. He was in a terrible state, poor man.'

'What did he tell you?'

'Oh, none of the gory details—he said he'd been asked to keep them to himself. But he said it was the work of a sadist. There's no one like that here. Not now.'

Briony wondered how shrewd the warden's judgment was on this. Good natured people often had difficulty believing anyone around them could be dangerous and, as she'd learned at Hendon, it was common for murderers to be people well trusted by those who knew them. She decided to try another tack.

'You said there's no one on the residence list now who might commit a crime like this. Has there ever been, that you can remember?'

The old man suddenly got up from his chair and started looking about him, patting the pockets of his jacket as he did so.

'Matches. What have I done with them? Mind if I have a cigarette?'

'Not at all. Take your time, Mr Perrin, but if there is anyone you can think of…'

'Well, there is, as a matter of fact. Now what did I do with the darn things? Just a minute. I'll have to see if I've got some in here.'

There was another pause while he raked through a drawer and fished out a squashed box of matches, then lit a cigarette from a pack of Players Number 6 on the table.

'Since Colin came and talked to me—day before yesterday, that was—it's been bothering me. There was someone a few years ago. 1967 was when he left. Yes, I'm pretty sure. He took his exams in June that year and failed. Never heard any more of him since. I expected to, mind. For a couple of years I was afraid he'd turn up again, but he never did. Touch wood.'

Briony had written down the date and sat with her pencil poised as Perrin frowned at the desktop in front of him. She decided to prompt.

'So his name, Mr Perrin?'

'His name was Mathew Quin. He's the only one I've ever had here who I'd say had a really nasty streak. Well, maybe I should put that a bit more strongly. A lot of young lads have got a nasty streak, but it's just like a dash of pepper in the system. On balance, they're all right, unless they're the worse for drink. I'd say Quin was a nasty piece of work. He was a bit young for university. A bright boy, you know. Got his A levels at sixteen and did so well he persuaded them to take him in the following year.' Perrin dragged slowly on his cigarette. 'He certainly was bright, I'll say that for him. Used to spook me the way he knew everything.'

'What kinds of things?'

'Well, all the comings and goings round here, for a start. He seemed to know everyone's business and remember everything about them. I reckon any time of the day or night, if you'd asked him he could have told you exactly who was in and who was out. And half the ones who were out, he'd know where they'd gone.'

Perrin stopped and the pause grew longer as he sat staring ahead of him. Briony wasn't sure if he'd lost the thread or decided there was something he didn't want to tell her and she knew that it was important to keep the casual tone in her voice as she prompted.

'What first made you see him as different from the other students?'

'There was an incident put the warning lights on for me not long after he came.

'I used to do the night patrol sometimes. Now it's done by a security officer because I'm the only warden here, but then we had two junior wardens and the three of us used to alternate so there'd be someone on duty twenty-four hours. We did patrols about one o'clock and then again about three or four in the morning. The lads aren't supposed to be out after midnight without permission, but of course some of them break the rule, and then they sneak back in through the side door and go up number four staircase, without turning the lights on. And we don't know anything about it, supposedly. But we get a pretty shrewd idea of who's up to what. It's pretty dark down that end of the building, so they have to grope their way, but you wouldn't hear from the office here. Well, this young lad Mathew, he evidently intended to play a sort of practical joke on another student who was sneaking in late. In the passageway near number four staircase there's a row of old brass hooks where a lot of the students leave their coats. Anyway, Mathew Quin took one of these coats—a great bulky thing from the army surplus stores—and I suppose he waited till the lights were all out and he laid it on the stairs, near the top. I don't know if he invented that trick, but it was pretty effective. The other student was drunk and he tripped on the coat and fell back down the stairs.'

There was another pause, as the faded blue eyes stared at the whirl of smoke rising from the cigarette he held between finger and thumb. Some ash fell on his shoe, but he didn't seem to notice.

'Anyway, what seems to have happened next is he vomited as he fell—fine mess there was everywhere—and knocked his head on the stair rail at the bottom. Lucky for him I came by with the torch and heard this funny noise, which was him struggling to breathe through the vomit in his nostrils. I had to do mouth to mouth, which wasn't very pleasant in the circumstances. When I'd got him breathing again and cleared some of the muck out of the way, I sat back there for a minute to get me own breath before going to phone the ambulance, and this voice spoke—right close by—'Well done, warden'. I looked with the torch and there was Mathew Quin, right there near the bottom of the staircase, smiling.

'"What are you doing there?" I said. "Don't just stand there, phone the bloody ambulance." But he didn't move. He just went on smiling. When I came back from calling the ambulance, he'd gone.'

'How do you know it was Quin who put the coat there?' asked Briony.

'He admitted it. There was an inquiry and he admitted it. Said it was just a joke, not meant to harm and all that kind of stuff and nonsense. But the ambulance men reckoned the other student had lain there a good ten minutes before I got to him. So what was Quin doing in that time?'

'What do you think?'

'I'll tell you what I think. He stood there listening to the other feller struggling for breath—it was an ugly sound, I'll tell you—and waiting for him to die. And he was smiling about it. Course, we couldn't prove that. He said he was worried about what might happen and crept down the stairs to see. But that's not true. I would have heard him. He was right there within a few feet of me, all the time. Well anyway, the inquiry let him off with a warning. They took into account that he was younger than the others—barely past his seventeenth birthday—and might be having a bit of trouble adjusting to the new environment.

'After that he always used to grin at me in this knowing way. Sometimes he'd stop to tell me something, or ask me a question, but it was like some kind of a provocation. Usually it was something nasty—he wanted to see my reaction, I suppose.'

'Can you give me an example?'

'He'd tell me about some corpse that had come into the anatomy lab—what injuries there were on it, what had happened to it. I used to pretend I wasn't listening, but you can't not hear, can you?

'He had all these drawings pinned up on the wall in his room.'

'What kinds of drawings?

Perrin looked at Briony, then at the cigarette still burning in his hand.

'Anatomy.'

'But surely all the medical students do anatomy drawings. We had to do them for our anatomy course at Hendon.'

'Oh, yes. Sketches. I seen that type of thing. Technical drawing, they call it here. All the medical students have to study that. But these were different. There was often something about them that made your flesh crawl. He'd show the face of the person being cut up, looking out at you with open eyes. Sometimes he'd draw animals. Then the cleaners complained about a set of drawings of a woman with her skirts thrown high, showing the lower half of her all cut up. Quin said an artist friend had given them to him. Didn't look much like art to me. I seen a few things in my time, but I was shocked, I tell you. I made him take them down.'

He took off his glasses and began to clean them with a grey looking handkerchief. He seemed to have come to a halt. Briony drew breath to start the next question, then heard the voice in her head. Hold it. Bide your time. Perrin stuffed the handkerchief back into his jacket pocket, held the spectacles up to the light, then used both hands to position them back over his ears. He looked at Briony.

'It's no work for a woman, in my opinion. Investigating murders. I don't like talking about this kind of thing to a young lady.'

This time Briony did rush in. 'Mr Perrin, I can assure you I—'

'Tough nut, are you? That what you're going to say? I suppose you must know what you're doing. See that window? Get up and take a look out, because you can't see the courtyard from where you're sitting.'

The window ran the full length of the outer wall, but started at chest height. It was badly stained. Streams from this morning's rain had dried against a patina of old dust. Looking out, she saw a large paved square with a stone fountain in the middle—a couple of hundred years old, she guessed. It must have been there before they built the hall. A student was sitting on a bench reading some papers, and two others were crossing.

'Any birds out there?' asked Perrin.

'A few pigeons.'

'I like the birds,' he said. 'I go out and feed them in the mornings, specially in winter. I've always done that. And they get to know who their friends are. They never run away from me, the birds out there. Quin's room was on this side of the building. Well, one morning when I was crumbling up a bit of loaf I had with me, I had this distinct feeling that I was being watched. You know they say your spine creeps—well, I pretty much felt that something was crawling up my back. I looked up and he was staring at me through his window.

'Next morning, he was there again. So I started going out there different times of the day. Quin came back early in the Christmas vacation one year—in fact he came back early most vacations—but this particular time I remember it was a week or so before term started and there weren't many others around and I was just sitting in here as usual doing one of the regular jobs, checking the cleaning roster or something, I forget exactly what, and I heard this commotion outside. Squawking and shrieking. I looked out and there was Quin, with the pigeons milling all round him, and he was stamping on their heads. Laying about him like a maniac. And they were huddled together in a panic, silly creatures, instead of getting out of his way. I banged on the window and yelled at him, then I ran out fast as I could go and I met him by the door. He was walking in cool as a cucumber. I let him have it, I tell you. I would have knocked his head off if I'd had my wits about me, but I did a fair amount of shouting and told him he was a raving lunatic and he'd better pack his stuff because he wasn't staying in hall any longer. Well, he just stood there and waited for me to finish. And then he gave that nasty little smile, and he said, "They were sick, Warden. They had the mange."

'He'd killed eight of the poor creatures and one was still fluttering there on the ground. I brought it inside but it died a couple of days later. Anyway, I made sure a complaint went up to the discipline committee and he was asked to make a statement—which he did—complete with technical drawings and medical references, explaining the condition these birds were supposed to have, and how he was just putting them out of their misery and trying to stop it spreading further. The committee report said that in future he was to express his concerns to the warden first so the problem could be dealt with in a more appropriate manner. That was it. Hardly even a rap over the knuckles.

'By the end of that term I wasn't the only one who thought he was a maniac. I got a lot of complaints from the other students that he was being anti-social. Sometimes he got funny about people even looking at him. Used to swear and threaten them if he caught their eye. Then other times he'd walk around smiling at everyone like the Cheshire cat. He was taking a lot of drugs, I know that, but it was very hard to prove. And of course he wasn't the only one doing that. We caught a couple of them out because they were foolish enough to leave the stuff in their rooms and they got sent down for the rest of the term. Quin was too clever to get himself caught that way, but something must have snapped because blow me if I didn't get a notice in the middle of the exam period to say he'd been excluded from his degree.'

Perrin's story had been slowing down over the past few minutes and he was visibly exhausted now.

'Would you like a break, Mr Perrin?'

'I'd rather get it over and done with if it's all the same to you.'

'Whatever you prefer. I'm ready when you are. So what happened?'

'Failed his anatomy exams, according to the report. But I think there was more to it than that. He used to get top marks in anatomy. Always. But apparently he messed up the practical—rather literally, according to some of the other students, who said the supervisor came and stopped him because he was basically vandalising the body—slashing at it with cuts going in all directions.'

'Was this in the report?'

'No. As I say, this is what the other students told me. They were a bit shaken by it and they were worried it might have affected their own work, so they were asking my advice about an appeal. But as it turned out, they all did fine, so there was no need.'

'I see. So there's nothing of this on record—in writing—that you know of, Mr Perrin?'

'Well, whoever was the invigilator—I can't remember now who they said it was—would have made out a report of his own. And then the examiners would have seen what he'd done, so they probably made comments on the assessment sheets.'

'Would Professor Godwin have been involved?'

'He was chairman of the examinations board, so it would have been his signature on the letter telling Quin he was excluded.'

'And you've heard nothing about Mathew Quin since?'

'Nothing at all. But this nasty business that's happened… Who knows?'

'We hope we *will* know, before too long. Just one more thing. What did he look like?'

'His looks changed. When he first came he just looked like a schoolboy—slightly chubby, short hair, black framed glasses. Then within a few months he'd grown his hair, thinned down. He changed his glasses too, for those awful national health things with the wire frames that what's 'is name—the Beatle—made fashionable.'

'John Lennon.'

'That's right. I think he might have been trying to look like John Lennon. Then a year later he was trying to look like another one of those pop stars—even worse—with a great lot of curly dark hair. When he first came it was light coloured, I'm sure it was, and by the time he left it was dark. I don't know if he dyed it or what. Goodness knows what he looks like now. I can't be much help to you there.'

Briony put away her notebook and got up.

'You've been an enormous help, Mr Perrin. Thank you. Detective Superintendent Macready, who's in charge of the case, may wish to ask you further questions, but I've taken quite enough of your time this afternoon. Thank you again.'

'You take care now,' said Perrin as he opened the door for her.

13

As Donna walked into the café, ten minutes late and wearing a short leather coat that swung open over her belted mini-dress, Briony noticed how the men sitting at the tables near the door turned their heads to watch. She looked down at her own rather tired skirt and unpolished shoes, but instead of embarrassing her, they suddenly gave her a feeling of security. With weirdos like Mathew Quin wandering about, who wanted to be the one catching everyone's attention, she thought. Did Donna ever think about that?

'Hi! Mind my stuff while I get some tea.' Donna heaved a pink canvas tote bag onto the seat opposite Briony, strands of blonde hair falling forward as she bent to get her purse out of it. She brushed them back across her head as she stood upright, but they immediately slid forward again.

'Where's your helmet? I thought you said you had a motorbike helmet on this morning?'

'Left it at work. More to the point, Briony Williams, where's your umbrella?'

'I don't have one.'

'Exactly. But the word's getting around that something very

suspicious happened to Macready's umbrella and that you might be the one who can help the police with their enquiries.'

'Oh shit. Shit shit shit.'

'Another cup of tea?'

Donna returned with two cups of bright orange tea and an iced finger bun.

'So, you see, about four o'clock this afternoon, apparently—I wasn't there, but the desk sergeant told me later—there was a special late delivery from West End Central, containing just one item, which was Macready's umbrella. Someone had left it in the lobby.'

'How did they know it was his?'

'Everyone knows Macready's umbrella. It's an heirloom or something.'

'And why is it supposed to have anything to do with me?'

'Because Steve Latham was watching you through the window when you nipped out of the building in the direction of West End Central, with an umbrella that looked a bit too big for you.'

'I'm starting to hate that guy.'

'Well, he thinks you're sweet. He told me.'

'He thinks I'm dumb.'

'Let him. It'll give you a temporary advantage.'

Briony began pushing the scattered grains of sugar on the table into a small heap. 'But I can't let Macready think I'm dumb.'

'Nah. No fear of that. He's got your number exactly. I reckon he guessed you'd been through that file even before he opened it.'

'*You* seem to know everything about it, anyway.'

Donna leant back in her seat and sipped her tea, looking at Briony over the rim of the cup, which she then returned to the saucer with a sharp clip.

'I should think so,' she said. 'The whole case has turned now. Macready called all the DCs in at five today to brief us on what's in that file. I've got to work two locations now: mornings in the university, evenings in the Hanging Gardens. So no movie for me,

I'm afraid. I've got to be in Holland Park by eight thirty. You'd think they'd have changed the name of the pub after a thing like that happened, wouldn't you?'

Briony dented the small pile of sugar with the bowl of her teaspoon and started to develop a crescent shape.

'Maybe. But the pub's been there for three hundred years or something. Didn't you see that old drawing of it in the file? It had hanging baskets then. A lot of tourists go there because of the flowers—it's won all these awards. From what I could gather, that's mainly because of this guy Kendrick.'

Donna pointed a long nailed finger at Briony. 'Greg Kendrick, right? The suspect.'

'Right. He's interesting. He's a properly qualified botanist. And the last time there was an entry in that file—which was February this year—he was still employed at the Hanging Gardens, so the landlord must trust him.'

'Or doesn't want to lose him. If he's making the place look so good and it brings lots of extra business, they might prefer to think he wouldn't hurt a fly. Macready said that's one of the things staff at the Hanging Gardens said about him when they were interviewed. They say that about all the mass murderers.'

'You mean serial killers,' Briony corrected.

'Whatever you want to call him, this one's a real screwball. He must have the strength of an ape, too. How did he get that poor woman up there?'

Briony divided the granules of sugar into two parallel lines.

'Well that's the thing, you see—that's why Kendrick was the main suspect. Because he was used to managing these really heavy baskets, which have to be wired up and then hung from the girder under the roof.'

Donna shuddered. 'What happened to her exactly? Did you get to read the autopsy report?'

'I skimmed it.'

'Macready said he wouldn't go into that at this stage. He wants to check some details first. But tell me she was dead before he got her up there…'

'The autopsy report said not. She died from blood loss. But she was almost certainly unconscious. I was scanning through for some reference to formaldehyde. If that's what he used to put her out, then we've really nailed the connection between the two cases. But no such luck, I'm afraid. Anyway, he couldn't have done what he did if she'd been struggling, or screaming. Her mouth wasn't taped. And he'd made quite elaborate arrangements with the body, draping her with garlands of red geraniums, then passing the chains around the torso and between the legs so she wouldn't tip. It was raining, so when the blood dripped on the pavement a lot of it got washed away.'

'A bit of rain couldn't wash away that much blood.'

'No, course not—but diluted it, spread it around. What I'm wondering is whether he'd written anything at the scene. That's what could have got washed away.'

Donna had left the finger bun almost untouched. She poked it with a knife.

'Why did I choose this? I couldn't eat it now if you paid me. Jimmy, where are you when I need you?'

'Did you know it was Jimmy who put me onto the file? I hope he gets some credit for it.'

'I hope *you* do, but I think you may have blown it, Briony. You'll be in the doghouse for the next week at least.'

A wide grin crept over Briony's face as she swept the granules of sugar off the table into the palm of her hand and brushed them onto a saucer.

'See if I care. I got another lead this afternoon. A really good one. When you're talking to people in the pub or the college, you might try to find out something about a former student called Mathew Quin. He left the university four years ago. If it turns out he was known around the Hanging Gardens, I reckon we've got him. All we have to do then is find him.'

Briony launched into the story she'd heard from the warden and, by the time she had finished, daylight was fading fast and Lyons was about to close. Donna stood up and began to button her coat.

'Look, I feel very privileged being told all this, but are you thinking of letting Macready in on any of it?'

'Oh, I guess I'll point him in the right direction.'

'You're crazy. He'll take you off the case instantly if he thinks you're withholding information. Haven't you done enough to queer your pitch already? Do you really want to be sent out to Hackney or something, to spend the next five years dealing with break-and-enters?'

'No. But I don't want to be Girl Friday for Steve Latham, either. Donna, this man's going to kill again. And maybe soon. That's all any of us should be worried about. And you be careful, okay?'

'It's you who needs to watch it,' retorted Donna.

14

Briony didn't get much sleep. All the reactions she didn't have while she was talking to Donna started to work away in her as soon as she'd turned the light out. She should just have left the file alone. What had she got out of that rushed preview of it, anyway? Then: oh hell—why did she have to take the bloody umbrella?— As if she was *trying* to get herself into trouble. Her faced went hot in the dark. Stupid. So bloody stupid. Four days she'd been on this investigation—her first really major case—and already she'd got on the wrong side of the boss. Apologise. Go in there the minute he arrives in the morning and apologise.

She turned over and rearranged the pillow, then saw in her mind's eye the pigeons, huddling together in mindless panic, to get their heads stamped in. It was no good. She got up and put the kettle on.

When she finally got to sleep, somewhere around three in the morning, she dreamt someone was breaking into her flat. It was so vivid she was sure she actually heard the window pane crack and the glass fall through and a voice right by her ear saying, 'You got it coming to you now, haven't you?'

For the last few hours of the night, she slept fitfully with her old school hockey stick propped against the bedside table.

•

Briony splashed her face with cold water and tried unsuccessfully to conceal the effects of the past eight hours with some make-up, before heading out into brilliant early sunshine to wait for the bus.

When she arrived at work, Macready was already in his office looking as if he hadn't moved from there since the same time yesterday. He was a desk detective, Briony thought. He mainly left the street work to other people. Maybe there was something to be said for that. The investigation was getting more complicated by the day and somebody needed to be holding all the threads. She steeled herself and tapped against the open door to draw his attention from the papers he was staring at.

'Superintendent Macready?'

He didn't look up. 'What is it?'

'Could I speak to you for a minute, please?'

'I would very much prefer it if you could wait until later, Williams.'

'I'm sorry I—it's just that I have some evidence that might be important. From one of the interviews yesterday.'

Now Macready looked up. He gestured to the seat opposite him and glanced pointedly at his watch as Briony sat down. He checked it again, twice, during her attempt to retell the warden's story—which she did very badly, forgetting details and having to put them in out of sequence—but he did not interrupt her. When she got to the end, there was a long and very uncomfortable silence.

'Should I go now, sir?'

'Where exactly would you be going to, Inspector Williams?'

'To complete my interviews, sir.'

'I see. The ones on my list, or do you prefer to keep to your own?'

Briony went crimson and did not reply. After another stretch of silence, she got up to leave. Macready's gaze had returned to the papers in front of him and he appeared not to notice, but as she got to the door, his voice cut in.

'Kindly stick to the list you have been given, Williams. And kindly remember to return my umbrella next time you make use of it. I am particularly attached to that umbrella. There will be a case conference in my office at 4.00 pm today and a general briefing in the incident room at 4.30.'

Intending to gather her scattered wits, Briony went and sat at her horrible desk for a few moments and stared at the photographs on the wall. 'Mathew Quin.' She mouthed the words. It had to be. It had to be him. The stories the warden had told her fitted too well with the images she was staring at. A wacko anatomist who liked pictures of messed up bodies. Where was he now? What was he up to? What did he look like? Had he changed his name? She had to accept that it was not up to her to find the answers to these questions—at least, not unless or until she was instructed to do so—but what was the point in doing the interviews she had lined up for today without a photo of Quin to show them? There must be one somewhere in the college records. Maybe she could just— no. Maybe not.

She was gathering her things ready for the day's work, when Steve came in. He had his hands in the pockets of a blue corduroy jacket—the first time she'd seen him without a cigarette—and his shoulders hunched. He looked sideways at her.

'First you steal my chair, now it's Macready's umbrella. So what are you up to today, Briony Williams?'

Briony flashed him a brilliant smile. 'Oh, I think I'll go shopping!'

If he registered the sarcasm, he didn't show it. Steve slumped into his desk chair, legs stretched out in front of him, and frowned slightly.

'Did Palgrave tell you he traced that Tupperware? Interesting. It's from a picnic set they discontinued two years ago, but funny thing is, it was only distributed in the West Country—Devon and

Cornwall. So how did Walker get hold of it? Or did he bring it with him to London? Anyway, what *are* you doing today?'

'Why do you ask?'

'Coordination. We're supposed to be working as a team, remember?'

'Well, what are you doing, then?'

'First off, I'm talking to Chief Inspector Rutgers. He was in charge of the Hanging Gardens case. Then I'll start following any leads from there.'

'I'm interviewing Godwin's widow.'

'Oh. Right.' He looked at her a bit too intently. 'Say, Briony, you know what?'

'I think I know you're about to give me some advice.'

'Yeah. Don't get paranoid. Doesn't suit you.'

Briony shouldered her bag and stood up. 'Just because you're paranoid, doesn't mean they're not out to get you. See you at four.'

By four o'clock, she had advanced the inquiry with precisely nothing. The two people claiming to have seen someone loitering around the entrance to the college recorded conflicting descriptions and Mrs Godwin, who had been given far too much of some tranquilliser or other, had answered almost every question with, 'I can't imagine' or 'I've no idea'.

Briony could imagine that Mrs Godwin was someone without much idea at the best of times. There was a whine in her voice that sounded as if it belonged there permanently and it was hard to feel appropriately sympathetic. Godwin was evidently one of those men who did not bring his work home, since his wife had no idea what committees he was on, whether he had found any of the students difficult this year or whether there had been anything troubling him at work recently. She shook her head vaguely at Mathew Quin's name, fingering the brooch at the neck of her Liberty print blouse and staring at the polished surface of the coffee table beside her.

It was barely one o'clock when Briony drew the interview to a close. As she waited for the rickety Northern Line tube at Highgate, she thought to herself that she really would have time to go shopping, if she wanted to. But she didn't. Somehow she had to get Macready to take the Quin story seriously and she thought it might help if she got the notes typed up in full, because she realised, thinking back on it, that it was the way the story had been told to her, as much as any specific evidence it contained, that had convinced her of its relevance. What would really nail it would be the invigilator's report from the third year anatomy exams in the summer term of 1967, but she'd need a warrant to search through the college records for it. She had a thought. That was the year after Colin Oldroyd arrived. Surely she couldn't get into trouble for ringing him up to ask: as a DI, she had to use at least some initiative.

When she got back to Vine Street, she handed her notes in for typing, with the Perrin interview marked for priority, and went back to her desk to phone Oldroyd.

He answered straightaway and as soon as she said her name, remembered that she had been present at his interview. But he had no quick response to her question.

'1967? You must understand that I was pretty new to the college at the time. My fellowship started in the Christmas term of 1966, so I wasn't on any of the boards or committees until the following year. I really don't think I can be much help to you on this one. You'd have to go through the examinations records, but they're strictly confidential and I don't know who'd be in charge of them right now. Because, of course, it would have been Professor Godwin. But I'll ask around if you like, see if anyone remembers a Mathew Quin.'

'Thank you, Dr Oldroyd. If you can do that discreetly, I would be very grateful. I'm sure you'll understand that we need to avoid gossip and speculation.'

'Well, there's no shortage of that, I can assure you.'

•

The four o'clock meeting in Macready's office was nothing like the freewheeling discussion with which the investigation had begun five days ago. Extra chairs had been brought in as Jimmy was also attending and the stenographer had been asked to record the discussion.

'We are now fairly sure that we have identified a previous murder by the same killer,' Macready announced. 'Most of you were briefed on that yesterday—those of you, that is, who had not found ways of briefing yourselves independently. Second—'

The eyes rested only briefly on Briony, and with no detectable change of expression, before he continued.

'Some additional information about the Hanging Gardens case has come through today, as a result of inquiries by Inspector Latham. The body of the victim had been mutilated: the right hand was severed just below the wrist bone and the left ear was also removed. It is possible that one or both of these may have been sent to the police, since a package addressed to Chief Inspector Rutgers arrived six days after the murder. However, this was intercepted for examination by the bomb squad, who were sufficiently suspicious to have it destroyed unopened. So it remains, unfortunately, a matter for speculation.'

Well, you're ahead of me there, thought Briony. Someone had done quick work tracking that parcel. Palgrave's domain most likely.

Macready looked hard at each of them in turn, then fixed on Steve. 'Do you have anything to add on this matter, Latham?'

Latham swept ash off the edge of his corduroy jacket, but let another lot fall as he spoke.

'Greg Kendrick was the principal suspect and Rutgers's team were pretty keen on him, had him under full surveillance for three weeks, but they couldn't get any evidence that would stand up in court. We need to interview him again because he may be able to give us valuable information, but I think we can remove him from the suspect list. Last Sunday night he was in hospital having his appendix out. I'm working back through the list of other suspects, but most them were long shots and they're even longer for our case.

If we're going to reopen the investigation on the Hanging Gardens murder, we may have to start again at square one. It's looking very different now—'

Macready interrupted. 'Thank you, Latham. We will arrange some interviews on site for tomorrow. Palgrave, I understand you have some interesting information from the Tupperware company?'

Palgrave flicked over some pages of a spiral-bound notebook.

'According to the manufacturers, this is a non-standard item. It's a 4 oz container, designed as part of a picnic set that contained three such items. It was not available separately and only eighty of the picnic sets were sold, on a trial promotion in Devon and Cornwall. It was then discontinued.'

'This raises the question,' said Macready, 'of whether Walker is from the West Country and, if so, whether we should be checking unsolved cases in Devon and Cornwall. For the present, that won't be our priority. Our best course immediately will be to focus on possible links between the murders in Gower Street and Holland Park.'

15

On Saturday morning, exactly a week after her arrival, Nell at last woke at what for her was a normal time. She'd managed to sleep through on only a half dose of the Mogadon last night and even had some vague dreams, though she could hardly remember anything of them. Someone walking. City streets. Then sand. Nothing, really. Maybe a sign that she needed to be out and about.

What she could see of the sky through the window above her looked chalky and uncertain, but perhaps it would brighten up, so she and Julie could go boating on the Serpentine in Hyde Park as they'd planned. Poor Rita had to go to work.

Nell herself was starting work on Monday at a temping job Julie had found for her and next weekend she'd have to begin some university work, to prepare for term, so this last weekend of freedom was important. The Beatles song 'Here comes the sun' ran through her head as she willed a streaky blue patch in the clouds to grow larger. Instead, it started to fade again.

She sat up, bunched the pillow in the small of her back and took the Margaret Drabble novel from her bedside table. This wasn't one of her course books, but it was all about a girl at university. It was written in the first person, which usually Nell didn't like, but this time she loved it, because the voice seemed to be talking off the page in a vivid jumble of thoughts and plans and reactions. It was a bit like reading someone's diary and made her think that perhaps she should start keeping one. She could buy a notebook this morning. A nice one, with a hard cover.

She heard the twins getting up. First Rita, who opened and closed her bedroom door carefully and wore slippers so she didn't make much noise as she walked around. Julie, on the other hand, always liked everyone to know when she was up in the morning. She clumped out of her bedroom in platform sandals, crossed the room to the balcony, then went back the other way, through the front door of the flat and down the stairs for the paper. She came up again louder and faster, calling breathlessly as she entered the sitting room, 'Hey, Reet! It's in! They printed it! Nell!'

Nell's bedroom door was flung wide open and the newspaper thrust under her nose.

'See? Isn't that fantastic! And it means we get five pounds.'

The page Nell found herself staring at had three rows of photos under the heading 'Summer in the City'. One of the photos showed a girl in a beret, holding an armful of white flowers. 'Student Nell Adams among the flowers at Covent Garden,' said the caption. The photographs on either side showed a small boy pointing with an ice cream cone at the bars of the monkey cage in Regent's Park Zoo, and an old lady in an elaborate hat, looking up at one of the sentries outside Buckingham Palace.

'It's a sort of competition,' Julie explained. 'Well, not exactly competition, but you can send in your photos and the ones they pick to go in the paper get a five pound prize. See?' She bounced off the bed and went calling for Rita again, as Nell took in more of the print. 'Twins Julie and Rita Eldridge of Collingham Gardens snapped their cousin as she sorted through a cascade of fresh carnations at her favourite flower stall.'

But I've never been there before, said a voice in Nell's head, as if this little piece of misrepresentation were all she had to worry about.

'What?' Rita appeared in the doorway, half dressed, with one hand pushed into the leg of a pair of tights. She inspected the photo critically, then put an arm round Julie. 'Great! I didn't know you'd sent it in.'

'It was a secret.' Julie blushed and looked coy, but her expression changed as she noticed Nell's face. 'What's the matter? You are pleased, aren't you? What's the matter?'

Nell had started to cry now and couldn't stop.

'What's the matter?' Rita echoed, dropping the unravelled tights and sitting on the side of the bed. 'It's only a bit of fun, Nell. It's just one of those pictures, you know, and you looked so—just so right, you know? It's a perfect picture.'

Julie took the offending paper and folded it, still blushing but in a very different way.

'Look, I'm really sorry. I didn't—it's because you were in the papers before, isn't it?'

'But you should be getting over that now,' said Rita. 'This is a happy picture. It's completely different.'

Nell wiped her nose on the sheet. 'It's not the point. They should never have printed my photo before. They admitted that, afterwards. The police shouldn't have released it to the bloody paper. I don't know why they had to have a picture of me, in any case. I was only a witness. But I was on the bloody front page, don't you see? It went everywhere. Whoever did that murder knows who it was that found the body. And now if he sees this paper, he'll know where I am.'

'Oh, sugar!' Julie's hand went to her mouth.

16

The briefing on Saturday morning was mercifully short, as it was mainly to say that the whole team had an appointment with the landlord to be shown around the Hanging Gardens at ten, then to interview Greg Kendrick and any of the other staff who might be able to assist with the inquiry. The pub was in a narrow curved street just a couple of blocks back from Baker Street. It was the corner building in a row of neat Regency houses with low set deep oblong windows and matching blue doors with fan windows over them. Behind the houses were vast spreading trees, ancient oaks in their full summer majesty, their upper branches shooting high over the roofs. Although the buildings were four storeys above ground, they were in proportion to the width of the street so that the area gave an impression of easy seclusion. And the flowers were just glorious, dominating the whole scene in a blaze of luminous colour. Sprays of mauve, yellow and scarlet grew in all directions from the huge baskets, while glossy trails of flowering vine cascaded from vents cut underneath them.

The windows on the ground floor of the pub had been enlarged and were divided by thick marble pillars on which ornate carriage lamps were mounted. Entry was through finely ornamented swing doors set diagonally on a wedge cut across the corner of the building. According to the case report there was no forced entry and these were the only doors.

They'd tracked everyone who'd been in the pub the evening before the murder, and all had alibis except Greg Kendrick, who was now, at least officially, off the suspect list. He was short, round faced and had a nice direct smile as he came to meet them, though there were clear signs of tension in his movements as he arranged chairs for everyone around the largest of the tables in the bar. Briony thought he looked a little older than twenty-eight, and wondered if the straight-cut jeans and checked shirt were his best clothes.

'I can offer you a drink,' he said, 'but I'm not sure that's the right thing.'

'Some water would be very much the right thing, thank you kindly,' answered Macready, pulling off his overcoat and handing it to Kendrick.

The interview began with some uncharacteristic small talk from Macready.

'You are quite protected from the traffic here,' he said, looking out of the window and watching a small dog sniff its way along the pavement opposite. 'Is it always so quiet?'

'Pretty much. There's no short cuts through here—and the street winds around a corner so you can't drive fast.'

'Is the dog a local?'

'Millie? Oh yes, belongs to an old lady at number seven. There's a few dogs around here.'

'Do you have a dog yourself, Mr Kendrick?'

'No, sir.'

'Pity. I rather miss having a dog, but Piccadilly is no place for them. This really is a very pleasant part of London, I must say. You have worked here how long?'

'Three years.'

'And before that?'

'I was an assistant at Kew Gardens.'

The eyebrow rose and dipped. 'Indeed? You are a fortunate man, Mr Kendrick. I suppose an expert gardener such as yourself may take his pick among the better areas of the city to work in.'

'Well, in a way I suppose, but not necessarily, it's just—' Kendrick looked sideways at Latham, then at Briony. 'I'm not sure what you really want to know.'

Macready straightened up. 'Ah, yes. You are right to remind us of our business, Mr Kendrick. Inspector Latham will explain that to you.'

Latham, clearly impatient with Macready's opening strategy, dived straight for the main line of questioning.

'Mr Kendrick, as you know we want to talk to you again about the murder that took place here on the 14th of August last year. You knew the victim, Miss Sabina Melies, is that right?'

'I knew her a bit—'

'Was she a friend of yours?'

'She was just a very friendly girl. I'm usually a bit shy, but she wasn't. She knew everyone round here, really. The landlord or any of the regulars could tell you as much about her as I could. I only met her a few months before it happened. She hadn't been around here very long and she wasn't sure how long she was going to stay.'

'Tell us more about that. About any plans she discussed with you, for example.'

'She used to talk about going to join some kibbutz in Israel. She'd lived in a commune before, in America, but it broke up. That's why she came to England. She was getting quite well paid work as a translator. She spoke Spanish.'

Latham had the notes from Kendrick's previous interviews in front of him and he referred to them conspicuously before putting the next question.

'You said she wasn't a personal friend?'

'Not really, no.'

'But you slept with her.'

Kendrick looked down at his hands clasped on the table in front of him and frowned. 'Couple of times. It wasn't anything. For Sabina, anyway. She slept with a lot of people. She was—you know.'

'What, Mr Kendrick?'

'Uninhibited.'

'Might that have bothered some people, do you think?'

Kendrick met Latham's eye again. 'I'm sure it did. Lots of people. Sometimes it felt like half the crowd in here of a night were women whose boyfriends she'd raced off or blokes who resented her for dumping them. But she usually won them round again. You just had to take Sabina for what she was.'

'Would you say any of those resentments that you observed were serious?'

'Not really, no. I don't think so. Not from what I could see.'

Latham allowed the pause to hang there, while he checked his notes again.

'Mr Kendrick, when you were interviewed in August last year, you said at one point, "there's a couple of people I'd be suspicious of". You mentioned three people, in fact. Miss Melies's brother Andreas was one. Why were you suspicious of him?'

'Obvious reasons. He was a big aggressive bloke. I only saw him twice and both times he was looking to borrow money off her. The first time he came in here, he'd had a bit to drink and got a hold of her elbow and forced her to go outside. Then we all heard him yelling at her, calling her a slut, a tart—worse things. He left after she gave him twenty quid.'

'Cigarette?' Latham offered the pack.

'No, thanks. I don't smoke.'

'How did you know she gave him the money?'

'She said she'd give him ten, but she only had the twenty pound note and she was asking who could change it. She'd just been paid.

It was her pay. He was acting like he was ready to get pretty rough with her—and she just let him take the twenty quid.'

'And the second time you saw him?'

'Second time she wasn't here and he started threatening everyone in the bar, trying to find out where she was. The landlord had to phone the police, but of course he left before they got here.'

'Between the 4th of August and the 5th of September, Mr Melies was detained by the police in Sao Paulo after his involvement in a street brawl. Did you know that?'

'No, I'd no idea.'

'So who else did you suspect, Mr Kendrick?'

'Maybe that's too strong a way of putting it. But I didn't much like the sound of the people she was working for—some agency it was—sounded a bit shady to me.'

'In what way?'

'They warned her not to talk about her work to anyone. She had this stuff to translate and she wasn't supposed to tell anyone what was in it. But sometimes I could see it bothered her. She used to say she wanted to leave, but she couldn't earn as much anywhere else because she didn't have a typing speed. So it was twelve quid a week for bar work or the dole, basically.'

'The people Sabina Melies worked for were the Spanish embassy, Mr Kendrick. Confidentiality is a condition for all their employees.'

Kendrick, who had been mild mannered so far, suddenly kicked the leg of his chair. 'Are you just trying to make a fool of me? Why do you ask me about things you already know?'

Macready made a discreet gesture to silence Latham and cut in.

'I apologise, Mr Kendrick. Your recollections are important and no discourtesy was intended. Please continue. There was someone else you had a suspicion about, was there?'

'Sort of. It was a week or so before—before she got killed. She came in with this bloke—I can't remember his name, or whether she even told me it. Said he'd been part of a commune she'd stayed in for a while when she was living in California. He'd just come back. He wanted her to put him up for a few days, but she was obviously very uncomfortable about it, which wasn't like her. He had a drink with her for about half an hour then he went off on his own and she came and talked to me. She was all jittery. First of all she wouldn't say anything about him, then after a couple more whiskies she said something like—I can't remember the exact words—but it was like, this bloke was into the dark stuff. I asked what she meant and she said some of those communes had gone bad. And I said, is that why you left? And she said yes. Then she said—and here I do remember the exact words: "They got in deep shit". So I tried to probe a bit more—asked what was she scared of. I suppose I was a bit intrigued, really. All that Charlie Manson stuff came to mind, you know? But when I brought that up she started laughing. She seemed a bit hysterical in fact, so I dropped it. But she asked if she could stay with me that night.'

Latham came in again. 'So was that the first time you slept with her?'

Kendrick's mouth twitched. 'No. The first time was a few months previous, shortly after I met her. I was a convenience. I didn't really mind.'

'Can you describe this man who upset Miss Melies?' asked Macready quietly.

Kendrick took a deep breath. 'That's hard. Shaggy hair. The rats' tails look, you know? Kind of dirty brown. I'd say he was quite tall. Five eleven or so. Quite thin. It was a warm night, but he wore a duffle coat, I remember that. He was the edgy type—moved his hands and feet a lot, like people do when they're on speed, but he seemed very focused, which people usually aren't when they're on speed.'

'Did you notice the colour of his eyes?'

'Couldn't be sure. I had the impression they were dark eyes. Once he looked at me, when I stepped over his legs on my way to the toilet. Dark eyes, pale face—that's about the best I can do, I'm afraid.'

'And you really cannot recollect the name?'

'I keep thinking about that. And the more I go over it in my mind, the surer I am that Sabina didn't say what his name was.'

'Thank you, Mr Kendrick,' said Macready firmly, as Latham looked ready to launch into another line of questioning. 'If you do think of anything further about this man, or about what Miss Melies said to you concerning him, please let us know immediately. Now. We would like to see upstairs, please, and inspect your gardens at closer quarters.'

Kendrick seemed to be hesitating about making a move. He hunched his shoulders and looked down at the table. Macready prompted.

'Mr Kendrick? Is there anything else you'd like to mention?'

'Maybe. Just one thing. I may be wrong, mind you. Your memory can do funny things sometimes, you know? And I've been asked that many questions about what I remember, I sometimes wonder if— Well, anyway. Sabina was sitting with this guy over there.' He pointed to a bench on the far side of the room. 'They were in some kind of conversation, but they certainly weren't talking loud. I was collecting the glasses, so I had to pass them to fetch a couple from that table, just in front of them. And I heard their voices, but I didn't recognise any of the words they said. I thought they were talking in Spanish.'

17

Sometimes Walker spoke in the night, waking him with the close-up sound of his voice. Sometimes the voice was part of a dream, but not always. This time he heard it so clearly that it woke him, but he did not catch its words. That bothered him. He sat up and swung his legs over the edge of the bed.

'What?' he said. 'What?'

The voice hung there in the darkness, waiting.

He pulled on some jeans and a coat, put the things he needed in a bag that could be slung over his shoulder and left.

Outside, the air was almost still and the world had got larger, as if the sky had swollen, above the hulks of the empty warehouses. Walker's steps were silent for a time and sped fast until he reached Borough High Street, where two late drinkers swerved out from the edge of the footpath, their arms around each other. These he followed, one footfall at a time.

'Here! Who's that behind us?'

One of the men wheeled around, pulling out of the embrace. Another footfall echoed.

'Who's that?'

The other man, dazed with drink, swam on the spot and offered slurred words of reassurance. 'Aint nubuddy, you pissy ole tyke. Nubuddy here.'

They came together again and continued on their way. Walker stepped lightly, allowing an occasional scrape against the dirt to keep the attention, but as they crossed towards St Thomas Street, the echo came again and built until it rebounded from all the blank-eyed, empty buildings.

'I *said*,' The voice cracked as it strained for emphasis. 'I'm *asking* you, who the bloody hell are you? *Where* the bloody hell—'

Walker appeared in front of him for a moment, smiled and was gone from sight again.

'Bloody hell. Who was that, then? Did you see that? That's the bloody devil, that is. I swear I seen the bloody devil.'

The second man said no recognisable words, but shook and gibbered and wrapped his arms around his chest.

Walker continued his journey. Three in the morning. London was awake twenty-three hours a day but this was the hour when the city stopped. He could walk down the middle of London Bridge, between Southwark Cathedral and Magnus the Martyr, with only one set of passing headlights to distract him as he looked out across the black water. The deaths of London were many and varied, but of all of them the black water was the easiest. He could see it again turning to a soup of corpses here, but he was not interested. The barrier between life and death had to be made to flame bright, to roar and dazzle, so the eye might be satisfied with seeing and the ear with hearing. He passed the Monument. Remembrance of things past. But for Walker there was no past. He saw the inferno of Pudding Lane rage around him and ash float in the air like swarming moths. Fire was a stronger death than water, but lives were best plucked one at a time, albeit in close succession when the occasion offered. That way the terror could be seen to pass from one to the other.

Walker could cut across time, or move in it and with it. Step by step. Step by step up Gracechurch and into Bishopsgate, up Bishopsgate across London Wall, and on, house by house, each house with its hearing walls, waiting to be entered. But he ignored them.

In Brushfield Street, where he turned east, deserted shops and houses presented their blank faces on either side of him; everything failed here, on the border between two worlds. On the other side of the line, those who knew how to survive on the poisoned ground were no shopkeepers. Ahead of him loomed the massive body of the church, its steeple gashing the purple sky, its shoulders braced against the timid structures huddled around it. It was a different species from them. He'd once heard a story about the building of the church. Its foundations were dug in the plague pit, and the mason's son was killed in a fall from the steeple. Turn.

At the end of Brushfield, the road was strewn with cabbage leaves and other vegetable refuse from Spitalfields markets, shown up in the light spill from the Ten Bells. He came to a stop in Hanbury Street. Here there were no street lights and the darkness thickened in layers between the roofline of the cramped houses and the ground.

Jack had found Annie Chapman in Hanbury Street and she had found Jack. Leather apron. You'd need a leather apron for that sort of work. Walker laughed out loud, cracking the silence.

The place was a little further along, on the left, near the crossroads with Brick Lane, on a section of the pavement that was lined with rusting sheets of corrugated iron. Nothing marked the spot. So, opening the bag, he began preparations to rectify that.

Afterwards, retracing his steps a short way, he cut through via Wilkes into Fournier Street and skirted the vast blank side wall of the church. On this he had to leave something to keep the fuzz buzzing while he went about his real work a bit further away. He enjoyed the movements of the brush over the smooth stone. It was as if the design he knew so well was already there, waiting to be brought to the surface line by line.

When he had finished the job, he packed the bag and walked

across the road, and along Brushfield into Crispin Street, a narrow passageway to which a new concrete building showed its back, filling the spaces where there was once a sick mess of dives and alleyways.

This was where Jack got Mary Kelly and made his last work. If you closed your eyes, the whole scene was still there, the filthy mess in the little stinking room, floating in the dark. It was meaningless, doing that to a body: spreading it all over the walls like that, making the face into a hash, trying to get an effect with a botched disembowelling and ending up with something you might come across in any abattoir. Mary Kelly was Jack's last scene. After that, Walker had done with him. Took him to the river and made an end.

He had already decided what to do here and it didn't take him long. When he'd finished, he packed up again and set off for the other side of Jack's mile. That's what they called it now, but it was Walker's long before it was Jack's.

The alleyways were guarded by iron posts, to prevent cars from entering. You could get the bike through here, but that wouldn't be smart. Artillery Lane skewed at an unexpected angle, as if to confound horses and bikes, and the uneven brick paving was no friend to either. He stopped. This was where it all began, the sprouting warren of misaligned alleyways in which human low-life germinated like some outgrowth of the dirt. He stood there, feeling the shapes of the stones against the soles of his shoes, sensing the static in the air, trying to gauge the direction of the current. When he turned slightly so he was facing towards the church, he lost it, but another quarter turn and the charge travelled clean through him so his fingers tingled and the soles of his feet were hot. Yes, this was the axis, running diagonally across the mile, between Hanbury and Mitre Square.

Coming out onto Bishopsgate again, he looked up at the darkened windows and smiled. Nothing going on behind those. Bodies lying asleep, having dreams that told them nothing, showed them nothing, all through the dead hours. He turned into Houndsditch, a wider road that looked as if it belonged in the twentieth century, and passed two cars, the first traffic he'd encountered since he entered the mile.

More cars were turning through from both ends of the road as he cut across to Duke's Place, back into the last chopped off corner of the old world.

18

'Spitalfields,' said Macready. His pronunciation of the word was dry-mouthed and precise. 'We are going to pay a visit to Christchurch in Spitalfields, where it appears someone has made a copy of the art work we found in Gresham. A painting, I'm told, on the church wall. The constable in the office took a call from a Mr Fisher, the sexton, who was instructed to notify us by Whitechapel Station. Williams, check the call please and find out who Fisher spoke to at Whitechapel. Palgrave, get the soco team on the case. Latham, we will go ahead in the first car. It is time to be up and doing, as my mother used to say.'

I don't blame her, Briony thought. Having spent most of Sunday sitting in Macready's office listening to interview tapes and picking over the case notes with Steve on one side of her sucking smoke into his lungs and Palgrave on the other making strange shapes with his bony hands, she was thinking she'd be crawling up the walls if she had to spend another morning in there. Even the work in the files seemed like a refreshing prospect by comparison. Not that they hadn't been working—the level of concentration Latham and Macready maintained as they went back and forth over some detail or other made her head ache—but it was such a claustrophobic way of doing things.

The investigation seemed to be heading everywhere and nowhere, with too many clues producing leads in too many different directions and Macready was determined to get to what he called 'the nub of the case'. She still hadn't managed to interest him in the story of Mathew Quin.

'It is 8.30, so we will still have to contend with rush hour traffic. Williams, you can follow us with Palgrave after you have spoken direct with Mr Fisher. Be sure to instruct him to leave everything untouched.'

Briony went to the front desk in search of a London telephone directory, wondering whether she should look under Church of England, or parish churches, or what, when a very young looking constable in a gleaming new uniform came out from one of the administrative offices.

'Inspector Williams? I've got a telephone number here I'm supposed to give you. For the sexton at Christchurch.'

'Ah, good! Was it you took the call?'

'That's right. He sounded quite distressed, poor man. Said they'd had an anonymous tip-off. It was hard to get a word in edgeways, actually. You can use the phone just there on the left.'

Briony copied the number into her notebook before dialling it. Fisher answered the call himself.

'Police, you say? I thought they'd be here by now, not ringing me up with a lot of silly questions. It's a terrible mess here. Worse than last week. And I can't find Reverend Burroughs, which is very unusual. I see him every morning at eight in the rectory, but there doesn't seem to be anyone there.'

'Superintendent Macready is already on his way to you, Mr Fisher,' said Briony. 'You mentioned some kind of tip-off to the officer you spoke to first.'

'Somebody rang up about a quarter to eight just when I was

having my breakfast. He said there was a message for us in Fournier Street. So I went out there—and—well, I hope I never see another message like that.'

'Did he say anything else?'

'That was it. Put the phone down. So I went straight across to the rectory—then, when I couldn't find Reverend Burroughs, I phoned the police in Whitechapel and when I told them what it was I seen on the church wall, they said to phone you.'

'Thank you, Mr Fisher. We'll be with you very soon. We need to be sure no one interferes with the site before we get there, so please keep watch for us.'

'Oh, I'll be keeping a watch all right, but I need to find Reverend Burroughs. I wondered if he might have gone into the church. It's kept locked, you see, because there's structural damage and we can't afford to repair it so it's too dangerous to have people in there. That's the state things are in, you see, in this country.'

'Is the church locked now?'

'Yes. Yes. I told you. It's always locked. But what if he went in there and locked the door behind him and had an accident or something. He could have gone in there to check everything was all right, or something, see. If he'd got the same kind of a phone call, I was thinking, that's what he most probably would have done. But I can't get in there now, because it's a heavy bolted lock and we've only got the one key.'

'All right, Mr Fisher. We'll check the church as soon as we get there. Who did you speak to at Whitechapel Station?'

'Several people. They hand you round from pillar to post there. Last time I had to phone them up—about the vandalism—they made me explain it to three different people. Then it took them two days before they got around to paying us a visit. Apparently they weren't interested in obscenities and splashed paint, but this is something different.'

Briony was looking at her watch and getting anxious about

how long this was taking. She tried to keep the impatience out of her voice.

'Just briefly, Mr Fisher, can you tell me who at Whitechapel Station told you to contact us here at Vine Street?'

'Inspector something or other. I didn't get the name. He said to give the details and tell them to inform Superintendent Macready.'

'Thank you, Mr Fisher. We'll be there very soon.'

Briony went in search of Palgrave and found him on the phone in the incident room, giving instructions about who was to do what, then ticking them off in a small black notebook with an improbably short stub of pencil, which he licked each time he'd made a mark with it. It took a particular kind of person to hang onto a pencil long enough for it to get that short, thought Briony. In fact, there were very few pencils around that were less than half the length of a new one. So what happened to all those half used pencils? When he'd finished the call, Palgrave tucked the stub into the elastic band on his notebook and deposited them in the upper pocket of his jacket.

'The car is waiting, Inspector Williams, and the others are already in it. I'll join you when I've seen the desk sergeant.'

It was an uncomfortable drive. Palgrave took the front seat and Briony was squashed in the back with Jimmy and one of the pathologists. When the car drew up in Commercial Street outside Christchurch, it made the fourth in a row of police vehicles. There was a yellow cordon across the entrance to the churchyard, but when Palgrave approached it, the officer on duty pointed to the left.

'That way, Inspector. Just round the corner.'

Another cordon was being put up along the side of the church, where there was evidently some kind of mess on the wall that had drawn the interest of Macready, Latham and several uniformed police who Briony assumed must be from Whitechapel Station. As the new arrivals approached, Macready signalled for everyone to move back and waved Jimmy through.

There were no obscenities. There was no splashed paint. Here, again, was Hogarth's drawing: the contorted face with the knife in its eye, the skull with a bolt through the forehead, the attenuated limbs of a disembowelled body. It was done in thick brushstrokes that gave only the bold outlines of the image, but it was remarkably effective, the more so as you drew further back towards the other side of the road.

Latham, standing several paces behind the others, beckoned to Briony with a movement of his head, then walked towards a side street leading off to the north. She caught up with him.

'See what you think of the one up here,' he said, leading the way round into Hanbury Street and out into the full morning sun. It had been quite chilly under the shadow of the church and Briony wanted to stop there for a while to feel the warmth across her back, but Latham was already three paces ahead, crossing the road diagonally to the right. About fifty yards further down the street, two uniforms were standing guard by an expanse of industrial fence that was screening some kind of building site. There was another cordon. The words on the fence were painted in evenly spaced, regularly formed letters:

A TIME TO DIE

'Get it?' asked Steve.

'Get what?'

'To everything…'

'A time to be born, a time to die. It's Bob Dylan, isn't it?'

'The words are from the Bible.'

Briony looked at them, bending over the cordon to get closer.

'So does this go with your cult theory?'

'What do you mean, cult theory?'

'You know, that stuff about the Freemasons.'

'It might. But don't you know what this place is? 29 Hanbury

Street. Site of the second Ripper murder. Victim was Annie Chapman.'

'So who's the victim this time? We should get back to the church. I have to talk to Macready, report on the call to Mr Fisher. Should have done that first. He was worried about the rector when I talked to him. Reverend Burroughs. Said he seemed to have gone missing.'

'No point in rushing. They're already searching the rectory. And it will take them a while to get in to the church. Door's got a bloody great brass lock on it, two centuries old. They have to find the key or get the right locksmith out, and there aren't many of those who specialise in eighteenth century brass work. Nobody's game to break a stained glass window for a quick way in. I reckon we got a bit of thinking time. Let's walk to the end of the road.'

Briony had always preferred walking to standing around, although Hanbury Street didn't exactly offer much to look at: building site on one side; row of ugly little houses on the other. Some had lace curtains.

'I reckon this place would turn *me* into a raving psychopath after a while,' said Steve. 'Can you imagine going home every night to one of those little places? They're like fucking cupboards. Close the door and forget the world. Makes me claustrophobic even to look at them.'

'I dunno. This whole area's like a kind of warren. I read about it at college. Perfect conditions for brewing up the next underground movement. Could be all kinds of interesting weirdos in those houses. I think we should get back.'

'In a minute. Like I said, this is thinking time. So what do you make of the graffiti artist?'

'He's a bit too good at his work. Probably is an artist, or at least had some training.'

'Got his A level, you mean?'

'Something like that. Anatomy students do technical drawing, you know. And Mathew Quin had a bit of a flair for that, so Mr

Perrin told me. He upset the cleaning staff by putting his work up on the bedroom walls. I think we should ask Perrin to come and look at what's on the church wall over there. See if it rings any bells.'

'We got so many bells ringing already I'm practically deaf. We're drowning in clues. Why do you fancy this guy Quin so much?'

Briony drew a deep breath. 'I thought I'd explained that over the weekend. To a load of deaf ears. Couldn't we at least interview Perrin—all together—so you and Macready can hear the story first hand?'

'We're going to have a pretty long list of interviews after today.' Steve blew smoke into the misty sunshine, then turned and smiled at Briony. 'But I'll back you, if you want to put it to Macready again.'

This was a big concession, after the tensions of the past week. She smiled back.

'Thanks.'

'You're nice when you smile. You should do it more often.'

'Do you say that to Macready?'

'Don't be cheeky. Can't you see when someone's being nice to you?'

They turned back, passing Palgrave and Jimmy, who were followed up by two other socos carrying their black bags. As they reached the corner of Wilkes and Fournier Street again, Macready crossed to meet them.

'One of the cars has just found another painting exercise. In Crispin Street, across the way. We can walk.'

Macready's stride was long and fast, forcing Briony into an undignified trot to keep up. Again, she felt like the tag-along in the team as the two men walked shoulder to shoulder, talking in low voices so she couldn't catch any of what they were saying.

A police car was parked across the entrance to Crispin Street, which was also blocked off from the sun by a very solid looking building on the east side. An officer got out of the car to greet Macready, and led them to a double wooden gate about halfway down the block.

It was another brush sketch, painted across the divide between the gates. A woman lay on the ground, her head bent back and her exposed throat marked with a deep, open gash. Macready turned to Briony, the eyebrow raised and one side of his mouth along with it, in a sardonic smile.

'Hogarth again, eh Williams?'

Briony suddenly didn't feel too good. Her mouth and lips felt dry and her forehead hot.

'I don't recognise it,' said Steve.

'Not as well known as *The Reward of Cruelty*,' said Macready, but part of the same series. This is one of the *Stages of Cruelty*. The reward is what happens to the perpetrator of the stages after he has been caught. He's hanged and then anatomised. The latter was considered the ultimate indignity.'

The picture was smaller, cruder, but so much more real than the baroque design of the anatomy. It was like an intimate message. Briony was concentrating on her breathing, which was getting very shallow and she had to edge back a couple of paces to lean against the wall.

'Away from there, Williams!' Macready's voice was like a gunshot. 'There may be valuable evidence…'

But Briony was already on the ground, pulled suddenly against it by the weight of her own head.

19

Caroline was only five minutes late for work but there on her desk like a reprimand was a note from the sub-editor who was never less than twenty minutes early and liked to let you know when he'd had to take a phone call for you. Of course he could just have left the phone ringing, since no one would have been surprised that it was unanswered at this hour, but that would have been missing an opportunity to score a point. She sat for a minute, staring at the neatly folded paper before picking it up, and planned how she could present her resignation letter, by staying late so she could leave it on his desk for him to find first thing next morning. She couldn't expect a reply from the *Sunday Times* before this time next week at the earliest, but maybe, if it said what she hoped, she would leave a copy of that too.

'Caroline,' said the blue pencil. Doesn't he even have a lead pencil, Caroline fumed to herself. She would leave him a whole bundle of them, 'for office correspondence' as a parting gift. 'There has been another incident of graffiti.' You can't have an incident of graffiti, she thought, wishing she had a blue pencil herself. 'We have decided to cover this one as there is a threat of violence implied. You are to go to Christchurch Spitalfields this morning. Tony will join you there. So will the Reverend whatsit. He advises there are delays this morning on the Metropolitan Line, so I have approved ten shillings cab fare, for which you are to take reimbursement on arrival, from the rector. I am assuming you will return by bus.'

What does he mean by threat of violence implied, muttered Caroline, apart from the fact that Lennie Meyer couldn't write a sentence with the words in the correct order. As if there wasn't an implied threat of violence the first time, what with the beheading of the angel and all that pig's blood. Goodness knows what it must be this time, to spark his interest at last. And it had to be something pretty urgent to make the rector offer to pay a cab fare. An odd sort of arrangement, really, but it suited her just fine.

She hurried down the stairs and was lucky enough to catch a taxi almost as soon as she stepped out onto the street. The driver's screen was open, but fortunately he wasn't the chatty type. Considering the rate at which he managed to keep moving through the thick of the city traffic, diving into spaces nobody else seemed to be able to find, he was probably using all his concentration. They passed Bank after less than fifteen minutes and Caroline had to hang on to the strap by the window to steady herself as the cab accelerated up Leadenhall Street, then took a sharp turn into Duke's Place.

'Excuse me,' said Caroline, 'I think Christchurch is the other way, isn't it?'

'Short cut,' snapped the driver, swinging left, then left again. He stopped in a laneway. 'Twelve and six.'

'But this isn't the church.'

'Can't stop there. No parking. You have to get out here.'

'But I don't even know where I am.'

'Creechurch Lane. Church is just over there, the other side of Mitre Square.'

Caroline was annoyed and decided that he was not going to get a tip. He may have been an efficient driver, but there was no excuse for rudeness. She counted out twelve and six exactly, then wondered why the hand held out to receive it was cased in a rubbery white glove and why the door of the cab was opening. And as she saw the face of the driver and the funny way he smiled at her through his shaggy hair, reminding her of that hippy staring at her in the park the other day, she tried to make herself run, but her legs didn't seem to know quite how to do it and her high heels slid against the rounded edges of the brick paving.

He moved very slowly: watching her as she regained her balance and scuttled into Mitre Passage, as she tried to muster her breath to call out, then bumped against the wall and put her hands up to keep him away from her face. He caught them together by the wrists with his own rubbery hand and made a strange movement which caused a snapping noise that echoed in the passage. She felt herself sliding down the wall as the glove moved to take a confident hold on the side of her neck, and another snapping noise resounded.

20

'Just breathe slowly. That's it.'

Briony was sitting on a wooden chair, bent double with her head between her knees. The voice belonged to someone with solid legs in policewomen's shoes and stockings.

'That's it. Breathe deep. Keep your head down and your shoulders loose. Good. Two more nice long breaths... Now bring your shoulders up, but leave your head loose—Right! Now lift your head. Slowly, mind.'

Briony found herself looking into the big-boned, middle-aged face of a policewoman in a sergeant's jacket.

'Well, at least there's a bit of colour in your face now. You'd better stay another half hour at least. And here—make sure you drink this glass of water. All of it, mind.

There was a light knock on the door and a young woman poked her head round it.

'Sergeant Thomas? They need someone to direct a traffic diversion. Duke's Place and Houndsditch are being blocked. Inspector Palgrave's asking if you're free yet.'

'Tell him I'll be there directly.' The sergeant fixed Briony with a penetrating look.

'You should take the rest of the day off. I'm sure that will be DI Palgrave's advice.'

Briony made her way out to the toilets and splashed her face with cold water. The combination of red eyes and ashen skin that she saw in the mirror made her feel like crawling into a hole and an attempt at a quick repair job with the mascara and Boots moisturiser in her handbag didn't make much improvement, but she was determined not to give up and go home. She looked at her watch: 9.45. Perhaps she could pick up some information from the officers setting up the incident room and get a cup of coffee, which was surely all she needed to get back on form.

Luckily the four people in there when she made her entry were far too busy arranging phones and typewriters to even look her way and they'd already set up a kettle with mugs and instant coffee on the bar. There was also a plate of arrowroot biscuits, which she didn't fancy in the slightest, but she made herself eat one just to help fend off the risk of another blackout. The female officer who'd come in about the traffic diversion was testing a phone on the other end of the bar and when she put down the receiver, Briony edged towards her.

'Do you know where I'd find Superintendent Macready?' she asked.

'He'll be in Mitre Square, I should think. Check this plug's in properly, would you? Just the other side of the counter there. The line's still dead.'

The phone socket was hanging off the wall by a couple of exposed wires, and it was hard to reconnect the plug without wrenching the whole thing out. Eventually she managed it.

'Bingo,' said the officer. 'Dial tone.'

'How far is Mitre Square?' she asked.

'Fifteen minutes on foot if you walk fast and know where you're going. You're on the Vine Street team, aren't you? Why don't you get them to drive you?'

And meet Sergeant Thomas again at the road block, thought Briony. There was an A to Z in her handbag, so she figured out the quickest route, set off and took a long cool look at the painting on the gate in Crispin Street as she passed. Yes, she was better now. Back in control.

Mitre Square was crawling with police and a growing crowd of spectators had gathered round the cordon across the entry from Duke's Place. An ambulance was parked in the square, blocking the view to whatever it was that interested the crowd. The street directory showed another entrance in Creechurch Lane and Briony thought she might get in that way more discreetly, but the first person she saw as she came round the corner was Steve Latham, crushing a cigarette butt with gratuitous force under his rubber soled shoe. When he looked up, the expression on his face froze.

'What the heck—Who let you come down here? I thought they were supposed to be looking after you.'

'I'm fine. So what's up here?'

'Look, Briony, honestly, you're not—'

He approached awkwardly and took hold of her arm, which she gently twisted free again.

'I'm fine.'

'Look, don't come all tough-girl on me, Briony, please. You gave us a helluva shock just now. It's been a bit of a day for shocks, as a matter of fact, and I'm sure the one around there won't do you any good. This is a really ugly case. One of the worst I've been on. Even Macready's affected, I can tell.'

'Round here, you said?'

'At least let me come with you.'

Around the corner was a small brick paved yard, with an arched passageway leading off to the right. There was a cordon across the passageway, guarded by three uniforms, and several figures were moving around on the other side. Socos with their kitbags. Macready, fortunately, didn't seem to be among them. The smell of blood was unmistakable and trickles of it had found their way out between the paving stones. She turned to Steve.

'No formaldehyde this time?'

'You've got a point. It's not reeking like the last one, but we won't be sure till forensics have done the work.'

Ignoring the tell-tale dryness in her mouth, Briony headed straight for the cordon and showed her ID card to get through. Steve stood behind as she took in the scene, so close that she could feel his chest against her shoulder.

The victim's blonde hair looked clean and alive and her face was unmutilated, but her neck was cut through so deeply that the spine was exposed. A vertical incision stretched from the middle of her chest down to the pubic bone and the skin either side was peeled back, autopsy style, as if it had been an extra layer of clothing. The lower ribs had also been broken outwards, so the chest cavity gaped like a crimson pond.

On the smooth curved stone of the archway above her, words were painted in sharply angled letters.

A TIME TO KILL

She looked back at what was on the ground, at the ruined pink suit and the white handbag splattered with blood. The girl's hands, broken at the wrists, lay at odd angles like those of a puppet, but her shoes were still on her feet.

'This is recent, isn't it?' she asked in what she hoped would be a clear, steady voice. It came out as a strangled quaver.

'Very. Probably happened about an hour ago, while we were admiring his art work further up the street,' said Steve. 'Looks like he meant to take the heart but it was a bit too ambitious for a rush job. Basic butchery is all he managed. Had enough?' And, without waiting for an assent, he steered her firmly out again into the sunshine, towards a low wall on the other side of the yard, where she sat down obediently. There was cold sweat on her forehead again.

'Hello. You look like I feel,' said Jimmy, walking towards them and taking his seat on the wall next to her. 'There's more dirty work over in the Spitalfields church, apparently. They got in there a few minutes ago and the boss's just been called over, which means I'll be wanted as well. More excitement than a day at the races, isn't it? Oh, now, here they come.'

A siren was audible in the distance, then another. As they grew to a crescendo, it sounded like six sirens, the ambulance screaming over the top of the police chorus.

A camera flash went off to the right of them and Briony turned to see two pressmen being physically restrained from entering Creechurch Lane. They were taking pictures constantly, even as they were manhandled back around the corner to make way for another ambulance that was turning into the yard. Steve swore and got up to talk to the driver.

'We've already got an ambulance,' he said. 'It's through on the other side.'

'We're back-up,' said the driver.

'I don't see how one body can use two ambulances.'

But the team were already getting out. A female paramedic wearing a formidable arrangement of shoulder bags with red crosses on them came across and looked pointedly at Briony.

'Anyone need treating for shock?'

'I'm fine,' said Briony tonelessly.

'What's the treatment?' asked Jimmy. 'Would I like it?'

The ambulance officer crouched in front of Briony and took her wrist in one hand while she held a stopwatch in the other.

'Not good,' she pronounced and Briony found herself being frogmarched into the ambulance, an officer on either side of her. They made her lie down, then looked in her eyes with a torch, examined her tongue, put a tourniquet around her upper arm and took her pulse again. After that came a string of questions: what's your name, what day of the week is it, where do you live, date of birth, when did you last eat, have you any history of asthma, diabetes, blood pressure problems, is there any history of heart disease in your family, are you on the pill? When they had scribbled their way through an elaborate set of printed forms, they gave her tea in a yellow plastic cup and allowed her to sit up and drink it. Briony felt confused one minute and irritated the next, but the irritation soon won out. While she was stuck here talking about what day it was, Jimmy and Steve would have gone back to the church and, yet again, she'd have to follow up like some kid who'd been left out of the game.

'I need to go now,' she said firmly. 'I've got work to do. I'm on the investigation team and we've just heard there's another incident.'

'That's what we're here for,' said the nurse. 'To keep you on your feet. You haven't blacked out or anything, have you?'

'No.'

'Good. Take these.' She handed Briony two shiny blue pills, and poured more tea into her cup.

'You've got low blood pressure, did you know that? See your doctor about it as soon as you can. I suppose you won't feel like eating right now, so I'll give you some glucose sweets. Keep one in your mouth all the time.'

'I have to go now,' Briony repeated, as if to herself this time.

Another ambulance officer holding an intercom appeared in the doorway.

'When you're ready,' he said. 'We've got to move again. They want us up the other end of Commercial Street.'

'I guess we're all going to the same place, then,' said the nurse, taking the cup from Briony's hand. 'Sit tight.'

The crowd had been moved back from around Mitre Passage and were lining Aldgate High Street, pushing up towards the steps leading into the churchyard entrance. A string of uniformed police were holding them back, and Brushfield Street opposite now looked like a police parking lot. Here she managed to lose the ambulance officers, who met up with two of their colleagues patrolling the spectators. Cameras were flashing intermittently and Briony was careful to keep her face turned away from them. Jimmy was standing at the church door adjusting the settings on his own camera. She gave him a glucose sweet.

'Oh. What have I done to deserve that, then?'

'It's part of the shock treatment,' said Briony. 'The rest is just third degree interrogation. So what's happened in there?'

'Some bloke been strung up over the pulpit. I wouldn't go in if you don't have to.'

'Of course I have to.'

The lock on the church doors had been removed completely, leaving big holes in the wood, which was being brushed for fingerprints. She stepped through into a cavernous space with a small floodlit area at the far end and recognised Macready and Latham amongst the small inner circle of police gathered there. They had their backs to her and seemed deep in discussion, but she had a clear view of the body. In the centre of the floodlit area was a heavily built canopied pulpit, raised about four feet off the ground and there, apparently standing in it, was an elderly man with his hands resting on the pages of a Bible propped up on the lectern, as if to start reading. Except that his mouth was wide open and thick dark blood had poured from it all over his text.

21

The shoes felt fine when Nell put them on in the morning, but by the time she'd got to the end of a day spent running errands over three floors of a large office building, they felt like instruments of torture. Apart from giving her blisters on both heels, they pinched her toes and forced her to tense up her arches to keep them on when she went up and down stairs. It was stupid to borrow other people's shoes, she told herself repeatedly through the morning. She should have known it was a bad idea, but Rita insisted she couldn't go to her new job in her old lace-ups. She'd intended to go out at lunch time and buy some smart sandals, but she found that it was part of a Girl Friday's job to collect the lunches from the café down the road, so that just meant more blisters.

Was it worth all this for eleven pounds fifty a week, Nell asked herself as she hobbled down the stairs of Leicester Square tube station with the rush hour crowds at the end of the afternoon. Mum had sent a twenty pound cheque for books, so if she lived on cheese sandwiches for the next three weeks until her grant came through, she probably wouldn't need to get a job at all. But Julie had been determined to help her at Brook Street Bureau and Rita was planning a budget wardrobe that would set her up for the winter term.

Besides, here she was pushing her way into a tube train, just taking it as part of the day's work. Maybe it was a good thing to have no time or energy for qualms. Hanging onto the strap in the middle of the carriage, she tried to read the back of someone's newspaper, but he was holding it at the wrong angle. When she got out at Gloucester Road, she was surprised to find that the news-stand had sold out of evening papers.

Rita had Mondays off, so she was at home already after her afternoon's shopping, watching *Doctor Who*. Nell thought the twins watched far too much TV, but she did like to see the six o'clock news and was quite taken aback when Rita suddenly switched it off.

'So. How was your day?'

'Fine. Can't we watch the news?'

'What, after your first day at work? You're supposed to be full of news yourself. Tell me about it while I make some supper in the kitchen. I'm going to do a tuna pie which has to go into the oven for half an hour, so I'd better start now.'

An hour later, when Julie came home, Nell switched on the television assuming that they would watch it as usual while they ate, but Rita switched it off again.

'I've got a bit of a headache,' she said, giving Julie a funny look.

Then while Nell was doing the washing up, it was obvious the twins were having some kind of argument in the sitting room. Suddenly, the penny dropped. There was something on the news that they didn't want her to see. Something had been in the evening papers, sensational enough to cause a sell-out. Deciding to tackle the issue head-on, she dried her hands and went through.

'So what's happened? Is it a bomb somewhere?'

The twins glared at each other. Obviously they'd disagreed about what to say or not to say.

'Just a horrible story in the paper,' said Julie. 'You don't need to know anything about it. It'll only upset you. By the way, Rita says you were complaining her shoes hurt. Why don't you try those clog sandals of mine? They're not the most elegant things, but they'd be better than your lace-ups.'

'I think part of the problem is that my feet are bigger than yours. They're broader, anyway. So what's happened?'

'Somebody got murdered,' said Julie. 'But it was right over the other side of London, in the East End.'

Next morning, the twins walked Nell to the tube station, frog-marched her, practically, one on either side, hurrying her past the placards saying 'Whitechapel Murder—latest' and 'Ripper Rides again'. But once she'd got on the train, Nell was on her own, surrounded by people carrying newspapers, holding them up in her face so the headlines stared her in the eye. And when she got to the office, everyone was talking about it.

'He cut her heart out,' she heard one girl say, although that wasn't quite true, 'like Jack the Ripper. We'll be scared to go home from work now.'

Nell picked up the incoming mail and began to sort it, as she'd been shown the previous day. Before she'd finished distributing it, another delivery came with four big boxes of stationery, which she had to stack in the cupboards, checking it off against the order sheets. If she kept moving, she could keep out of the conversations around her and luckily Julie's clogs were a lot less uncomfortable than Rita's shoes, so she could get around faster.

The most difficult moment in the day came at lunch time, when she went to collect the sandwiches.

'Sorry, love,' said the woman behind the counter, 'I'm a bit behind this morning. Should be ready in a few minutes.' She continued steadily buttering bread, laying on slices of meat and lettuce, or cheese and tomato and making a diagonal cut through each round with an unnecessarily large knife.

'Well, I'm glad I don't live in the East End,' she said. 'My brother's over that way, working for the National Westminster in the Mile End Road and my sister-in-law's that worried about the children. She was crying on the phone last night. Awful, isn't it? In broad daylight, can you believe it? You have to wonder about which way the police were looking, don't you? I just hope they catch him, that's all. It's dreadful to think of someone like that running round on the loose. Makes your flesh creep.'

'Yes,' said Nell. 'I hope they catch him. Shall I come back in five minutes?'

'Make it ten. Sorry love. It's just been one of those mornings, you know?'

Nell slipped back out into the sunshine and began walking round the block. I hope they catch him, said a voice in her head. I hope they catch him. I hope they catch him. The words chimed in with the pace of her footsteps as she walked faster and faster, scaring off the city birds that were pecking at invisible things on the footpath around her. She passed a newsagent and, on second thoughts, doubled back to buy a copy of the *Guardian*. There was going to be no hiding from this story, so she might as well read the facts from a reliable source. She found a bench in the shade and stared at the headline: 'Double Murder in Whitechapel.'

In what seems like an eerie replay of one of the darkest episodes of the Jack the Ripper story, two people were brutally murdered in the Whitechapel area yesterday morning. The mutilated body of journalist Caroline Staines was found in a passageway off Mitre Square just after 9.30 am, and by 10.30 police had discovered a second body, that of the Reverend Burroughs, the rector of Christchurch in Spitalfields.

Miss Staines was reporting on a recent episode of vandalism at the church and left her office at the *Evening Standard* first thing yesterday morning to keep an appointment with the Reverend Burroughs. A grotesque painting found on the side wall of the church this morning shows a mutilated body in the style of Hogarth's *The Reward of Cruelty*.

Like the Ripper, this is a killer who works quickly and with great skill. Police have declined to release details of the mutilations. A press release from Vine Street Police Station, where the investigation is headed by Detective Superintendent Macready, states that the police 'are keeping an open mind' about possible connections with the Gower Street murder committed on 14th August, but they believe the killer has professional medical knowledge and may have links with the West country.

Professional medical knowledge. What did that mean? She remembered those very words being used by a fat sergeant in Plymouth, when one of her interminable interviews with the police had stalled again and they started arguing among themselves.

She turned to the inside pages, where the report continued. 'Anyone who saw anything suspicious in the areas of Spitalfields, Whitechapel or Aldgate yesterday morning or on Sunday night is asked to contact the police on...' She wrote the phone number on the inside of her wrist. An article on page four headed 'The Dark World of Hogarth' was accompanied by a photograph of the painting that the killer or killers had copied on the church wall.

Nell was surprised at how calm she felt. For years, she realised, she had wanted to talk to the police again. Talking to counsellors just made it all seem like something inside your head, but what it was really about was catching the killer. The police in Plymouth had interviewed her at length, but she couldn't tell them what they needed to know and they never told her anything about their investigation. Once the newspapers had dropped the story, no one spoke of it again, except her counsellor, and by then it had become Nell's problem, something that had taken up residence in her head, instead of something that had actually happened out there in the world.

Maybe there was no connection. Why should there have been? Maybe the police would have no interest in her story; but the feeling of calm meant something. She always knew it was going to happen again and not knowing where or when was what spooked her.

22

Vine Street on Tuesday morning seemed to be in complete chaos. Some of the staff had been drafted to the incident room in Spitalfields, but Macready had decided to base himself in his own office and was giving tasks to people right, left and centre. Briony didn't know where she was supposed to be based herself, so she looked for an opportunity to catch Macready and get a couple of things sorted out.

Seeing the stenographer leave his office at around ten, she knocked on the door.

'I'm busy,' he called. 'Who is it?'

'It's Williams, sir.'

The door was flung open and Macready stood there in his shirt sleeves, glaring at her in a way that almost made her turn and run.

'You are better, then? Come in. Sit down.'

He closed the door sharply after her.

'I need to get one or two things clear, sir.'

'I expect you do. I am very sorry you are in this situation, Williams. This is no case for a young woman. It has taken a turn that none of us could have anticipated and I have decided it would be much better if you were assigned to some other investigation, where your considerable abilities would be more suited—'

'No it wouldn't.'

'I beg your pardon?'

'Sir—even if I *am* a novice, I've worked as hard as anyone on this case. I've found some good leads already and I can find more, but I feel as if I'm constantly being excluded.'

'On the contrary, Williams. The mistake was to include you in yesterday's expedition when it was clearly too much for you.'

'It's up to me to say what's too much for me, sir. I was taken ill, that's all, and if you and Latham hadn't been so rude as to keep your backs turned to me all the time, maybe it wouldn't have been such a sudden shock to you.'

Macready looked stunned.

Both sat in silence, until there was a knock at the door.

'Go away!' barked Macready and footsteps could be heard scuttling off down the corridor. He raised an eyebrow and looked sideways at Briony.

'How is that for rudeness, Detective Inspector Williams? As you can see, I specialise in it. Do you have any further reprimands to deliver?'

'No, sir, but I have a request. I need a warrant to go back through the records at Senate House. I'm convinced that the man Greg Kendrick described was Mathew Quin, but I need your endorsement to make the enquiries to establish that.'

There was a further silence.

'It is against my better judgment,' Macready said, 'to licence such independent action on the part of a junior team member in a serious investigation, but I will allow you to pursue that line of enquiry provided you keep me informed of your progress on a daily basis. If your sense of independence exceeds the bounds of propriety, you will be removed from this case without further discussion. Is that understood?'

'Yes, sir.'

'And your other activities on this case will in future be restricted to interviews, as directed by me or Inspector Palgrave. You will not be involved in any further crime scene work. Is that also understood?'

Briony took a bit longer to answer this time.

'Is that understood, Inspector Williams?'

'Yes, sir.'

She got up to leave.

'Oh, and Williams—you are fully recovered, are you?'

'Yes, thank you, sir. Completely.'

'I was actually rather distressed by what happened. So was Latham. I am very sorry.'

Briony found parts of this conversation replaying in her head for the rest of the day and reacted to them by turns with seizures of embarrassment and renewed surges of indignation. Palgrave delivered the warrant to her after he returned from Whitechapel in the afternoon, but didn't seem inclined to discuss it with her.

•

The college records for the previous ten years were kept in the senate house building, in a cavernous room on the seventh floor that was filled almost entirely with long ranks of metal shelving. Faced with a vast sea of buff coloured folders and no clear labelling system, Briony tried to get some help from the clerical staff, but there was evidently no one around who understood properly how the records had been organised. After spending nearly an hour with a friendly but not very bright temporary secretary who took twice as long as she did herself to work out that the arrangement was neither straightforwardly chronological nor alphabetical, she decided she would just have to start at one end of the first shelving unit and go through it until she could see some kind of pattern.

This was what Macready had originally wanted her to be doing after all, she thought, being a glorified filing clerk. She deposited a pile of folders on one of the trestle tables by the wall and scanned the front page of each. It took her over an hour to figure out that admissions were divided into years and sequenced according to the number allocated through the UCCA system, so she had to find Quin in the examination records first in order to get his number. Examination results were organised by subject and also by ranking, but since students did not always start their degrees in the year they applied, a set of continuous numbers might be distributed across two or even three years. With any luck, Quin's admission record should have included a passport photo.

It took her another two and a half hours to locate the set of files covering the examination results in anatomy for 1967, then to find Mathew Quin's record sheet, kept in a separate file because he was unranked. The word *Excluded* was written in longhand across the results column, but there were no further comments or details. Finding the invigilator's report was a job for another day, she realised now, but at least she had Quin's UCCA number.

Most of the medical students took four years to get to their finals, so Briony started going through the admissions files for 1963, taking them in batches of twelve, which was about as many as would fit on the small table. Just as she was starting to pick up speed and conviction, the temp came hovering into view.

'I'm off now,' she said. 'It's five thirty. Will you be staying much longer?'

'Could be.'

'If you're here after six, you'll have to contact security, because that's when they set the alarm. And you'll need to get one of the security officers to show you the way out. The lifts get switched off—fire precautions they told me—so you have to leave by the back stairs.'

Terrific, thought Briony. Oh well, tomorrow was another day.

In any case, perhaps it wasn't a bad idea to pay a visit to Vine Street before she went home. It was vital for her to keep in touch with all the new evidence coming in.

She got back to find the incident room packed and waiting for a major six o' clock briefing from Macready. Already the photographs of the Gresham College murder had been moved to the back wall and replaced by a large map of the Spitalfields area showing the two new murder sites and a display of photographs.

Of course there would be a briefing—she should have assumed that. But why hadn't she been told? Then it dawned on her. Maybe to all intents and purposes, she really had been dropped from the inquiry and the warrant to search records at Senate House was just a sop, a way of keeping her busy at something that would have her out of the way of the mainstream process of investigation. Now she had to go through the humiliation of trying to follow the briefing from a position over near the back wall, squashed behind a group of uniforms who'd obviously been drafted in that day, while Palgrave and Latham stood with Macready by the main desk at the front.

'I think it is well known,' Macready began, 'that I prefer to keep my investigation team to a minimum. You are all here this evening, however, because this inquiry has developed rapidly along several different lines and if we are to follow these up speedily, we are going to have to work in close coordination on searches being conducted in three different areas of the city.

'However, yesterday's murders are our most immediate concern. First, the timing. Preliminary reports from the autopsy on the Reverend Burroughs indicate that time of death was 5.30 am at the earliest, when it would have been dark. Burroughs had no torch with him and the way between the rectory and the church was along an unlit path. Taking all factors into account, the most likely time for the murder was between 6.30 and 7.00.

'A phone call for Caroline Staines was received at the *Evening Standard* at 8.45, presumably the soonest she might have been at work. She was not. When she arrived twenty minutes later, she was given the message by Mr Leonard Meyer, her immediate superior, who instructed her to take a cab. It transpires that this idea was introduced by the caller, who specifically requested that Miss Staines take a taxi as it would halve the journey time and offered to reimburse the cost. A little unusual, perhaps, but Mr Meyer was not suspicious. A pity, since there has emerged strong evidence that a taxi may have been used to lure the victim to the scene of her death.

'We have in the last hour recovered a cab that was stolen in Appold Street, behind Liverpool Street Station after the driver, a Mr Edward Gordon, was knocked out. He too is being interviewed, but has been unable to provide a description of his assailant, who approached from behind as he was on his way to the toilets at the petrol station on the corner of Appold Street and Sun Street.'

Macready pulled down a second large roll-up map next to that showing the murder sites and pointed to the junction with a wooden marker. 'The attendant who was filling Mr Gordon's tank at the time claims he saw nothing. The toilet is round the side of the building, out of view of the area where the pumps are located. Payment was made on account and since Gordon had already signed for it, the attendant returned to his workshop after having filled the tank, without observing who drove the taxi away.

'That was at 8.10 am, pretty well exactly. The attendant recalls he had just finished listening to the radio news when the taxi drove in. This puts the latest possible time for the murder of Reverend Burroughs at 7.45, allowing for the time it would take him to walk from the murder site to the petrol station. It is likely, however, that he would have spent some time waiting for an opportunity such as Mr Gordon presented him with. How long? Taxi cab drivers do not keep accounts with every petrol station in London. Mr Gordon was a regular at this one, though his calls did not take him round that way more than twice a week on average, at varying times of the day and night. A dozen other taxi drivers kept accounts there, with similarly random patterns of use. The killer was fortunate if he waited less than half an hour for an opportunity, even at the start of the rush hour, when there was a higher than average likelihood that a cab driver would decide to fill up. We must appeal widely for anyone who may have seen a person loitering in this area.' He drew a ring around the area behind Liverpool Station with a wooden pointer. 'We will also need to check all vehicles parked there early this morning.

'Latham, I believe you have other details to report on.'

Macready checked his watch as Latham came forward. He might as well have said, 'Be brisk!' and for a moment Briony actually thought Steve looked a bit self-conscious and awkward and wondered if the pressure was getting to him in some way he couldn't quite smooth over, until she realised the problem was only the fact that he didn't have a cigarette in his hand. He stuck closely to his notes, rarely looking up as he spoke, and delivering the information in a near monotone.

'First victim: the Reverend Thomas Burroughs, aged sixty-three. Been rector of Christchurch Spitalfields since 1942. Lived alone. Person with whom he was in most regular contact was the sexton, Mr Andrew Fisher, who reported to him every morning. Mr Fisher was interviewed this afternoon at 1.30. He was in a state of some distress and confusion so we stuck to a couple of points. First, means of gaining entry to the church. The front doors are the only doors and they're locked with the original system, designed by some crack locksmith who installed a brass bolt on the inside that can be shot closed or opened from the outside with this key.'

He held up an evidence bag containing something the size of a soup spoon and probably ten times as heavy. 'Very clever. The bolt's serrated on the underside, and the key turns a grooved wheel below it that catches on the teeth and makes it slide one way or the other. Fisher says you practically need two hands to turn the key and he can't imagine anyone managing to shift the bolt any other way. We had to remove the entire wheel to get any purchase on the bolt and gain entry. It took the local locksmith with a specialist toolkit twenty minutes and he was pretty upset with us for requiring him to damage what he called a masterpiece. Burroughs was in there with the key tied round his waist.

'So that leaves us with two alternatives: either Burroughs let the killer in with him and one or other of them shot the bolt when they were inside, or Burroughs went in there alone and the killer found some other form of access, a way that was not even known to the sexton, who'd worked there for twenty-five years. But however you look at it, he had to get himself out without disturbing the bolt. We're checking the floors for possible underground access. The question has been put to me—' Here Latham looked up from his notes and glared at Jimmy, who was standing just to his right. 'What if the killer was still in there with the body when we found it? Well there's a short answer to that. If he was in there then, he's in there now, because we've got a guard on the doorway and three officers inside to ensure that the crime scene's undisturbed until the Socos have taken their toothcombs over every flagstone and panel in the place.'

He moved to the next page of notes and the room was so silent you could hear the papers shuffle as his hand shook slightly. It was the longest Briony had seen him without a fag clutched between his fingers. He'd be going cold turkey soon.

'We don't have much on Burroughs yet. The Whitechapel force are interviewing local churchgoers and will be doing a routine door-knock early tomorrow morning. One thing we do know about him at this stage is that he'd had two appointments with Miss Staines, who evidently thought she was on her way to a third when she took a cab to Whitechapel yesterday morning. Staines was a journalist at the *Evening Standard*, where we interviewed her immediate boss Mr Leonard Meyer, the sub-editor, and a photographer, Mr Tony Childs, who'd accompanied her on the second of her visits to the Spitalfields rectory.

Meyer took a phone call at 8.35, purporting to be from the Reverend Burroughs and describing in some detail the art work on the side of the church and hinting at its relationship to some violent crime. Meyer left a note for Staines, directing her to follow up on it as soon as she arrived. Her two previous interviews with Burroughs were, according to Meyer, on her own initiative. They were about graffiti in the churchyard, which he had not thought newsworthy. A report she made last Tuesday was spiked. Meyer insists he doesn't have a copy of it, so we're going through all Miss Staines's papers looking for one. What we do have at this stage are the photographs that were to accompany it, taken by a freelance photographer, Mr Tony Childs, who worked regularly for the *Evening Standard*. Jimmy?'

Jimmy had arranged the shots on a separate board, which he propped up on the table. There were six in all, in two rows.

'The top row is the pictures that were initially chosen to accompany the article,' said Latham. 'Before it got spiked, that is.' One showed a beheaded statue and the others were of what seemed to be its head, sitting on a tomb on which some dark liquid had been spilled. Latham pointed to it. 'This,' he said, 'is most likely pig's blood, but we're still waiting on forensic tests to confirm that. And here,' he moved the pointer to the second row, 'there's more of it. Now these weren't the shots the paper was going to print, but they're pretty interesting to us. These gravestones carry a message, which you can see most clearly here.' He pointed to the last picture, where the word TURN was legible on each of three stones that stood side by side. And now,' Latham's voice came through, with a distinct note of triumph, 'we can put together something that gives us a vital clue. Jimmy?'

Jimmy put the first board on the floor and lifted up a second, showing a new set of photos. One was of the graffiti on the fence in Hanbury Street.

A TIME TO DIE

And next to that was the word on the tub next to Godwin's corpse. TURN.

And next to that was a page of lines in large print. Latham read them out.

He added that they were from *Ecclesiastes* although most people thought they were by Bob Dylan.

For some reason this didn't seem to hit the right note with Macready.

'Thank you, Latham. We will stick to the details of the case for now, since time is of the essence as the good preacher tells us, and we may be sure he is indeed a good preacher whose message is not sinister, even if it is somewhat grim in places, especially when it is misquoted. Is there anything further we need to know at this stage about the interviews you conducted today?'

Latham's jaw had a tense set now.

'No, sir. I wouldn't consider the rest of the information particularly relevant to the officers here, not at present.'

23

Briony was looking alternately at the dial on her watch, lying beside her on the doctor's desk, and at the blood pressure gauge.

'Is it serious?' she asked.

'I doubt it. You can roll your sleeve down now, thank you.'

The doctor folded the rubber cuff and put it in a drawer. 'Your pulse is a bit slow, but low blood pressure is rarely a serious problem in a young person. However, if your blood count is low, we need to do something about that. Where were you exactly when you fainted?'

'Oh just—standing in the street. We were inspecting a building.'

'I see. Did you get any early warning signs— shortness of breath, dizziness, anything like that?'

'Not until just before it happened.'

'And you've never fainted before?'

'Once, at a school speech day. Are there any more tests?'

'No no, that's it.'

What a waste of bloody time, Briony hissed to herself as she marched down to the tube station. She'd figured out that the tube would be the quickest way to get to Russell Square. No time for breakfast now. It was ten already and she was determined to find

Quin's admission photo by lunch time, but she bought a cheese and tomato sandwich to tide her over.

Just as well, because the admissions numbers were all out of sequence and by two she had still not struck paydirt. The temp wasn't there and the regular member of staff, a severe looking woman with a pair of gold spectacles on a chain round her neck, was not about to help things along.

'1963.' She sighed. 'No, I'm afraid I can't explain the order. That is the very worst year. Some of the shelving units were pulled over during the sit-in a couple of years ago and that was one of them. I have had no time to rearrange them and it would be much better if they were left undisturbed. I suppose this is absolutely necessary?'

'I'm afraid it is, yes.'

'I see. Please don't try to put them in order yourself. How many do you have there?' She frowned at the pile on Briony's table. 'Two at a time is the rule. The girl who was here yesterday obviously didn't explain things to you very well. Hopeless!' There was a distinct hiss at the end of the last word.

Two at a time made for very slow going and after a while Briony resorted to standing by the ill-lit shelves and pulling out the documents one by one, her sense of expectation getting duller with every half hour. It was ridiculous, wasting her time like this. She wasn't game to ask Macready for an assistant, but if she didn't have something worth taking back to him by the end of the day, it was going to confirm his opinion that this was a wild goose chase. After all, was there really anything to go on in Perrin's story? How many undergraduates might be guilty of cruelty to pigeons, or of laughing when their drunken friends fell down stairs?

'Mathew Quin' said the page in front of her. She had got up such a rhythm of opening, turning and closing that she'd reversed the sheet almost before she realised what it was. There was a small black and white, passport-sized photo stapled to the top. 'Bingo!' said Briony out loud.

Placing the file on her table, she sat down and stared at the small face. Just a boy. You could hardly believe he was even seventeen. Short dark hair, regular features, a round chin, straight, unsmiling mouth. What colour were his eyes? Jimmy might be able to tell. The name was written underneath the photo in careful longhand and an address. Quin was from Saltash, in Cornwall. West country.

'Yes!' she exclaimed under her breath. 'It's gotta be.' The cursed Tupperware connection was paying off after all. She put the whole sheet into a transparent plastic envelope. The chances of there being any retrievable fingerprints were surely remote—but then, those automatic photo booths delivered the pictures in sheets of four, still sticky from the developing fluid, which retained prints very well. A boy like that might just plant his thumb firmly in the middle of the image when he picked them up. Or when he cut them.

She stared again at the face, under its covering of plastic.

'I'm going to find you, Mathew Quin,' she said.

24

When she got back to Vine Street, the place seemed worse than usual because of some noisy repair work going on outside the fourth floor. She headed for the incident room at the other end of the building, where the drilling was at least reduced to a background noise.

Donna was there, inspecting the photos of the painting on the church wall.

'Hi!'

'Oh, hello Briony. I heard you were sick.'

'I'm better. I just blacked out, that's all. And Steve Latham tried to make out it was a big deal.'

'Are you sure you're better? You don't look too hot.'

'Gee, thanks.'

'You know what I mean. Don't be difficult. This case is giving a lot of people the jitters, including me, to be honest. I'm just wondering, who's next, you know?'

'Well, I think I might have made a bit of breakthrough. Look—'

Briony got out the plastic envelope she'd brought back from Senate House and handed it to Donna. 'Mathew Quin.'

'What? You mean this is the guy the warden told you about?'

'That's him. Failed his anatomy exams three years ago—or, to be more precise, was expelled from the examination for making a mess of his practical. My next job is to find the report from the invigilator. That should finally convince Macready to put him on top of the suspects list.'

Donna looked closely at the photo and frowned. 'I doubt it.'

'What do you mean?'

'I doubt it will convince Macready. Anyway, Macready's not the type of person who lets himself be convinced. He thinks what he thinks and it's best not to try and interfere with the way he sees things.' She handed the envelope back to Briony. 'You sure you're not just—'

'Just what?'

'Well, just pushing a bit too hard with this case.'

'What can I do? They're trying to push me out.' Suddenly, unexpectedly, Briony felt tears welling up in her eyes.

'Come off it, Briony. What gives you that idea?'

'Oh, I dunno.' She couldn't say any more because her bottom lip refused to do the work of forming the words and a tear suddenly fell on the plastic cover right over the little face of Mathew Quin.

'Hey, what's up? Look, I didn't mean to upset you. What's up?'

Briony shook her head as more tears came, humiliatingly, out of her nose this time. She wiped them away with the back of her hand. Donna swiftly confiscated the folder.

'Rule number one,' she said, dabbing it with a clean tissue and handing another to Briony, 'don't use your most precious piece of evidence as a hanky. And what about those other rules? Don't get fazed. Keep coming back. I've adopted them myself. Simple, but effective. Now come on, tell me what's the matter.'

Briony took a deep breath and launched right into the middle of it. 'I don't understand. I've witnessed autopsies. I've been at crime scenes after murders—nasty ones. I've seen photos of just about everything you could think off, then suddenly I have to black out in front of a crude drawing of a woman with her throat cut. And the two key witnesses to the event are Steve Latham and Detective Superintendent Iain Macready. It's confirmed all their prejudices now. They'd like to get me off the case altogether. Macready because I'm an embarrassment, and Steve because I'm trespassing on his territory. I just—I just can't get treated as an equal.'

Donna leant on the desk and folded her arms.

'Well, there's no such thing as equals in the police force. You should at least know that by now. Everyone's got their place in the pecking order. You are the junior on the team, you know. Maybe you're expecting too much too quickly.'

'Maybe I am. But do they have to be so obvious about it? They might at least talk to me while we're walking along the street, instead of leaving me to stare at their backs.'

'Ah, well that's different. That's common rudeness. You should tell them that.'

'How can I tell them?'

'You speak English, don't you? Just tell them, straight out.'

'I thought you just said I was too pushy.'

'Not in that way. You're pushing too hard on the case. If you can't talk to Macready, talk to Palgrave. He'd find the right way to pass the message on.'

'But he's the last person—I mean—I'm just not his type. I didn't come up through the ranks like he did. He thinks I'm a Hendon upstart. I'm sure he doesn't agree with putting a woman on a major investigation team in the first place.'

'Well, maybe that's *your* prejudice. He's been very fair to me whenever I've worked for him. And he's quite used to dealing with ambitious women. He's got two daughters, you know—and one of them's a Hendon upstart, as you call it. Topped her year, she did. And he's very proud of her.'

'No kidding.'

'You know what? I think you should give *this* to Palgrave.'

She held out the envelope containing Quin's now carefully wiped face. 'He's much more likely to take an interest than Macready, specially right now, when everything's happening at once.'

Briony got to work tracking the address of Quin's family. She phoned through to the telephone exchange in Saltash, but the name and address no longer matched in the listings. So they had moved. At least it wasn't such a common name. In the present phone book for Saltash, there were two Quins, for whom she took down the details. But the family might well have moved elsewhere. It could turn into an expanding search—a job for the uniforms—and then she'd certainly need Palgrave's collaboration.

When he came in a couple of hours later, Briony held up the sheet with Quin's picture. He wasn't interested enough to take a close look, but the brief nod of his head was some kind of acknowledgment, she supposed.

'Give it to the Identikit team. They'll make a drawing and age it. How old would he be now?'

'Twenty-five, I think.'

'At any rate, we wouldn't get anywhere releasing a thing like that to the public. What you might do is try with the passport office. If he's been issued with a passport in the past few years, they might have a more recent photo.'

'I've also got the lead on a family address, but it's no longer current.'

'Good. The local branch should be able to trace them easy enough. Give me what you've got so far.'

He turned his head at an exaggeratedly skewed angle, trying to make out the jigsaw puzzled writing on Briony's desktop. 'Can't read a word of that. You could improve your note-taking practices, you know. What are those little pigs doing?'

'Just an association. With one of the Manson murders.'

'Interesting. Give me those details, too, translated into plain English. Where are you going now?'

'I was hoping to find DS Macready.'

'He's over in Whitechapel. Due back at six. If you're free till then, you can help me with some interviews. There's a queue building up out there. Some of them are regulars—nutcases who come in every time we put out a call for help with our enquiries—but there's a couple of people who look as if they might be worth talking to. In particular, a young woman in a red beret, who looks rather nervous. She might be more comfortable talking to you than me.'

'I'm not sure about that, you know. That type usually want to talk to someone they see as an authority figure. As a matter of fact, it's not exactly true that I'm free right now. I need to make as much progress as I can with tracing Mathew Quin, because DS Macready's sort of got me on trial. I need to get results, or he'll put me on some other case. As a matter of fact, I was wondering if I could ask your advice about something.'

Briony tried to ignore the fact that Palgrave had stuck a finger in his ear as she was talking and was rotating it meaningfully, as if this was some kind of aid to concentration.

'Ah,' he said. 'Are you sure it's advice that you want, Inspector Williams? You don't strike me as someone who likes advice very much.'

'Well, maybe I'm not very good at taking it, but that doesn't mean I won't try.'

'Then my advice is to leave the steering to the people in the front seat. You and I are in the back. You'll no doubt get your turn at the wheel in a few years time, but I'll be staying where I am until I retire. In this business, you can't afford to be too proud to spend your time tracing a piece of Tupperware to its point of origin. That's what it's all about. As a matter of fact, we've also traced the industrial screw that was put through Godwin's skull. Would you be interested to know how we did that?'

Briony did not think she could face listening to a long story as she stood there in the incident room, surrounded by images of

Caroline Staines's open eyes and twisted hands, while Palgrave was trying to excavate his ear-drum.

'Sure. Yes, I would. Could we have a cup of tea, do you think? What about going to the canteen?'

'So you're not so very pressed for time after all?' He looked at his watch. 'Ten minutes is what I can spare, since I'm evidently not going to get any help with those interviews. Let's hope the service is a bit quicker than usual down there.'

The queue shuffled painfully slowly, so Briony had the opportunity to make a detailed study of every sweating bun and collapsed cake on offer. Palgrave hardly gave them a glance before picking out a jam donut. The jam had leaked heavily against the cellophane wrapping. Briony chose a dry looking scone and teamed it with a half melted portion of butter. Just ahead of them, a woman in a pink cotton cap was pouring tea from a large pot across a row of mugs assembled on a grill, so that she didn't have to raise the spout between one mug and the next.

The scone was a bad idea, because it was so dry it sucked her mouth together. That meant she couldn't talk, so had to listen while Palgrave rambled on in his flat voice about how they'd traced the iron bolt. She tried to focus her eyes somewhere behind him as he sucked jam off the end of the finger that had been in his ear a few minutes earlier and she spotted Jimmy sitting at a table near the window, reading the paper. She had to talk to him about Quin's photo. But it would be rude to just get up and leave Palgrave, especially while he was in the middle of his story, whose details she really ought to be following. She made an effort to listen, while monitoring Jimmy with peripheral vision in case he should make a move.

'... but there's not many ironmongers left, you see. Not much call for them these days, I suppose. We found one near St Pancras, but all the others were south of the river. Interesting, that. Because, you see, a lot of the parts they deal in are for bridges. They all told us roughly the same thing. You wouldn't use a bolt like that in a scaffolding girder. It's from a bridge. But that's just about all we could get out of any of them, till we found this old feller in Lambeth. Well, he knew a thing or two, I tell you that. He measured the thread with a special gauge he's got and he said, "Suspension bridge". Straightaway, just like that. It's an unusual thread, you see— a bit looser, to allow for the swing of the bridge, but it locks in, so it can't work its way free. Course it's not used on the top of the bridge. It's for the supports underneath. This feller in Lambeth, he noticed there wasn't much rust on it. "It's been treated with an inhibitor," he said. Now this is a technique they developed in the war, apparently, because of the rust problems they were getting in some of the gun boats, so he reckoned this bolt had been manufactured during or after the war. "I'd say it was custom made," he said, "which means you're looking for a suspension bridge built in the last twenty-five years. That narrows your options a bit, I should think." He was right, of course. We've got it down to three.'

Jimmy was folding his paper and getting up.

'Sorry,' said Briony. 'Would you mind if I just—would you excuse me just for a second?'

'I have to be going now myself,' said Palgrave, adjusting the limp collar of his jacket. 'Anyway, the educated guess is that it's the Tamar Bridge. Fits with the Tupperware connection. I've got five pound on our Walker being a Cornish.'

'What?'

'I said I think our boy's a Cornishman.'

'Mathew Quin's from Saltash,' said Briony and sat down again, heavily, staring at the remains of the scone as if it were something from another world.

25

It hadn't been easy getting off work early. Girl Fridays were not entitled to privileges and were not expected to ask for favours. 'Toothache, is it? Very sad. You can go at three thirty after you've filed the invoices,' said the manager. 'That's two hours, but we'll have to count it as two and half out of your pay packet, because of the extra time it'll take the wages clerk to alter the pay form.'

He didn't even look at her as he said it. You're a nasty little man, thought Nell as she watched him staring out of the window. He sat unnaturally upright and his collar stood sharply away from the back of his neck.

'Thanks,' she said, and went back to tidying the store cupboard.

She left at three fifteen on the dot and resisted an impulse to turn and wave at his window as she walked down the street. He'd be sitting there, she was sure, checking his watch. I don't need your pathetic job anyway, she thought, as she quickened her pace.

When she rang up this morning, they'd told her to go to Vine Street police station in Piccadilly.

'If you walk westwards along Piccadilly from the tube station,' said the woman on the phone, 'you'll pass an alleyway called Piccadilly Passage. Just go down there and you'll be in Vine Street.'

There was really no need to take the tube. Piccadilly was only one stop from Leicester Square anyway, and the walk would help clear her head. Nell wasn't sure, now, what she should say. They might think she was nuts, coming to see them about something that had happened three years ago, in another part of England. Besides, she didn't even know how to tell the story. She never had told it, actually, not to anyone. The Plymouth police had interviewed her, but they already knew what she'd found, so all she'd had to explain to them was how she'd got in the carriage, and why she hadn't noticed anything wrong straightaway.

She found Piccadilly Passage easily enough, but when she got into Vine Street, she nearly turned and went home. It was a hideous cul-de-sac, with the backs of three tall, characterless brick buildings at its blind end. There'd been no rain, but thick brown water was pouring down the gutter from a whole line of downpipes on the wall facing her. Some kind of building work was going on. There was scaffolding three-quarters of the way up and there were ropes dangled from it into the filthy water on the ground. Why so many pipes? All the buildings seemed to be turned the wrong way round and they loomed up, shutting out the sun. There were three police cars parked to the left of her, as if to point out where she was supposed to go. She took a deep breath, and plunged through the entrance into the gloomy building.

'Sorry about the noise,' said the policewoman on the desk, almost shouting above it as she took Nell's name and address. 'They're drilling. They said they'd be finished by four. Take a seat on the bench over there. We'll get someone to talk to you as soon as we can.'

There were five other people waiting, all staring at the cracks on the brown lino floor, deafened by the drilling noise. She looked at her watch. Twenty to four. Ten minutes later, just as she felt the drill had become something inside her, screaming through her nervous system, the noise stopped. The policewoman came in and called the man next to her, then the man opposite, but Nell figured there were still three people to go before it was her turn.

Just as she'd prepared herself for another half hour's wait, pulling *Hard Times* out of her bag and thinking the boss at work would go well in a Dickens novel, she was called.

The policewoman led the way down the corridor, her shoes squeaking on the lino. She showed Nell into a small cubicle room with a table and two chairs and a bare lightbulb. The only daylight came from a strip of window well above eye level.

'If you'd just take a seat, Inspector Palgrave will be along to talk to you.'

Was this where they interrogated the murderer suspects? Just sitting here made you feel like a suspect. She put the book back in her bag and on a last minute impulse, took her beret off and smoothed her hair.

There was another ten minute wait before the inspector turned up, and when he did, Nell thought at first it must be someone who'd got the wrong room. He didn't look at all like the police inspectors she'd met in Devonshire and it wasn't just because he was wearing an old illfitting suit instead of a uniform. Was this really the right person for her to be talking to? It was too late to change her mind now. He shook hands with her rather limply and sat at the desk, then took a form out of a drawer and a stub of pencil out of his jacket pocket.

There was a set of routine questions and he wrote the answers letter by letter, as if he wasn't used to writing at all. Name. Address. Phone number. Date and place of birth. Occupation.

'Well, I'm going to be a student soon, but right now I'm a Girl Friday.'

'Oh, really? So what does a Girl Friday do?'

'Well, um, sort of a bit of everything.'

'What, like Man Friday in *Robinson Crusoe*, you mean? I used to watch that on TV with my daughters. You build the huts and till the soil, do you? Mend the boats, eh?'

'It's more like sharpening the pencils, actually. It's office work. Just temporary. Till I go to university.'

'I see. So what have you got to tell us, Miss Adams?'

She launched into the story in a rush, but as she got to the part that took place in the train carriage, she felt herself slowing. Her face muscles seemed to be freezing, so only her mouth would move, and her lips were dry, and she was sure she was leaving out details, mixing things up. And the inspector was clicking the end of the pencil against his teeth, which was very distracting. She stopped.

The inspector leaned forward, elbows on the table.

'Miss Nell Adams. You're nineteen now, that right?'

'That's right.'

'So you would have been fifteen years old at the time of this incident?'

She nodded, working hard to keep her face in order.

'It must be very distressing to go back over it. I tell you what, Nell. Instead of asking you for the details now, I'll contact the police in Devonshire and get the records from them. Which station was it that dealt with the case?'

'Um, I'm not sure what you mean.'

'Where were you interviewed? Which police station?'

'In Torquay first of all, because that was the nearest to—to where the train stopped. Then some policemen came to talk to me at home—at my aunty's house in Exeter. But they were from Plymouth. Once they asked me to go to the police station in Plymouth, because they had an identity parade.'

'And did you pick anyone?'

'No, because—because they all looked the same. I didn't see his face at all. Just this tall skinny man in a duffle coat, with long hair.'

'And you say they never arrested anyone?'

'No, I don't think so. I don't really know, because they said I shouldn't have any more to do with the case. Because it was too upsetting. They sent me to a psychiatrist. A counsellor, you know. Because I was having panic attacks.'

'And are you still seeing a counsellor?'

'No. I don't—that's not what I want.'

'You don't want to go on talking about it. You just want to see this man behind bars. That right?'

She felt some of the tension go out of her. 'Yes. That's right. But maybe—maybe it's got nothing to do with—with what's happened in London. I wasn't sure if I should come.'

'You did the right thing, I'll tell you that for certain. When I've got the details from Plymouth, we may need to talk to you again.'

'Do you think there really might be a connection, then?'

'I couldn't say at this stage. But it is possible. Thank you for coming to talk to us.'

Nell got up to leave, then hesitated.

'Um. There's something else. If there is a connection, if it is the same man, I'm worried about—I'm worried that he could trace me.'

'How's that, then?'

She explained about the newspaper coverage at the time and the recent feature in *Summer in the City*. Palgrave took down the details, then put away the notebook.

'I'd set your mind at rest on that score, Miss Adams. The likelihood of his coming to look for you is very remote indeed. But if you have any worries, give us a ring here. You can ask for me personally.'

26

Briony was summoned to a six o'clock meeting in Macready's office, which she hoped was a sign that she was properly back on the team again. Maybe Palgrave had put in a good word for her after all. She went to collect Quin's entrance form from the Identikit team to take with her and took a look at the image they were working on. The bland little face from the photograph was coming into relief, with a contoured jawline and deep-set eyes. It was the eyes they had got right. The brows were widely spaced, angled slightly downwards at the outer edges and the bridge of the nose finished high, so the eyes themselves seemed to be forced apart. Framed by heavy upper lids and a strong lower lid line, they looked out at you with a kind of defiance, their large dark pupils accentuated.

Macready was brusque, nodded at her without smiling, and Steve Latham seemed preoccupied. Or perhaps he was just avoiding her eye. Cigarette in hand, he sat and stared at his feet, occasionally brushing his hair away as it fell forward. Palgrave was late, so for the first twenty minutes of the meeting, Briony felt stranded. Her case for getting Quin taken seriously was very much stronger with the Tamar Bridge connection, but she wasn't sure enough of her ground to make it without Palgrave there.

In uncomfortable silence, Macready arranged some papers on his desk, laying them out like the cards in some oversized game of patience. Eventually, he selected one and began speaking rapidly.

'This latest episode has been exactly planned. We know that Walker did something of a tour of the backstreets in Whitechapel on Sunday night to leave his messages and probably also to choose the locations for his crime.'

'He didn't choose them,' Steve said. 'At least, not Mitre passage. That was Jack the Ripper's choice.'

Macready glared at Steve, put the page to one side and took up another.

'Motive. These, I believe, are your notes, Latham. Would you care to take us through them?'

Steve raked a thick clump of hair back as he sat up and brushed ash off his knee.

'There's no straightforward pattern in his choice of victims. He's killed two women and two men. Neither of the women was raped or otherwise sexually assaulted. That is unusual. He imitates Jack the Ripper in this, as in other things, but he's more sophisticated. He's picked these victims—got something against them personally. Find the motive and we'll find the killer is my punt. In the case of Godwin, the likelihood is that it's some kind of ritualised revenge killing. Godwin had a lot of power. He made decisions that affected people's lives. I reckon this guy's got a fierce ego. He's resentful. Bears grudges. Greg Kendrick's story about the old acquaintance who was looking for Sabina Melies is interesting. He asked her to put him up—maybe there was something sexual, maybe not—but she thwarted him and got out of his way. He wouldn't like that. So we have to ask what might have linked him with Staines and Burroughs, which means as like as not what connects him with the story Staines was following up on. Now her first article on the vandalism—the one that got spiked—mentions repeated episodes of vandalism in the churchyard. Forensic reports this morning identify the substance used on the gravestones as pig's blood.'

'Pig's blood?' The eyebrow arched fiercely.

'Yes, sir.'

'But you already knew that, Latham. You mentioned it at the briefing. What led to you to think it was pig's blood?'

'The interview with Tony Childs, sir, the *Evening Standard* photographer.'

'I see. And what led Mr Childs to assume it was pig's blood?'

'Caroline Staines told him. And the Reverend Burroughs told her.'

'Almost a game of Chinese whispers, Latham. And yet the rumour turns out to have been correct. What other knowledge did Mr Childs pass on to you by this circuitous route?'

Steve dragged deep on his cigarette and let the smoke come out with his words. 'Mr Childs is a bit embarrassed, I reckon. Caroline Staines had been trying to persuade her editor that she was onto something with this story about church vandalism. She thought there was more to it and it seems she was just starting to get a lead. Burroughs was offering to talk to her and volunteering some kind of special information about previous incidents. Childs wasn't interested. She called him and persuaded him to go to the second appointment with Burroughs but he didn't want to go, and didn't stay long enough to hear any of the details.'

'I asked you what Mr Childs *did* hear from Miss Staines, Latham, not what he didn't. This whole affair is set about with a quicksand of pointless anecdotes. We have no time to sink into them. Please keep to the relevant details.'

'I'm afraid I can't tell the pointless anecdotes from the relevant details quite as sharply as you, sir,' said Latham. 'What I'm trying to explain is that Mr Childs was only able to give fragmentary information, isolated details, because he gave only occasional and reluctant attention to the story Caroline Staines was following. He took in the mention of pig's blood because it related to what he saw and photographed. The only other thing he remembered being told was that the tomb had been opened once before and the vandals seemed to have been looking for something that wasn't there. And it wasn't there because the bloke who was rector at the time had removed it for safekeeping.'

'What was this something?'

'He thinks it might have been some kind of diary.'

'And when was the tomb opened previously?'

'He doesn't know, or doesn't remember. It's one of the most frustrating interviews I've ever done. I think that guy wouldn't notice the getaway vehicle if he witnessed a bank robbery. But I'm working on the assumption that Caroline Staines took notes. She had a handbag with her when she was murdered and her notebook was inside it.'

'Then why don't we have it?' Macready's voice was dangerously quiet.

'Forensics won't release it yet. It's being fingerprinted and photographed.'

'Since when were the forensics officers in charge of this investigation, Latham? Tell them to deliver it on my orders, without further delay.'

Macready picked another page from the layout in front of him.

'Report from Detective Constable Donna Caldwell. Latham, I believe you can also fill us in on what this is about?'

'DC Caldwell has been working in plain clothes at Gresham, talking to students. She got talking to a girl who had a story about a friend who'd got pregnant the previous year and had an abortion.'

'This is strictly relevant, I take it?' asked Macready acidly.

'Oh very strictly, sir. The boyfriend was an intern, a recent graduate of Gresham, and he'd arranged for the abortion to be done by someone he'd met while studying for his degree. As a consequence, both of them got thrown out of the local Freemasons' lodge. By Godwin. Colin Oldroyd is supposed to be a member as well. The gossip is he and Godwin did a double act, excommunicating undesirables. At the least, this gives us a new range of possibilities for motive and it may indicate that Oldroyd was holding things back when we interviewed him.'

Macready's right eyebrow arched sharply. 'That is, if this proves to be anything more than gossip. I hope your obsession with the Freemasons justifies the time you have devoted to this line of enquiry, Latham. It seems to me to border dangerously on fantasy. Dangerously for your career, that is.'

Latham didn't turn a hair.

'Did you know that Hogarth was a Freemason, sir? And according to one school of thought, so was Jack the Ripper.'

'And so are many of the civic dignitaries in Edinburgh and London. Perhaps you would like us to add the Prince of Wales to the list of suspects?'

'What, is he one of them as well?'

'I have no idea, Latham. It is none of my business, or yours. In the past, it has been something of a tradition for the Prince of Wales to hold high office with the Masons. I merely intend to illustrate the absurdity of your line of reasoning.'

'I've called Oldroyd in for another interview, on Thursday morning. Would you like to be present?'

'I will conduct the interview myself.'

Macready took up another page from the desk, then looked at his watch. 'I have here a report from Palgrave on the murder weapons. There has been significant progress in tracing the origins of the bolt driven through Godwin's forehead. Since Palgrave isn't here to report on the work of his team, I propose to defer this part of the briefing until later on.'

'Where is he?' asked Steve.

'Following up on some vital information gained in an interview he has just conducted. He may be here presently. In the meantime,

Williams, I think we will move on to your report. Kindly be as brief as possible.'

'I've traced Mathew Quin's admission form, sir. Here it is. You'll notice there's a home address in Saltash.'

'Has Palgrave seen this?'

'Yes, sir.'

'Very well. Quin is to be formally added to the list of suspects. How do you propose that we should further our researches into this fresh faced youth?'

'The address is no longer current, but Inspector Palgrave has contacted the Saltash police to trace the family. He's complaining they've been a bit slow off the mark. I've also made enquiries with the passport office, in the hopes of getting a more recent photograph, but they've been slow as well. On another tack, as I said before, sir, I have a hunch that Quin is the man who came looking for Sabina Melies at the Hanging Gardens.'

'And what are the grounds for this hunch, as you call it?'

'A hunch is something you don't have grounds for, sir, exactly.'

'You don't?'

'No, sir. Not exactly.'

'We will pursue the enquiries in Saltash, and at the hall of residence, Inspector Williams. That may at least give us some facts. If you intend to speak to Mr Kendrick again, you must have someone with you. If Latham or Palgrave is not available, take one of the detective constables. There are to be no more urgent leads arising from unwitnessed interviews, is that understood?'

'Yes, sir. Can I attend the interview with Dr Oldroyd?'

Macready collected his papers before he looked up to reply.

'Very well.'

Latham cut in. 'I don't think that's a good idea, sir. The Freemasons take their secrecy very seriously, from what I've read, and they don't admit women. Oldroyd may be much harder to crack if Inspector Williams is present.'

'Latham, I have no intention of trying to crack Dr Oldroyd, as you put it, or of inviting him to reveal the secrets of his order.'

At this point, you could have cut the tension in the room with a knife. Macready used silence as a punishment and he kept this one for a good two minutes until, mercifully, Palgrave made his entry, to tell the story he'd heard from the girl.

27

Sitting in the bus on her way to work next morning, Briony felt flat and a bit depressed, in spite of her breakthrough in getting Quin onto the suspect list.

Donna was right, she realised. She'd been trying to force her way into the centre of the case and was so fixated on her own idea of how to get to it that she'd actually turned down the chance for interviewing the girl in the red beret and so getting on to what might be a prime lead. Some information telegraphed from Plymouth late yesterday indicated that the link with Walker was possible. The location and timing certainly were suggestive. If Quin left Gresham in the summer of 1967, an unsolved murder committed in early autumn in a train that had passed through his home town had to be checked out. Sabina Melies was killed in early September 1970. That was a three-year gap and, as Steve had reminded them last night, one possible suspect was a guy who'd been in a commune with her in America. Now there were three more killings in late August. The pattern was too strong to ignore. So if it was all the work of the same man and he'd been in California for three years, maybe he'd committed more murders there.

Catching Steve in the incident room when she arrived, she ran the argument past him. He listened with no expression on his face, then shrugged his shoulders.

'Obviously. But not necessarily.'

'What's that supposed to mean?'

'Means it's an obvious line of reasoning, but not necessarily the right one.'

'I see. Thanks.'

'Look, Briony, I don't mean to be rude, but I'm a bit preoccupied right now with some possibilities that are much closer to the evidence in hand.'

'What evidence in particular?'

'Caroline Staines's notebook. There are pages missing. It's a spiral bound notebook and pages have been torn out. You know when you tear a page from a spiral bound book, it leaves those annoying little bits of paper caught in the spiral? And sometimes they fall out on the floor? Forensics picked up fragments of the paper at the murder site. The murderer must have torn them out himself, right there, then returned the book to the handbag.'

'Why would he do that?'

'There must have been stuff in those pages that he really didn't want anyone to read.'

'No, no.' Briony was getting caught up in this now and lost the disinterested tone she'd been determined to maintain in answer to Steve's indifference to her own lines of evidence.

'What I mean is, why would he bother to tear the pages and return the notebook to the handbag? Why not just take it, if there was something in it he didn't want us to see? Why not just take the handbag, for that matter, and muddy up the motive patterns? It was a big risk for him, messing about finding pages in a notebook—over the body of someone you've just butchered in broad daylight. And what about all the blood? He must have been spray painted with it, including his hands. Was there blood on the notebook?'

Steve held up his hand in a stop sign. 'Hold on, hold on. Hold your horses, Briony. Now, that's pretty good, I must admit. You got the point straight off. Yes, there were blood stains on the notebook and the handbag clasp. But he's pretty skilled at controlling the mess, this guy. He wore gloves again—we're guessing they're professional, surgical gloves—but they can't have been exactly dripping. He must know how to keep clear of the arterial spray which, as you saw, hit the roof of the passageway as well as the walls. According to forensics, he was facing her when he broke her wrists, then got behind her to cut her throat and stayed behind her for the follow up work. I hope this is not upsetting you, by the way?'

Briony didn't deign to reply.

He continued. 'The handbag was thrown up near her head. So it was easy for him to get to. Now your other question—why tear the pages out instead of just taking the notebook. My point exactly. My theory is, that's his whole way of working. He's teasing us with evidence, laying trails for us to follow and taking bits out so we can't catch up with him. He's making a story with pieces missing. He knows how to motivate *us*, you see. Some murderers are clever because they leave no evidence. This guy's planted evidence to come at us every which way, so we get lost in it. So the challenge for us is—stick to the trail and don't get distracted. What we can deduce, quite plainly, is that Burroughs was giving Staines some information that got Walker seriously annoyed with both of them. So what was it?'

Briony was drawing breath for some kind of considered reply, but Steve cut across her. He usually preferred answering his own questions, anyway.

'Almost certainly something to do with that tomb and quite possibly something more general to do with the history of the church. We know she was interested in the architect, Nicholas Hawksmoor. Contemporary of our friend Hogarth, as a matter of fact. The team over in Whitechapel have been over every inch of that tomb. The top can be moved—and there's evidence it's been moved recently—

slid about six inches to one side. What's inside it? Nothing. Who's tomb is it? Ah, now here it gets interesting. The rector says he knows, but there's no name. Now that's pretty damn fucking freaky, wouldn't you say?'

'Maybe it isn't. There's lots of old graves with no name on them. Names get worn away by the rain and the wind.'

'But this isn't worn away. It's just—well there never was any kind of inscription. That's—bizarre. Macready's over there supervising an inch by inch search of the rectory, hoping to come across something that will point to what the big secret is. But I'm thinking of taking another tack. You see, I'm starting to think this guy we're looking for may have been deeply familiar with the church and everything about it.'

'Oh, why's that?' Briony came up with the gratifying prompt despite herself.

'This business of the lock on the church door. Now my guess was there's some kind of subfloor access to the church that the sexton didn't know about. Is that what you guessed?'

'Well—by process of elimination.'

'Trouble is—that option's now eliminated as well. Every flagstone has been examined individually. Forensics say there's no chance that there's any form of trapdoor or opening. Zilch. None of the windows open. They're high up and made of stained glass. Any breakage you'd spot immediately.'

'Roof?'

'Damaged. In fact, the structure's so fragile the workmen can only do repairs from the underside. If he'd got up there from the outside of the building, he would have dislodged all kinds of stuff. Besides which, you'd need a specialist extension ladder to get that high. He'd have had to haul it up after him when he left. So, I've got this theory.'

Steve paused for effect, before delivering.

'You know that Sherlock Holmes maxim—when you've

eliminated the impossible, whatever remains must be the truth. Well, we list the impossible.' He counted off the options on his fingers.

'Impossibility number one: no access by the windows, floor or roof. Number two: the murderer's human—can't fly or pass through walls. Ergo—he got in, and out, through the door. Bolt was shot after he left and the only means of shooting it was a key. Murderer had a key. Impossibility number three: it couldn't have been the rector's key, because it was found around his waist. So.'

Steve paused theatrically, as if he were about to complete a magic trick. 'Solution is: there are two keys. Whoever made that lock made two keys. And when you think about it—well, you would, wouldn't you? If you'd gone to all that trouble to design the ultimate locking system, you'd be inclined to cast a back-up key.'

'Not necessarily.'

'Don't be obtuse, Briony. Let's just suppose that's the case. Just suppose. It would be absolute inside knowledge, the second key. Did Burroughs know about it? Evidently nobody else did, because look at all the palaver we had to go to to get in. So what I reckon is, trace how the murderer knew about it and we'll be well on the way to tracing him. So I'll need your help to do some searches in the parish records, see if we can find out who this locksmith was.'

'Don't look at me,' said Briony, stony faced. 'I've got as many leads as I can chase already. Can't one of the DCs do it? After all, it's a pretty long shot you're taking.'

He stared back, equally stony. Luckily, his phone rang just at that moment and gave her a chance to escape from the confrontation.

She marched off to her desk and picked up her own phone to make a reminder call to the passport office. Just as well, because they'd evidently lost the details of her request and she had to go over them again, which did not improve her temper. She went to get a cup of coffee.

The drilling had started again and was almost ear-splitting down in the little kitchenette at the far end of the corridor, where there was white dust over everything, including the kettle and the top of the coffee tin. She wiped them with the teatowel, then stood looking out of the window while the kettle boiled. A tap on the shoulder startled her. Steve. He mouthed an exaggerated hello, got out a second mug and put in two heaped spoons of the dusty looking powder.

The noise stopped for a minute and was replaced by the rising noise of the kettle. Briony gestured to the tin. 'Shouldn't have too much of this stuff. You know they put detergent in it, don't you? To make it dissolve.' Before the remark was out of her mouth, she knew it was a mistake.

'Is that the effect it has on you?'

'What do you mean?'

He grinned. 'Oh just, you know—I don't know why you have to act so frigid.'

The drilling started up before she could quip back, so she just stood there, mouth set, staring at the bench top.

Steve switched off the kettle and poured water into both mugs, which frothed suspiciously. Then he held up the sugar bowl in a gesture of enquiry. She shook her head. The drilling stopped.

'Sure? You could—'

'Do with a bit of sweetening up? If you make one more smart remark I'll rip your head off,' she snapped. For a moment he looked almost stunned. His stare hardened, and to avoid it, she turned back towards the window. A pigeon had stalked along the ledge outside and was pecking at the rotten wood on the bottom of the sash. It continued without flinching when the drill started again.

Steve was the first back to his desk and was leaning over to buckle his briefcase when Briony came in. She bit the bullet.

'I have to talk to you. I mean, I think we should have a chat.'

He looked at his watch. 'I haven't got time.'

'Yes, you have,' she said. 'I checked the schedules this morning and there's nothing on yours till the interview with Kendrick this afternoon.'

'Something's come up. I have to go to Whitechapel.'

'Then I'll get Donna to come with me to talk to Kendrick, shall I?'

'You can't. She's working undercover over there anyway, remember? I'll do the interview on my way back. I can take one of the Whitechapel DCs with me if need be.'

'No you won't.' Suppressing an impulse to shout, she pronounced each word with separate emphasis.

As Steve stood up, Briony positioned herself between him and the door. 'That's what we have to talk about. I'm sick of you trying to shut me out of this case.'

He sat down again and pushed a hand through his hair.

'Oh, Jeez! Tantrums now, is it?'

'That's right. I'm going to throw a nice big psychedelic tantrum and you're going to sit and listen.'

Out came the cigarette pack. He struck a match, cupped his hands round his face to light up, shook it out and flicked it into the waste paper basket right beside her and inhaled sharply.

'Give me a cigarette,' she said.

'You don't smoke.'

'It was you who told me it would be only a matter of time. Well, maybe now's the time.' She took one from the pack he held out and looked at it. 'Do these really help? You know, with all the hassles?'

He shrugged.

'What I don't understand is,' she continued, 'why we can't just work together. It's getting me down. I really want to do this interview. Why would you try to take it away from me? Why did you have to try and stop me sitting in on Oldroyd's interview tomorrow? It's like you have to get all the breaks or something.'

'Look, Briony, I think you need to keep your personal hang-ups out of this case. It's complicated enough already. Oldroyd might clam up if there's a woman in the room because the Freemasons are strictly bound to keep their secrets among the men. Simple as that.'

'Is it? Truth is, I don't think *you* like working with a woman. Not a woman DI, anyway. You think we're there to make the coffee and do the typing.'

'Hang on, it was me made the coffee just now. You trying to tell me I'm a male chauvinist pig or something?'

'Yes.'

'Christ. You're just so uptight, you know? You wouldn't understand if I explained it to you.'

'Try me.'

He got up and fetched another chair, lifted it high over the desk and plonked it down next to her.

'Sit down. I can't talk when you're standing over me like that. You going to actually smoke that fag or what?'

'In a minute. First I want the explanation.'

'Macready had this theory that a woman DI might be good at interviews. If we trained her up. I didn't agree with him. Women can make good DCs, especially for undercover work like Donna's doing, but the real detective work—it's like hunting a predator. You have to find their tracks. Then you have to stalk them. Then you have to choose the moment to close in, quick and fast. It's a man's job.'

'I get it,' Briony cut in. 'You wouldn't send a woman on a lion hunt.'

'Right. And I mean, this guy's really dangerous.'

'Well, I see it differently. You're scared I might be a better tracker than you are. *You're* the one who's got all uptight about it.'

He glared at her. 'Don't get bitchy.'

'I'm only using the words you used.'

She got up and went back to her desk and there was an awkward silence for a couple of minutes. She stared at the cigarette.

'Got a light?'

He sighed, pulled the matches out of his pocket and came over.

'Put it in your mouth, then. You can't light a fag in mid-air. Got to draw on it, soon as it's lit. Ready?'

She nodded. The matched flared, she breathed in, then coughed violently her eyes watered.

'I can see you're going to be slow learner,' he said.

28

The day was quite overcast and the Hanging Gardens looked more subdued than she remembered. The flowers in the baskets seemed to be thinning out, in anticipation of changing weather conditions. Briony had deliberately got there ten minutes early, hoping that before Steve arrived she might catch an informal chat with Kendrick. He was obviously still wary about his place on the suspect list and she wanted to get his confidence. She was convinced he was holding something back.

'We can sit out there,' he said, pointing to the open back door of the pub lounge room. 'In the garden.'

The garden was a brick paved courtyard, with dozens of baskets stacked against the walls on both sides.

'End of season,' explained Kendrick. 'I'm just doing the autumn planting. Sorry about the mess. Will your colleague be long, do you think?'

'Only a few minutes.'

'What about a glass of lemonade?'

While he went to fetch the drinks, Briony walked over to take a closer look at the baskets and disturbed some small birds who had been pecking at their contents. She wondered how many newly planted seeds they might have found. A heap of discarded overblown geraniums was mouldering in one corner, giving off a distinctive smell. Bees were hovering around it. For a split second, the sketch of the woman with the cut throat etched itself on her mind, as if it were right there in front of her.

Kendrick returned with a tray on which were a jug, three glasses and a saucer with slices of lemon. He put the tray on the ground, poured a glass and handed it to her.

'It must have been a terrible shock for you,' said Briony, 'finding the body.'

Kendrick didn't reply, but looked at her, waiting to see where she was leading.

'I still find it a shock myself, the sight of a murder victim. I don't suppose you ever get used to it. Some of those older men in the force, you know, the ones who've attended just about every crime scene you can imagine, I often wonder if they have nightmares.'

'Oh, the nightmares.' Kendrick stared into his glass. 'Nothing is the same,' he said. 'I've lost my feeling for this work. All the flowers look dead to me. Flowers and graves. They belong together, don't they? I'm thinking of leaving here, as a matter of fact. I've been getting a bit of freelance work. Got to know someone in the advertising industry who's helping me to branch out. Flower power is a very commercial proposition now, he told me. Not that I'm looking to get rich or anything. I just need a change.'

'Still,' said Briony, 'it seems a shame to leave here.'

The front doorbell rang and Steve was shown in by one of the other staff. He accepted a glass of lemonade and knocked it back in two large gulps.

'Thanks.' He gasped theatrically. 'I was parched.'

Briony could see Kendrick's guard had gone up again and just when he was starting to relax. If only she'd been allowed to do this interview on her own, simply by leading him into conversation, building the confidence as she went along. Instead there was Steve, fussing with papers, jarring the nerves with his smoker's cough, about to take over with his formal list of questions. He started right in on them, as if it had never even occurred to him that Briony might have her own list.

'Mr Kendrick. When we last interviewed you, you said you had your suspicions about a man who came looking for Sabina Melies here one evening. Someone she'd known in America. You said you thought they might have been speaking to each other in Spanish. I've been working on that lead, but we really don't have much to go on. We may need to make more contacts. Does she have any friends here who are from Puerto Rico?'

'Not that I know of. Her brother's the only connection she has from there as far as I know.'

'She seemed frightened of this man. She said—I have the words here—"he was into the dark stuff". Is there anything else—anything else at all—you can remember her saying about him?'

'Like I told you. It took me a while to get even that out of her. She didn't want to say anything.'

Steve paused a moment, then took out the Identikit drawing of Quin and handed it to Kendrick.

'Do you recognise this man, Mr Kendrick?'

'No. Can't say that I do. Should I?'

'His name is Mathew Quin. Does that name mean anything to you?'

Kendrick shook his head and Steve looked pointedly at Briony, as if to say: so, that's it then.

Now it was up to her to rescue the situation. She leant forward and looked Kendrick in the eye.

'If you leave here,' she said, 'won't you miss the place?'

'In some ways. But I've already stopped coming here in the evenings. I don't drink here any more. It's changed.'

'How do you mean?'

'It's gone cold. It used to be just a very friendly local pub. There was a lot of regulars and that's what gives a pub its spirit. Most of them have stopped coming here now. It's just—it's gone upmarket. The suits come here. Not the kind of people you can have a conversation with, unless you want to discuss the price of real estate.'

'Would you say Sabina Melies was one of the regular crowd?'

'Yes.'

'Did she ever talk about her past? You said in your interview with us that she'd met this man—the man you were suspicious of—at a commune in America. Is that the only time she mentioned the commune?'

'No, come to think of it. She told a few stories. It was near Haight-Ashbury in California. She called it Hashbury. I think they practically lived on the stuff. She made us laugh, the way she described them all getting stoned out of their minds and wandering into people's houses, just walking through the front door, you know, saying, "Hey, man, far out."'

'Did she think it was funny, too?'

'Hard to tell. She liked getting a rise out of people—laughter, curiosity, surprise—but she'd get you going on something, then suddenly change the subject, as if she didn't want to talk about it after all.'

'But she *was* afraid of something, connected with this commune.'

'I told you, she was afraid of the bloke who turned up. Shit scared, more like it. Possibly, looking back on it, she was scared before that. She was the jumpy type, she'd get full of enthusiasm for something, then suddenly drop it. I just thought it was the Latin American temperament. But looking at it another way, she could have been just jumpy. Nervous. All that stuff about not trusting the people she worked for. Maybe she'd got a bit paranoid, generally.'

'Can you remember her saying the names of any of the people in the commune?'

Kendrick didn't answer straight off this time. He stopped and stared into the empty glass he still held in his hand.

'No. Only once when I asked her what kind of commune it was, she said it went bad because these new people came in on it. They were supposed to be nomadic, walking across the globe, or something, but evidently they didn't move on fast enough for Sabina's liking. Course, like all those hippy groups around Hashbury, they probably weren't actually going anywhere.'

Briony concentrated hard, avoiding Steve's eye.

'Was she afraid of anyone in this nomad group?'

'Look, I wouldn't know. I hardly remember? I don't think she actually mentioned anyone in particular. I assumed they were your standard bunch of hippy scroungers.'

Kendrick stopped again, stared into the glass and frowned.

Briony watched him, but let the silence do its work. The Macready treatment. Suddenly, Kendrick squirmed in his chair, as if something had bitten him.

'Is this really important, this stuff about the commune?' He looked directly at Briony for the first time.

'It is of the most urgent and serious importance, Mr Kendrick.'

'See, I don't know if this is relevant, but when the bloke in the duffle coat turned up—and, like I told you, she stayed the night with me—she gave me this diary. Made me swear I wouldn't look at it or tell anyone about it. It was an old diary she'd written in California and she didn't want this bloke to get his hands on it.'

'And you didn't look at it?'

'Course I looked at it. But it's in Spanish.'

'Why didn't you mention this before?'

'I thought about it. I probably should have told the police straight up, when they first talked to me last year. But when they got it into their heads it was me that killed her, I got a bit paranoid myself. Because I had no idea what she'd written in there, you know? What if she'd said something about me? That might have made it worse. For a while, I really thought I was going to end up in the clink. Then the longer I kept it, the worse it looked that I hadn't told them about it. So when they wanted to search my room, I hid it.'

He put his glass back on the tray, stood up and walked slowly over to the baskets stacked against the wall. He moved two from the top layer, took out one from the second and brought it over.

'I'm pretty sure it's this one,' he said, putting it on the ground near the tray. As he tipped it upside down, the edge of a plastic bag was clearly visible in the heap of soil.

29

'It's a Booby Trap!' shrieked Julie, as Nell held up what looked like a pair of lime green tights and tried to figure out the shape. The pack was clearly labelled 'Booby Trap' and had a large Mary Quant flower on the edge.

'You still haven't twigged, have you?' said Rita. 'Here, let me show you.' She made fists of her hands and stretched the lime coloured nylon over them. 'See? It's a bra. I've got you a purple one as well—you can pay me back at the end of the week. They're amazingly cheap and you can buy pants to match—so you can chuck out all those nasty white things you've been draping around the bathroom.'

Nell looked at the Booby Trap with new eyes, stretching it this way and that. 'Clever,' she said. 'I like it! Thanks, Rita.'

'It's very sexy on,' said Julie. 'Much sexier than no bra at all. All you need now is something to wear over it!'

The twins were getting ready to go out to a party in Holland Park and had been working hard to persuade Nell to go with them.

'There will be students there,' said Rita. 'Just your type—you know, glasses, floppy hair, great long skinny legs.'

Since Nell had avoided one party already, she could feel this one closing in on her. Besides, she didn't really feel like an evening on her own in the flat and she'd just done a bit of shopping herself on the way home, since the West End shops were open late on Wednesdays.

Retreating to her room, she unpacked her tote bag and inspected the new sandals. They were soft brown leather with low heels and big square buckles. She had bought a shirt, too, in shiny blue satin material with silver crescent buttons, like moons. It didn't really go with the shoes or, now she came to think about it, with anything else she had, but she couldn't resist that deep midnight blue. She'd forgotten how much pleasure you could get from buying clothes and how much worry. Really, she should have spent the money on books for her course. She was letting the twins influence her too much.

After trying on just about everything in her sparse wardrobe, Nell settled on a long Laura Ashley skirt with Victorian flounces around the hem. It was white cotton with a pattern of dark blue sprigs, so it looked okay with the sandals and more or less okay with the blue shirt—at least, she thought so—and she came out of her room feeling quite pleased with herself.

'Don't tell me you're going in *that!*' said Rita. 'It makes you look about twelve.'

Rita herself was dressed to kill, in black hipster slacks with a chain belt and gold knit top, sleeveless with a polo neck. Her hair was blow-dried into a sleekly curved bob and her gold sandals added at least three inches to her height.

'I think Nell looks pretty,' said Julie. 'Just because Cliff wants you to look like Emma Peel, doesn't mean everyone else has to lay on the glamour.' This was a generous comment, since it was obvious that Julie had herself been laying on the glamour and that her short black jersey dress had been carefully picked to complement Rita's outfit.

Nell guessed that there was a plan to fix Julie up with one of Cliff's friends and sincerely hoped that no such plans had been made for her. She'd spent her A-level years as a kind of recluse, only going out occasionally to the cinema with other girls. She avoided the eyes of boys on the street. Often she had thought that she would like a boyfriend, someone you could really talk to about all kinds of things, but on the few occasions she had got talking to a boy, the conversation usually ran dry rather quickly. Boys were much more interested in trying to kiss you, which most of them did very badly.

The ones Julie and Rita knew were much older—not boys at all, really—men in their mid twenties, who drove sports cars and had a completely different way about them, but impressing them was clearly hard work and Nell didn't feel up to it. She decided to be firm.

'I'm afraid I'll just have to do. Or stay at home, which would really be fine with me. I could watch television—'

'Nonsense!' interrupted Rita, as she checked the contents of a tiny patent leather shoulder bag. 'You never like what's on television. You need to get out more. Anyway, it's too late to change now. Cliff will be here any minute.' She snapped the clip on her bag and went to shut the balcony doors.

Cliff's white convertible drew up a few minutes later, its hood folded back and its chrome gleaming in the evening sun.

With his right arm across the top of the steering wheel and his left fist around the gear stick, Cliff negotiated a succession of back streets with sudden bursts of acceleration so that Nell and Julie, packed into the back, were thrown against each other with every turn.

'All right in the back there, girls?' Cliff called out as he yanked the wheel sharply to the right, then pushed it just as sharply left again. Rita giggled in response.

'Tell us some more about Guy,' she said.

'Guy Waterlow? He's Roger's brother. Roger's going to be the lawyer, Guy's the doctor. He qualified last year and he's been too busy running around emergency wards to meet any girls, so tonight might be his lucky night.'

'Who's Roger?' asked Julie.

Rita half turned from the front seat, which caused her hair to blow violently across her face. 'Roger's the man whose party we're going to, silly. Honestly! I must have told you that three times, Julie. Roger and Galina. It's their housewarming party.'

'I thought you said it was a flat.'

'It *is* a flat. But housewarming is the expression. It's just an expression you use, isn't it, Cliff?'

'What's that?' Cliff was whistling to himself and had obviously lost interest in the conversation.

He parked the car in front of a row of Regency terraces and helped the two girls out of the back, deftly freeing the hem of Nell's skirt from the gear stick as she climbed over. Then, with a bottle of champagne trapped under one arm and Rita hanging on the other, he sprinted up the steps and rapped out the rhythm of 'I'm sorry I'll read that again' on the ornate brass door knocker. A tall man with smooth glossed hair and a very pink face appeared.

'Cliff!' he chortled, in an alarmingly deep voice. 'Thought I recognised your signature tune there. And who are all these gorgeous women you've managed to collect? I know Rita, of course.' He kissed Rita's hand. 'So this must be the famous twin, eh?'

'Julie,' said Julie. 'And this is our cousin Nell.'

'And this is a damn good bottle of bubbly, by the looks of it. Cliff's a man you can always trust to pick the wine. Come in, then, come in!'

'Is that Roger?' Julie whispered to Rita as the man led them down the hallway.

'Of course it is, silly!' giggled Rita.

As Nell edged her way into the crowded room behind Julie and Rita, she felt like a child at an adult's party. There was nothing of the beery smell or pulsing music she remembered from the few parties she'd been to with the twins in Exeter. People stood around holding wine glasses and talked in low voices. Everyone seemed to be tall and expensively dressed. Nell's midnight blue shirt looked like something from the limp end of the bargain rail compared with the splendid deep burgundy satin shirt Roger was wearing. He had his arm around a willowy blonde with heavy eye make-up, who shook hands with Julie and Rita without smiling, then pecked Cliff on the cheek.

'Fantastic,' she cooed. 'Fantastic.'

'What would you like to drink?' asked Roger. 'Glass of champage? Or would you like to try Galina's fruit punch? She's been cutting it up for days, haven't you, darling? It has fresh peaches in it. And what are those other things called again?'

'Nectarines.'

'Nectarines. Anyway, if you'd like to try it, it's steaming away on the Aga in the kitchen. Galina insisted on the Aga, didn't you, darling?'

'I must say,' said Cliff, 'you've made this place look amazing. Galina, you're a genius.'

'Isn't she!' Roger beamed and glowed and kissed Galina on the side of her neck.

'Galina's just finished decorating this room,' Rita whispered to Nell. 'Cliff advised her on the colour scheme.'

What colour scheme, Nell wondered to herself. Everything seemed to be cream: the rugs on the floor, the armchairs, the cushions, the heavy tasselled curtains, even the long-haired cat that was winding its way among the black trousered legs of the guests. She bent down to stroke it, but it backed off.

'We're on top of pretty well everything except the garden now,' said Roger.

'It's not a garden,' said Galina. 'It's a courtyard.'

'Courtyard. Yes. That's it, really. Too small for a garden. We were thinking it would look nice with a sculpture in the middle, you know, one of those stone fountain arrangements and stone pots for the flowers. Job for a specialist, I think, don't you, Cliff?'

'Not my line, I'm afraid,' said Cliff. 'I only do interiors. We won't worry about the garden for the photo-shoot. Just this room and the kitchen should do it. All right if we start on Tuesday?'

Galina nodded solemnly.

'Terrific,' beamed Roger. 'Glasses. I'll get you some glasses.' He disappeared and Galina took Cliff's arm. 'I have to introduce you to my sister Tamsin,' she said. 'She's dying to meet you.'

Rita, Julie and Nell were left standing in a little trio by the door. Rita hunched her shoulders, drew in her breath and smiled bravely.

'Doesn't the room look fabulous? It's going to be featured in *Vogue*.'

'Cliff arranges rooms for advertising shoots,' Julie explained to Nell.

'He's an interior designer,' Rita corrected her.

'So what's happened to this famous brother of Roger's?' asked Julie. 'Called away to an emergency, I suppose. Doesn't matter. Something tells me he wouldn't be my type.'

'Where's the kitchen?' asked Nell. 'I'll go and get us some punch.'

The kitchen had a cream tiled floor and cream cupboard doors with black handles. It was full of people and she had to push past to get to the stove. A man with thick glossy hair and sideburns was ladling pink liquid into a glass.

'Hello,' he said. 'Come to get some of the good stuff, eh?'

He handed her the glass and began to fill another one.

'I'm afraid I need three.'

'Then you'll need a tray. I'm Guy, by the way.'

'Guy Waterlow? I've heard about you.'

'Sounds ominous. So who are you?'

'Nell Adams. I came with Julie and Rita—you know—the twins. They're my cousins.'

'So where do you live, Nell?'

Nell thought quickly. This was getting awkward. She didn't want the man who was supposed to be Julie's date chatting her up.

'I live with Julie and Rita,' she said and made a quick getaway.

30

He was walking on sand: cold, white, flat and smooth as paper, with no horizon to distinguish it from the white sky, which threw an even blanket of light without gleam or shadow. But somewhere in the furthest reaches of this scene the wind blew. He could hear it, like the constant passing of distant traffic. Keep walking, said the voice, so close to his ear that he could feel the breath on which the words came. Keep walking.

It was hard to set up an even pace because the sand drifted beneath his feet, leaving him always on the same spot, while behind him the wind gathered speed. Then the angle of the ground began to change, to slope upwards, to swell in a giant wave and his feet slid against lumps in the sand, hard nodules from which tufts of grass grew. The wind came closer, whipping at the strands of grass, stirring the surface of the sand, revealing dome-shaped structures beneath it. Skulls. It was not grass that bristled from them, but strands of dead hair. Clean white bones lay beneath the sand, which was looser now and gave way under his feet. Keep walking.

He could make some slow progress by digging his heels into the hard bone, but the wall of sand rose higher and higher before him, threatening to close over his head so that his bones, too, would be captured in the white field of death. Now, said the voice. Turn.

As he turned, the world darkened and the wind blew deep into his body, like breath, warming the blood in his veins. The sand tumours shrank into black cobbles under his feet. Weak lamplight reflected from the walls close on either side of him, revealing their patina of coal dust, streaked with old beer and piss. Walking was easy here. He knew these streets like the lines on his own palm, knew where Hanbury crossed the deeper crevice of Brick Lane, where Vallance Road forked into Durward Street and knew how to negotiate the dense cross-hatching of Fairclough, Back Church Lane, Berner and Christian Streets so that the one he was after could be overtaken and headed off in a moment.

She swayed, putting out a hand to the wall. Footsteps approached from behind and he drew aside at the corner of George's Yard to watch the man pass. So did she, letting her ragged coat fall open as she greeted him. Only sixpence, to you. The man quickened his pace and she spat in his wake before sliding down the wall to sit on the ground.

Moving quietly towards her, he collected a red flower that had fallen from the lapel of her coat and held it out to her. As she raised an unsteady hand to take it, the knife came across at the speed of lightning so the flower was hit with purple spray.

He heard the sound of a horse and cart. The blade had not finished its work, not by any means, yet he had to withdraw, leaving things as they were. The knife was hot in his palm, demanding more.

The second one steered her way into his field of vision, making fire engine noises, interspersed with snatches of tuneless song. In Duke's Place she shouted at the copper on the beat. Show us your truncheon, Curly. I bet it's too small to hang your hat on. The copper crossed into Houndsditch, and she, turning and turning in her crazy song and dance, found her way into Mitre Square. Here some serious business could be undertaken.

But the work was hack work and the darkness leaked away and the white sands drifted in again to form a great curved bowl at the centre of which stood a white figure, ancient as the cracked earth through which the sands were gradually draining.

He woke in the daylight. Jack's botched work was finished with, now. Compare his random slashes, done with no sense of the difference between one organ and another, to the exact, clean cut with which the ear now added to his own collection had been severed, so that there was not the slightest damage to its shell-like form. Even the tongue which, however cleanly you clipped it, was always a vile thing, was still unmistakably a tongue, fit to carry a message.

31

'He's not worth it. Honestly, Rita. It's good riddance.'
Julie was struggling to keep up with Rita, who was almost
running. The broken rhythms of the two sets of high heels clatter-
ing against the pavement almost drowned out their voices.

'Good riddance is exactly what *he* thinks, I expect. I know what
he thinks of me. He thinks I'm just a little shop girl, good for filling the gaps between real girlfriends.'

'Well, what's so special about him, anyway? There's lots of other
men in London who have sports cars.'

'I don't care about the bloody sports car!' Rita's voice broke as
she said this, and started to come out in a high-pitched whine. 'I
thought he cared about me. Last time we went out he was so nice
to me. I really liked him. I really did.' Her pace slackened a little as
the sobs took over, so that Nell, with folds of skirt bunched into her
fist to keep it out of her way, was able to catch up.

'Julie's right,' said Nell. 'He's not worth it. Some people know
how to act nice and they just turn it on and off to manipulate you.'

'What do you mean?' The words came out in a squeak from
Rita's twisted mouth as she searched in her bag for a tissue.

'I mean I don't think he's nice at all. And neither are all the beautiful people up there in that flat. Roger should be in Pseuds' Corner. And Galina acts like she's got a key in her back—and she talks like she badly needs winding up. So what if her stuffy white living room's going to be in *Vogue*?'

'Champagne. The colour scheme's called Champagne.'

'It would be. Whatever it is, I hope someone's got the sense to spill some red wine on it.'

Rita, having failed to find a tissue, was transferring large amounts of wet mascara to the back of her wrist.

'Do you know what I heard them call us?' she sniffed. 'The dumb brunettes.'

'How incredibly witty,' snapped Nell. 'The trouble with you, Rita, is you're so easily impressed. Then when people insult you, you take it too seriously.'

'It's all very well for you. You're going to university and everything. They just think we're nothing, Julie and me. They just think we're stupid. That's what you think, too. Isn't it? Really? Why don't you be honest?'

'Why don't I try and get us a taxi? It's too late to be catching the tube. Which way is the main road?'

'Holland Park Road's that way,' said Julie, pointing back the way they'd come. 'I was trying to tell you you were going in the wrong direction. And these shoes are killing me.'

'I'm not walking back past Roger and Galina's. We'll have to go round the block.'

Rita suddenly veered across the road without looking and forced a moped rider to swerve so sharply he almost fell off. Nell made a determined sprint to catch up with her, while Julie was left limping several yards behind them.

'Anyway,' she said, as she captured Rita firmly by the elbow, 'what about me? Where are all those long legged student types you promised me?'

'Cliff said Roger had a lot of friends who are still at university.'

'Nonsense. I think they're all chartered accountants.'

'What about Tamsin?'

'Her too. How did she get so stiff looking?'

'She's a dancer. She trained with the Royal Ballet. Galina's always talking about her.'

'Sounds to me like she may have been plotting this Cliff–Tamsin thing for a while. So how well do you know these awful people? I think I'm going to have to start choosing your friends for you. Since you insist on choosing my clothes, that seems pretty fair to me. Is it a deal?'

Against her will Rita's mouth was twisting into a smile now.

'You don't know anyone in London.'

'Not yet, I don't. But there's a big dance on next week for new students. I'll buy three tickets, shall I?'

32

'Hello, Mr Perrin? It's Briony Williams here.'

'Good morning. I was wondering how long it'd be before the next onslaught. I had a long chat with your people yesterday. Just about wore me out they did.'

Well, thought Briony, they might have got her in on the follow-up with Perrin, since it was her lead in the first place.

'Just one question,' she said. 'Did Quin know any Spanish?'

'They asked me that yesterday. I wouldn't have a clue.'

'Thanks, Mr Perrin.'

Thursday got off to a frustrating start. The Saltash police had evidently lost the trace on Quin's family and concluded that they had moved out of the area. That is not a conclusion, Briony fumed to herself. The diary had gone to a translator, who promised to have the first two thousand words ready by Friday morning. That was also when the case file on the train murder was supposed to be arriving from Plymouth and when the forensic reports were due on the search of the room Quin had occupied in the hall of residence. A partial thumbprint had been found on the photograph from his entrance form, but there were no matches so far from the search in criminal records. The breakthroughs had been coming thick and fast, yet everything seemed to have stalled. Steve, sitting at his desk, going through books about William Hogarth, seemed to take it in his stride. But then, maybe he had high expectations of the interview with Oldroyd, booked in for eleven. Since Oldroyd had already told her he'd never heard of Mathew Quin, she didn't anticipate any new revelations from him.

Still, she had better be prepared. She got out her copy of the notes from his first interview, but her mind started wandering before she was halfway down the first page. Moments from yesterday afternoon were burned on her mind, and kept replaying themselves, as if they still had urgent business to do. The baskets with their rich black soil; the little birds taking flight; the basket Kendrick took out, with its strange secret planted in the dry caked earth; the small blue book in its cocoon of plastic. And over all these images hovered that of the painting on the gate in Crispin Street, executed in rapid, cruel brushstrokes. Why did she find this more real and more threatening even than the images of Caroline Staines that surrounded her here in this room? It was like a secret promise, that there was more to come, always more.

She got up, left the room and headed for the toilets, intending to check her appearance before the interview. Donna was in there, combing her hair.

'Hi, Briony! How are things?'

'Complicated. But better than they were. You were right, Donna, which is very annoying of you. So watch out—any opportunity to pay you back with some good advice, I'll be snatching at it. But there's something else I want to ask you about. You still watching the Hanging Gardens?'

'No. They de-prioritised it. The clientele's changed there and Palgrave didn't think I was getting any useful information. Makes my days a bit easier, anyway.'

'You haven't come across anyone there who speaks Spanish, then?'

'Nor anyone who knows Mathew Quin. Sorry, Briony. Those two leads are stone cold on my beat. Not a thing.'

'Oh, well. I guess we just have to keep working it from every angle. You know we're interviewing Oldroyd again this morning, because of your report?'

'Oh yeah? I'd be interested to hear how that goes. He's not liked, you know, Oldroyd. Bit of a stuffed shirt. Carries the rule book up his sleeve.'

'I can imagine. I've got permission to sit in on the interview— no thanks to Steve Latham—so I'll tell you what I can.'

'Good. Because the general briefing won't be till Friday morning and I need to be right on the ball for an arrangement I've got for eight tonight. Meet me at Lyons at six?'

At six o'clock on the dot, Briony was sitting at a table in front of a plate of bangers and mash with baked beans and a large mug of tea, with a Mars bar to follow.

'You'll feel sick,' Donna warned.

'Rubbish. We had this every day when I was at college and anyway it's going to save me from a fate worse than death—a piece of cold raw liver, lying in wait in my fridge. Doctor's orders. Now I need your advice about Steve Latham again, Donna. I just can't make him out. One day he comes over all sweet and friendly—'

'Flirting, you mean,' Donna interrupted.

'I suppose, maybe. But it isn't the usual sort of flirting. It's as if he really wants to get on with me. Then he'll suddenly do something to undermine me. Yesterday I tried to have it out with him.'

'Good for you! So what happened?'

'Bit of an argument. Then stalemate. We went to talk to Kendrick in the afternoon and at least he let me take over the interview. Got some good stuff, too. I was going to tell you—'

'Right now I'm more interested in hearing about what Oldroyd had to say for himself.'

'Wasn't exactly a showdown. I'll tell you in a minute.' Briony prepared a forkful of beans. 'First you have to answer my question. What do think Steve Latham's up to?'

Donna pushed away her half eaten plate of cheese and egg salad. Then she opened her handbag, took out a small cosmetic mirror and her mascara and began to do her eyes.

'Know what?' she said. 'I think you fancy him.'

'I do not. I wouldn't mind being proper friends, but I can't trust him.'

'That's right. Got to watch yourself around Steve Latham. He used to chat me up when I first came. He was very intense—you know the kind of thing—when they act like they can't take their eyes off you, but they're too humble to make a move. Then the minute they get a bit of encouragement, they make out it's you that's doing the chasing. Little power game. Seen it a few times.'

'He was trying to be nice to me the other day, when I was sick. Then the next time I see him, he's sitting in Macready's office and won't even cast a glance my way. Then he comes up with this put-down about having a woman in the interview room. When I tried to talk to him yesterday it was all over the place, you know? I absolutely couldn't get through to him.'

'He probably thinks he can't get through to you. You don't wear mascara, do you?'

'Not unless I'm going out. I'm always in such a rush in the mornings. I don't usually bother with make-up.'

Donna's eyelashes were looking like beetle's legs, Briony thought.

'You should, you know. You got lovely eyes. But you shouldn't wear those glasses. They're out of fashion. Get some contact lenses, that's my advice.'

'Yeah, well, maybe. But it's not the kind of advice I'm asking for. Are you telling me I should be fluttering my eyelashes at him?'

'He's a bloke. It's the language they understand. Here. Try some.'

Briony put down her knife and fork, removed her glasses and

took the mascara brush, which was coated in what looked like blue shoe polish.

'It's got bits in it.'

'That's lash lengthener—the fibres cling to the ends of your lashes. Makes them longer and thicker. It's brilliant.'

But as soon as Briony touched her lashes with the brush, one of the flecks got in her eye and caused her to blink, which made a blue-black smudge along her lower lids.

'Oh damn! Look, I'm not in the mood for doing this right now.'

She dabbed at the smudge with the tissue Donna handed her, then gave back the mirror and returned to her sausages.

'Anyway,' she said, 'I agree with Germaine Greer. We shouldn't be trying to turn ourselves into whatever it is they like to have fantasies about.'

'Don't you ever have fantasies yourself?'

Briony pointed at Donna with a greasy knife. 'None of your damn business. So do you want to hear about this interview?' She put the Mars bar in her pocket. 'I'll save this for later.'

'You're a lost cause, Briony Williams. One day somebody's going to have to take you in hand.' Donna flicked her hair over her shoulders and leaned forward. 'Okay. So tell me.'

'Well, first of all Macready said he was doing the interview himself. He was quite narky with Steve for setting it up and I think he wanted to make sure he didn't get too heavy with Colin Oldroyd. In fact, you know, I got a hunch—strictly off the record—that Macready's a Freemason himself.'

'They've got a special way of shaking hands. Did you notice anything like that?'

'No, they had their backs to me, as usual, when he came in. At first I thought the interview wasn't going anywhere. Macready took Oldroyd back over the things he'd already told us. He asked again if anyone might have a grudge against Godwin and got pretty well the same answer we got in his first interview. But then he began to push it a bit—you know—was he sure there was nothing he might have forgotten—the standard soft-line probe—and Oldroyd didn't answer. He just kind of clammed up. So Steve went straight for it. Said it had come to our attention that there was some gossip around the college about Godwin—that he was a member of an organisation from which some people had been expelled. Then you could just see Oldroyd tensing up. He said, "I'm not at liberty to speak about that." And Macready came right back at him: "If you have information relative to this case, Dr Oldroyd, you are not at liberty to remain silent." Macready had that real killer look in his eye, you know?'

'So did he tell? About the Freemasons?'

'Eventually. He beat about the bush a bit first—talking about "a club" he and Godwin belonged to that had to exclude some members. Then gradually he started spilling the beans. Talked about "the lodge". Godwin was Grand Master apparently, a few years ago. Oldroyd said there was a tradition going back to the eighteenth century of admitting student members, if they were recommended by the right people, but there'd been some trouble with some of them and Godwin had to chuck them out. So Macready's asked for a list of the names. Oldroyd's supposed to be getting it for us by tomorrow.'

'I might beat him to it,' said Donna, tossing a strand of hair back over her shoulder. 'I got a date tonight. Want to guess who with?'

'What? Not the guy who did the abortion?'

'No. The one who got the girl into trouble. Alec, his name is. I had lunch with him today and he's not keeping secrets for anyone. Told me he hated Oldroyd. Said he never wanted to be in a club with all those old guys anyway, but—here's the interesting bit—turns out the Freemasons' rejects have got a little club of their own going and Alec's under pressure to join. They call themselves The Invisible College. Freaky, huh?'

'You want to watch yourself, Donna. Don't get into anything

you can't handle. Anyway what about this man's girlfriend? The one who got pregnant?'

'It's not *really* a date—not like that, anyway. He said he might be able to arrange for me to meet one of the Invisibles.'

'And I'm the only one who knows about this? Look, Donna, you don't know what these guys might be like. You were sharp enough with me the other day for acting on my own initiative. Shouldn't you have cleared it with Palgrave or Macready first?'

'They were in Whitechapel this morning—couldn't get hold of them on the phone.'

'Well, I don't like it. This case really spooks me, Donna. Walker or whoever he is is one step ahead of us all the time. Sometimes I think he's watching us. It gives me a bad feeling. Don't go. Please.'

'I'll be fine. Honestly. I know what I'm doing, Briony.'

'Then you have to promise to phone me first thing tomorrow morning. If I haven't heard from you by nine, I'm going to raise the alarm.'

Briony ate the Mars bar as she walked to the tube station, threading her way through the crowds that were milling around the theatres in their best clothes. She felt cold in her cotton shirt and Piccadilly looked gloomy under the fading sky, in spite of its perpetual light show. Autumn was coming. The entrance to the tube suddenly struck her as an ugly dark cave. Instead of plunging into it, she crossed the road to the island and sat under the statue of Eros, instantly attracting a crowd of pigeons. She broke the remains of the chocolate into chunks and began to throw it to them, watching how the scramble for the pieces brought out the bullies and the victims among them. Identifying a lame one on the outer edge of the huddle, she aimed directly towards it, but just as it got the prize in its beak, it was attacked by a larger bird with brilliant purple neck feathers. A burst of indignation shot through her and she jumped up. 'Get away!' she hissed at it. A few heads turned among the crowds on the other side.

33

In her dream, Briony was looking through the glass door panel into the waiting room where several people were sitting. One of them was Donna, wearing a red beret, and opposite her sat a man whose face was a paper mask drawn up like Quin's Identikit portrait, but with holes cut out in the eye sockets. Briony was tapping on the glass, then calling out, trying to warn Donna, but couldn't make herself heard above the drilling noise. Then she was out in the street and could see the red beret ahead in the Piccadilly crowds, with the masked man following. But Briony herself was surrounded on all sides, and couldn't move fast enough to catch up. She made a frantic effort to shout a warning as Donna headed into the tube station with her pursuer only a couple of steps behind, but it was no good, only a useless croaking noise came out, and it woke her up. She switched the lamp on and looked at the clock on her bedside table: it was only two thirty.

This nightmare was trying to tell her something, she was convinced. It was too real to be just a dream, too urgent. What if Donna didn't ring? Daylight was a long time coming, with several hours of sleeplessness eventually giving way to another dream, this time about looking for things in the fridge, using a fingerprinting brush on assorted packets of leaking meat and suppurating vegetables. The alarm cut in as she was trying to force the door shut on them.

Briony got up and stared at the real thing in the kitchen. She picked out the liver and dropped it in the bin. And the lettuce. Then she tried to boil an egg, but it cracked in the water and made a frilly, frothy mess. That went into the bin as well. She set off for work, intending to stop at Lyons for a cooked breakfast, but the bus got stuck in traffic and it was eight thirty by the time she got to Piccadilly. She had to be at her desk in time for Donna's call.

Nine o'clock went by. Then five past. Then ten. Briony dialled Donna's home number, but there was no answer. To make things worse, the clock on the wall was four minutes faster than her watch. The minute hand jerked and clicked as it changed position. When the phone rang at 9.22, her heart thumped so violently she could hardly speak into it. It was Macready. He wanted her in his office immediately. She could put it off no longer, anyway. She'd rather have reported to Palgrave first off, but it was hardly going to make much difference, since Macready would eventually have to know.

The door of his office was wide open and before she reached it she heard the sound of a camera. Jimmy, with one foot up on a wooden chair and his shoulders at an awkward angle, was photographing something soft and pink in a plastic container on Macready's desk. Oh, hell. Another parcel. Of course. Steve was looking at what must be the note, contained in a plastic cover. He passed it to her.

This speaks for itself. Walker

No one was saying anything. She walked out of the office and leant against the wall with her eyes closed.

When she opened them, Steve was standing a few feet away, hands in his pockets, watching her.

'Hey, you okay?'

'Donna Caldwell's gone missing.'

'How come?'

'She had a lead and went out last night with a bloke who had information—'

'What, on a date you mean?'

'Yes. I didn't like the sound of it. I tried to stop her and I told her to call me this morning at nine—so I'd know she was all right—but she didn't call.'

'Probably just forgot. Donna's been round the block a few times. Knows how to handle herself. She's not like you, Briony.'

'Thanks.'

'Oh, you know what I mean.'

'Do I? I know I've got to report this to Palgrave.'

'Let me deal with it. I'll make a few checks, see if she's turned up at Gresham. If you report her missing and it's a false alarm, you'll just look daft. There's too much else to worry about.'

'Can I have that advice on the record?'

Steve looked at his watch. 'I'll be back around twelve with the first instalment of the translation. Better be here.'

When Briony got back to the incident room, the phone on her desk was ringing. Donna's voice came through loud and clear.

'Where have you been? This is the third time I've rung! I need to talk to you, but not at the station. Can you come to Gower Street?'

'I suppose I could. You owe me a coffee at least.'

'What for?'

'For giving me a nervous breakdown. You were supposed to ring me at nine.'

'Never mind. There's an Italian café just round the corner from the college, in Torrington Place. I'll wait there for you.'

It was better than hanging around at Vine Street to watch the rain streaming down the windows, Briony had to admit. There was nothing especially useful for her to do until the translation of the diary came in and the atmosphere was suffocating. She left a note for Steve—'Donna okay'—and swept the stray notes on her desk into her bag, so she could go through them on the tube.

Out in the Tottenham Court Road, the rain was light but persistent, splattering on the café tables and chairs that had optimistically been put out on the pavement. The area was getting trendy, despite the ugly concrete buildings and heavy traffic. On the other side of the road was Paperchase, with its window display of boxes and notebooks in brilliant colours. She remembered the small blue diary filled with close lines of handwriting. Sabina Melies was probably full of hope when she had bought it, choosing the bright turquoise with a feeling that the world was opening up to her and that she should keep a record of her own unfolding story.

Briony spotted Donna through the window of the café, sitting warm and dry in the orange glow of the lamp above her table, reading the paper. Well why was I ever worried about you, Briony muttered to herself as she pushed the door open.

'Cut above Lyons, isn't it?' said Donna, smiling broadly. 'Would you like a cappuccino?'

'What's that?'

'I'll get you one. You'll love it.' She went up to the counter, and Briony picked up the newspaper. The Whitechapel murders had gone off the front page, which carried a picture of victims from the latest bombing in Belfast. A large quantity of gelignite had been found in a house in Reading and another London bombing campaign was being anticipated. A Scotland Yard superintendent had been appointed to lead a team of fifty officers in an anti-terrorist squad, targeting the Angry Brigade. It all made Walker look like a small-time crim, but what he did seemed more evil, somehow. He had no cause to fight for and no enemies except in his own mind.

Donna came back with an oversized yellow pottery cup full of froth, which Briony started to spoon out onto the saucer.

'What are you doing?'

'Looking for the coffee.'

'Don't be silly. It's all coffee. Just drink it.'

'Will you tell me if I get foam on my nose? So, why the under-cover game? Why are we meeting here?'

'I found out some stuff, but I'm not sure whether to report it, so I thought I'd talk to you first. You know I told you yesterday that the bloke I was going to meet—Alec—is under pressure to join this group—'

'You mean the Invisible College? Yes, so—'

'So he's now totally paranoid. A lot of the students are saying they killed Godwin.'

'Then report it immediately.'

'No, Briony, you're getting the wrong end of the stick. Just wait till I've finished telling you.'

'The students from the Invisible College can't have killed Godwin. Their alibis have been checked and they're rock solid. Emergency ward duty—that kind of thing. Four of them were over at a music festival in Wales and they were actually performing on stage that night. They've got a group. They got back here on Tuesday and they've been heavying Alec to join the Invisibles. There are only two who could have been in London, but I double-checked their alibis this morning. That's why I was late phoning you.'

'How did you get all the names? It's not exactly subtle asking for that kind of detailed information. Wasn't Alec suspicious?'

'I'd already told him who I was. He *wants* to talk to the police. Off the record, of course. So does his friend. Guy's been a member of the Invisibles for a few years and knows everything. Guy's training to be an ENT specialist.'

'What's ENT?'

'Ear nose and throat. Now there's someone I wouldn't mind a real date with. Anyway, he told us the Invisibles were around before the lodge was established—it was started as a student organisation—for sharing knowledge—way back in the sixteen hundreds. At that time the only bodies they could get were from the gallows and the Invisibles found a way of preserving them, which gave them an advantage over all the other students. When the lodge started up a couple of centuries ago, most of them joined the Freemasons, but some of them left again soon after because they were losing their independence. There's been a kind of stand-off between them ever since. The Invisibles have been picking up the lodge's rejects for generations, because they're the kinds of people who are more likely to be adventurous and independent minded. But they've got a few hassles among them because of different interpretations of what that means.'

'So did you get the names we're looking for?'

'Yes. Hate to disappoint you, Briony, but Quin's not one of them. He was never a member of the Invisibles and almost certainly never a member of the lodge, either.'

'You give me a nervous breakdown thinking you've fallen into the hands of some psycho, then you bring me all the way over here in the rain to tell me my favourite suspect's not showing up in the evidence? Thanks a lot, Donna.'

'I didn't say he's not showing up in the evidence, did I? According to Guy, he tried to join the Invisibles, but they didn't want him. They thought he was a kid, basically. He had one meeting with them and tried to sell them this grand plan about how they could become more powerful than the lodge, but evidently he didn't impress anyone. When he left, they voted against him and Guy had to give him the news the next day. This time, he said, Quin didn't say a thing, but afterwards he disappeared for a couple of days and they eventually found him wandering about near the Blackfriars Bridge. Guy said he was "seriously disturbed" and he tried to persuade him to get treatment.'

Briony pushed away her cup, took off her spectacles and cleaned them with a tissue.

'Why don't you want to report this?'

'I'll tell you. One, I didn't report that I was going out last night with Alec and, as you were keen to advise me, that could get me into a bit of trouble.'

'But that's not—'

'Just a minute. Let me finish. Two, I blew my cover, which is a much more serious breach. It was the only way I could get the information.'

'Exactly, so there's no—'

'I said let me finish, Briony. Three—and now you get to the more serious stuff—Guy's shit scared that if it is Quin who's been doing all this free-range anatomy, he may be targeting old acquaintances, specially if he thinks they might have grassed on him. Guy doesn't want to be the next on the list of bodies. He's trying to lie low.'

Donna paused and frowned, staring at the table in front of her.

'Then, see, when I thought about it, what's to be gained from reporting it? What Guy's told me about Quin is pretty well what Perrin told you—basically, he's a psycho. Prime suspect material.'

'So does that mean you've risked your career for nothing? It was you who told me that Macready won't tolerate outriders who fail to keep him informed.'

'Yeah, well, maybe I'm coming under your bad influence. Now, how about another coffee? You owe me this time.'

Briony got up and went to the counter, where two more cappuccinos cost her nearly the price of a full meal at Lyons. As she watched the gleaming metal machine bubble and steam its way through the process, a question was nagging at her. There was something not quite right about Donna's story.

34

Why had Guy Waterlow gone out of his way to talk to Donna? Why had he given her that information about the Invisibles? Without some kind of follow up, what Donna had told her was really not of much use. Waterlow had probably learnt more from her than she had from him, so maybe that was the intention. Maybe he just wanted to find out how much the police knew and Donna had fallen for it—or, rather, for him.

Back at Vine Street, Briony found that Waterlow was on Oldroyd's list, along with seven other names. So was *that* a complete list? Steve would probably be checking it out already, but it was important that he ask them about Quin.

Steve didn't seem to be around—in fact the whole station was uncomfortably quiet, now that the drilling had stopped—but a small pile of blue carbon typed pages had been left on her desk. Sabina's diary. This could be the heart of the case, or a big disappointment. She flicked through. The evenly spaced blocks of print looked very remote from the scrawled pages of the original blue notebook and there was nothing to immediately suggest that it was a diary of any kind. There were no dates or divisions between the days. A note at the top explained that some pages were missing and that the handwriting deteriorated badly towards the end of this part of the translation.

The next instalment was promised for 'soonest possible'. According to Steve, the translator was himself a bit of a hippy type and, from what they'd heard about Sabina, should be well suited to the job. Maybe a bit too well suited, Briony began to think to herself as she read through the first ten pages. They were a confused set of ramblings about the Human Be-in and Golden Gate Park, interspersed with the fragments of song lyrics in English, mostly from the Grateful Dead or the Incredible String Band (thoughtfully identified by the translator). Then there was the story of a group of them, including some small children, driving in an old bus out over the hills skirting San Francisco Bay and down through the San Joaquin Valley, finding deserted ranches that provided convenient stopping places.

The bus eventually came to the end of its journey in an abandoned fruit orchard with two makeshift huts that had once been used by the workers. The trees were in fruit and there was a convenient water supply from a nearby creek, which marked the border onto some wetlands. Somewhere in the San Joaquin Valley—or maybe they'd gone on, further than that—wherever it was they'd stopped, it was apparently on a hippy trail, with groups of people straggling through, stopping to trade drugs and sometimes leaving one or more of their members behind to swell the numbers of the commune. Some character called Neb kept large amounts of marijuana, which he planted, all around them and also held 'a stash of acid' which he used to purchase a car from one of the visitors, so he could return to Haight-Ashbury for other trading missions.

Briony read with growing disappointment, seeing nothing to connect with the case. Until, about halfway through. The commune had reached a low point, with the food supply running out, and her attention picked up as she sensed a new intensity coming into the narrative.

We only have oranges now until the grapes ripen, the potatoes have rotted in the ground. Everyone is sick of oranges. Hayley made orange and lentil soup but two of the children vomited it up, the little ones that still shit in the camp area. I noticed later it gave them diarrhoea too. They sucked their mothers to try and make up for it but the milk surely tastes orange by now. At sunset I walked out into the dunes to get away from the sweet stink. I like to sleep out there, the sand is so warm.

Agate and Hayley asked me if I want to leave with them and go to the Scientologists where they give you bread every day and soup made with vegetables. Hayley is worried about Midge because he is the oldest of the children and he is not growing. Tomorrow we're leaving they said. Dead set. Erien says bullshit they will still be here next week and after.

I think he is right. No one is going anywhere, because the bus is grounded and Neb says only he's allowed to use the car because the breaks are fucked. Sometimes Erien talks about going. He says he will find an army truck and hotwire it. Then we can drive to Florida. Instead we went to the dump, where occasionally we find some food that is not gone rotten yet. Once we found boxes with half frozen pies. Dozens of them. Another time there was a load of mouldy bread. This time we found nothing but broken furniture, and had to run most of the way back because we heard rifle shots.

The army shoots all day some days, over in the wetlands. You can hear them from the orchard. When we go on long walks we pick up the shells. We even found a couple of old rifles which Neb keeps in the locked store, but nobody's tried to see if they work any more. Think if we could lock up all the rifles. All the rifles in the world. One day I'll get shot out there, says Erien, or they'll catch me and send me off to Nam to get my head blown off, so I'm going to blow my mind first.

I don't know why he wants to go to Florida. Everyone wants to go somewhere but no one goes anywhere. I can remember when all anyone wanted to do was be here. Forever. Peace. That's what we thought we'd found and it was true but I don't know why it didn't last it was so perfect for a while and sometimes it still is but only for a few moments at a time. Hayley says it's gone completely for her. She thinks it was an illusion in the first place but I know it wasn't. Isn't.

Neb used to be known for the biggest holdings in Golden Gate Park, which was one of the reasons we had so many visitors for a while. But that's all run out and we haven't had any visitors for... well I don't know exactly. Lots of months. Maybe six. If Neb wants acid now, he has to take the grass back to Haight and trade. That's what he went to do this morning.

It's hot in these days and the sun stays late. We sit out and wait for the moon to come. Erien and Pascal do the same riffs over and over again on their guitars and we dance for a while, but mostly everyone is too smashed to dance or to sing. When there's no real food but the hash is good, there's not much action.

Neb came back in the night and everyone got up in case there was food. He brought a cheese and a sack of apples. And he said there were some people coming.

'They should be here in the morning.'

'What do you mean?' asked Waltraut. 'Where were they?'

Neb said they were camped near the road about 5 miles away, but they were planning to move on at dawn.

In the middle of the day the people came. Three women and two men. Who knows how they got here—maybe they hitched a lift or something—but we just saw them walking over the hill, carrying all this stuff. One of them was pushing 3 little kids—babies really—in a home made cart. They had tents with them, which they put up on the other side of the stream, but they have not brought any food. None of them has told us their names yet.

Hayley invited them to come eat with us and a couple of the women came over but they acted shy, would not sit down but stood behind and ate in silence. After we'd finished the meal, we heard calling out and whoops from the trees. It was Neb and Guillermo, with sacks over their shoulders. They have lifted bags of rice and a big tin of coffee from an army supply drop, said they left them some grass in exchange.

I've tried to talk to those women, but you just can't get anywhere with them. What's your name, I ask. Where are you from? They give you one word in answer and they don't ask any questions back, just smile like zombies. It seems only one of them is supposed to do the talking—this ratty looking guy with little red eyes and hair in corkscrews. 'Dreadlocks' Hayley says they're called in English.

Here a note said 'pages missing'. And for Briony, something was starting to add up. If the pages had been removed on purpose, as with Caroline Staines's notebook, to leave a fragmented story as a lure, then whoever ripped the pages out of Sabina's diary must know Spanish. Was 'the ratty looking guy' Mathew Quin? She read on.

Today the trouble starts. I knew it was coming.

They have made a fire and taken one of our big cooking pots. A couple of us went over to see what they had found to put in it, since there was an incredible smell coming. It was rabbit stew.

Their men have been out catching rabbits. One of the women offered us some. We're vegetarians I told her and she didn't say anything, just gave the bowl to the rat man, who gave me this look that sent a charge through my spine. How can you be vegetarians he said when you've got no fucking vegetables. He said it in English. Then in Spanish he said, 'You need meat to make blood. You got no blood in your veins, woman!'

Down by the creek they'd hung the rabbits on a wire, skinned. There were wood pigeons too. The other man was down there, the ratty one. I saw him cut the legs off a dead pigeon. When he saw me, he cut the head off and drained the blood into his mouth. Then he looked me in the eye for a long time and didn't blink. I stared him out.

That nails it, thought Briony, immediately remembering the warden's story about Quin and the pigeons. And the next paragraph delivered the confirmation.

I told Neb we want them to go. I don't know why he brought them. We don't own the place, he said, we can't stop anyone coming if they want to come. They're Walkers, so don't try to mess with them. I didn't know what he was talking about. When I left the tent I saw Hayley crying outside. They're right, she said. We're all going to die here, if we don't get real food. Waltraud and Guillermo are coming with me. We're going to live in the tents. We're taking all the kids. They said they'd give me protection. I said—From what?

I went to find Waltraud. I was feeling mad. I wanted to get her by the hair and make her see some sense. I found her down by the stream, doing some washing. What do you think you are getting into, I said. These are dangerous people. That guy with the rat's hair is insane. We need to get them out of here. She just sat there staring past me like I was invisible. Then I turned around, and there he was, grinning all over his face. And he said something to Waltraud, very quietly, in German, and she got up and went back to the tent like she was his dog or something.

I wanted to get as far away from him as I could so I went up to sleep in the dunes. Erien found me up there. He brought some of the new acid and persuaded me to take it with him. It was incredible. It made the sky blow up like a balloon. The stars went off like fireworks and the dunes were like the middle of the ocean. Round and round goes the wind, said a voice in my head, or maybe it wasn't in my head. Maybe it was just out there, blowing across the sand.

When I woke up it was day and Erien was gone. Back at the tents, I couldn't find Hayley or Agate. I sat and listened to the flies, which made an endless empty noise like death. I don't like trips. This trip is turning bad I thought, but I could hardly think because the flies had

taken my thoughts away. After a while I noticed someone was sitting next to me. I heard a man's voice. If you
pull their wings off they still make that noise, it said. I fell
asleep again and I heard the voice in my sleep. It's all
turning to death here, it said. Turn, turn. Round and
around goes the wind. The voice went on, speaking sometimes in Spanish, sometimes in English. And there were
some things in a language I don't recognise. And I was
walking in the dunes and there were old white bones in
the sand, it was a whole field of death.

But all the time I was still sitting there, and when
I realised I was awake again the sun was nearly gone.

Here the typing broke off, and the translator's scrawly handwriting announced again 'pages removed'. The next page began in mid
sentence.

or if I might be getting sick. As I walk around, I think
everyone looks sick. Pascal says their women are on smack
and I wonder if they have been giving it to Hayley. She
won't even look at me when I pass her. Waltraud stayed
in their tent all day yesterday, so only the children have
been running between the camps.

Midge came up to me and said he wanted to show
me the new game the Ratman taught him. You play it
with orange pips, says Midge. You take a handful of
orange pips up onto the dunes. Then you make a trail,
one for each footstep, counting the number you leave
on the sand. I can count up to a hundred, he says. After
a hundred, you turn back and try to find them. See how
many you can find. So, I said, what about the ones you
can't find? Those are the ones the Walker has taken, said

Midge. When you leave the trail, the Walker comes to follow you.

Who's the Walker then? Midge said he was Walker the Wizard. I told him he should stay clear of Walker the Wizard.

Guillermo and the rat man have gone. At first I thought Erien must have gone with them but he came back in the night, shivering and totally freaked out. Said he'd had a bad trip and stayed out in the wetlands because he was surrounded. Surrounded with what I asked. I was very angry with him. He's going to get shot out there. He said don't get uptight, don't put that neurotic trip on me.

In the morning I saw Waltraud picking oranges, but she moved further away, then next time I looked she'd gone. Later I tried to talk to Hayley. I know she and Waltraud have been shooting up and I reminded Hayley when we decided to join the commune we swore to each other that we would never do smack. No shooting up. And if things started going bad we'd leave. But I couldn't get any talk going. Not about anything. I told her I'm worried about Midge but all I got out of her was, he's okay.

Some days have gone since I wrote in this. The Ratman came back yesterday, without Guillermo and without the Cadillac. He just walked in over the hill. No explanations. I have been crying a lot. First I stayed out in the dunes but then I came back to be in the tent with the others. Neb has joined the Walkers. I knew he would. Maybe he was always one of them. So. OK. Who cares, said Agate. But Erien is getting totally paranoid. He is no help to us, he just sits there for hours, his hands shaking. I talked with Agate and Pascal about getting out, taking Erien with us if we can. We would have to take the dune buggy, when we can get the petrol.

More 'pages missing'.

cutting up the rabbits in front of the children. He takes the eyes out Midge said, with the point of his knife, then looks at them through a black thing that makes whirring noises. What does he mean? Binoculars? A microscope? A camera, perhaps. Does the rat man have a camera? I realise Midge would never have seen one of those, at least, not since he was old enough to know what it was.

I feel sorry for Midge. He looks lonely and worried, the other children are too young for him to play with. He followed me out to the trees and helped me pick the fruit, and he was even trying to cheer me up, telling me the grapes would soon be ripe. He was counting the grapes in the bunches. I can count to five hundred now he said. When we got back he showed me his treasure. Orange pips, dried white in the sun and tied in one of the cloths. There are five hundred of them, he told me. He had another cloth, full of dried animal bones. Probably rabbit, but who knows?

Neb is starting to spook me. When I found the store was open and rifles were gone I went to look for him and eventually I found him up on the dunes wandering around and looking as if he was smacked out of his mind. I bawled him out for going over to the Walkers. He acted like he didn't even hear me. Stared at me as if I was someone from another planet.

Pascal has found an old can at the dump with some petrol left in the bottom of it. He's buried it under the bus, till we can get some more. We have to go out and see if we can siphon some from one of the army trucks. We searched all day yesterday but didn't find one. There's an army road, a track really, on the other side of the dunes, about two hours walk away, and sometimes you see trucks parked there. But we haven't been lucky the last couple of days. We're worried Neb may have figured out what we're trying to do. What if Erien tells him? We don't talk in front of Erien now, because he can't keep his mouth shut. He just lies around and talks shit all day like a total junkie.

Midge has gone missing. It's a whole day and a night now. Hayley screams and cries for a while and goes off shouting for him, then she falls asleep. She doesn't even know when she last saw him. I have been all over the dunes, calling and looking for tracks. The Walkers are mainly hanging around their tent. I went over and yelled at them. Told them they were a bunch of useless freaks and they should get out there and help with the search. I called Neb to come out but he didn't answer, so I thought I'd go in and get him, but the Ratman stood in my way. He took hold of my wrists. Said he'd snap them if I didn't shut my mouth.

Briony stared at the last lines on the page, as if somehow she could will more lines to appear. We've found him, she muttered to herself. He's right here.

She did not want her concentration interrupted right now, and wasn't keen to get caught up in conversation with Donna, who came flouncing in a few minutes later, obviously in search of a sounding board for her latest discoveries.

'I had lunch with Alec,' she said. 'He was hanging around me all morning and I'm starting to worry he's going to get people asking the wrong kind of questions about me. Besides, I'm also starting to get this vibe from him—you know—he's a bit too interested in me.'

'What do you mean?'

'I mean he's a bit too interested in me for a man supposed to be involved with someone he just got into trouble.'

35

It was raining when Nell left work on Friday. Her hair was awful in wet weather. It reacted by crinkling and expanding, then blowing in all directions as the wind caught it. She twisted it into a thick coil at the back of her head and captured it under the beret. Rita had lent her a nice beige raincoat—trench-coat style with a wide belt—but her sandals were hardly the right thing for this weather. They were looking a bit the worse for wear already.

The entrances to Leicester Square tube station were jam-packed with people, pushing their way in or out and annoying each other with their wet bags and umbrellas. She wanted to buy an *Evening Standard*, but couldn't battle her way across to the seller on his stand, which was protected with a large sheet of transparent plastic. This didn't stop the wind getting through and whipping at the edges of the piled up newspapers. They were trapped under a brick so they wouldn't blow away. She saw a hippy with straggly hair lifting the brick to read the front page and being shooed away. As he turned, his hair blew across his face and a shadow flickered across the screen of Nell's memory. A second later he was gone, sucked into the crowd.

The flat seemed dingy and cold when she got back, so she switched on the reading lamp and the little electric fire that was so far the only heating they had. It was an hour till either of the twins would get back. Rita worked ten till six at the Way In, an hour later at either end of the day. Julie had a longer journey, so it meant that every day except Monday, which was one of Rita's days off, Nell had an hour to herself in the flat for reading or playing records that the twins didn't like. It was her favourite hour of the day.

Equipped with a cup of instant and two ginger biscuits, she sat crosslegged in front of the fire with the table lamp aimed over her new copy of *Hard Times*. It was one of the texts for the history of the novel course in first semester. So was *Anna Karenina*, and that meant she was a step ahead. The letter from her department said all students would be expected to have read it before term started.

Nell thought she would like to sit there and read all evening. She didn't feel like going out again, especially not to some noisy dance with a lot of people she didn't know and she was sure the twins would not like Pink Floyd. But since she'd already paid for the tickets, they'd have to go through with it now. At least they wouldn't have to leave before eight and Rita and Julie would take at least an hour to get ready so she might have two hours for reading. Nell was starting to keep a little ledger of hours in her head. 'A good English student will do at least four hours reading a day,' said the letter from her department.

She was just getting into the story, imagining the streets of Coketown and the little cramped schoolroom where the children were drilled in facts and definitions, remembering some of the primary school teachers she'd hated, when the lamp suddenly went off and the fire started to make low twanging noises as its glowing bar faded.

Damn, she thought, the meter must have run out. But then, on second thoughts, it couldn't have run out. They had put in a pound in five pence coins before they left for work, because they wanted to be sure there would be plenty of hot water for baths before they went out this evening. Maybe there was a power cut. She walked around the flat, trying a few switches. They were all dead.

Then she thought she heard the sound of water running in the bathroom, so she went out to check and found the hallway full of steam. The bathroom was thick with it and she could hear the bath tap at full bore. The hot water was all going to waste down the plug-hole. It must have been on for ages to have got through all the money they'd put in the meter.

Furious, she switched it off and went to bash on the door of the other flat. There was no answer. Maybe they just put the bath on, then went out and forgot about it. She called, loudly. No answer. She stood for a minute, not knowing what to do or to think. Then she heard the front door and Julie came stomping up the stairs. She must have got off work early.

'What's up?'

'I found the bath running. It's wasted all our hot water. Plug wasn't even in. They must have switched it on and gone out or something. All the electricity's gone off. It's run the meter dry.'

Julie went to look, and Nell followed. Julie turned the tap on again and the water came out cold.

'What a nerve. I mean, what a bl—blinking nerve. I hate sharing the bathroom with them. They complain all the time, about every little thing, then they go and use up all our hot water. Just like that. They never pay their share of the hot water. Well, they're going to have to pay us back this time or I'll dob them in to the landlady. I'm dying for a cup of tea and now we can't even put the kettle on. I haven't got a single five pee left now, because I put them all in there this morning. I don't suppose you've got one, have you?'

'One,' said Nell. 'At least it'll let you boil the kettle. Shall I go and get some change? The fruit shop will still be open.'

'I'll go. I've still got my coat on. You make the tea.'

Nell went back into the sitting room, picked up her book and coffee cup and took a couple of steps towards the kitchen. But something was wrong. She turned round and there was a man standing in the doorway of her bedroom, a tall man with long straggly hair.

'Hello, Nell,' he said.

The face that she never saw, never could see, even in her dreams, was staring at her now. She took a couple of steps backwards, fighting for breath. Then, still clutching the book and the coffee cup, she stumbled out into the hallway and half ran, half fell down the stairs, dropping the cup as she scrabbled at the catch on the front door and tore her fingernail. Next she was on the pavement, screaming for Julie, who had only just crossed the road and now stood staring at Nell in blank disbelief, the terror catching at her too, like some instant contagion.

36

After she'd read the translator's first instalments a second time, and a third, Briony's mind was going round in circles. The document could certainly do with some improvement as evidence: there were no places identified, no names and few identifying details, other than the observation that the Ratman looked liked a rat and had a taste for cracking wrists and lifting eyeballs out of their sockets. And the languages.

It was now even more urgent to find out whether Quin had been issued with a passport in the past couple of years and—more particularly—with a visa for the United States. She picked up the phone and dialled the passport office again.

'What name was it again? Just hold on a minute and I'll see if there's any information yet.'

'It is urgent,' said Briony. 'I made that clear when I put in the search request the day before yesterday *and* when I gave you a reminder call yesterday.'

'Just hang on a minute,' said the girl on the other end, as if Briony had been complaining about a mixed up appointment at the hairdresser's. Briony counted to ten while she waited, but could feel her temper rising. She drew heavily on a piece of scrap paper with her biro and got the thick sticky ink on the ends of her fingers. 'Stupid cheap bloody things,' she said and pitched the biro across into the waste-basket.

'Beg your pardon?' asked the girl, returning to the phone.

'Nothing. What have you found?'

'Nothing yet, I'm afraid. We've been a bit busy with applications. We'll have a look for you next week, all right?'

'Absolutely not,' Briony snapped. 'I need to speak to the head of your department, please.'

'Just a minute. I'll see who I can find.'

Surely Macready never got messed about like this. Briony had had enough of not being taken seriously and was ready to give someone a rocket.

'Hello, can I help you, Miss er—' The voice conjured the image of a hefty male civil servant, the kind you'd see getting his shoes polished in the Burlington Arcade.

'Detective Inspector Williams of the Metropolitan Police. On Wednesday I sent a request for information through to your office, marked high priority. It seems no action has been taken yet. I need the information by the end of this afternoon without fail.'

'I see. Perhaps you could just give us the details again, Inspector Williams.'

She drew a deep breath and exhaled audibly down the phone, before reiterating her request.

'I'd like to know by five this afternoon, please.'

'Well, that may not be possible. We'll do our best, of course.'

'This is a murder inquiry. It's essential we have that information without delay.'

An hour later the phone rang.

'Inspector Williams? Nicholas Trench from the passport office. It seems we may have found a record here. Passport and visa for the United States issued to Mr Mathew Quin of Gresham College residence hall, Russell Square on the 20th of September 1967. Date of birth on the passport is the 20th of May 1946. Would you like copies of the documents dispatched to you?'

'Immediately,' said Briony.

She went and knocked on Macready's door, then Palgrave's. Neither of them was there. Jimmy walked past, carrying a large corkboard. She followed him back to the incident room and watched him awkwardly manoeuvre his way through the door.

'Don't lift a finger or anything, will you?' he said.

Obediently, she took one end of the board. 'Sorry. I'm in a daze. Efficiency of some people just blows your mind, you know? You wouldn't believe how long it took—'

'It's going on the wall over there, see, where I've cleared the space?'

She passed the screws to him one by one and watched as he fixed the board to the wall, grimacing at the last turns of the screwdriver.

'Okay. Ready for the photos. In that envelope and make sure you don't get them out of order. Top one first.'

They were photographs of Walker's latest parcel.

'Know what?' said Jimmy, speaking with a tin tack between his teeth, 'I reckon this Walker or whatever his name is—' he took the tack in his fingers and stabbed it into the board '—has got something like this over at his place, wherever that is.'

'What do you mean?'

'A pin board. I wouldn't be surprised if he keeps pin-up photos of his little achievements, you know? He likes the look of what he does, this one.'

Briony had to force herself to look steadily at the sight of the bloody pink mess that had once been the Reverend Burroughs's tongue.

'What you got to remember, see,' Jimmy paused to capture another tin tack in his teeth, 'is that he keeps the best bits to himself. He sends the eye, then the tongue. The messy bits. But he's got quite a collection of other things. A finger, a kidney, an ear.'

'What makes you think he takes photos?'

'Nothing, really. Just a hunch.'

'Don't try telling Macready that. You'll have to be more specific. Go on—think harder. What makes you think he takes photographs?'

'Obvious. He's a bit of an artist and artists take pictures of their work. He's a collector and photography's a collector's thing, you know. Anyway, what are you doing here at six o'clock of a Friday night?'

'Just had a breakthrough.'

'Oh yeah?'

'Have to tell Macready first. Where is he?'

The phone rang again.

'Inspector Williams? I was hoping you'd still be around. It's the desk here. I've got West End Central on the phone for Palgrave, but he's over in Whitechapel doing interviews. Can you take it? Apparently they need to speak to someone straightaway. It's from one of the radio cars.'

'You can't get Palgrave on the radio?'

'Afraid not.'

As she waited for the call to be transferred, Briony signalled to Jimmy to stay, but he was already on his way out.

'Yes, hello? PC Welland from West End Central. We've got a situation here on which I'm seeking advice from Inspector Palgrave. I understand he isn't available.'

'That's right. This is Inspector Williams. Can I help?'

'Situation is, we were called over to a flat in Collingham Gardens on a report of an intruder. No sign of him when we got there and we haven't found any evidence of a break-and-enter. Occupants of the flat are three young women. Only one of them actually sighted the intruder and this particular young woman, name of Miss Nell Adams, is in a bit of a state. Now one of our female officers has had a chat to her, tried to calm her down and so on, and this officer is of the opinion that the young lady's story is confused and a bit as you might say highly coloured and there's very likely some boyfriend trouble at the bottom of it. Those are the essentials of the situation as we see it here. Now the reason I'm consulting you is, young lady in question mentioned Inspector Palgrave by name. Claims she was interviewed by him last week in connection with a murder inquiry. Said she went to Vine Street on Wednesday and was interviewed on the premises. Would you be able to confirm that?'

'Yes. We did have a witness called Nell Adams come forward this week. Inspector Palgrave was very interested in what she had to tell us. Is she suggesting there's some connection between the intruder and the murder cases we're investigating here?'

'Fact of the matter is, Inspector Williams, that's exactly what she's suggesting. Miss Adams is most insistent that she's in danger and wants to talk to Inspector Palgrave immediately.'

'Where are you? I'll call a car.'

37

'And you're absolutely sure you didn't turn the bath on yourself?' It was the third time the policewoman had asked the question.

'Absolutely.' Nell wanted to scream with frustration, but she was trying hard to get a grip on herself. She could see exactly how things looked to the others. The easiest thing for them all to think—even Julie, who was closest to the situation—was that Nell had come home, switched on the bath and forgotten about it, then got herself into a panic when the electricity cut out and imagined she'd seen the man she was still having nightmares about. In a way, it would be easier for Nell herself to believe that. Then instead of fearing that the murderer was after her, knew where she lived and could get into the flat any time the mood took him, she'd only have to fear she was going nuts. But every nerve in her body protested against that way of looking at it.

She knew the killer was here, in the world, planning his horrors in the privacy of his own mind. Only his victims were as close to him as she was. The woman in the nightmare with her throat cut was trying to tell her story. She couldn't tell it now, but Nell could. This was not about nightmares or delusions or irrational fears or getting over it or learning to live a normal life. It was about what was going to happen next and who it was going to happen to. That was what she knew. When the panic came, it was because the knowledge was getting lost. Because people were trying to get her to suffocate it.

Talking to the policewoman was no good, because all she did was to go around and around over the same questions and answers, trying to pull Nell's story into the version that was easiest to believe. Now they were all sitting there, waiting for this other policewoman to arrive, instead of Inspector Palgrave. It was going to be no good talking to anyone except Inspector Palgrave. Maybe she should just say so.

She could see the twins were upset, especially Julie, who was avoiding her eye now. Rita glanced at her but it was a funny look, as if they'd suddenly become strangers. Nell had grown used to the fault-line that ran through her life, but the shock was new to them, the sense that something had happened that you couldn't control or predict. Maybe they were living with someone who was going crazy. Maybe they were living with someone who was being stalked by a killer.

The constable stood in the corner, tapping the flat end of his pencil against his little black notebook and looking at his watch as if he were timing an egg. No doubt this was all normal and boring to him. At last they heard the front door downstairs.

Inspector Williams didn't look like a policewoman at all. She was tall and a bit gawky and she was carrying too many things. As she came through the door, a bulky leather bag slid from her shoulder and landed against the straps of a tote bag carried over her forearm. A wet raincoat slid from under her other arm as she tried to push the strap back up over her shoulder. The constable picked up the coat and stood holding it as he made the introductions.

'We'll just leave you to it, then,' he concluded. 'We'll be forwarding a copy of our report to Inspector Palgrave first thing on Monday.'

'You haven't called in a soco?'

'No, ma'am. I don't have authority to do that. It's actually not usual in a case like this, as a matter of fact.'

'You've checked all the possible entry points?'

'Yes, ma'am. As I mentioned, none of the doors has been forced. The balcony doors over there have got an inside bolt. Very secure.'

'Fingerprints?'

'No, ma'am. We haven't checked for prints. We didn't actually see it as necessary in a case like—'

'We'll definitely need a soco. Would you radio Vine Street and tell them, when you get back to the car? Thanks, Constable—'

'Welland, ma'am.' He handed back her coat.

The WPC also rose to leave.

'Perhaps I could have a quick word with you outside, Inspector Williams,' she said.

Nell saw the twins exchange glances as, for a minute, the three of them were left in the room together.

'I'm sorry,' she said. 'I'm sorry I've messed things up for you again. Maybe I should go and stay in the youth hostel for a while or something.'

'No,' said Rita. 'We're in this together. I believe you, Nell.'

'So do I,' said Julie.

Inspector Williams came back in, stopping to take a close look at the door handle as she did.

'Do you mind if I have a look around?' she asked.

'Here,' said Rita. 'Let me take your things. Do you want to see in the bedrooms?'

'Yes. But don't touch the door handles.'

Rita looked confused. 'But we already have. At least, we closed the door to Nell's room.'

Inspector Williams turned to Nell.

'So the door was open?'

'Not when I got home. But when I came back into the room,

after I'd been out trying to see what was happening in the bath-room, when I saw the man—my bedroom door was open behind him. I'm sure it was.'

'And you're sure you didn't open it yourself, after you came home.'

'Quite sure. I didn't go in there.'

'You said something was happening in the bathroom.'

Nell told the story all over again, but it felt quite different this time. The inspector took her and Julie out into the hallway and got them to stand exactly where they were standing before.

'You came up the stairs at about what time?' she asked Julie.

'About half past five. I got off work half an hour early. Other-wise Nell would have been here on her own.' Julie shuddered. 'Then what might have happened?'

Inspector Williams paused for a minute, looking intently at Julie, before she resumed the questions. 'Tell me what you saw when you got to the top of the staircase.'

'Lots of steam. And Nell standing by the door of the other flat.'

'Who lives in that flat?'

'John and Karen. They're away for the weekend, Rita says. Karen told her this morning. But we didn't know that.'

'Do they often go away at the weekend?'

'Quite often.'

'So you were standing there. And you saw Nell just where she is now.' Inspector Williams switched the lights off. A narrow strip of window above the stairs let in the last of the daylight, but every-thing was in deep shadow. 'It's ten to eight now, so it's close to sunset. Was it much lighter than this?'

'A bit. But not much, no.'

'And there was steam everywhere. If I move over here—' She walked to the far corner of the hallway. 'Can you see me now?'

'Just,' said Julie. 'I can see a sort of shadow. There was a lot of steam over there. I remember. It must have drifted across and got trapped there. You mean he might have been standing there and we didn't see him?'

'It's possible. There's a lot of condensation on the walls here, so I suspect you're right about the steam drifting to this end of the hall. Nell, what can you see from where you're standing?'

'Not much. But I do remember a great cloud of steam there.'

The inspector walked back across the hall to the open door.

'Then you both went in here? Did you go right into the bathroom?'

'Yes,' said Nell. 'We were looking into the bath. Julie turned the tap and it ran cold. Then we talked for a minute, then Julie went to get some more change for the meter and I went back into the flat.'

'How much money was in the meter?'

'A pound,' said Julie. 'We put a pound's worth in there this morning.'

'Judging from the condensation in here there'll be no fingerprints to spoil,' said Inspector Williams. She turned the tap on full blast.

A torrent of water spurted out and the heater made glugging noises. She turned to Nell. 'Would you adjust the tap to the volume you think it was on when you found it, please.'

'It's hard to say exactly. There was so much steam. From the noise, I'd say it was on pretty hard.' Nell adjusted the tap slightly. 'About there, I should think.'

Inspector Williams put the plug in and looked at her watch. 'How much money would be used up, normally, if you ran one bath?'

'About twenty pee,' said Julie.

The bath filled rapidly. 'Three minutes,' pronounced the Inspector. 'By my arithmetic, if you get five baths for a pound and it takes three minutes to run a bath, you could run the meter out in fifteen minutes. How hot is the water?'

'Boiling,' said Julie. 'Well, nearly.'

'I had the heater on,' said Nell. But that shouldn't have used more than ten pence. We'd have had that left in the meter anyway, before we put the coins in this morning.'

They went back into the sitting room, where Inspector Williams jotted down some notes. She fired off more questions as she wrote.

'Nell, you came home at what time?'

'I got in about ten past five.'

'You put on the heater and the kettle straightaway?'

'Yes.'

'Did you notice what time the electricity went off?'

'Not exactly. Must have been about twenty-five past, I suppose.'

'Julie, you say you were home half an hour early, so you would normally get into the flat at six?'

'Pretty well.'

'Nell, what's your usual time for getting back?'

'Five. But on Wednesday it was later because I went shopping.'

'Rita?'

'I get home at six thirty, except Mondays. I work Saturdays and have Mondays off.'

'And, Rita, you're last to leave in the morning. You lock up. Do you remember bolting the French windows?'

'Yes.'

'What about the other windows? I'd better take a look at the windows in the bedrooms.'

She took a white rubber glove from her handbag and put it on to turn the handles of the bedroom doors. In Nell's room, she immediately took an interest in the skylight.

'Do you leave this open all the time?'

'Yes,' said Nell. 'Otherwise it gets stuffy. It doesn't let the rain in unless the wind's blowing right towards the opening.'

'Okay. I don't want any of you to go into this room until we've checked for forensic evidence.'

'What's that?' asked Julie.

'Fingerprints, footprints, signs of entry, traces of hair or fibre that might have been left, that kind of thing. Now. Nell. This man you saw, have you ever seen him before?'

'Yes. I saw him at the newspaper stall at Leicester Square tube station. This afternoon. I'm sure it was the same man. I think he followed me.'

'You could be right,' said the inspector. She took her glasses off and started to clean them with the end of her scarf. 'Was he carrying anything? A camera bag, anything like that?'

Nell frowned and shook her head. 'Don't think so. But it was his face I was looking at.'

There was a knock on the door.

'Ah,' said Inspector Williams, 'That'll be the soco.'

38

It was Palgrave, with two socos in tow. Briony was torn between feeling suspicious that this was some kind of statement of no confidence in her ability to manage the situation, and feeling gratified that she'd been sent serious back-up. But there was no mistaking the relief on Nell Adams's face as Palgrave shook hands with her.

She left them to talk for a few minutes while she briefed the Socos on the intruder's movements and went over possible entry and exit points. The skylight in Nell Adams's room became an immediate focus. The bathroom was less promising, but one of the officers perked up as he looked closely at the tap.

'Hello! What we got here? Biro ink!'

'Yes,' said Briony. 'I'm afraid that's me.' She held up the offending fingers. 'I assumed there was too much condensation on there for prints, anyway.'

'Unless of course he had biro ink on his fingers, which would have been very considerate of him.'

'I'm glad I've left my mark on something to do with this case. I'll let you get on with it, then.'

She went into the hallway and met Palgrave coming out of the flat.

'So,' he said. 'We've had a visit from our friend, have we?'

'Seems like it.'

'Sooner or later they start taking risks. That's when you catch them.'

'But what are we going to do about these girls? They'll need police protection. He's obviously been following Nell Adams. She's the one at risk. Can we get her into some kind of secure accommodation for a while?'

'What you got in mind, Williams? Pentonville Jail? There's no easy answer to this. What is it that makes you think he's following her?'

'Well, circumstantially, he couldn't have worked his little practical joke without knowing the lay-out of the flat and the regular patterns of coming and going from it. But I can do better than circumstantial. She spotted him at Leicester Square tube station.'

'I see. But we're still on shaky ground connecting this incident with our case,' said Palgrave.

'What about showing her the Identikit of Quin?'

'There's no explicit connection yet between Quin and these murders. I'd rather get the Identikit team to build up another picture from her description. Then we can compare them. It's more objective.'

'I suppose so.'

'That can be done tomorrow morning. I'll arrange for a car to keep this place under observation overnight.'

'He's going to know we'll put the place under surveillance.'

'If he does, that's all to the good. It'll discourage him from trying to pay any more visits.'

'Or it'll encourage him to study the net and slip through it.' Briony moved to make way for one of the Socos, who went across to the corner where she guessed Walker had been standing and began scraping at the carpet with a steel comb.

'Thing is,' she said, 'I don't think the officers from West End

Central were taking this seriously at all. When they rang up in the first place to ask me to come here, they described her as a confused young lady who probably had boyfriend trouble. Wanted to give her a sedative and get on to the next call. No police officer would authorise an expensive protection program on the basis of the story she's told us, not without the benefit of the background we've got on her possible involvement with the suspect. Unless Walker's aware that she's already known to the Vine Street team, he's probably banking on the assumption that she won't be able to interest the police in looking after her. But how much can we bank on that?'

'Come again?' Palgrave's forehead was creased every which way and he stuck his finger in his ear.

'I mean, it's a gamble we're talking about, isn't it? He thinks that we think, so we think that he thinks. If he thinks there's no protection for her—or he figures out what the regime is and how to get around it—he's going to come after her again. And, in a way, that's exactly what we want because that's how we can catch him. So what we do is, we put a dummy surveillance system in place—like a patrol car that checks every half hour. Then we anticipate he'll work around that, and we're ready for him, with a team planted here in the flat all the time.'

'Softly, softly eh? Do we enlist the secret service in this plan of yours? How long do you propose to keep it up for? Can't be done, Williams. It's too complicated.'

'Why?'

'Best answer to that question is a few years experience in uniform. You learn not to take long shots. They have a habit of going astray and tying up all your resources when you need them somewhere else in a hurry. Now we need to go in there and make an arrangement.'

Rita was drying Nell's hair with a bright purple hair dryer. She switched it off when they came back into the room.

'Sorry to keep you waiting,' said Palgrave. 'We just needed to organise a couple of things. I'll arrange for an officer to be stationed outside on the landing there overnight, all right? So you can have some peace of mind and a good night's sleep. In the morning, Miss Adams, we'd like you to come in to the station to do some identification work with us. You're welcome to bring your cousins with you for moral support. Would you like us to send a car?'

'What, a police car?' Julie was literally open mouthed.

'It'll be here at ten. Now where are those forensics boys?'

Palgrave opened the door to Nell's bedroom, from which loud scraping noises had been coming.

'Whoa!' he called. 'Stop a minute, will you? Now how long you going to be?'

'Another five. You want me to secure this skylight before I finish in here?'

'That's a very good idea,' said Palgrave. 'All right, ladies, we'll be off now and these boys will leave you in peace in another five minutes. You have a good night's sleep, eh?'

On the way downstairs, Briony asked Palgrave about Macready. 'Where is he, d'you know? There's something I need to show him. Urgently.'

'I'll tell him about this, first thing tomorrow.'

'No, something else.'

'Things moving thick and fast, eh? He's been over in Whitechapel all day. I'll tell him you need to talk to him. Shall I say what it's about?'

'A document we've come across in connection with the Hanging Gardens case—actually mentions Walker by name.'

'Does it, now? Sounds promising. Have you told Latham about it?'

'He's got his own copy. I'm assuming he's read it by now.'

Briony went home and lay in the bath. Her bones felt greedy for the kind of warmth you could only get from deep hot water. Poor Nell, she thought. She's never going to feel safe in that bath now.

Or at least, not until Quin is safely locked up.

His turn would come. It'd gone his way for too long. The face of the seventeen-year-old floated in front of her. What was he thinking about, then? A boy hardly out of his childhood, going to university to learn how to be a doctor. Did part of him, once, really want to be a healer? Does part of every doctor want to be a killer? Turn turn turn. It made her dizzy to think about it, as she hauled herself up and out into the cold air. Damn. Forgot to go and collect the results of those blood tests. A strange pulse throbbed in her neck, and something lurched suddenly inside her head. Damn. She grabbed at one of the towels on the rail as she slumped down across the wet tiled floor, her head hitting the edge of the basin as she went.

39

The patients were planted there on their trolley beds as if suspended in time, while the nurses moved around them at the double, their wide shoes squeaking on the floor, trolleys rattling in front of them.

Briony's whole day had been spent waiting. After waiting half an hour to see her GP this morning, she had been sent to St Pancras Hospital to be x-rayed for mild concussion. There was a two hour wait for the x-ray, which was followed by forty minutes wait to see the doctor who was supposed to be monitoring her case. He said he'd like to keep her under observation and would see her again on his next round. She was brought lunch on a tray—orange squash and shepherd's pie with peas—and a large pile of tatty magazines, each of which took her at most two minutes to read. Passing nurses did various things to her: stuck a thermometer in her mouth; put a needle in her arm and drew out a syringe of blood; took her pulse; looked into her eyes with a torch; got her to blow into a cardboard tube; weighed her.

'When will I be able to go?' she asked every time one of the nurses came within range.

'Shouldn't be too long,' was always the answer. But when they had questions for her, they went for it. They had whole sheets of them, attached to clipboards. By the middle of the afternoon they knew everything from her address and date of birth to the date of her last menstrual period, what she'd eaten since breakfast the day before yesterday and what time she usually got up in the morning.

An oversized clock on the wall opposite marked the passing of every minute with a jerky shift of its long hand and, by four thirty, she'd had as much as she could stand. It was no easy matter getting off the trolley, as it was at least a foot higher off the ground than any ordinary bed, so you were supposed to call for a nurse to help you down if you needed to go to the loo. That meant, of course, they knew exactly who was going where when. The Met could learn a few tricks from St Pancras Hospital, Briony thought. Cross-questioning, identification, detention, psychological control. She swung her legs out and jumped to the floor. No she was *not* dizzy. Absolutely not. She set off at a brisk pace towards a door marked with an exit sign and met a nurse coming through it, pushing a trolley laden with steel implements and white cloths.

'Toilets are that way.' The nurse pointed to the double doors at the other end of the ward.

'I know. I'm just going for a stroll.'

'Not here, you're not. This is a staff-only section.'

'It says it's the exit.'

'That's an old sign.'

'Can't I even go for a walk?'

'Ask the doctor when he comes round. He'll tell you if it's all right.'

'I've been waiting for him for two hours. I feel fine. I'd like to go now, please.'

'Can't go until you've been signed out.' The nurse, whose blonde hair was swept back under an armoured cap welded with pure starch, stood her ground like a seasoned commandant. Briony tried to outstare her and lost.

'I can discharge myself. That's my legal right.'

'I wouldn't advise it. If you do that, you may be refused treatment next time. I'll get the ward sister to come and talk to you.'

Briony went back to bed, feeling about seven years old, and promptly fell asleep.

When she woke up, there was a subtle change in the light. Not that daylight was detectable in the mix before, but the strips of high window were now black and the fluorescent glow was more yellow than white. She smelt food, heard trolleys moving around and felt suddenly very hungry.

A tray was placed on the bridge-like structure over her bed, which was then wheeled up under her nose. Tomato soup, two slices of buttered white bread and a wedge of apple pie. The elderly woman in the next bed looked over and made a face.

'Not even any custard,' she said. 'You'd think they'd give you custard, wouldn't you? This National Health Service is a disgrace.' She began to spoon the tomato soup into a tiny, lipless mouth.

'Do you come here often?' asked Briony.

'Too bloody often. Gets me down, I'll tell you. High blood pressure. It's the bane of my life.'

'Mine's supposed to be too low. Funny, that.'

They drank their soup in synchronised rotations: spoon to bowl, spoon to mouth.

'Not too bad, though,' said the woman as she tipped her bowl to extract the last teaspoon's worth. 'Low blood pressure's not such a bad thing. I'd much rather have low than high. But you're young, see. It's not so bad when you're young. He's a nice doctor, don't you think, Dr Mills? You were asleep when he come round. Fast asleep, you were.'

Shit, Briony thought. Sugar and shit. She'd missed the warder's rounds and now she was going to be stuck in here overnight. Discharging herself might be the only option. Maybe she could get Macready to give her a character reference: desertion on grounds of dedication to duty. When a nurse came to collect her tray, she asked to see the ward sister.

'The ward sister won't be back till seven in the morning,' she was told. 'You can speak to the matron on night duty when she comes through, about a quarter to nine.'

The matron on night duty was a slow moving, bulky African woman. She cruised majestically up to the side of Briony's bed and looked at her for a while before speaking.

'You asking to see the night matron?'

'Yes. I'd like to go, please.'

There was no readable expression on the matron's face. She took a measured walk to the end of the bed, collected the clipboard that was attached there, and returned to Briony's side.

'Got to get back to work, have you?' she asked.

'Yes. I'm involved in an urgent case.'

'You're going to be involved in an urgent case if you go on the way you are, that's for sure. I'll read you the report, shall I?'

Briony nodded.

'That a yes, is it?'

'Yes. Yes, please.'

'What it says here: Miss Briony Williams, aged twenty-nine. Miss Williams is essentially a healthy young woman, whose only clinically significant problem is anaemia, probably attributable to a short menstrual cycle and heavy periods. The condition is exacerbated by a poor diet, irregular sleeping habits and chronic overwork. Her haemoglobin count is at present thirty per cent below normal. In moments of stress, this may lead to hypoxaemic respiratory failure, associated with hypertension. You want me to translate this for you, Miss Williams?'

'No. I think I get the message.'

'I'm sure you do. But what you going to do about it? That's the point. I'm not interested in keeping you here in the ward against your will. We need the beds for other patients. But if you go now, how soon will it be before we see you back here again? That's the point. You don't seem to have a lot of common sense about your health. You only get one body, you know. You need to show it some respect. You understand what I'm saying now?'

Briony stared at her hands, clasped in front of her on the colourless blanket.

'I can't help the work,' she said. 'It's a kind of emergency.'

'You think you's the only one dealing with emergencies, ma'am? Every night here we get car crashes, stabbings, cardiac arrests, little children suffering from third degree burns. You see me fadin' away here? I look after myself so I can look after other people. It's a basic responsibility. You understand what I'm saying?'

She put a thermometer in Briony's mouth and took hold of her wrist.

'Very well now. Pulse returnin' to normal. Anaemia related to menstruation's very common you know. You on the pill?'

Briony shook her head.

'No time for leisure activities, eh? Going on the pill sometimes helps with your sort of condition. There's a family planning clinic attached to the hospital. Opens Saturday afternoons, so you just missed it. But you could ask the doctor for a prescription when you see him in the morning.' She took the thermometer out and shook it. 'Temperature's just fine. Time to put on a happy face.' Suddenly the matron beamed. 'Happy face. See the difference?'

Briony laughed. The matron wrote something on the record sheet, then studied her patient again for a minute.

'You look a lot better when you smile, you know that? What kind of emergency work you do?'

'Police work.'

She nodded slowly. 'You can leave in the morning, after you've seen the doctor.'

40

Neither Inspector Williams nor Inspector Palgrave was at the station when the girls arrived. When Nell asked for them, she was told Inspector Williams was sick and Inspector Palgrave had gone to Plymouth, so she was left with a new person—a young male detective, who didn't seem to be taking her story all that seriously. Although the forensics officers had found signs that someone had climbed out through the skylight in her bedroom, Inspector Latham obviously wasn't convinced it was the same man who was wanted for the murders and the twins were very ready to be influenced by his suggestion that the intruder might have just been some crank, some drugged-up hippy who'd spotted Nell in the crowd and liked the look of her. Inspector Latham seemed to be impressed with Rita and she was flirting away with him, as Nell was led out to talk to the Identikit team.

She puzzled over the two pictures they had assembled. One of them might have looked like the face she'd seen, in a way, but then again it didn't really look like anyone. It was just a drawing. She was still confused by all the dozens of sets of eyes, noses, eyebrows, mouths and chins she'd had to go through. The face that resulted was a mix-and-match. She couldn't see it as a whole. And it didn't look like the other face at all. The eyes were different.

No. The man wasn't here. He was slipping away again and where did that leave her and the twins?

Tonight they would be on their own in the flat again, with only the promise of a visit from the patrol car when she got home from work on Monday—to 'reassure' her, Inspector Latham had said. A bloody great padlock had been put on the skylight, but that wasn't much comfort either.

Julie suggested they go to see *Ryan's Daughter* in the afternoon, to take their minds off their troubles. For Nell, it didn't quite work that way. The story took you to another place, another time, but it was full of tensions that played on those she was trying to cope with herself and the music surged through her, drawing up feelings she'd rather not have had right now, so that by halfway through, she felt she just couldn't sit there any longer. Julie and Rita seemed completely absorbed in the film and if she left, they'd insist on going with her. She began to feel trapped as she watched Sarah Miles in a wisp of white nightdress, running across the hills in the dark to meet her lover.

'Got to go to the loo,' she whispered to Julie. She edged her way along the row, whispering 'sorry—sorry—sorry' to all the people who had to gather up handbags and twist their knees to the side to let her past. As she came out into the aisle, the light reflected from the screen brightened and flickered so she could see for a second where she was going. A few rows further up, someone else had made their way out from the seating bank and was heading for the exit sign at the back, a tall man in a short coat. As she got nearer, she saw he'd stopped to hold the curtain aside for her. No, said a voice in her head.

She turned back towards the screen, which was now filled with raging waves. Wind howled, water crashed and sprayed, voices called out in desperation. Something was going to happen. Something

terrible. Nell spotted another exit sign on the other side of the audi-
torium and shot towards it and out into the glaring daylight before
she had time to think. She'd emerged behind the cinema, which rose
as a great blank wall right along the narrow street. Run, said a voice
in her head.

Her lungs were pumping hard already, as if trying to force her
into a headlong dash regardless of direction. At the corner of the
building to her right, she thought she saw someone, a tall figure
with an arm raised, as if waving. She ran the other way, then left at
the next corner, where Eros appeared on the skyline, flying high over
his island in the midst of the traffic that streamed past. Nell dodged
a bus and two taxis to cut across at the next junction as she bolted
down towards Trafalgar Square. When she turned at the end of the
street, Nelson's Column rose up ahead of her with its great black
lions forever on guard.

It was harder to cross the road this time. There were three lanes
of traffic, all flowing fast. A slow moving bus gave her the opportunity to scoot through a gap in the first lane, and in the second
she forced a car to a screeching halt, before nearly colliding with a
motorcyclist in the third. People standing at the bus stop on the
Trafalgar Square side of the road stared at her and a couple of them
yelled out. An elderly man in a hat actually left the queue and came
towards her, yelling. 'What do you think you're doing, you silly cow?'

But Nell was back up to full speed now, running towards the St
Martin's Church end of the Square, where there were wide steps
leading down through the pigeons.

The birds were milling in all directions, but they seemed to have
a good advance warning system, and as Nell came hurtling down
the steps, a bevy of them took flight and landed above her on the
backs of the lions. There were plenty of people here, too. A group
of student travellers with backpacks were taking photographs; some
children were feeding bread to the pigeons while their mothers sat
near by, chatting; there were people meandering across the square

in all directions, in twos or singly. Heads turned at the sound of Nell running, but the attention lapsed when she drew to a halt, her lungs heaving painfully. 'Stitch,' she muttered to herself, clutching her side and leaning heavily on the low stone wall by the fountains. Lions on their great pedestals sat either side of her.

Okay, she thought, he can't get me here. If he comes, I can see him but he can't do anything. The pigeons converged again, several coming up to peck the ground around her hands. She wished she had something to give them. It was amazing that birds could be so tame. Suddenly, one of them fluttered, took off, and landed on her head. Its sharp claws pierced the fabric of her beret and lodged in her hair.

'Ow,' she protested, putting a hand up to try and brush it off.

'Wait. Wait. Don't move,' said one of the backpackers, his camera raised at the ready. Then there were five, six of his friends around her, all snapping away.

Nell felt embarrassed, confused, awkward. Her lungs were still hurting when she breathed and every nerve in her body was on the alert for a pursuer. Eventually, the bird itself had had enough of the attention and took off again.

'Sorry,' said the first backpacker. 'Hope you don't mind. It was just such an opportunity, you know. I seen them land on people's heads before, but on the red hat—it's like it was deliberately posing.'

Nell pulled off her beret and swung it between her fingers.

'I think I'd better go,' she said.

'Why? Look, we didn't mean to drive you away. We're going now, anyway. You can have the fountain to yourself.'

She looked around the square and couldn't see anyone like the man she was running from. But an idea was forming in her mind.

'Where did you buy the camera?' she asked.

'Germany. Why?'

'Are they very expensive?'

'What, cameras in general? Silly question. Anywhere between five quid and five hundred. You want to buy one?'

'I'm thinking of it.'

'Why don't you just go to Boots over the road there? You can get quite a good cheap camera from them.'

'Thanks. I might try there.' She got up. 'See ya.'

As she set off back up the steps, there was still no sign of the man who'd been following her. She was beginning to worry more now about what Julie and Rita were doing. They might have come looking for her.

When she got back to the cinema, she found them in the foyer talking to a man in a suit.

'There you are,' shrieked Julie. 'Where on earth have you been? We've been having kaniptions here.'

'So this is your cousin, is it?' said the man in the suit. 'You want to let your friends know where you're going before you disappear, you know. These young ladies have been very worried about you.'

'I'm sorry.' Nell really meant it. 'I only meant to go out for a couple of minutes. I was feeling claustrophobic. But then I got— it's a bit hard to explain. Can I tell you later?'

'You can tell us over a cup of tea,' said Rita. 'There's a Lyons over the road.'

41

The first thing waiting for Briony on her return to work was the package with copies of the second part of Sabina's journal. A note from the translator warned that some of the words were illegible, because the handwriting was deteriorating and the pen also seemed to be missing letters.

> It's the middle of the day. When I got back to the tent I found someone has been in here, going through all our stuff. They've torn pages out of my diary. From now on I'm keeping this with me all the time.

> We're leaving here, as soon as we've found Midge. Please God we find Midge. Please God. A voice in my head has been saying that all day and all night. Pascal is going to search in the swamp, while Agate and I go back up on the dunes again. We've already been looking since sunrise and if I close my eyes I see sand and even when I walk on hard ground my feet seem to be sinking, but we can't stop looking as long as there's daylight.

(illegible) ... I've got sand in this pen ... (illegible) ...
try again. I want to make a record of this. We've been
finding orange pips, even where the wind has taken the
footprints away. But we can't be sure these are a trail ...
(illegible)

... thought I had lost Agate. I don't often go this
far out, so I don't know the landscape here. I get
confused easily. We whistle to each other because our
voices have got hoarse, but it's whistling down the wind.
Round and round goes the wind. Once I heard a
piercing whistle that seemed nearby. When I ran in the
direction it came from, I heard calling behind me. It
was Agate, far away in the other direction. We decided
to stay together now, because the sun is low and the
dunes are already throwing shadows. The wind is
driving us crazy.

We have found what we think are drops of blood ...
(illegible)

The torch will not last much longer, so if we do not
go back soon we will be lost ourselves, at least till
morning.

Pascal has come. He went right into the army base and
told them we needed help to search for a missing child.
They are starting a helicopter search. (illegible) They have
given Pascal some signal lights so he can indicate to
them where we are. I have not (illegible) ... any of them
to ... (illegible) of it.

(Translator's note: The rest of this page is blank. The handwriting improves on the next page, and is in a different pen.
The last few entries have dates.)

27th August 1970

For months I haven't known the date. I didn't even care what year it was. But hey, hello world. I even bought a newspaper this morning.

Waltraud has gone to a refuge with the little kids. She wouldn't even talk to me. I guess they all think we sold them out to the cops, because it was us who got the army in to look for Midge. When the cops interviewed us we told them everything, everything we could think of. I said I was sure the Ratman did it.

Hayley is in rehab so I am looking after Midge, who's starting to get over it now but he still wakes up in the night screaming. Who knows what he went through. The shrink says he'll tell in his own time. I wake up in the night too, when in my dream I see him there, half burrowed into the sand, too scared even to cry, with Neb's blood sprayed across his face. And Neb. Neb with his throat gaping open and a great black stain beneath his head and a black hole where his stomach was. Neb with his eyes wide open, staring at the dead sky, and all around him the writing in the sand.

20th August

The Haight has changed a lot. I remember when I first walked up there and went out on the Panhandle, the flower children were like angels in a new world. The whole place sang. You didn't need drugs to be flying. People sat on the grass and when it rained they turned their faces up to bathe in it. Now they huddle at the edge of the sidewalk and when it rains they pull sheets of black plastic over their heads. The flower children are shooting up and their faces look grey and everyone wants to talk about Charlie Manson and the Family.

Haight-Ashbury is a poor sick place. Hashbury-Trashbury they call it. When Hayley is straightened out we're going. Sometimes I think about the writing in the sand. Or, I don't think about it, it gets in my thoughts and sticks there. A time to love, a time to hate. A time to live, a time to die. A time to heal, a time to kill. The last one's supposed to be the other way around, Pascal says, the healing comes after. But not for the Ratman.

3rd September

I went to see Erien today. He is so fucked up. I just sat there and cried. He and the Ratman have been charged for possession of smack, and Erien's up for dodging the draft as well. They charged the Ratman with murder but they need more evidence to get it to stick in court. They tried to get a story out of Midge but it shook the poor kid up so much asking him about it that the shrink told them they had to give up. And no one can get anything out of the Rat, not even his name. We were told that since he was arrested, he's not said a single word.

4th September

There's been no sign of the rest of Walker's people. It's as if they'd vanished off the face of the earth. I've asked around a bit, but no one seems to even have heard of them.

Today I asked Pascal, 'Do you think the Ratman is Walker?'

He shook his head.

'Then who is Walker?'

Pascal stared at me in a funny way.

'Why would you even want to know?'

'I want to know because he's dangerous. He could be out there stirring up more of this…'

'This what?'

'Evil.'

'Evil? That's everywhere. Just look around you. Yesterday I saw a girl dead in the street, from an overdose. Hardly more than a kid. Know what I think about Walker? He's nobody. Doesn't exist. A spook. A legend to make crackheads think they're going somewhere because someone—or something—is leading them on. It's paranoid, that's all. A mind fuck.'

5th September
I'm glad Erien is safe in jail, because the Rat has got out. I am trying to get Hayley released from the clinic so we can leave. Pascal has already gone, and he hasn't even told me where he's heading. He's the one the Rat will come after first.

8th September
Every night I take Midge to a different place to sleep. There's still plenty of places in Haight-Ashbury where you can doss. I changed my clothes, too, and last night Gretel—one of the Diggers, who let us sleep on her floor—cut my hair for me. But I'd still be easy to recognise when I'm with Midge. The Rat may be looking out for us when we go to see Hayley, but we have to go. Tomorrow. I can't stand this any longer.

9th September
We talked to the counsellor at the rehab centre. She says she can find Hayley and Midge a place at a women's refuge centre in LA, but I won't be able to be with them.

So Midge has stayed with Hayley and they are being transferred tomorrow and here I am back on Gretel's floor trying to explain why I can't stop crying all the time, without telling the story. Gretel knows someone who can get me a flight to London half price, and I have written to my lousy brother to ask him to send the fare. Maybe, just maybe, he will do that.

42

Briony found Steve Latham going through some papers. She held
up the package. 'You seen this?'

'Yup.' He gave her a searching look. 'Heard you were ill again.
You okay now?'

'Fine.'

'No more fainting fits, I hope?'

'They weren't "fits". I said I'm fine. Has Macready read this stuff?
Has anyone started chasing up the Walker connection?'

'Yeah, sort of. But don't get too excited. Macready had a couple
of phone conversations with the San Francisco police. They don't
bite on Walker's people—say there were literally hundreds of small-
time cults or sects around the area in the late sixties.'

'Don't tell me anyone's going to try and dismiss this as a
coincidence.'

'No,' said Steve, 'but it's no God-given case cracker either. If
there is an American episode in this, it's going to be hard to make
any headway on it and nothing's going to happen in a hurry. Cops
over there say it will take a week at least to find the post-mortem
reports on the murder in the San Joaquin Valley. All they've got

immediately is a report that says the principal suspect escaped from custody.'

'Great. Do they have a name for this guy?'

'Nope. Like Sabina tells us. He refused to speak.'

'Well, that's just brilliant.'

'All right, don't get narky. Seen these?' He showed her the two Identikit drawings. 'This one's Nell Adams's pick and mix. Not much resemblance to the one based on your photo, is there?'

'It's not *my* photo. Anyway, the photo we want is the one on his visa. Have we got that yet?'

By way of an answer, Steve brought over two small photos and the Identikit image.

'Okay. So this is Quin at seventeen, on his way into college. And this is Quin aged twenty-one, on his way out of college and off to America. And this is Nell Adams's attempt at the jigsaw puzzle. Oscar Wilde's eyes. Anyone would pick them a mile off. Now you see them.' He pointed to the first and second pictures of Quin. 'Now you don't.' He handed her the Identikit.

'I don't think those things are reliable, anyway. Where's Palgrave?'

'Long story. He went to Plymouth on Saturday morning—drove down with a couple of the DCs, to do some interviews and chase up Quin's relatives. And of course he's going to go through the police files on the train murder. Can't rely on the stuff they've sent us. It's full of holes. To start with, there's almost nothing about the victim. Trouble is, Saturday afternoon we hear on the radio there's a force eight gale across the south-west. He rang here about four to say they'd arrived okay, but the storm got worse overnight and by yesterday morning most of the roads were flooded. So he hasn't got his interviews done and he can't get back till the motorway clears. Haven't heard from him this morning, but the papers are full of pictures of the flooding. Macready's spinning out about it. Palgrave's like his right arm.'

'So who talked to Nell Adams on Saturday?'

'I did. Think you're barking up the wrong tree, Briony. I don't think the intruder was our man. There's nothing to connect him.'

'Nell's the connection.'

'Remote possibility. Anyway, I've made sure the patrol will keep an eye on her.'

'What does that mean?'

'They'll be there when she gets home from work tonight.'

'That's useless. Look, you know what Walker's like. You know how he followed Caroline Staines. It's the same pattern. Nell Adams is at risk.'

'Don't get emotional about this, Briony. Macready asked me to assess the situation and my assessment is that the risk's low. Like I said, there's nothing to connect her with Walker.'

'But there is—she found a murder victim on a train out from Plymouth.'

'We can't hold Walker responsible for every murder west of Exeter.' He held up a hand as if to stop her interrupting him. 'I'm not discounting the risk. But it's low. We can reconsider if new evidence comes up.' He looked at his watch. 'Gotta go. I've arranged some interviews.'

'With who?'

'People from Oldroyd's list of the lodge rejects. Haven't been able to contact all of them, but I've got three of them booked in for this morning.'

'Is one of them Guy Waterlow, by any chance?'

'Yeah. You know something about him?'

'Donna got introduced to him last week, as a matter of fact—remember I was worried about her going on that date? Man she went out with introduced her to Waterlow. It was all a set-up. She doesn't know that, though. Do you mind keeping it quiet?'

'Guess not. So what did she learn about Waterlow?'

'That he knows Quin—or did. I'd like to be in on your interview, if it's okay. It could be important.'

'Don't see why not. He finishes his shift at Bartholomew's Hospital at twelve, so I'm meeting him there. I'm talking to Kevin Battersby and James Johnson first. They're in general practice in Guildford Street.'

Battersby and Johnson were both men who looked thoroughly settled in their profession. The main office of the practice, with its polished wood desk and chintz seated chairs, showed no trace of influence from the changing world outside. Johnson, who was balding gently, wore a brown tweedy looking suit. Battersby's slight paunch rather spoiled the effect of a pale sports jacket and bright red tie.

She let Steve make the running with the interview and didn't notice any signs of tension as he got to the matter of their expulsion from the lodge. Battersby responded to the question with an awkward chuckle and opened a tin of miniature cigars, which he offered to Steve.

'Yes, I was a bit of tearaway. Weakness for the horses, you know. Gambled away half the family silver before I was twenty-one, then started failing exams. The Masons did me a favour, really, throwing me out. It woke me up a bit—got me to start pulling myself together just in time to complete my degree and here I am.' He lit the two cigars, and blew a column of woody smoke towards the ceiling. 'Johnson doesn't smoke, do you, man? Go on, your turn to tell them about your vices.'

Johnson beamed widely. 'Wrong sense of humour,' he said. 'Couldn't help it—I found all those rituals side-splitting. Tried to control myself, but it only made things worse. Disgraced myself by suddenly snorting like a rhinoceros in the middle of an initiation ceremony and the Grand Master called me in the next day to give me my marching orders. Quite right, too. Shouldn't have joined in the first place, but I had an uncle who took a lot of trouble to get me in. Convinced me it was an essential career move. Bit of an embarrassment for him, of course, when I botched it up. Never

mind, he hasn't cut me off his Christmas card list. Not yet, anyway.'
He winked at Briony.

'And you and Dr Battersby were both expelled in the same year,
is that right?'

Johnson nodded. '1960. Sort of threw us into each other's
company.'

'After you left the Masons, was either of you approached by an
organisation known as the Invisible College?'

Johnson demonstrated the rhinoceros snort.

'What a hoot, eh? *Boys' Own* stuff. They sounded us out, but I
think we were too dull for them. They liked to think of themselves
as a bit adventurous. Rather glad they steered clear of us, actually.
Sticky organisation to get out of, I've heard.'

'What exactly *have* you heard, Dr Johnson?'

'There was a bit of gossip around. Stories about chaps who'd
wanted to leave and been threatened. Chaps who'd been involved
in shady goings-on, then blackmailed. All highly imaginative, no
doubt, but I'm sure we were lucky not to have got involved. It did
get a bit nasty a few years ago, when a couple of them were pushing drugs.'

'Do you happen to know who they were, Dr Johnson?'

'Quin was one of them.'

'Was he a member of the Invisibles?'

'Come to think of it, I couldn't say. I assumed he was because
he was always in company with—who was that other one, eh Battersby? Oh damn, now, what was his name? Tall chap. Fancies
himself. Still see him around occasionally. He's gone very straight
now, of course. Used to be a fully-fledged hippy.'

'Waterlow,' said Battersby, looking as if he'd just won a raffle.

'That's it! Waterlow.'

Steve didn't find the double act amusing. 'Can you tell us any
more about either of these men?'

Johnson looked at Battersby, then picked up the cue himself.

'Well—Quin—never knew him personally. He's a good five years younger than me, so we never coincided as undergraduates. He's no longer around. Took himself off down the hippy trail—went abroad somewhere.'

'And Waterlow?'

'Wouldn't trust him. Smart arse, not to put too fine a point on it. He's oh so respectable these days. Aiming for the Royal College of Surgeons, I should think.'

'Do you know why he and Quin were expelled from the lodge?'

'Drugs, is my guess,' said Battersby. 'But now wait a minute—' He turned to Johnson. 'Wasn't there someone else? Another of those hippy types from the college, that they used to hang around with? Damn me if I can remember his name. Possibly I never actually knew his name; scrawny looking character.'

'Maxwell Tremlay,' said Johnson.

'That's right, that's him. Gave me the creeps.'

'Thank you,' said Steve.

'You've been very helpful,' said Briony.

•

The main waiting room at Bartholomew's Hospital wasn't a very cheerful place to sit, especially after Briony's experience at the weekend. Steve was not in a talkative mood and there was no point in picking up any of the magazines, because during Saturday she must have already flicked through every one that had been published in the past two years.

When Waterlow finally emerged, at twenty past twelve, he was still wearing his surgeon's gown. He showed them into a small office separated from the main area by a glass panel and left them again while he went to change. Steve sat uncharacteristically silent.

'Can I lead off with this one?' Briony asked. 'I think I've got an idea about how to approach him.'

'Feel free,' he said.

Guy Waterlow was six foot two with model bone structure and

wavy brown hair, and he reappeared dressed like a Jaeger model. Money, thought Briony. He's dripping with it. She was willing to bet there was a new sports car outside in the hospital parking lot. He smiled like someone who was used to making an impact and he held Briony's hand just a second or two longer than necessary as she introduced herself.

As she went through her first set of questions about himself and his connections with Gresham College, his answers were easy and fluent and gave the impression that he liked the sound of his own unusually deep voice. It wasn't until ten minutes into the interview that he showed any signs of tension, when Briony moved to a more pointed line of questioning.

'Dr Waterlow, is it correct that you were excluded from the Freemasons' lodge?'

He gave Briony a searching look. Perhaps he'd twigged already that she'd been talking to Donna, or on the other hand, maybe that was just what he'd intended.

'Yes, I was. There was a disagreement on a medical matter.'

'Would you mind elaborating?'

'The lodge was opposed to the contraceptive pill when it was first introduced. I was strongly in favour of it. I made my views known.'

'You're an ear nose and throat specialist, Dr Waterlow. Is that right?'

'Training to be one.'

'Does your work involve prescribing the pill?'

'Not really, no. No, I can't say it does.'

'So your views on it didn't arise from any professional interest?'

'Yes, they did, in a more general sense. There is a range of health and welfare issues associated with use of the contraceptive pill. I think it helps prevent a lot of serious problems—abortions, unwanted children, complicated births in older women.'

'That sounds reasonable. Were the Freemasons so unreasonable that they threw you out for holding views like that?'

Waterlow shifted in his seat.

'As I said, the members of that lodge were extremely conservative.'

'The Invisible College was not as conservative?' Briony looked him in the eye and smiled. Waterlow flashed a fine set of teeth in response.

'The Invisibles were a very different kettle of fish.'

'Go on.'

'We were all rather young—in our early twenties. We got a bit wild sometimes.'

'Was Mathew Quin a member?'

This question produced a theatrical frown. 'I think so. If I remember rightly.'

You're lying now, thought Briony. She decided to lead him on.

'So you didn't know him well?'

A large hand swept through the abundant hair.

'I knew of him.'

'What did you know?'

'Not much. He just had a bad reputation.'

'What for?'

'Drugs. A violent temper. He was too young to be doing a medical degree and used to get out of hand.'

'Did you see evidence of this?'

'Once or twice. It's my opinion that he was seriously disturbed.'

'Disturbed enough to commit murder?'

'I really couldn't say.'

'Have you seen him in the last twelve months?'

'No.'

Steve was starting to fidget now and Briony could sense he was going to cut in at any moment. She tried one last shot.

'Did you or anyone you know have cause to be afraid of Mathew Quin?'

'Some people may have been. His behaviour was at times deranged. He could get violently excited and impulsive. He bore grudges.'

Here Steve did cut in, looking at his notes. 'When did you join the Invisible College?' he asked.

'1966.'

'Tell me why you joined. What attracted you to this organisation?'

'It's an organisation with a long history, as I've said. In the past, it's had some distinguished members. It has fostered experimental science and a generally innovative attitude to life. At times that may have gone a bit too far, but it created a sense of excitement. As a scientist, I knew the need for experiment and as a student I was drawn to this excitement. In the past couple of years, though, some of us have been trying to calm things down a bit, to make the Invisibles a more mature and professional association. I suppose you could say we've grown up.' Waterlow flashed another smile.

That speech was prepared, Briony thought.

'Can you give an example of the kinds of experiment going on in 1966?' asked Steve.

There was obviously no ready answer for this one. The words fell over each other on the way out.

'Well, of course it included all kinds of scientific experiment. We discussed the work we'd done in the lab, surgical techniques and equipment, new theories, that kind of thing.'

'Hardly on the wild side,' said Steve in a monotone. 'Nothing a bit more way out? Drugs, for example?'

'There was a bit of experiment of that sort. A kind of madness got into the student community around that time. I wouldn't say we were immune to it.'

'Exactly what form did this madness take in the Invisible College, Dr Waterlow?' Steve was leaning forward, ready to throw the net.

'There was some experiment with hallucinogens. I don't know a great deal about it because I left London in 1967 to do postgraduate work at Berkeley in California, and by the time I returned a year later things had taken a new turn. In 1968 there was a great deal of political tension among the students in London. People were debating and organising demonstrations rather than blowing their minds. I had a student from Prague sharing my flat for three months. Hearing the stories of people like that was a sobering experience.'

It was a neat side-step, but Steve was ready to counter it. He held Waterlow's gaze and kept his tone steady as he changed tack.

'Does the name "Walker" mean anything to you, Dr Waterlow?'

'Can't say it does, no.'

'Did you ever hear Walker's people mentioned, when you were in California?'

The frown again, as if he were earnestly searching his memory. 'Don't think so. No. There were the Diggers, the Process people, the Scientologists. But there were dozens of others whose names I wouldn't remember.'

'Thank you, Dr Waterlow,' said Steve. We may need to talk to you again later.'

Walking back across the parking lot, Briony spotted a red Aston Martin.

'I knew he'd have one of those,' she said. 'I bet you he's dripping with money. Thinks the world revolves around him. He slipped the net there, didn't he? I think he's telling us a load of bull.'

'He's shit scared of something. If I can get him down to the station, I'll get it out of him.'

'I don't think he's scared,' said Briony. 'He's just a bloody great ego on legs. I think he's embarrassed. He's not telling the truth about why he got expelled from the Freemasons. He's done something he's embarrassed about, betcha. And there's the California connection again. This is really shaping up now.'

Steve quickened his pace, so she almost had to run to catch up. When she did, he turned on her with sudden virulence.

'You think you know it all, don't you?'

43

Back at the station, Briony went to get lunch while Steve made phone calls. She couldn't think why he was in such a shitty mood, but decided to bring him back a ham sandwich as a peace offering. He was still on the phone when she returned from the cafeteria and, from the way he was stubbing his cigarette out, it was obvious his temper hadn't improved. It was impossible for her to concentrate with an explosion imminent on the other side of the room, so she pretended to tidy her desk, picking up what she could of the phone conversation.

'By four o'clock. At the latest. Waterlow. Yes.' Steve spelt the name out.

'Nineteen *sixty* seven. No, we need *all* the records checked. Everything you've got.' He covered the receiver with his hand. 'And if you fuck me about any more—yes, I said fuck. F-u-c-k. Would you like a definition?' There was a pause, then, 'Hello. Yes. Fine. Goodbye.' The receiver went down with a crash.

'So what's got up your nose?' asked Briony.

Steve slumped across his desk, both hands pushed deep into his hair.

'What?' she said. 'What's the matter?'

She went across and put the lunch bag beside him.

'Hey, it's not the end of the world, you know. I bought you a ham sandwich.'

The head came up a few inches, but stayed locked between his hands.

'How do you know it's not the end of the world?'

'Because I say so and I know everything. You just told me.'

'I said you *think* you know everything. This fucking case is just a pan of spaghetti. It's depressing the hell out of me. It's the worst case I've ever been on. Even Macready's rattled. The investigation's a total fuck-up. We're not getting it, and Walker's going to turn somebody else inside out any minute.' He straightened up and looked at the paper bag.

'Hey, you really bought me a ham sandwich? That's the nicest thing anyone's done for me all week.'

'And it's only Monday lunch time. Look on the bright side. Anyway, I don't think we're doing so badly with the leads. Berkeley's in San Francisco, isn't it? It's too much of a coincidence that Waterlow was there at the same time as Quin—and Sabina Melies. We have to find out what he was really up to.'

'We have to find out what he was up to before he left for California,' said Steve. 'This cult stuff comes from England.'

'But it's exactly what was going on in California—Sabina's diary reeks of it. Surely you've read about what the Manson Family believed? It was part of the whole drug culture gone wrong.'

'No. The stuff we're dealing with is English. I'm sure of it.'

'*Now* who thinks they know it all?'

'What we know is that the killer is getting off on the *Book of Ecclesiastes*.'

'So was Bob Dylan,' said Briony. 'I don't see what's specially English about it.'

'The fact that it's mixed up with bits of inspiration from William Hogarth and Jack the Ripper. It's the way they go together that's

English. Think about Hogarth—wandering around the London streets and picking up on all the horrors. Then the Ripper. I'd never realised before how those two worlds fit with each other. London cruelty. Maybe our friend was exporting it to San Fran in exchange for Peace and Love.'

'I don't suppose it was quite that simple.'

'Of course not. But you get my point, don't you? The first murder happened here. In England. Whatever it was that made this guy kill, he didn't get it from some cult meeting in Haight-Ashbury. My bet is it came out of the Invisible College, and the Walker stuff goes way back. And I bet Waterlow knows plenty about it.'

'But—'

The phone cut in and Steve picked it up. 'Oh hi, Donna—Yeah, but—Not now. Gotta go out. Here's Briony.'

He handed her the receiver and kept his hand over the mouthpiece. 'Better talk to her. Sounds like she needs girl talk, you know?'

He patted his pockets briskly, checking for keys and cigarettes, then left.

'Briony? Got time for a cuppa?'

'Not really. I'm on a lead and it's complicated. Got to follow up on some things.'

'I've been trying to talk to Guy, because I'm sure there's a lot more he can tell me. But Alec's always hanging around, like his minder. I thought if you came as well—'

'—it would be a cosy little foursome. I don't work like that, Donna. And nor should you. It's not safe. I wouldn't trust Guy as far as I could throw him.'

'I'm asking for back-up, Briony, not pep talks. Forget it.' The line disconnected, and Briony stared for a minute at the offending receiver before hanging up.

44

Don't show your face to me again, Nell muttered as she put the film in the camera. Just don't try it. She held the lens up to her right eye and saw all the things in her room—the dressing gown on the back of the door, the bedside table with the clock on it, the books and papers strewn on her bed—as if they were much further away. Yesterday she'd got a bit of practice using the flash, but she wouldn't get the film back till the day after tomorrow, so she couldn't be sure she'd got the hang of it.

She attached the flash, inserted the bulb and took a photo of the dressing gown. There was a satisfying flare and a click. Good. It was all working. She wound the film on and put the camera in her tote bag, then put on her old mac. This was not Rita's smart military style number with the wide belt, but a shapeless grey nylon thing, regulation summer rainwear at her high school. Now for the headscarf. The effect when she looked in the mirror was worse than she'd expected.

'Come on,' called Julie, 'I'll be late.'

Nell closed the bedroom door after her and locked it with the key, as the police had recommended, then presented herself. 'So, what do you think?'

'Are you really going to go out looking like that?'

'It's all in a good cause. Admit it—even you wouldn't recognise me, would you?'

'That raincoat's a fashion crime. And it's not even raining. Why are you taking that lumpy old tote bag?'

Nell patted it. 'Camera.'

'Come on, then. Haven't got time to argue.'

They had worked it all out on Sunday: Nell would change her times and her routes to and from work and go in company with the twins wherever possible. Julie was working in the Baker Street office of the Bureau, so her usual routine was to get the Piccadilly Line and change at Piccadilly Circus on to the Bakerloo. It was quicker than the Circle Line, even though that went all the way round to Baker Street with no changes, because the tubes were more frequent on the Piccadilly. But this morning, she and Nell left the flat together—ten minutes earlier than Julie's usual time for setting off, so as to allow for the slower journey—and they both caught the Circle Line. At Notting Hill, Nell changed to the Central. She was on her own now.

At Tottenham Court Road, she got off and came out onto the street. Even allowing for the fifteen minute walk from here, she was too early for work, so she found a café. A handwritten board above the counter listed the breakfast menu: beans on toast, egg on toast, sausage and beans, bacon and tomato with fried bread, double egg and bacon. Her stomach was in a tight little knot. She couldn't imagine eating any of those things, so she ordered some coffee and took it to a table by the window with a clear view of the street in both directions. The hippies and students weren't up at this time of day. All the people walking past were smartly dressed: the men in suits and the women in high heels and fitted dresses. Office workers. The man with his shaggy hair would stand out a mile among them. It was going to be much harder to keep him off her trail on the way home.

Thank goodness this was her last week working at the office. It was harder and harder to keep her mind on the job and there were so many people who wanted to play the boss and couldn't resist the opportunity to point out constantly what she was missing or doing wrong. She would so love to tell *them* a few things, to shake them out of their silly little world where a broken pencil sharpener or a cracked coffee cup had to be reported on two different forms. There was still plenty of talk about the Whitechapel murders. Some of the women, Nell suspected, rather enjoyed thinking they were in mortal danger every time they stepped outside the building. She couldn't resist barging into one of these conversations.

'Why would he wait till you got into the street? It would be much easier to get you up here, behind your desk. That's more his style, I'm sure.'

'You've got a morbid imagination, Nell Adams.'

'It's got nothing to do with imagination,' said Nell. 'Here's your typewriter ribbon. You have to sign for it, if you don't mind.'

But it had everything to do with imagination, she thought as she dusted the filing shelves. Now she'd given herself the idea, she could see opportunities for the killer everywhere she turned. Why take all that trouble to stop him following her to work, when he could so easily get her *at* work. He could just walk right in and people would think he was one of the delivery men or something. A lot of them were student temps with long hair.

In her tea break, she used the coin-operated phone on the stairwell to ring Vine Street. If she could only get on to Inspector Palgrave again, or Inspector Williams, she was sure they would not leave her without any kind of police protection. Neither of them was available.

'Can you tell me when Inspector Palgrave will be back?' she asked.

'Can't say for sure, I'm afraid. May not be for a couple of days.'

Nell continued to hold the receiver to her ear for a minute or two after they had hung up on the other end, looking down the gloomy concrete staircase as she listened to the dial tone. What if he came up those stairs, right now? She pulled the camera out of her handbag and checked it. She'd be ready for him. He'd be walking right into the picture frame, the one place he surely didn't want to be.

After replacing the receiver, she walked a few steps down the stairwell in the semi darkness, as if to test herself. Her stomach still felt tight, but her breathing was steady. She was doing well.

When she left the office at the end of the day, the headscarf and raincoat didn't look so out of place because heavy clouds had gathered. She'd arranged to meet Julie at Knightsbridge, so that all three of them could go home together when Rita finished work. Going back into the flat would be the hardest thing. That and having a bath, arrangements for which they'd discussed at length last night.

She wanted to try another call to Vine Street but, finding that the phones at Knightsbridge station were all in use, she crossed the Brompton Road to the post office. There was nobody around here. She had a choice of three phone boxes all to herself, in a side street just back from the main road where some post office vans were parked. The traffic still made it hard to hear clearly, so she picked the booth furthest away from the Brompton Road. This time she was lucky enough to get through to Inspector Williams. As a double decker bus rumbled past, she pressed the phone hard against her ear and put a finger in the other ear to reduce the noise.

'It's been okay today,' she said, 'but I'm worried about when we get back to the flat. Could you ask for someone to be there, do you think, to check it out before we go inside?'

'Of course somebody should be there when you get home,' said the inspector. 'I'll come round myself. There are a few more questions I'd like to ask you. It's half past five now. I'll have a car outside the flat by six thirty.'

'Good. Thanks,' said Nell, feeling the tension begin to drain away from her. But as she was about to put down the receiver, a hand was placed over hers and another hand came around her neck, forcing its rubbery fingers right inside her mouth so she couldn't make any sound come out.

45

Macready sent Briony home in one of the cars at nine, almost pushing her into the back seat. Even he was looking pale and worn in the yellow light of the street lamp. As the car lurched out, spraying blue and red light over the massive shadows of the trees, Briony started to wonder if this was what a bad trip felt like. The whole world seemed to have turned and, for the first time, she felt they were losing the case. Steve was right. Walker was always three steps ahead of them. The investigation was a fiasco and the next to be turned inside out was going to be little Nell, so Briony was going to be the last person the victim had spoken to. Everyone had failed. Everyone. Steve should have ordered full police protection. Palgrave shouldn't have left it to someone else to follow up when only he knew Nell's story first hand. Briony should have kept her on the phone till the police got to her in Knightsbridge. As for Macready, he was looking like a second-rate operator on a case that called for nothing short of genius. There had been some rumours that his instalment at Vine Street was an unofficial demotion and Briony had dismissed them as petty back-biting. Now, they weren't so easy to ignore.

The Socos, at least, had done their job well. It had taken them less than an hour to confirm which phone box Nell had used. The forensic side of it would be a dog's breakfast, since it meant getting the relevant set of fingerprints off the receiver of a public telephone that had probably been in constant use during the day, but on the floor of the booth they'd found a long crinkly hair that exactly matched samples taken from Nell's bedroom.

When Walker pulled her out of the phone box, he must have had a vehicle nearby to get her into. It was a crowded area and although he might have been unobserved in the side street where the phones were, he couldn't have taken her out onto the pavement of the main road without someone noticing. He couldn't have been following her by road, because Nell hadn't taken her usual route home on the tube. How could he have known where she'd surface from the underground? To spring her where he did, he'd have to have been stalking her on foot, catching the same trains. Then when she'd conveniently cornered herself, maybe he'd spotted some vehicle nearby and broken into it. According to Macready the booth from which Nell made her phone call was next to a post office, so a post office van was the first possibility to be checked out.

Well if this investigation team had failed Nell, so had the one in Plymouth, just as the police in San Francisco had failed Sabina. Or maybe they had all simply been defeated by something no police operation could have forestalled: a turn to the bad. She thought of Sabina, one of the hundreds of flower children at the Human Be-in four years ago, dancing in the rain, believing that the world had finally woken up to peace and love. Thinking that the Golden Gate had opened onto a wonderful world. Maybe, in a way, it had. But something else had slipped through the opening. Something charged up with the wrong kind of force.

Briony had read about those weirdos in California, taking over old abandoned ranches in the desert, pickling their brains with bad chemicals and making up elaborate stories about the end of the world. Manson wasn't unique, he was a type, as one of the lecturers at Hendon had insisted. He was both, Briony thought. So was Jack the Ripper. Probably. And Walker. Typical product of a culture gone bad, but with something extra.

She closed her eyes and leant against the side of the car, feeling the jolts and vibrations as a kind of soothing distraction, until she saw again in her mind the crude little image of the woman lying in the street with her cut throat exposed like a great ugly smile. Nell. Oh, please, not Nell Adams. Of all the dead bodies she'd seen in her career, she'd never seen one that belonged to someone she'd encountered close up, as a living breathing human being.

46

The alarm woke Briony at seven and she was almost ashamed to realise that she had slept like a log. No waking up in the night, not even any dreams that she could remember. She had gone into complete oblivion for eight hours during which Walker's next victim, if she was still alive, must have been in a living hell. And what kind of a night must Nell's cousins have had? Well, it was no help to them if the police felt defeated. Don't get fazed; keep coming back: the two golden rules now took on a whole new meaning. This was when they kicked in seriously—when everything was taking the worst kind of turn.

She went into the kitchen, where sun was streaming through the windows. Down in the High Street, a girl in a flowered dress and straw hat was waiting at the bus stop. To cap the irony, this looked like being one of the last true days of summer. A long day. It was going to be a long, long day.

Well, a good night's sleep was one thing, but, in the circumstances, breakfast was another. Briony took a cold egg from the refrigerator, weighed it in her hand for a moment, then put it back in the egg box. Instead of forcing herself to eat now, she thought, she could walk to work and stop on the way for breakfast once she'd got up an appetite. If she walked fast, she could do it in forty-five minutes, she reckoned. It would get her thinking.

As she walked, she had a song on the brain: 'Monday Monday.' It was Saturday Saturday, actually, but it might as well have been Monday. There was going to be no weekend at Vine Street. The others were probably already at work and had probably been there most of the night. She lifted her pace, so the song turned to a characterless rhythmic gabble in her head.

The first thing to do when she arrived, Briony decided, was to get onto Palgrave in Devonshire. Surely by now they should have been on Quin's trail. Palgrave should have found a lead to his whereabouts, or at least his habits.

The new Wimpy bar on the corner at Warren Street was open early. She went in and bought a hamburger, which she squirted with sauce from a large red plastic tomato on the table. As she ate, she stared through the window, watching the people herd in and out of Warren Street station and noticing that there were police officers at each of the exits, using walkie-talkies. There had been a lot of bomb threats around here, so maybe there was some kind of alert this morning. It had got to the point where people saw the threats as merely a nuisance, something that got in the way of their daily business, rather than as the prospect of real danger. We all make that mistake, thought Briony. It was the kind of mistake Walker had been wise to.

His luck, and our mistakes, she thought, that's what keeps him going. The post office van—that was where his luck came in. They were everywhere. She could see two of them through the window from where she sat. The ideal vehicle for his purposes. And the combination of a phone box and a van might be found around any post office, but it was the luck of the devil that walked into the perfect trap like that. Then again, if he'd had that kind of luck unexpectedly, it might have prompted him to go for the capture sooner than he'd planned. He was taking more risks, as Palgrave said. There was some hope, maybe, that right now his preparations weren't fully in place. His luck, his mistake.

Out in the street again, Briony wondered what might have turned up in the past few hours. The sun had held out, but there was quite a cold wind blowing, so it was good to walk fast, dodging around the other pedestrians. At Oxford Circus, she crossed to the west side of Regent Street to avoid the crush around Carnaby Street. Shopping crowds were already gathering on Regent Street itself, so she cut through to Hanover Square, thinking it would be quicker to find her way along the back streets. Here the dry leaves on the trees scraped noisily against each other; some fell on the path, where they were bowled along in a chaotic spin. The wind made everything seem unsettled and jumpy. It was the turn of the seasons. Briony thought of the girl in the flowered dress, standing at the bus stop. She was going to regret having worn that to work. And the straw hat would have been blowing off her head by now.

A Rolls Royce, moving slowly across into Grosvenor Street, forced her to stop and wait at the next crossing. Briony stared at its darkened windows. You could have cut someone's throat in the back of that and no one would ever have known, probably not even the chauffeur, professionally minding his own business on the other side of a soundproof glass screen.

47

'Clueless,' Jimmy pronounced. 'Whoever took them didn't have clue. I mean, what do you make of it?'

Briony peered at the row of photographs he'd laid out on her desk.

'Where did these come from?'

'Palgrave brought them back with him from Plymouth. Train murder. Could be Walker's debut, Palgrave reckons.'

The pictures were very dark and it was hard to make out even the outline of the body against the fabric of the seat. The head was slumped forward, so you couldn't see the face, just grey hair in an untidy perm and the collar of a sheepskin coat. The sides of the collar, over the shoulders, were still white at the edges, but a dark stain had seeped in from the neck.

'Throat's cut, yeah?'

'Like the others. And an ear cut off.'

'Who is she?'

'How should I know? I expect we'll be told in a minute. I wouldn't be too sure that this is the work of the same bloke myself—it's a different type of victim. Why would he go for a poor old biddy like this?'

'Has Macready seen them? Where is he?'

'Holed up in his office. He's spent all night on some errand, off on his own in the wee small hours. I've never seen him look so rattled.'

Jimmy nearly collided with Steve Latham as he got to the door. Jimmy was moving fast and Steve slowly, but it was Jimmy who had to side-step. Steve looked like a zombie. He leant against his desk and fixed Briony with the blue eyes.

'Palgrave's back,' he said.

'Yes, I heard. Has he found any leads on Quin?'

'Zilch, apparently. Hasn't been seen for four years. They tracked down his mother in Taunton and a sister, but they got no new info. He seems to have written him off as the black sheep of the family.'

'So what've you been doing?' she asked. 'You look like you've been up all night.'

'Pretty well. I've been over in the library belonging to the Freemasons' lodge in St Pancras. They have an interesting archive of papers, going back to the date of its foundation—1722. Among the founding members were W Hogarth, N Hawksmoor, T... Ascham and C Glade. Christopher Glade. Locksmith by appointment to the King. Glade's papers are still held at the lodge. They include an order from Nicholas Hawksmoor for a lock for the door of the new church in Spitalfields and a drawing giving the specifications. Two keys.'

'So you were right. You *were* right.' Briony sat down heavily, still staring at the page with its curled handwriting. 'Then where do we go from here?'

'That's not the only lead I got. The Masons have been very co-operative. They've located some of Godwin's private papers, including a file of his correspondence. He had an office on the premises which he seems to have used quite a bit.'

Steve held out a document in a transparent sleeve. 'Read that.'

It was a letter, dated 15th August, 1971.

Dear Godwin,

Thank you indeed for the notice. I myself have the diary in safekeeping and have apprised no one else of its whereabouts. I know I can rely on your absolute discretion in the matter. If it proves impossible to prevent further disturbances to the grave, at least we may rest assured that the trespassers will be frustrated of their aims.

Sincerely, as ever,

R Burroughs

Briony's thoughts were racing. 'Burroughs knew Godwin. How?'

'They were both members of the lodge.'

'And the diary he's talking about is the one that was in the tomb, right? So whose is it? Whose tomb is it? Surely we can find that out?'

'Macready's ordered a search of the parish records. He should have the results by now, but I haven't had a chance to talk to him—like I said he's been off on some all-night hunting trip.'

'Who's gone on a hunting trip?' asked Donna, marching into the centre of the room like some kind of store mannequin and turning to collect the full intensity of Steve's gaze. 'You know what?'

Briony obliged with the necessary prompt. 'What?'

'Macready's acting like he's got a screw loose. He called me into his office this morning because he wanted to know more about Guy Waterlow. At first I thought he was going to rap me over the knuckles for making that date with him, but that doesn't seem to have bothered him at all—except, you know what he asked me?'

Donna looked at Briony, waiting for the next prompt.

'What?'

'He said, "Do you think this young man Waterlow is attracted to you, Detective Constable Caldwell?"' Now Donna turned to Steve for a reaction.

'I was flabbergasted. I mean, you don't expect that kind of line from Macready of all people.'

Briony obligingly prompted again. 'So what did you say?'

Donna actually blushed, now, catching Steve's eye as she bowed her head so that a cascade of newly washed hair fell across her face. 'I said maybe. But I think Guy Waterlow's got his mind on other things. Like his career. I don't know why he offered to talk to me in the first place.'

Briony wondered whether Donna was really as naïve as she pretended or, alternatively, what game she was playing.

Donna stood there as Briony and Steve turned their attention back to Burroughs's letter, then seeing she was not going to get any more attention, made a parting speech.

'That bloke Alec's a bit of a creep, you know. That story about him getting his girlfriend pregnant—turns out it's a lot of baloney. Wasn't even him; it was somebody else. He used the story as a way to get talking to me. Funny way to make a play for another girl.'

Briony waited for her to be out of earshot before she put the next burning question. 'So what about this diary?'

'Dunno. I haven't had any luck with that, but, like I said, Macready's been onto something he won't talk about. Maybe he's figured out where to look for it. You know, I'm a bit worried about Donna.'

Donna was the last thing Briony wanted to discuss right now, so she didn't respond, but he continued. 'She seems to have lost the plot. It's not like her.'

'Well, maybe we're all a bit out of our depth on this case.'

The general briefing was mercifully short and practical. After an all-night search, the Socos were satisfied that there wasn't a body anywhere in the area, so there was a possibility that Walker had departed from his usual practice and kidnapped his victim with the intention of keeping her captive. The fact that he'd made such efforts to track her down suggested that she had a significance for him quite different from that of his other victims, Macready suggested. As the witness to what was probably his first murder, perhaps she was not chosen to be a victim, but to be a witness again. At least that gave them some hope of rescuing her if they worked fast and got the right leads.

As Briony had guessed, the main focus was on the post office vans parked near the phone she'd used. But to find out whether one of them was missing involved going through a central registry in which all regular vehicle routes were recorded.

Palgrave reported on his findings from Devon and Cornwall. Mathew Quin's father was dead and his mother, who had moved to a cottage outside Taunton to live with her daughter, had not seen him since August 1967, when he had visited her to ask for money. The sister, three years younger than him and still at school at the time, believed he had been on 'hard drugs'. He'd returned to Cornwall with some other students and they'd only stayed in the town for a couple of days before going across to Tintagel, where some kind of big hippy gathering was supposed to be taking place. The story checked out: there had been a minor rock festival at Tintagel on 28th and 29th August, 1967, featuring some groups from America. Palgrave had managed to find a young couple who had been there and now ran a local pub. The festival was meant to be linked with the Great Human Be-In in San Francisco, they said, to celebrate the spread of the Flower Power movement across England. Many of the people who attended, though, had chosen instead to follow the movement back to its source in California.

Quin remained a prime suspect, said Palgrave, because he could still have been in Cornwall on 10th September, when the train murder was committed. Briony then gave the details of what she'd learnt from the passport office about Quin's visa for America and pointed out how this fitted with the timing of the events recorded in Sabina Melies's diary.

There was no evident link, though, between Quin and the victim of the train murder. She was a Mrs Doris Anglesby, a widow from Falmouth who had been on her way to London to see her sister

May, in hospital recovering from an operation for cancer. May had been interviewed shortly after the murder, but no useful leads had come of it. The interview notes, said Palgrave, were sparse. She had died in November 1967. The only other relative Palgrave had been able to trace was May's son and Doris Anglesby's nephew, Philip, whose statement was being used to draw up a victim profile.

The next meeting in Macready's office was far more intense. Steve was ten minutes late, because he'd been trying to get onto the passport office again. He'd found out that Guy Waterlow had been issued with a visa for the United States in the same month as Quin—September 1967. Macready greeted this news by smacking the desk hard with the flat of his hand.

'I want Waterlow in for questioning, Latham.'

'Yes, sir.'

'Within the hour.'

'I don't see that we can do that, sir. Unless you can issue a warrant for his arrest and we don't have grounds.'

'Threaten him with arrest. Tell him he's obstructing our enquiries. Now, Palgrave. This victim profile. What do we know?'

'She was fifty-nine years old. Husband Gordon Anglesby died in 1960. He was the local publican. The Red Lion has been in his family for several generations, apparently, and Barbara Anglesby went on running the place after he died. Story is, everybody knew her, everybody liked her and no one can imagine anybody wanting to do her in. She employed a couple of bartenders—one an elderly man who'd worked at the Red Lion since the end of the war; another was a local feller who was actually in charge of the place the day Mrs Anglesby was murdered. Nephew Philip inherited the pub, but it's now run by Berni Inns so he doesn't have much to do with it. Obviously he stood to gain by the death of his aunt, but he was in surgery all day when the murder was committed. He's never heard of Mathew Quin and I can't find anything to connect Quin to Mrs Anglesby or the Red Lion. The officers conducting the original investigation were firmly of the opinion that Mrs Anglesby was murdered by a stranger.'

Macready leant forward across his clasped hands.

'Might this pub—the Red Lion—have been a place for drug trafficking?'

'Most unlikely, I'd say, sir. Until the new management took over, it seems to have been your traditional local, where everybody knew everybody else.'

'Very well. Thank you, Palgrave. I had better study this statement from Dr Philip—' Macready drew the file towards him to read the name. 'Dr Philip Tremlay.'

Steve shot out of his seat and grabbed the file. 'Dr WHO?'

'No one so mysterious, I think, Latham.' Macready showed a flicker of humour for the first time in days. 'Though I must say, there is a curious coincidence of names here. The occupant of the tomb in Christchurch is one Bartholomew Tremlay, an early member of the Invisible College.'

'Then what the—!' Steve was stopped in his tracks for a moment. 'There's no coincidence, sir. Can't be. We talked to some people yesterday who said there was a Maxwell Tremlay who hung around with Quin and Waterlow. This is clearly something we must look into immediately. Perhaps Briony—I mean, DI Williams—could hunt up his college records while we give Dr Waterlow the third degree.'

Briony was fuming as she headed back from Macready's office to the incident room. When Steve appeared a few minutes later with two cups of coffee, she was ready to throw them at him. She also had a little prepared speech.

'Let's get one thing clear, here. I am not the filing clerk. If you want a records search on Tremlay, you can lodge a request in the usual way and Palgrave will find someone to do it. I have more important things to do in this case.'

Steve put both cups of coffee on his own desk.

'Suit yourself,' he said. 'I just thought, since you knew your way around the weird filing system up there in Senate House—'

'Weird filing systems are not my priority in a situation like this. I need to be in on the interview with Waterlow. He knows more about Quin than he's letting on. Anyway, what we really need to know about Tremlay is whether he took a trip to California. I'll get onto the passport office again, while you phone Waterlow.'

48

Macready had had a shave and generally spruced himself up for the interview with Guy Waterlow, but when Briony was invited to sit beside him at the interview table, she could sense the tension in his muscles. Steve, on the other side of him, lighting a cigarette from the stub of the previous one with a shaky hand, was no better. And he certainly hadn't shaved.

'I'll lead the questioning myself,' said Macready. 'If a point should arise that either of you especially wants to pursue, you may signal like this.' He put his pen horizontally on the table above his notepad.

The interview began almost casually, with Macready affecting a look of boredom as Waterlow trotted out his answers. Then, gradually, the questions began to bite.

'You've emphasised that you regard the Invisible College as a strictly professional association,' said Macready. 'But it is also a secret association, is it not?'

'That's part of its tradition, probably because in past centuries the members had knowledge that might have got them into trouble.'

'Are you implying, Dr Waterlow, that this is no longer the case? You have, in other words, nothing to hide?'

A flicker of hesitation was evident before the reply. 'I wouldn't say we have anything to hide, no. But there are things that are kept confidential, as in any professional organisation.'

'Of course. Is your membership secret?'

'It's confidential.'

'But you would, of course, be prepared to discuss it in relation to a police matter, and provide any requested contact details?'

'I'm not sure I'd be in a position to do that.'

'And why is that?... Dr Waterlow?'

'It might be a case of—of people being hard to find. Some people move away from London, you know, and one loses touch with them.'

'Are you still in contact with Mathew Quin?'

'No.'

'When was the last time you saw him?'

'I can't remember exactly. A few years ago. Some time in 1967, I should think.'

'Was Mr Quin taking drugs at that time?'

'I wouldn't know for sure. People said he was.'

'People?'

'Just—people in general. The other students.'

'Were *you* taking drugs, Dr Waterlow?'

'I smoked a bit of hash. We all—experimented a bit. Some of my friends were experimenting with hallucinogens for a while, but that was a while back.'

'Who did you buy these drugs from? Were they traded through the members of the Invisible College?'

'Look I can't—'

'Can't what, Dr Waterlow?'

'I'd prefer not to discuss the affairs of my friends and colleagues.'

'We may require you to disclose the information regardless. Would you prefer to do that now, or when we have completed the formalities?'

'I'd like to have a solicitor present.'

Waterlow's solicitor turned out to be his brother, who was stockier, with blunter features, but the same voice. Roger Waterlow looked as if he'd been polished all over, face included, and he smiled all the time, though this only made him seem more ill at ease.

'Before the interview recommences,' he said, 'I'd like to clarify something. Is my client being interviewed as a suspect? I might remind you that Dr Waterlow was on duty in the emergency ward at St Bartholomew's Hospital on the night of Professor Godwin's murder.'

Macready leant forward. 'We are well aware of that, Mr Waterlow. But your brother must also be aware that this is a serious and urgent case. I am sure Dr Waterlow is here now, after what must have been a hard night's work, because he wishes to assist us in every way possible.'

Guy Waterlow nodded curtly. 'That's right. But I hope you will understand that I'm in an awkward position when it comes to discussing my friends' affairs.'

'We are trying to catch someone who has murdered at least four people and may kill again at any time, Dr Waterlow. Anything you can do to assist us in eliminating names from our enquiries will be appreciated. I will repeat the question I asked you earlier. Were members of the Invisible College trading drugs?'

'Some of them may have been.'

'Maxwell Tremlay, for example?'

'He may have been.'

'How well did you know Mr Tremlay?'

'He was an acquaintance.'

'Are you still in touch with him?'

'No.' A hand swept through the waves of hair, revealing hard frown lines on Waterlow's forehead. 'He's not around. He went to America.'

'I put it to you, Dr Waterlow, that you were dealing drugs in collaboration with Mr Tremlay.'

Waterlow exchanged the briefest of glances with his brother before replying. 'No. No, that's not how it was.'

'Did you ever sell drugs to Mathew Quin, or he to you?'

'I was not a drug dealer.'

'Answer my question, Dr Waterlow. Did you ever sell drugs to Mathew Quin?'

'I might have sold him some hash occasionally. That was just the way it got around. We all sold each other small quantities from time to time. I never had more than a small amount of it in my possession. I was never a dealer.'

Roger Waterlow intervened at this point.

'My client is here to assist with a murder enquiry,' he said. 'He is not, I take it, being charged with drug offences? I can't see how an inquisition about trivial and commonplace instances of soft drug use four years ago can be relevant here.'

Macready didn't even bother to look at him, but kept his gaze firmly on his brother as he drew out a document from the small pile of papers in front of him.

'Dr Waterlow, you travelled to America in September 1967, is that right?'

'Yes, I did. I went to do some postgraduate work at Berkeley.'

'Did you go alone?'

'I travelled alone, yes.'

'Mr Mathew Quin also travelled to America in September 1967. That is a coincidence, is it?'

'Yes.'

'He flew to Los Angeles three days after you did. That is a coincidence, is it?'

'Yes.'

'Dr Waterlow, did you ever see Mathew Quin in California? Did your paths cross?'

'No.'

Steve placed his biro horizontally on the table and Macready leant back in his chair, as a way of giving the okay.

'By further coincidence,' said Steve, 'it appears that Maxwell Tremlay flew to Los Angeles in September 1967. Did you see Mr Tremlay in California?'

'Mr Tremlay visited me once, in my rooms at Berkeley.'

'Tell us about the visit.'

'Just a social one, really. He said he was staying in San Francisco with some friends. It didn't surprise me. He was a hippy. We talked about the San Francisco peace movement. A lot of the Berkeley students were involved, as I'm sure you know.'

'Did Tremlay mention having seen Mathew Quin?'

Waterlow looked down at the table and his frown deepened. 'No. I can't remember that he did.'

'Yet they were on the same flight. Is that a coincidence, do you think? Dr Waterlow?'

Waterlow was obviously losing his composure. An involuntary muscle was twitching at the side of his face, pulling his mouth askew.

Macready leant forward again, speaking slowly and in a low voice. 'I put it to you, Dr Waterlow, that you are not telling the truth. I put it to you that you travelled to California knowing that Quin and Tremlay were also going there and that the three of you were in each other's company a great deal at that time.'

There was no answer.

'I am sure, Dr Waterlow, that it will not do your career much good if you are charged with obstructing our enquiries. A young girl's life is at stake at this very moment. If there is anything, anything at all that you know that may assist us in identifying the man who has kidnapped her, it is your most solemn duty to disclose the information.'

'I'd like to talk to my brother for a minute, in confidence, if that's all right,' he said.

Macready got up immediately. 'By all means. We will leave you for ten minutes.'

When the interview resumed, both Waterlow brothers seemed to have lost their gloss. They looked pale and drawn and, if anything, Roger seemed the more stressed of the two.

'I'm afraid I need to do some explaining,' Guy Waterlow began. 'I'm afraid I was not being entirely frank just now when I said I had not seen Mathew Quin in California. I apologise. It was never my intention to mislead the police, but Mr Quin is someone I prefer to dissociate myself from. I have a reputation to care for these days—a professional reputation. In my youth I made the mistake of allowing myself to be drawn into company that I would now be careful to avoid. Mr Quin was making some unsavoury connections in San Francisco, connections which, I believe, may have led him into criminal activities.'

'What criminal activities, Dr Waterlow?' asked Macready.

'I don't know exactly. He was involved in some kind of cult. They were dealing heroin and I suspect they were trying to blackmail people.'

'And did they try to blackmail you?'

'Not directly.'

Briony placed her pen in the signal position and Macready made a small hand gesture of invitation to speak.

'Was Quin one of Walker's people?' she asked.

The face opposite her went a whiter shade of pale.

'Yes.'

'In our last interview, Dr Waterlow, you said you had never heard of Walker's people. That was incorrect, was it?'

'Yes. Yes, it was. I was confused and to be honest I—well, I was confused.'

'To your knowledge, is or was Walker an actual person?'

'I don't really know. I just heard talk about him. The hippy culture tended to produce these cult figures—anyone with a bit of charisma and some crazy philosophy could draw together a bunch of followers. Quin was very susceptible in that way. He was immature, lonely—a sociopath, really—so he was easily led into other people's paranoias, especially when he was helped along by a cocktail of bad chemicals.'

'Do you think Mathew Quin would be capable of murder?'

'Quite possibly he would have been.'

Macready cut in.

'Would have been? That is an interesting choice of tense, Dr Waterlow.'

There was a very long pause. Waterlow was staring at his hands, and frowning intently. Eventually, he looked up.

'Mathew Quin is dead.'

49

It was dark and Nell found herself lying somewhere cold and hard. As she sat up, she still felt some of the comfort of deep sleep around her. She could just lie down again and get back into the cocoon, where she wouldn't notice the coldness of the floor or the difficulty of finding a place for her shoulders and hips against the hard surface. She couldn't see anything. Nothing at all, not even her hand when she held it so close to her face that she could feel her breath on it. She pulled up her knees, put her arms around them and noticed that she was still wearing her old nylon raincoat.

This would be the time and the place to panic, but it was as if her mind had not quite caught up with her body—or was it the other way around—and she didn't feel that this was real. More sleep would be nice. She leaned her back against what must have been the wall and let her eyes close and her thoughts slip away.

Then her head jerked heavily to one side and woke her again. Keeping her body against the wall so she wouldn't lose her balance, she stood up, leaning against her hands. The raincoat crackled as she moved. Maybe it would be better to take it off, so there was no sound. She started to pull at it, but one of the sleeves was stuck to her arm, her left arm. There was some sticky stuff on the inside of her elbow and it hurt when she tried to peel the fabric away from it. Eventually she succeeded, but the last bit tore violently at her skin and nearly made her cry out. She felt a trickle of blood run down her arm. It's okay. You're okay. Just breathe.

Somebody had given her a jab in the arm. She remembered now. The hand was over her face and its fingers were pushed into her mouth, holding it wide so she couldn't get any pressure to bite and then both her arms were pulled back and she was crushed hard against the dense glass of the telephone box. She felt a needle go right in. It must have been something to make her go to sleep. Maybe she wasn't supposed to wake up yet.

She didn't want to make any noise. If he knew she was awake and moving around, he might come and tie her up, even put a gag in her mouth. Thinking about that made the panic start to rise. She counted her breaths. First the in breath, then the out breath. Nice and steady. One, two, three, four.

The voice in her head started giving advice. Explore a bit. See if you can find out where you are. She edged a step or two along the wall, feeling to either side of her with her hands. After several more steps, she came up against something that felt like the side of a bookcase or cupboard. Exploring it with her hand, she found it was a cupboard with lever style handles. A metal cupboard, like the ones in the office. Maybe you should try to open it, said the voice, but not yet. It might make a noise and if he hears you moving around—No, that was the kind of thinking that brought the panic.

She took one step outwards from the wall and explored the space with her hands. Nothing. She took one step back again and, facing the cupboard, made her way to the other side of it.

Count the steps. It was important to remember how many steps. That was how blind people found their way around at home. Twelve steps before you reached the corner. This had to be quite a big room. A basement of some kind, perhaps. It would have to have a door. Unless it was a cellar and the only door was in the ceiling, where you wouldn't be able to reach. Please let there be a door, a proper door, in the wall. Even if it was locked, a door would be such a good thing to find. It might be made of wood and wood was better than metal and concrete. Wood came from trees, that grow in the ground.

Two steps in along the next stretch of wall, the back of her head brushed against something. She felt with her hands. Something was stuck on the wall with tape. Some kind of paper, with a smooth surface. There was another one, next to it, with one below that and one above it. Perhaps there was one above that again, but she couldn't reach that far. She took a half step away from the wall, guiding herself now with her fingers rather than the palms of her hands, so as not to disturb the things stuck on the walls. Eight more steps. That meant ten from the corner. Still no door. But this was a big room. If it was a whole basement area, it might still be quite a long way to the door.

Nell began to lift her feet rather than slide them. That way, it was easier to move silently and her muscles were not so tensed up. Fifteen steps. Her right foot came down on something. She bent to feel with her hand. A piece of cloth of some kind, crumpled on the floor. Her scarf. The one she had been wearing on her head. It was easy to recognise by the size and texture and the way the knot was tied. It's blue and purple, Nell said to herself, imagining the bright design. She undid the knot, made the scarf into a neat roll and tied it around her arm, trying to make it tight so it would not slip off, but it was hard to get the bandage firm with one hand.

Fifteen sixteen seventeen. No door yet. A door would be the best thing in the world. If there wasn't one, perhaps it would be better not to know that, not just yet. Perhaps it would be better to sit down again for a while and see if some plan came to her, if she could think her way out of this. She remembered an old joke from school.

How did the prisoner escape from a dungeon with nothing in it but a table?

He rubbed his finger on the wall until he got a sore. Then he sawed the table in two halves, then he put the two halves together to make a whole, then he climbed through the hole. Tears started coming out of Nell's eyes, then out of her nose, so she had to breathe through her mouth.

She decided to move a bit further towards the middle of the room, with small steps, counting each one and keeping her hands braced in front of her. If your scarf was dropped here there's a chance your bag was too, she whispered. It was probably all right to whisper. The sound of her own voice was nice to hear. She whispered the count. Eight steps towards the middle, then eight steps back to the wall, then three steps along the wall, then eight steps towards the middle—

When she reached the next corner, there was another metal cupboard, at right angles to the way she was moving. It seemed to be exactly the same as the first. Same handles, same size. But next to it, on the other side, was something lumpy. Her bag. She sat down and felt inside. The camera. A packet of mints. Her mascara and new lipstick. Her book. *Hard Times*. A pencil. A comb.

It was hard to figure out which way round the camera was, because the back and the front felt the same and it took her a while to identify the various buttons. The button to take the photos. The wind-on lever. The flash. She switched the flash on, held the camera up near her face and took a photo. At first, it just blinded her, but for a split second, there was an after image. A square shape in the middle of the room.

Perhaps you should take a few in succession, she told herself, then you might get used to the dazzle. Better stand up to do it. And you might get a better view of the room if you go further in to the middle. She took eight small steps away from the wall, wound the film on, and pressed the button again. This time she did see a little bit. The square thing was a table and there were other things against the wall opposite. Perhaps another shelf or cupboard, but not as high. More like the height of the table. Another flash, facing at a slightly different angle, showed the wall to her left, with a rectangular shape in the middle of it. A door.

Backing up to the wall again, she moved faster along it, with more confidence, reaching the next corner without bothering to count her steps. Now she was against the wall with the door in it. This time she would count. Eight, nine, ten—Something was in her path. Another metal thing, like the cupboards, only wider. A low hum was coming from it. It was a fridge, with a handle like the one on the fridge at home. She opened it and a light went on inside, revealing rows of small plastic containers with their lids on.

50

After a second ten minute recess to allow the Waterlow brothers to consult and Macready to catch up with some new information from Palgrave, the interview resumed, with Macready facing Guy Waterlow alone across the desk. Steve and Briony had been relegated to the sidelines, literally, with their chairs moved against the wall under the window, which was now spattered with raindrops. The weather seemed to have changed to suit the mood in the room.

Macready opened quietly.

'Dr Waterlow, before we proceed further with this interview, I will offer you and your brother a formal assurance. We have no interest in pursuing charges against you for drug related offences. However, if you withhold information from us that is in any way relevant to the murder cases we are investigating, I will charge you with anything and everything I can find against you, including being an accessory to the crimes. Is that understood?'

'Yes, sir.'

'We have established, then, that you knew both Quin and Tremlay before you went to California. Bearing in mind what I have just told you, please tell us what you knew of their association with each other.'

'As I said earlier, Quin was immature and easily led. He was far too young to be a medical student in my opinion. He should not have been admitted to the degree before he was eighteen, but he had strong support from his school, Pendragon. The major public schools still carry a lot of weight with the university. His psychological health was precarious, but the warning signs were evidently ignored by the people who taught him. Tremlay was interested in him—I think they'd known each other slightly before Quin arrived at Gresham. Both were from Cornwall and they were at Pendragon together, though Quin would have been a couple of years behind. Mind you, as you know, Pendragon is a big school, and very formal. There wouldn't have been much contact between boys in different years, unless they were brothers. At first I thought Tremlay was trying to help Quin, but then I became concerned that he was using him as a guinea pig for new drugs. To try out anything interesting that came his way. I challenged him about it.'

Here Waterlow hesitated. He looked sideways at his brother, then at Macready, who simply waited for him to continue. He stumbled on.

'Yes, so I challenged him about it. Tremlay said that he hadn't given anything to Quin that he hadn't first tried himself and that, in any case, Quin needed no persuasion—that he was a genuine experimenter. I think that was supposed to be a dig at me, because Tremlay thought I was a bit tame in that regard. He reminded me that some of the most famous members of the Invisible College had been the leaders of the scientific revolution in the 1660s and had tried all kinds of experiments and substances on themselves. Robert Hooke drank opium and solutions of mercury and took various other metallic compounds. He recorded the effects in his diary.'

'This is Robert Hooke the microscopist, we are talking about?'

'Yes.'

'I see. We will come back to that in a moment. But first let us return to Tremlay. You say he was encouraging Quin with some hallucinogenic experiments. What were the results?'

'Not good. Quin was right on the edge. Taking those trips was going to send him over.'

'And that is what happened in California?'

'He took an overdose in Golden Gate Park.'

'This will be news to his relatives, you realise? You are sure that this is what happened?'

'I was there. I got a phone call asking me to come and help, but I was too late. By the time I arrived he'd been dead for twenty minutes. But I doubt I could have done much if I'd been there twenty minutes earlier.'

'Why weren't his relatives informed?'

'I've no idea. There are official procedures, of course, but I didn't think it was any of my business to follow it up. Tremlay dealt with the papers.'

'Did he now? And where is Mr Tremlay these days?'

Waterlow shrugged. 'I assume he stayed in America. He didn't like England.'

'Why was that?'

'It's just what he said. He said the English were uptight.'

'A highly original view, I'm sure. And was Mr Tremlay—it was Mr Tremlay, was it—not Dr Tremlay?'

'That's right. He may have qualified since then—I don't know.'

'Was Mr Tremlay one of Walker's people?'

'I don't really know.'

There was a pause, as Macready adjusted his position in his chair and looked through some papers on his desk.

He resumed the questioning with a brief smile. 'Let us return now to the fascinating topic of the Invisible College. I am told you are something of an expert on its history.'

'Hardly that. I have an interest in it.'

'You are too modest, I think.' Macready drew from his briefcase a small pamphlet with a worn grey cover and put it on the table. 'On the basis of this, I would say you were something of an expert.' He turned some of the pages. 'There is considerable research behind this work.'

Waterlow had frozen completely. The silence hung there. Briony heard herself swallow, then heard Steve do the same. She watched the second hand on her watch as it went round the dial, then round again. It was Roger Waterlow who spoke first.

'I'm afraid my brother needs a break. This is distressing for him.'

Macready leaned back in his chair and crossed his legs, without taking his eyes off Guy Waterlow.

'Speaking of distress,' he said, 'somewhere in this city a young girl may be being held captive by a serial murderer whose work she was unfortunate enough to witness once before. Can you imagine her distress, Dr Waterlow?'

Waterlow shook his head.

Pressing the pamphlet open at the first page, Macready began to read.

'"The Invisible College was founded by the Rosicrucians or Rose Cross Fraternity in the second decade of the seventeenth century and thus precedes the foundation of Gresham by over thirty years."'

He looked up. 'So the Invisible College is also an older organisation than the Freemasons' lodge in St Pancras, older by a century.' Waterlow nodded.

'"The brothers of the Rose Cross were a group of esoteric scholars, experimentalists who shared secret knowledge of alchemy, astrology and mathematical magic. They believed this knowledge to be dangerous and powerful and therefore guarded it jealously from the uninitiated.

"However, in the 1660s a new generation of scholars came to the fore, who devised more advanced instruments of investigation of which they were justly proud. These scholars wanted to give their experiments a public face. When the Royal Society was founded in 1660, many of them joined it, welcoming the publicity surrounding its activities and the opportunity to display their inventions to an admiring audience of fashionable gentlemen. They also continued their secret work with the Invisible College. In the well attended theatres of the Royal Society, they performed vivisections to demonstrate blood transfusion and the operation of internal organs, exposing the living, beating heart to view for the first time; in their more private quarters they experimented with mercury and cinnabar, attempting to create the philosopher's stone and its by-product, the homunculus or alchemical man.'"

Macready laid the pamphlet flat on the desk, and paused for a moment. 'Very interesting, I am sure. And some of these secret experimentalists were quite prominent men, like Robert Hooke, curator of experiments for the Royal Society, no less, and friend of Christopher Wren.' The eyebrow went up and then down into an exaggerated tick as Macready continued with the list. 'And now, among the—I would assume—third generation of membership is one Bartholomew Tremlay, a specialist in chemical experiments. According to the parish records in Spitalfields, Bartholomew Tremlay is the occupant of the unmarked tomb recently vandalised in the grounds of Christchurch. Tremlay. Not a common name in the twentieth century. Have you any comments to make on the coincidence of names, Dr Waterlow?'

Waterlow shook his head, and Macready scrutinised him for a moment before continuing.

'These men engaged in some curious correspondence. And

here—' He turned several pages of the pamphlet. 'Here you have a most useful appendix that includes extracts from letters between Bartholomew Tremlay and Timothy Ascham, then president of the Invisible fraternity and a member of the newly established lodge. The letters concern an experiment, if I recollect correctly, from which Mr Tremlay reported a somewhat dramatic outcome. What happened?'

'He claimed to have—' At first Waterlow's voice came out in a whisper. He cleared his throat and started again. 'He claimed to have produced a homunculus, an alchemical man. He was probably just hallucinating.'

'But evidently his friend Ascham did not think so. For the benefit of my colleagues, who were asleep in their beds in the small hours of the morning while I was locked deep in the archives of Gresham library,' Macready gave them a sideways glance, 'let me read Mr Ascham's letter.

"Sir, I have begged of you that you would not try this recipe in this phase of the moon but, perforce, you must go against all my urgings in the matter and now who may vouch for the consequences? The Walker is abroad again."

'The letter is dated 1st of September, 1728. The reply is short and prompt. "*The sons of men are snared at an evil time, when it suddenly falls upon them.*" The words are from *Ecclesiastes*. On the 8th September, Timothy Ascham was found murdered in his bed, with both eyes neatly removed and placed in a silver bowl on his table. And a message written in blood on the parchment beside them: "*That ye may see the business that is done.*"'

Macready closed the pamphlet and placed it on the desk in front of him. He let the silence reign again for a full two minutes before cutting into it with a voice that was pure steel.

'Dr Waterlow, where is Maxwell Tremlay?'

51

Her watch said 10.20 but she had no way of knowing whether it was morning or evening. Nell held the door of the fridge wide open, to let as much as light as possible out into the room. She could see the table in the middle quite clearly now and the square outlines of pictures pinned to the wall on her right. The other shapes she'd seen by the camera flash, over against the wall on her left, were harder to make out. Since the fridge door swung shut when she let it go, she had to memorise where they were and make her way across in the dark to investigate. Two big stone washing tubs, like the ones in the kitchen at home. She could feel the shape of the taps and the plugholes in the bottom. Next to them was the door. Of course it was locked, but it was there.

She sat for a while with her back to it, listening. Once or twice she thought she heard fluttering noises near the ceiling, as if there were birds somewhere. Was this a basement or an attic? If it's an attic, said the voice, there's a better chance someone might hear you if you yell out. But it would be better not to yell out now, in case he comes with the knife.

Nell rested her head on her knees, closed her eyes and tried to remember the story of *Hard Times*, detail by detail, from the beginning, but it was hard to concentrate because every couple of minutes she thought she heard something—perhaps a bird—or perhaps sounds of someone moving around somewhere else in the building. Or perhaps she was just imagining it. But after a while, who knew how long, she did hear something. Her muscles froze and her heart started to beat violently. It was a door opening and closing, then footsteps. She crawled back to the other side of the room, where she had been lying and found her mac. Then she lay down on the floor and pretended to be asleep.

A torch beam shone hard into her face.

'I thought you might be back in business. Been creeping around, eh? Wouldn't do that, if I were you.'

Nell was lying on her side and tried to turn her face out of the glare of the torch beam, but she could hardly move. A knee was pressing so hard into her ribs she thought they would crack and a hand pushed down on her shoulder. It hurt so much she was going to have to scream any second, but she couldn't get the breath to scream and let out a kind of sob instead. Then suddenly she was released.

'Get up. I said, Get up! Stand up.'

Slowly she made her way to a standing position, her back against the wall. The torch beam followed her as she rose, but at least now she could raise her arm to protect her eyes.

Something gleamed for a second across the torch beam. 'See that? Know what a scalpel is, Nell? You'd think it was for taking scalps, wouldn't you? But it's much more versatile than that. Mind you, your scalp might be worth taking.' A hand grabbed her hair and twisted it violently above her head, so she squealed. 'Don't tempt me, will you?' He let go. 'I've got a few things to see to. If you stay nice and still, nice and quiet, I might not even need to tie you up. You strike me as an intelligent sort of person, so I'll put you in the picture. This is a cellar. Soundproof.' The voice made a wolf howl. 'See? You could hold a rock concert in here and no one would know. And there's no way out. The door's double panelled and there's an exclusive designer bolt on the other side. So if you want to shuffle around a bit—as you have evidently been doing—that's fine. But don't waste your energy trying to get liberated. I want you nice and alert for a scene that's coming up. You're a very lucky girl, Nell, as a matter of fact. Not many people have seen what you're going to see.'

The beam snapped off, but its after-image continued to dazzle her.

52

Macready had allowed a fifteen minute break and when she got out of the room, Briony felt as stiff and tense as if she'd been in the hot seat herself. She stretched her fingers and rolled her head slowly, with her eyes closed, to stretch her neck. When she opened them again, Steve was standing in the corridor staring at her.

'Cup of coffee?'

Before she could answer, Macready swept past. 'My office, please. Palgrave has things to report.'

Palgrave had managed to get Philip Tremlay on the phone and learnt, as he put it, 'a few things we should have picked up on before.' Like Maxwell Tremlay was Philip Tremlay's cousin and the nephew of Barbara Anglesby, the train murder victim.

'He should have been on the suspect list in the first place,' said Palgrave, 'if the investigating team had done their homework properly in 1967. All the connections are there. Admitted to Gresham as a medical student in 1963, but withdrew in 1966 without completing his degree. In February that year he was charged with possession of LSD. Let off with a fine that was paid by his aunt. Philip Tremlay admits there may have been some tension over this, especially as she went through his things looking for more drugs and found some papers that upset her. She rang him up in a state, but wouldn't say what was in them. Dr Tremlay's impression was that she was overreacting to something a woman of her generation couldn't really cope with. Student lifestyle. He didn't like his cousin, but insists it never occurred to him that he would commit murder. He assumed he was in London and hasn't, in any case, seen him since Maxwell Tremlay was twelve years old. As for helping us to trace him now—well, I'd say Philip Tremlay was one of those people who doesn't see much beyond his own front fence. We might shake something out of him in a face-to-face interview, but he's useless to us at this stage, from this distance.

'I've requested a search through Barbara Anglesby's letters—luckily for us those at least were put in safekeeping as evidence during the first investigation. We can see if there was any correspondence with Maxwell Tremlay, or even any indication of where he was living. The Whitechapel team have put in a lot of work trying to find out whether he's local to the area. He knows it like the back of his hand.'

'And he clearly has a proprietorial interest in the grave next to Christchurch,' Macready cut in. 'A motive pattern is emerging. All the victims knew of his esoteric activities and their macabre results, or at least—like Caroline Staines—they were in danger of finding out.'

Palgrave resumed. 'Now we know more certainly who we are looking for, I'd say the best thing is to launch a big television appeal on the evening news for anyone who might recognise him. We've got the passport office hunting out his photograph. And we'll need Waterlow to do a new Identikit before you start on him again, sir.'

'You may have him for half an hour.'

After Palgrave left, Briony feared that Macready was going to keep her and Steve there in his stuffy office in silence, like two kids being punished by the headmaster. She decided to use the old schoolroom tactic for escape.

'Sir, could I be excused for a moment, please?'

Macready waved a hand. 'Yes. By all means, make yourself scarce, both of you.'

Steve took her by the elbow as they were walking back down the corridor. 'Let's get that coffee.'

The sound of the jug boiling in the kitchenette was almost soothing. Steve stood with his back to the window, smoking with deep concentration, while Briony leant against the cupboard and stared at her shoes. It was Steve who spoke first.

'We need to know more about Tremlay.'

'We're doing our best—or rather Macready is. How much more do you think Waterlow knows?'

'Plenty. But that's not what I meant. I meant the other Tremlay. Bartholomew. This guy's repeating history, right?'

'I suppose so. In a way.'

'Calling himself Walker—I mean—that's a clear sign he's reliving the earlier Tremlay's adventures. What do you think the connection is?'

'How do you mean?'

'Well, it must be his ancestor, I suppose. That's one of the things we should be finding out.'

Briony tried not to sound exasperated. 'I'm sure that would be fascinating, if we had a week to spare. We have to find out where he is. Now.'

'Okay. But my point is—let's put it this way. One of the things we're certain about our Walker is that he knows London like the back of his hand. He went to California and he could have sunk there without trace after he escaped from jail. He could have gone out in the desert with another bunch of wackos and lived happily ever after, shooting up and occasionally disembowelling someone when he got the shits. But he didn't.'

'He came back to London.'

'Right. Now he's not London born and bred, because we know his family's from Cornwall, but he's chosen London. It's his hunting ground. It's where the Walker got released. Now where exactly do you think that was?'

'Because wherever it was, it's going to be a really important place to our Walker.' Briony was getting excited now. 'We can find that out. Surely we can find that out. The pamphlet Macready's got is quoting from letters—letters Waterlow must have seen in the original. I guess they didn't put neat little addresses in the right hand corner then, like we do now. But we don't have time right now to go ferreting around trying to locate Bartholomew Tremlay's papers.'

'Now it's your turn to chop off the promising lines of enquiry eh? Waterlow would know where the papers are. And, more than that, he'd know what's in them. He probably knows where Tremlay lived and where he did his experiments. So instead of giving him the third degree about Maxwell Tremlay and risk him giving us the run-around for another two hours, we backtrack and get him to tell us everything he knows about Bartholomew T and his experiments.'

Briony was just thinking she would grab an early lunch so she'd be prepared for a long afternoon in the interview room, when Jimmy appeared at the door.

'Typical!' he said. 'I might a known you two would be in here arguing about the price of fish when it's bedlam down the other end of the corridor. I should watch out, if I was you. Macready's got his umbrella and he's looking for somebody to impale.'

'Why? What's up?' she asked.

'Lord Byron's given us the slip, that's what.'

Steve was on his feet, stubbing out a half smoked cigarette. 'What are you talking about?'

'Waterlow. Disappeared from under our noses.'

'But how?' asked Briony.

Jimmy straddled the corner of Steve's desk and put one foot on the chair.

'*How* is what they're trying to figure out right now. He was in the front office doing an Identikit and they left him what you might call a window of opportunity. One of the blokes there went out to get lunch and the other one was called to the phone on the front desk. He goes back in the room—and there's nobody there.'

'Shit,' said Steve instantly, 'the scaffolding!'

Briony followed him to the scene, noticing as she passed that the young officer she'd spoken to about Quin's Identikit was standing alone in the corridor looking as if he'd just witnessed a bad accident. Roger Waterlow was among a small group of uniformed police by the front desk, beetroot red and muttering words like 'flabbergasted' and 'completely flummoxed'.

Palgrave had already figured out the window option and was leaning through it at a dangerous angle, ignoring the gentle drizzle and looking upwards to the roof. Steve joined him. When they pulled their heads back into the room, both looked flushed and disoriented. The rain was like beads of sweat on their foreheads. Palgrave beckoned Briony over and got her to stick her own head out, looking first up, then down towards the ground.

'There's a suspended platform just down there, see,' he explained. 'Basically just a plank with ropes on each end. It's operated with a pulley. If he had an accomplice, he could have been out of the room and on the ground in seconds. Even working it on his own wouldn't have taken him more than a couple of minutes.'

'How long's he been gone?' asked Briony. 'He can't have got far.'

'Doesn't need to,' said Palgrave. 'A dalek in a leopardskin hat could lose himself in the Piccadilly crowds at lunch time.'

53

'You know things are getting desperate,' said Steve, 'when Palgrave tries to be witty. Come on—at the risk of getting skewered, we'd best go find the boss.'

Macready was sitting in his office with his overcoat on, his umbrella hooked over the edge of the desk and reading Waterlow's pamphlet. The small window rattled in response to a sudden squall of wind, and rain lashed against the glass. He did not even seem to register Steve and Briony's entrance into the room, but after a minute, he said, 'I hope you have brought your macintoshes, as I have no intention of sharing my umbrella, especially with Inspector Williams.'

'Where are we going?' asked Steve.

'I am endeavouring to determine that, Latham, if you would be so kind as to allow me to concentrate.'

Steve got out his cigarette pack and offered it to Briony. She took one and he lit it for her, then reached for the ashtray from Macready's desk and balanced it on his knee, so they could both use it. Not even pretending to smoke it, Briony watched the cigarette burn into a long column of ash, and listened to the rain as it settled into a steady pattern. It was Steve who broke the silence.

'Is there any indication there, sir, of where Bartholomew Tremlay did these experiments of his?'

'Ah, Latham, I see we are thinking along the same lines again. There is a reference to the place of his birth, in St Swithin's Lane, Cheapside, an area now converted to office blocks. I have checked it already. But, of course, he was born before the great fire of London. If his laboratory was kept there, it would have been razed to the ground.'

'So he would have moved after the great fire. Where?'

'Across the river, very likely, but he could have moved back again as the city was being rebuilt. We can't easily narrow the options.' said Macready.

Steve was deep in concentration, issuing columns of smoke from both nostrils. 'So what type of place are we looking for? Has to be somewhere old. There are plenty of buildings in London that go back to 1720, but they're pretty special buildings.'

'It may be more complicated than that, Latham. Think of all the houses in London that have been partially rebuilt. What kind of place are we looking for?'

'Jimmy thinks the murderer may be a photographer,' said Briony. 'In which case, he'd need a dark room. You couldn't take photographs like that to the chemist for developing. Maybe he's got some kind of basement place. And I was thinking—you know this Tupperware stuff he uses? Well, according to Palgrave, it's discontinued. He must have acquired it a few years ago—maybe he took it from his aunt's place, or something—so he had it before he went to America. I bet he's kept stuff, somewhere, somewhere in London, somewhere he knew he could go back to.'

Steve interrupted. 'Then why did he ask Sabina for a place to stay?'

'Do you think that's really why he sought her out? Turning up like that was a warning. He came to intimidate her. He didn't go to all that trouble to make her a colourful end, just because she wouldn't let him doss down on the living room couch. He had deeper scores to settle. I don't believe he was looking for a place to stay at all. That's a red herring.'

She held up a hand to stop him interrupting again. 'Just—just suppose for a minute he *did* have a place he could hang onto even while he was away for several months. You wouldn't do that with an ordinary flat. But if it was some kind of cellar, or store room—'

There was a knock on the door and Palgrave appeared.

'Excuse me, sir. Several people noticed a post office van drive down Vine Street half an hour ago. It passed one of our cars. Unfortunately, nobody got the number. We've radioed all the cars within a ten mile radius and asked them to report the location and registration number of every post office van they see. If there's any grounds for suspicion about any of them, they're to tail it.'

'Just a minute,' said Steve. 'I should have thought of this before.' And he bolted from the room.

Macready tapped the end of his pencil on the desk briskly, as if making up his mind about something. 'Perhaps you had better go too, Inspector Williams. Find us a map of London in the early eighteenth century. The library staff at Senate House should be able to help you.'

54

Nell was sitting on the floor. She had taken off her tights and was feeding one leg of them into the other, to make a thicker sleeve. Into this she pushed the camera, right down to the end and tied a knot to secure it.

A sling. She would have to hit him straightaway, the minute she could see where he was. If he had his torch switched on as he came in, then she would see him before he saw her. It would be a momentary advantage. To strengthen it, she could leave the fridge door open—that would draw his attention and he'd probably move into the room towards it, so if she flattened herself against the wall by the doorway, she'd have a chance of hitting him from behind. Then she'd have to get out and close the door after her, double quick, and bolt it before he could recover.

But she knew she was not going to be a good shot. She might only whack him on the shoulder or in the middle of the back, then he would be able to grab her before she could try again. What if the bolt was hard to move and he got through the door after her, to chase her through whatever dark passage was on the other side of it?

What she needed was some way of tripping him, to be sure he actually fell as she hit him. A booby trap. Her heart beat faster. The

Booby Trap. Maybe you saved my life, Julie, with your lime green underwear, she thought.

She stood up and slowly removed the scarf which she'd used to bandage her arm. The blood had dried now and there didn't seem to be much of it, but her arm was still stiff and felt swollen, so removing her shirt was an awkward process. Not as awkward, though, as unclasping the bra with her left hand. It had a stupid little clip that refused to disengage, no matter how she pushed and pulled. Eventually she had to do it the way she'd been shown by the fitting specialist in the department store where Aunty Pat had taken her to buy her first bra: pull the straps down off your shoulders and take your arms out, then swivel the whole thing round so the clasp is at the front. And undo it. Who but a blue-rinsed corseted old fusspot like that would ever bother with such a routine, she'd thought at the time.

It was a relief to get the shirt on again. She went over and opened the fridge. Her watch said 1.15. Day or night? He could be back any minute, or not for hours. She crouched down and looked under the fridge. Not that she could see, exactly, since there was no light at all at floor level, but she could feel where the legs were, and that they were those old fashioned thick iron legs, that curved outwards slightly. Perfect. The fridge was hard to lift, but she only had to raise it a fraction of an inch, for a couple of seconds, to slide one of the shoulder straps of the Booby Trap underneath it.

The table was heavy as well. That was a good thing. Very heavy. Very good. But it was a slow and strenuous business to manoeuvre it into position, so that the corner formed one point of a triangle between the fridge and the door. She slid the other bra strap under the leg of the table, then pushed it back until the Booby Trap was stretched completely taut, forming a trip line about three inches above the ground.

All she had to do now was wait.

55

The Senate House library staff put the passport office to shame. Within an hour of Briony's phone call, two books containing early maps of London were delivered by cab. Markers had been set considerately at the pages most likely to be of use.

Briony took them straight down the hall to Macready, who was still sitting in his overcoat.

'Williams. Have you seen DC Caldwell today, by any chance?'

'Donna? Yes, sir. I saw her this morning, just before the general briefing.'

'She was due to report to Palgrave ten minutes ago. She has failed to do so.'

A chill went up the back of Briony's neck.

'To tell you the truth, sir, I've been concerned—'

'So have I, Williams, which is why I have had DC Caldwell followed for the past two days. If she has set off on any unauthorised expedition, I expect DC Atherton to telephone with a report at any moment. If a trap has been set for her, she may lead us directly into the heart of it.'

'Then with any luck we won't need to spend too much time on these,' said Briony, as she deposited the books on Macready's desk.

'On the contrary. We will continue to pursue all avenues. Palgrave and I are at present checking the coordinates of no fewer than twenty-seven post office vans. So you may take the books back to your own desk—and this—' he handed her Waterlow's pamphlet. 'Do not let it out of your sight. See what you can make of it. Latham may have something to contribute when he returns. And, Williams—be ready to leave immediately on report of a location.'

'Yes, sir.' She lugged the books back to her own desk and dumped them with a satisfying thud. They were heavy and awkwardly mismatched in shape. She opened the first at one of the places that had been marked and stared at the maze of streets and out-of-scale buildings. It would all have been fascinating no doubt if you had a couple of days to spare and somebody's life didn't depend on your knowing what you were looking for. And where the hell was Donna? Had she gone looking for Waterlow on her own initiative? Hopefully the officer assigned to tail her would call in soon. She looked at her watch. 2.15.

As she turned the pages of the first book, the maps stared back at her like a crazy jumble, so she closed it and turned her attention to the pamphlet. At the back the pages were in different type. These were the ones containing extracts from Bartholomew Tremlay's correspondence. There were also some passages from his diary.

This also is vanity and striving after wind, saith the Preacher, that vain fool.

The Preacher cometh first but the Walker who casteth no shadow in the sun cometh after.

And the Walker entereth to do his work with the Preacher's

hands and to make his way in the Preacher's steps. So all shall be turned to the way of undoing.

Vanity of vanities, saith the Preacher, and the Preacher hath a vain tongue.

There is a time for the tongue in the mouth and a time for the knife in the hand. And the Walker maketh his way through time and none shall stop his course, even to the hundredth generation.

The wind goes around and around and all things shall be turned to the way of undoing.

A time to pluck out, and a time to rend,
A time for hate, and a time for war,
A time to kill, and a time to die,
Better to be amongst the dead who are already dead
Than amongst the living who shall meet their end at his hands.
For there is evil under the sun
And he casteth no shadow
And he entereth where he will
And his knife speaketh in the dark
And he shall cast off one vessel to enter another

And the man that is entered shall take on the look of his eye
And the breath of his mouth and the way of his coming

And who so inviteth him in, shall know all things and remain alive in him, even to the hundredth generation, for death is no threshold for him, and he casteth no shadow in the sun.

Somebody should take this stuff and burn it, thought Briony, or rip it up and flush it down the toilet. Just reading it made her feel there was some malevolent presence in the room with her, so she had to force herself to look up and around to confirm that she was alone. But she didn't feel alone.

She stood up, intending to march down the corridor to find Jimmy or Palgrave or anyone, just to exchange a few words and shake off the creeps, but she remembered Macready's instructions—don't let it out of your sight. So she had to take the nasty thing with her, clutched in her hand. It ought at least to have been in a plastic sleeve. Not that fingerprints were worth bothering about, when it had been in the library for God knew how long, but something was needed to restrict its contaminating influence.

She was raking through her desk drawers, looking for a stray evidence bag that she might have thrown in there, when Steve came back with an evidence bag in his hand.

'Get some gloves,' he said. 'I need you to help me go through this.'

They sat on either side of his desk and laid out the contents of the bag. The papers were very old: thick and mottled and written on in brown ink which had perhaps once been black. At first it was hard to make out any of the words at all. The writing was a slanted scrawl with some of the letters put in above the line, in miniature.

'What are they?' she asked.

'Christopher Glade's papers. Glade was the locksmith who made the contraption on the Christchurch door. The Freemasons have kept his papers. So I had this thought. If Walker or Tremlay or whoever he is—this sick fuck we're trying to track down—has got a key to the Christchurch lock, maybe the connection's important in other ways. And look at this.' Steve pointed with a gloved finger at a page ruled into two columns of unequal width. One seemed to have names in it. The other was crammed with words in smaller writing. 'See here,' he indicated a name near the bottom of the second column.

Briony squinted. '*B Tremb*.'

'Right.' Steve's voice caught as he spoke. 'And here it says *2 lockes of brasse wth key of same*. And here—' he pointed with an unsteady finger at another sheet, also ruled in columns. Three columns. One had dates: 22nd June, 30th June, 4th July, 4th July, 18th July. Another names. She saw again *B Tremb*. The third column was addresses. Steve put a ruler across the page under Tremlay's name, slanting it to follow the heavy diagonal of the writing. *4 Laman ^St.* 'This must be some kind of delivery sheet,' he said. 'I need an A–Z.'

'No you don't,' said Briony. 'You need these.' She went across to her own desk and started going through the first book of maps, looking at the back for an index. There wasn't one. She sat down. 'Looks like we have to do this the hard way. These are old maps, from Tremlay's time. Some of the streets are named, but not all of them. I'll start looking; you start praying.'

56

The plot of *Hard Times* was easier to remember than the plot of *Anna Karenina*. She got stuck a few times in both, but there were parts of *Anna Karenina* that had disappeared completely from her memory. Most of what happened in the middle, in fact. Yet some scenes leapt to the front of your mind and stayed there. Like, of course, the scenes at the railway station, where the horror caught up with Anna and the horse race in which Vronsky rode like a madman and broke the horse's back. That was awful. Better to think about the horses in Mr Sleary's circus.

But really it was hard to keep her mind on anything. It kept jumping back to the present and the adrenalin was pumping through her, preparing her for when the door opened, or rather for when the first sound of someone on the other side of the door might be audible. It was tempting to do a walk around the room, which she could see a bit more clearly now, because the fridge light took away the worst darkness, even from the furthest corners.

But what if he came to the door just as she was at one of these corners? She had to stay at her post. She'd looked at her watch so many times. She tried to measure ten minute intervals, only checking it when she thought the ten minutes was up. Funnily enough, she did better the first few times; then her racing pulse started to confuse things and she was checking every three or four minutes. She went back into the classroom scene in *Hard Times* and tried to remember the dialogue about the definition of a horse, which she had thought very funny the first time she read it, but now it seemed quite strange and confused. And then there was a sudden sharp *clack* coming from the other side of the door and her heart started to thunder and thump so she had to gasp for breath as she got into position, flattening herself against the wall.

Instantly he reacted to the open fridge.

'Been fuckin around, have we?' he said, as he strode forward and Nell took a big step away from the wall, enough to make room for the arc of the sling behind her, exactly as she had figured it out and she felt the weight fly through the air and heard it crack down against the side of the man's head. Then he seemed to be trying to turn on her, but he had caught his foot in something and as she dived for the door, he fell towards her at an awkward angle, crashing against the table.

She got out and pushed the door shut, hard, behind her, leaning against it with her shoulder as she tried to find the bolt he had mentioned. But there was some complicated arrangement where the bolt ought to have been—some kind of metal wheel or something that she couldn't move. At any minute he could get up and come after her, so she decided to just run—or at least, go as fast as she could in the pitch dark, guiding herself with one hand against the rough wall on her left and still tightly clutching the sling in her right hand, so her knuckles ached and she could feel the sweat in her palm.

The ground was uneven and her feet awkwardly misplaced themselves at every step, so she kept stumbling. It was worse than trying to run in a dream. For all she knew, he could be after her already and about to reach out for her and grab her before she could even think of taking another swing at him.

Suddenly she fell, heavily and painfully, her hands catching against the hard edges of stone as they instinctively shot out to break the fall. The camera hit the stone with a *smack* so loud it echoed. Stairs.

She scrambled up them on all fours, until she reached level floor again. Here the walls were smooth and flat and the floor had been paved, so she could make better speed.

Then there was a break in the wall to her right. She felt around with both hands and determined that it was a corner, a junction with what seemed to be a second passage. Which way? She took some steps to the right, six exactly—it was important to keep count—and was about to retrace them so as to continue in the direction she'd set off, when she thought she saw a a faint spill of light ahead.

It grew clearer as she advanced. Yes. It was light showing under a doorway. Dim light, but a definite band. And when she got there, she could easily make out the edges of the doorway. There was a lock with what seemed to be a large key in it. It was hard to turn and she worried about it making a noise, which it did. A decisive *clunk* as the key moved clockwise. And a prolonged *creak* as the door opened.

She stepped through into a large room lit by candles. A giant candle stood in an elaborate iron stand in the middle and there was another of these in each corner. As she looked around, her whole body seemed to have gone into slow motion. In a continuous scan she saw paintings on the walls, books on shelves and in piles on the floor, benches with bottles and other kinds of oddly shaped glassware, thick cords hanging from the ceiling in great loops, tall ornate mirrors propped against the walls. And she saw a man asleep on a chair facing one of these mirrors and a woman with long drooping hair facing another mirror, with her hands tied above her head by one of the cords dangling from the heavy beam that spanned the ceiling. Her thoughts came in slow motion, one by one, as if from far away. Wake the man up. Untie the woman. Or find something to cut the ropes on her hands. Scream for help. Another thought said, see if the camera still works and take a photo. The woman's eyes were wide open and her mouth was covered with a broad tape or bandage. The man could be already dead, with his throat cut like someone else she had seen in that posture a long time ago.

Like someone wading through deep water, she forced her way two steps towards the woman, but then something happened. Something clamped itself over her nose and mouth so that she couldn't breathe, then a nasty sour tasting ball of cloth was forced inside her mouth and she was retching. There was a sharp ripping noise and a wide band of sticky stuff was stretched over the lower half of her face, pulling at her skin and barely leaving her nostrils free to draw air.

'Nice of you to find your own way up here,' said a voice. 'I thought I was going to have to transport you.'

Coils of rope—one, two, three—were passed around her upper body, pressing her arms against her sides and causing sharp waves of pain to surge up from the swollen arm. She fell sideways, but she didn't fall, she swung—until something yanked her back upright again and she was forced into a chair rammed against the backs of her knees.

'Won't be long now. Fifteen minutes. Twenty, maybe. We have to wait for Guy here to wake up to himself so he can appreciate the trouble I'm taking with him. I believe you met each other once before, by coincidence, or what you might call a chance turn of events. Of course, chance never has anything to do with the turn of events, not when you know how these things come about and can be made to come about, but I don't expect you to follow that. You're just here to watch the show. Guy helped me to find you, after your photo appeared in the paper. Said he'd run into you at a party.'

57

The earliest map that gave any useful street names was one for 1769, nearly fifty years after Tremlay's death, and judging from the much sparser layout of a map for 1700, a great deal of building had gone on during that time in most areas of central London.

'Well, that stands to reason,' said Steve. 'They were trying to reinvent the whole city after the great fire. They got pretty ambitious.'

With the aid of magnifying glasses they identified three Laman streets on the later map: one off Leadenhall Street, one near the Horse Ferry in Westminster and one in Southwark, not far south of the Bankside. None of these correlated with any of the six Laman streets in the current A to Z, so there was no straightforward way to point the location now. Leadenhall Street was an obvious first choice since it ran up to Whitechapel and ended close to Duke's Place, but Steve was sceptical. It was half a mile away from where the great fire started, he pointed out, and for anyone who had lived through it, was unlikely to have been the choice location for a laboratory containing precious materials.

'Southwark gets my vote,' he said, 'but, anyway, we're guessing. Let's take this to Macready. See if anything ties in with what he's got to go on.'

Macready had a street plan of the whole metropolitan area spread across his desk. He called Palgrave to join them, and proceeded with a rather gloomy report. Attempts to trace the still un-numbered post office van had come to nothing, while squandering the time of nearly half the Met's patrol fleet. Two dozen vans had been stopped for checks on the drivers and six stationery vans had been opened and searched. There was nothing suspicious about any of them. The patrols had also been asked to report on vans that had travelled outside the range of a normal delivery run. One that had been followed north up the Pancras Road then up Pancras Way and on beyond Camden Town turned out only to be making an express delivery. Another had gone a suspiciously long way around the Victoria Embankment, but they'd got it confused with two other vans in the spaghetti junction at Blackfriars and had given up on the chase.

More disturbingly, as Palgrave now reported, tapping his mouth with his fist between words, as if trying to knock back each phrase of the embarrassing news he was obliged to report, the officer tailing Donna Caldwell had lost her. She had answered a phone call and left Vine Street promptly afterwards, taking a southbound Bakerloo Line train to Waterloo. DC Atherton had lost her at Waterloo station, where she had gone into a Ladies that, unbeknown to him, had a street side exit.

'Very good, Palgrave,' said Macready tonelessly. 'We are excelling ourselves here, putting the Marx Brothers to shame. What other ingredients are in the Duck Soup?'

'None, sir, I hope,' said Palgrave, swallowing. 'The mistake was more understandable than it might seem. PC Caldwell was known for regularly making prolonged visits to the Ladies room to do her make-up, sir. The officer had no reason to suspect that—'

Briony's thoughts were racing and mounting excitement got the better of her. She interrupted in a rush. 'Southwark! It fits!'

'There is no need to shout, Williams.' Macready's eyebrow was back in action, which somehow looked like a good omen for once.

'And please refer to the map. Specificity is of the essence at this point.'

'We've found an address for Tremlay—Laman Street—and we've found three Laman streets on an eighteenth century map. One of them is somewhere here.' She pointed to the area south of the river between Blackfriars Road and Borough High Street. 'It's hard to pinpoint, because all the street names have changed.'

'There's a lot of old warehouses and disused sheds around here, near the Bankside power station,' said Palgrave. 'Some of them have got underground storage facilities or cellars. A lot of the cellars were dug out during the war, so's they would have somewhere to store all their stuff in the bombing. And of course they doubled as air-raid shelters for the local workers. Very secure. Wouldn't like to be shut up in one myself, not with our Walker for company. There's very few residents left in this area now.'

'Let's go,' said Macready. 'Palgrave, you had better stay here in case better information comes this way and proves we are on a wild goose chase, or duck hunt or whatever may be the appropriate metaphor for the occasion. Williams, Latham, you will each be in charge of a car with two patrol officers, doing house to house searches. Be sure you have high powered torches with full batteries. We will operate from three points of a triangle. Latham starts here, at the Borough Market end of Park Street and moves west, across the Southwark Bridge Road. Williams, you progress from the riverside end of Holland Street then eastwards along Sumner Street. I will begin at the junction between Blackfriars Road and Union Street and work through this block here and then on down Bear Lane towards the river. Report your location by radio after each search. If you find anything that requires investigation, order back-up immediately. Palgrave will alert the Southwark police, so that they are ready to render assistance.'

58

On Briony's count, they passed eleven post office vans on the siren ride between Piccadilly and Bankside. The wind had dropped but the rain was still coming down quite heavily, so the driver, a sergeant in early middle age with a solid, four-square look about him, needed to concentrate and no one attempted any conversation on the way. The second officer, a constable in uniform, was much younger and, Briony thought, looked rather tense. If they got into any trouble, he'd be the one to send for back-up. The traffic was slow across Waterloo Bridge and she wished she could get out and run. Anything rather than being trapped in this slow procession with the rhythm of the high speed windscreen wipers whipping her thoughts into a meaningless set of repetitions.

The driver took a left turn almost as soon as they were off the bridge, leaving the worst of the traffic behind and steering into a warren of streets lined by what looked like outsize garages. Most of them were visibly locked, with loops of chain through their handles. There were no people here and no footpaths for pedestrians, but as they rounded a bend the car was brought to a halt by a bedraggled dog crossing the street at its own steady pace and staring at them as if they were intruders on its terrain.

'Left again or under the bridge?' asked the sergeant.

Briony leant towards the windscreen and looked up at the heavy brick arch looming ahead. 'Left again. We'll check out this side as closely as we can before we go under the railway line. Not many of these doors look worth knocking on, but we may have to get out and try. Stop at the next corner there, by that green fence.'

The fence was chipped and rotten, with assorted bits of rubbish caught between the planks at its base.

'I'll get out, if you like,' said the constable. 'Take a look round.'

'So will I,' said Briony. 'You take this side; I'll do the other.'

The rain was unrelenting as it ate into the surface of her mac, so it got colder and heavier on her arms. Behind the fence was waste ground, with no structures of any kind on it. She walked back the way they'd come, hoping she might hear or see some sign of activity. If there was anyone around here, anyone at all, there was a chance they would have noticed a post office van passing, given that there was so little else on the streets to notice.

Nothing. She got back in the car and beckoned the constable to join her, but he called out, 'T's' all right. I'll follow you on foot. I got better waterproofs than you have, Inspector.'

He was right, of course. A cape, boots and a helmet were just the equipment for this job. They drove around the next corner at a slow crawl, passing a small shop with boarded windows. What an utterly dismal place. After touring two more blocks, they went back for the constable and found him standing in the road and staring at the ground.

Briony got out and he pointed to some fresh tyre marks where a vehicle had clipped the kerb and crossed a muddy grass verge.

'In too much of a hurry,' he commented, laconically.

The tracks led a short way into the next street, then turned into a garage with padlocked doors. Since the garage was built onto the front of a warehouse, chances were that there was an entry to it from the inside. That might be an easier bet than tackling the padlock.

But a walk around the back revealed that the garage doors appeared to be the only entrance to the whole building. A high fence ran down one side of it, barely a foot away from the wall; there would be no access that way.

Briony returned to the front and stared at the lock. 'Could we pick that, do you think?' she asked.

'Take a while, unless you had the right instruments,' said the sergeant, inspecting it at close range and spending what seemed to Briony an inordinate amount of time turning it this way and that as he peered at it and poked it with a crude looking penknife. She shifted from one foot to the other and looked at her watch intermittently as five minutes felt like an hour.

'Hey, hello!' said the constable brightly.

A sleepy looking pigeon had waddled out from the narrow gap by the fence, its feathers all fluffed up. They were dry. Completely.

'It's been inside there,' said Briony. 'There must be a hole in the wall or something. Constable Bellingham, get down and look.'

The constable obediently crouched on the ground by the fence and squinted, then edged himself sideways into the gap, until only his boots were visible, then he called for the torch.

He scrambled to his feet again, red in the face and breathing fast.

'There's a vehicle in there, Inspector, a van. Colour red.'

'Right,' said Briony. 'Thank you, Constable. Please return to the car and radio that information. Then remain here till Superintendent Macready arrives.' She looked sternly at the sergeant, to try and forestall any objection as she said, 'We are going to break into this place. Immediately.'

The sergeant was not the argumentative type. He brought a small metal box from the boot of the car and took out a chisel and screwdriver, then set about removing one of the asbestos panels from the wooden frame.

'Wouldn't it be quicker to just break it?' asked Briony.

'No, ma'am. Not with what I got available. You'd need a mallet. Here we are. Nearly done.'

He climbed through and she followed.

The doors at the back of the van were not locked and the smell hit her the moment she opened them. Formaldehyde. She hardly paused to inspect the interior, only took in that there was no body before moving to the inside end of the garage and searching with the torch for the way through to the main building.

The door frame was heavy and set low in the ground, so the base of the door was about four inches below the concrete floor of the shed. No lock on this door, either, but a big step down, as she opened it inwards. The floor on the other side consisted of ill-matched wooden planks, some of which had come loose and got out of alignment, making treacherous gaps through which you could easily put your foot. The whole place was just a shell. No interior walls and no ceiling. The torch beam dissolved into the cavernous space of the roof.

As they picked their way across the floor, the arrangement of planks became increasingly sparse and disordered until, about three feet from the far wall, it ended altogether, leaving what looked at first like a black hole. Briony lowered herself carefully to a crouching position and explored with the torch. The last plank was wider than the others and thicker looking, almost like a beam.

The sergeant took up his position a bit further along and lowered one foot over the edge.

'I think there's a step down here,' he said, then lowered the second foot and stood up to prove it. It was a narrow flight of stone steps, set against an underground wall that ran across almost midway between the outer walls of the building. The steps were worn into dips and hollows so you had to keep one hand on the wall to steady your balance as you went down.

And it was a long way down. After a dozen or so steps, the

sergeant whispered, 'Inspector Williams, hadn't we better wait for back-up?'

'I don't think we can afford to wait,' said Briony. 'They'll find us easily enough.' And she tried to quicken her pace, which meant concentrating hard to keep the pool of torch light angled so that it provided enough light behind her for the sergeant to follow, while allowing her to see where she was putting her own feet.

At the bottom of the staircase an archway ahead of them marked the contours of a passageway lined with stone and set at intervals with elaborately curled iron brackets, presumably to hold flame torches. Someone had taken a lot of trouble with the building of this. About ten yards in, a second passageway opened up to her left and she stopped for a few seconds to consider which way; there was no question of splitting up, in the circumstances. It would be best to continue in the same direction, she decided, otherwise they risked confusion if there were further alternatives along the way. The second set of steps took her by surprise and she would have lost her balance if the sergeant had not caught her arm in time.

Instinctively, they stayed much closer together as they proceeded along the next section of the passageway, where the ground had not been levelled and was set with jutting stones at odd angles, as if they were actually meant to trip you. The walls here were without torch brackets, so maybe the area was designed as a trap to confound intruders. Their own torch revealed a doorway at the far end, with an elaborate bolt. Brass, with a notched wheel and large keyhole, but no key. However, it was not locked.

She gestured to the sergeant to stay by the door as she explored. It was a large square cellar with a table and a fridge on one side and a double stoneware sink opposite. Beside the sink was a locked cupboard, but she knew what this was for by the now familiar smell of formaldehyde. It was a darkroom. A scan around the walls revealed dozens of photographs of varying sizes, from large glossy prints to polaroid snapshots. With a shock that registered like a violent strum through her whole nervous system, Briony recognised Donna, photographed near the entrance to Piccadilly station and coming out of the Lyons café and seen through the window—quite close up this time—sitting at one of the tables. Then there was Caroline Staines—not as Jimmy had captured her, all bits and pieces, but in a single shot taken directly above the corpse, like a parody of a Penthouse girl lying on her back with her throat arched.

'Pretty, isn't she?' said a voice, close by. 'I prefer them when they're showing what they're made of.'

Briony wheeled round and shone her torch in the face of a man with a thin face surrounded by straggly hair. He held up a knife from which blood was dripping.

'Shame about your friend by the door there. Didn't see me coming. But *you* will. Drop the torch and put your hands on your head.'

She obeyed, hearing the torch roll across the floor out of any easy reach. The man had his own torch, which he shone directly into her eyes, so that the knife blade was all she could see in the glare.

'Turn around.' He bound her hands behind her with tape that came off its roll in a searing rip and burned her skin as it crushed her palms together.

'Good. Now we can have a conversation. But only a short one, because I got people waiting. I'll introduce you in a minute, though you already know them really, especially one of them. Donna's a good girl. She comes when she's called. She seems to have taken a liking to the ear nose and throat specialist. I do a bit of ear nose and throat work myself, of course, as I'm about to demonstrate. But first I need you to fill me in on a couple of things. One. How did you find this place?'

Cooperate, thought Briony. Play for time.

'I was worried about Donna, so I got permission to tail her, with help of the officer—the officer over there.'

The enormity of being responsible for the sergeant's death, if he was indeed dead, was swimming amid all the other horrors she'd now walked into. She was having trouble just stringing words together. Any words.

'We followed her to Waterloo station and then we lost track of her, so we started doing a house to house…search in this area.'

'So which way—no, never mind. Answer to the first question, unsatisfactory, but it's enough to give you a choice on the second question. You can go first, second or third. Which will it be? Fourth is already reserved for Alice in Wonderland, who's been more adventurous than you have down here.'

Play for time.

'Can't I be introduced to the others first?'

'That was only a manner of speaking, Detective Inspector. You've already met them. I'll put you second. Let's go. And remember to walk steady. I'm keeping this—' he indicated the knife point, 'close to where your left kidney sits.'

She registered the sergeant's slumped body by the doorway. And blood, lots of it, still spreading across the floor. Then the treacherous ground leading to the shallow uneven stairs. A right turn into another passageway. Through another door. And a huge candlelit room where her bound hands were attached to a heavy cord swinging from somewhere above.

'Behave yourself during the entertainment,' said the voice. 'If someone were to pull hard on this—' he indicated by tugging at the rope so her hands shot out behind her and jarred her elbows and shoulders—'it would put you in the *strappado*, which will be pretty entertaining for anybody else here who's still got their eyes in place.'

He moved away from her and crossed the room towards the figure of a man who was bound into a chair in front of a huge ornate mirror. But then something else happened. Another man, tall and black coated, rushed out from behind her and raised what looked like a stick, held at both ends, over Walker's head, bringing it down and across his throat.

'Handcuffs!' roared Macready's voice and more men ran into the room, so that there was something that looked like a rugby scrum in the centre. Then it went still and Macready came towards her, flicking a pen-knife blade that caught the gleam of a candle. He cut the rope, then the tapes.

'Free the others,' he said, 'while I get our friend organised.'

59

As she sat in the back of the car on the return journey to Vine Street, Briony's thoughts still seemed to be moving in slow motion. She was not sure what questions she had already asked and had great difficulty taking in the answers. She kept remembering particular things that puzzled her, like passing the garage, from which the post office van had been driven out for full examination and noticing a large square opening in the floor. Perhaps she had asked about this, perhaps not. Maybe what she had pieced together in her mind was her own conjecture, or maybe it was a mixture of what she was figuring out and what she'd been told.

Tremlay had started to ask which way she came in. There had to be more than one entrance to his underground place. After all, he couldn't have got the unconscious Waterlow across the broken floor in the warehouse, down all those steps and through the tunnels. It would be a major operation, even with Nell, who was small and slight enough to be carried over his shoulder. The post office van was concealing a major entrance point.

'Which way did you get in then, sir?' she asked Macready, who was in the front seat, but for once turned round towards her rather than showing his back.

'Ah yes, you went the long way round, I think, Williams. There is a drop from the opening in the garage through to the tunnel just outside the room where Tremlay had secured his victims. He has made himself a harness for lowering things directly into his catacombs. We made use of it.'

She smiled. 'You made use of the umbrella too, didn't you, sir?'

'As I have on previous occasions. It is the best defence weapon a police officer may legally have about him, in my experience. I will present you with one of your own, Williams, since you have now more or less deserved it.'

'More or less.'

'But you must take good care of it. An umbrella of hand stitched double silk with a handle of polished scots pine is not to be trifled with.'

'No, sir.'

She went back to processing things in her mind and the smile faded.

'You okay?' asked Steve.

'Oh yeah,' she tried to perk up. 'Just a bit spun out, you know. There was a lot happening down there. What about the sergeant— it's awful, I never even got his name clear.'

'I told you,' said Steve, 'Sergeant Leigh. He's on his way to emergency.'

'So he's got a chance?'

'I told you. There was still a pulse. And Waterlow managed to do something to stop the blood loss.'

'Waterlow will need to do more than that to redeem himself,' said Macready, 'but it's a start. There have been many terrible things in this case, but losing a good officer would be one of the worst.'

'And Donna. I've been worried about her all along. I had a hunch, you know.'

'No injuries that we could tell,' Steve said, 'but of course she's badly shaken up.'

'He'd taken photos of her. He must have been tailing her. I knew he'd tailed Nell, but it never occurred to me that—'

The thought trailed away as another, quite disconnected, took over.

'That pamphlet,' she said. 'It shouldn't go back in the library. It needs to be burnt.'

'No chance.' Steve was grinning broadly now. 'That'll go into the Black Museum. It'll get pride of place, along with Bartholomew Tremlay's diary when we find it. Someone pinched the Ripper's letters from there a few years ago, but this will be a big compensation.'

'Who pinched the Ripper's letters?' asked Briony. 'I've got a hunch we're going to find them with Tremlay's diary.'

Macready turned back to face the windscreen. 'You have had too many hunches, Williams,' he said. 'And too little sleep.'

60

'It was Alec's voice, you see. I knew it instantly. It's one of those gravelly voices, you know? He just said—he said Guy Waterlow wanted to talk to me. He couldn't cope with Macready's interview style and he wanted to be able to explain his situation to someone quietly and calmly, because it was very complicated. So I—'

Donna's voice caught on the last part of the statement and Briony could see she was ready to crack at any moment.

'You don't have to talk about it now if you don't want to. Would you like to go for a walk or something? Get a bit of sun?'

This drew a surprisingly aggressive reaction.

'Of course I have to bloody talk about it! I'll be lucky if I get away with explaining all this less than twenty different ways to fifty different people by the time the trial's over. Anyway, I can't think about anything else. How can I? How can I think about anything else?'

The voice was unsteady again and Donna bit her lip and pushed her hair back from her face, only to let it fall forward again immediately. Briony noticed that it had not been washed.

'So I thought it might be a way to get the information that would save that girl's life. Nell, is that her name? It seemed to be a risk worth taking. Everyone was taking risks. And it didn't actually *seem* much of a risk. I thought that Alec bloke was just a bit of a twerp. He didn't know much. It was Guy who knew things.'

'But he deceived you. He told you all that cock and bull story about his girlfriend's abortion.'

'Did I say that? That was not what I said, Briony Williams!'

'Okay, okay! No need to bite my head off.'

'What I said was, someone else told me that story. A girl called Jenny English. About a friend of *hers* called Susannah. It was Susannah who was supposed to have had the abortion, which was done by somebody called Andrew Michaels. Now don't let anybody tell me I'm mixed up. I've sorted this out in my mind over and over again. I've got all the names clear. Nobody actually mentioned the name of the man who got Susannah pregnant. Alec saw me talking to Jenny. And he came up to me later, in the bar, and he said, "Jenny's told you the story, has she?" And I didn't want to dob Jenny in, but what could I say? So I didn't say anything, and *he* said, "It's okay." And he introduced himself and he said Susannah was just fine, but he'd heard that I'd been asking questions about the Invisibles and why did I want to know? So he never *actually* said he was Susannah's boyfriend, but he led me to make that assumption. Then he looked at me in a funny way and said, "Anyway I know something about you." Somehow he'd figured out I was a cop. He'd been watching me and he said he could tell all the signs of a plainclothes officer. I tried to ask him some more about that, because nobody else has ever sussed me out like that, but he wouldn't be drawn. He said I should know about the Invisibles and he had a friend who wanted to talk to someone and he thought he could get him to talk to me.'

'That was Guy?'

'Yes. Guy. So when Alec rang up for me at the station on Saturday morning, it was a bit like a repeat situation. He was playing the go-between for Guy and I just didn't—I should have thought.'

Briony prompted very quietly. 'And then what happened?'

'He told me Guy would meet me at this pub, near Waterloo station, the Green Man in Stamford Street. So I got to Waterloo and came out on the east side of the station.'

'After checking out the ladies' cloakrooms.'

Donna ignored this intervention. 'And I crossed the road and there was this van parked there and it was a post office van and Alec got out of it and for a split second I just thought, oh, he's come to collect me, you know, to give me a lift? Then I registered—post office van. And it occurred to me: Alec. I never thought it could be Alec. He was just such a—nobody. But there he was grinning at me in this nasty way and coming towards me and I turned to run, but he caught me round the neck and put this handkerchief over my face with this horrible stuff on it that made me choke and I was pushed into the van and then I must have blacked out, because the next thing I knew was—I can't.' The voice shook itself to pieces now and the lip trembled. 'I can't talk about that right now.'

'Come on,' said Briony. 'Let's take that walk in the sun.'

•

When it came to it, Donna did remarkably well in the witness box. She was subdued, but honest and clear in everything she said. From the police point of view, the trial of Maxwell Tremlay went smoothly. After all, they were not exactly short of witnesses and that meant that there was no point in the defence counsel working overtime to undermine any of them. So Donna, Nell, Greg Kendrick and Guy Waterlow got through without any real cross-examination. Tremlay was sent down for life.

It was a different matter during Waterlow's trial for being an accessory—before and after the fact. The prosecution case was built strongly around the evidence that he escaped from the police station of his own accord, with a pre-arranged rendezvous with Tremlay, who was ready to pick him up and drive him away. Waterlow claimed he'd been rendered semi-conscious with some kind of vaporous poison—formaldehyde, obviously—and pushed through the window onto the builders' platform, then into the van, which was waiting with its back doors open. But Waterlow was too big to be manoeuvred involuntarily through this sequence of transitions. The story just didn't hang together. On the other hand, he obviously was rendered unconscious once he'd been got into the van. And why should he have left the safety of the police station to put himself in the power of a man who'd given him every reason to fear and mistrust him?

The ambiguities of the situation were in Waterlow's favour, even if the practicalities were against him. Macready was convinced he was an active accomplice to Tremlay, taking care, no doubt to avoid knowing anything about his acts of violence, but fully complicit in keeping him informed and shielding him from scrutiny. Waterlow was a true Invisible—nobody could see where his principles really positioned him, because he didn't have any. He was an operator. 'Part of a new breed, I fear,' said Macready.

The circumstantial evidence against Waterlow had mounted to a pretty convincing level, but his family had money and connections and hired one of the best defence QCs in the business. He turned the police case upside down and inside out, reduced Donna to tears in the witness box and got Briony to contradict herself on a technicality during a forty-minute grilling. At the end of it all, when a split and exhausted jury finally came in with a not guilty verdict, one of the tabloids ran with a front page story about the heroic victim who in an exciting finale had escaped the killer's knife and saved the life of a police officer only to be persecuted by 'the Scottish Superintendent' and his henchmen. Only a month before, the same paper had built 'Macready of the Yard' up to super-hero status for successfully tracking down the Ripper's Disciple and putting him behind bars with a triple life sentence.

Jimmy took pleasure in using the newspaper to eat chips out of, bringing them round the station on a tour.

'Here, have some. They're hot, mind.'

They were, too.

'Did you fry these yourself or something?' asked Steve, shaking his fingers out after making the mistake of trying to scoop up a handful at a time.

'Not exactly. New place just opened up on the corner of Swallow Street. They do pizzas as well, but I don't exactly take to those. Don't know why they bother, anyway. These are the best chips in central London. Who'd want pizza?'

'I saw Donna eating one yesterday,' said Briony. 'I was wondering where she got it.'

'She would. Miss trendy boots. I 'spose she's seen this.' He pointed to the oil smeared face of Guy Waterlow, looking his most distinguished.

'Bound to have,' said Briony. 'She told me he had the nerve to ring her up. At home.'

Steve's ears pricked up. 'What for?'

'Said he wanted to apologise. For what she'd been through.'

'What particular part of what she'd been through?' asked Jimmy, his mouth full.

'I dunno. She still thinks he didn't actually know about the murders. She thinks he was naïve—a pawn in the game like Quin, but a very different type of pawn.'

'Who's talking?' said Steve. 'She must have been born yesterday not to suspect a man who was hanging around watching her like that.'

'Not necessarily.' Briony was starting to get annoyed now. 'How many cases do we know about where the killer gets really close to someone and it never occurs to them that he's the one. She may even be right about Waterlow. I reckon he's a deeply stupid bloke.'

'Stupid enough to get off scot-free when he's up to his neck in it?' Steve carped.

'Yes. The money does the talking for him.'

There was a pause while they finished off the chips, then Jimmy

twisted the newspaper into a corkscrew, tied it in a knot and pitched
it into the bin.

'Did Donna tell you she's leaving?'

'What—leaving the force?' said Briony.

'That's what she told me.'

'She didn't say anything to me about it.' Briony suddenly felt
quite hurt. She'd talked to Donna for an hour yesterday, in the little
café near Gresham where they'd met before and exchanged all sorts
of confidences, but Donna had never said a thing about resigning.

'Best decision,' said Steve, offering a cigarette to Jimmy. 'She's
not cut out for this sort of work, really. Not in the long run. What's
she going to do?'

'Public relations,' said Jimmy, putting on an affected voice. 'For
an advertising company. She gets her own car and something called
a grooming allowance, and double the pay she's getting now, I
shouldn't be surprised.'

'How come she didn't tell me?' asked Briony.

'Worried about how you'd react, I expect. She thinks you depend
on her.'

'*I* depend on *her*?'

'Women always depend on each other,' said Steve, 'until—'

'—until they hook some nice man like Guy Waterlow to depend
on?' Briony cut in. 'Anyway, I'm going to leave you two to gossip.
I've got to see Palgrave. Bet you he knew about Donna before any
of us.'

61

Everyone was surprised at Nell. Her parents wanted to come over, but she specifically asked them not to. The twins wanted to find her another counsellor, but she refused to make an appointment. Aunty Pat wanted her to come down and stay so she could get some good hot meals into her and see she had plenty of fresh air. But all Nell wanted was to get on with her life.

The killer had been found, identified and locked up, which was all she needed—all she had ever needed—to enable her to take control of her future. She wouldn't say get back to normal, as she didn't actually think that normal was normal anymore, but she had a growing sense that she could cope with whatever came her way.

Through all the endless conversations she'd been involved in about what happened, the person who seemed to understand her best was Inspector Williams, or Briony as Nell was now allowed to call her. When all the formal interviews were over, they arranged to meet for coffee one Saturday morning. Nell was halfway through her first term and halfway through *Bleak House*, having become addicted to Dickens. She was reading it when Briony walked into the café, fifteen minutes late and wearing exactly the clothes Nell had first seen her in.

'Don't you have any weekend gear?' she asked.

'Why? I'm plainclothes. So that's what I wear. I'm not into those frilly T-shirts.'

'I should get my cousins to sort you out. Rita's determined she could turn you into a glamour girl.'

'Is that what she tries to do to you?'

'Sometimes.'

'What you reading?' Briony reached across for the book and turned it over to read the blurb on the back. 'This is the one about the law courts, isn't it? We had to read it for our course at Hendon. Good stuff.'

'So you didn't go to university?'

'Nope. Hendon was a better bet for me. I always knew what I wanted to do.'

'How?' asked Nell. 'How could you always know you wanted to be a detective? Something must have given you the idea.'

Briony slumped in her seat, frowned and thought for a minute.

'You're good at getting stories out of people, aren't you? I had a cousin once. We used to play together quite a lot when we were little. Her mum was my mother's sister. When she was nine she disappeared. On her way home from school. Everyone just went crazy. I don't think my mother slept for more than an hour at a time for weeks. My aunt was just destroyed by it. When she'd got over crying all day, it was like the spirit had completely gone out of her, you know. She'd be sitting at the table, but there was nobody there.'

'So what about you?'

'I started playing detectives. I looked for her all the time, wrote lists of what I called clues. I didn't actually know what a clue was, but I knew the police didn't have any. She never was found. And in a way I've never stopped looking for her.' She straightened up, and took a sip of her coffee. 'Not that that's what the job's about, you know. You wouldn't get anywhere in this business if you were in it to try and deal with all your old hang-ups. I probably shouldn't have told you. I'd never tell the blokes I work with. Their attitude's bad enough as it is.'

Nell was amused by this. 'I can imagine. But you make a pretty good team, I reckon.'

'Didn't look like it for most of the case, but maybe we did in the end. What about you? Now everyone's patted you on the back and told you you're a brave girl—next thing they'll be telling you to get over it. There's no end to the trite little bits of advice you could come in for.' She gave Nell a searching look. 'You seem remarkably unfazed to me. Your cousins told me you had panic attacks. Don't see any sign of those.'

'I had nightmares and panics for a few years, but you know what? I think this has actually cured me.' Nell grinned. 'Shock treatment. No, but seriously. When the first thing happened—you know, on the train—like you said, everyone was trying to get me to put it behind me, get over it. I couldn't. It was part of my life. It was real. And so was the guy who did it and he was knocking around in the same world as me, knowing who I was. After he got into the flat that time, I thought—right—and I bought this camera. All those years not knowing what his face was like, if he showed it again I was going to shoot him with my camera. I never did get to take a picture, but I hit him with it.'

They both laughed.

'I'm interested in what you do,' said Nell. 'Since I've got drawn into it, maybe I'm developing a taste for it. You know, the clue business. Can you become a detective with a degree in English literature?'

'Probably,' said Briony.

Associate Professor Jane Goodall grew up in the UK, where she studied at London and Oxford Universities, and now lives in Sydney, Australia. She has written books and journal articles on drama and the history of ideas and is Research Director of the College of Arts, Education and Social Sciences at the University of Western Sydney. *The Walker* is her first novel.